Story of The Ghost

A NOVEL

CHARLES L. MAHONEY

SOTG *(Story of The Ghost)*
A Novel by Charles L. Mahoney
Second Print Edition

ISBN 978-0-615-96253-5

Copyright 2014

Cover Design & Formatting: Streetlight Graphics

TABLE OF CONTENTS

DECEMBER '80

IT TOOK THE WARDEN over twenty minutes to make it down from his second floor office and up to the cage of the guard tower located on the outer rim of the prison yard. The target he'd been so insistent on was still out there. Roughly a mile to the northeast, near the long toes of the Chappel buttes, stood a man in a dark-blue shirt, signature boots and dancehall cowboy jeans. The man palmed the back of his neck under the protected sun as the Warden stared at the tower guard on duty. "Why aintcha aimin' it?" he said.

"He ain't one of ours, sir," the guard answered. "That's a con-firm."

"Gimmie the thing," the Warden said as he controlled a Winchester 351 rifle by the barrel and leveled it through a circular gap in the cage. He adjusted the scope.

"He's got a truck, sir."

"Uh huh . . ."

"I ain't never seen him before."

The Warden tipped back his rancher's hat. "Just 'cause you ain't never seen him before don't mean you respond to me with fuzz on the reddy, kay."

The guard didn't speak. The Warden wiped his eyes and handed back the rifle, letting the silver hair under his hat breath for a bit.

"Yer conscience get the best of ya?" the Warden said.

"No sir."

"What is it then?"

"He ain't one of ours, Captain. And I don't know what he's doing over there. It looks like his truck is broke down."

"He's got a uni on."

"Half uniform sir."

"Well is due to him bein a Special."

The guard thought about something. "*Special*, sir?"

"The Specials is what we got goin on here now. Theys in them units we been buildin', kay. And theys the way we goin on with the future. I can't get into specifics with ya right now but what they is is for priznahs who behave and can rehabilitate themselves. This here's why . . . *Marcus*, you received yer raise as fast as ya did. Less expenses, son."

"Well I ain't never seen him in the yard before."

The Warden held his hat over his heart and closed his eyes, addressing his target. He sniffed the mid-morning air like a snake testing out its internal radar. There were noises coming from the middle of the yard and so the guard slid by the Warden to investigate. Just birds picking at the bales of hay and cackling at one another.

The Warden opened his eyes to the expanse of his private desert land and saddled back his hat. He turned around and snatched the rifle out of the guard's hand quicker than he had before. "Ya ain't qualified," he said.

The guard handed his utility belt with a puzzled look, his thumbs tucked down.

"I've been here for five years, in this very position. I won the shooters long range two times out of four, I'm qualified."

"What I mean is ya ain't shoot no priznah before."

"I don't want to shoot a prisoner."

A bird dove at the tower, panning its wings in a bid for the pavement of the parking lot - the only pavement until the highway.

"Let me ask ya somethin'," the Warden said. "Why ya here, son?"

"To protect the prison and the prisoners who don't cause nobody no trouble. I take my shots, sure, but if it ain't at the hay it's at the birds. And if it ain't at the birds it's at the snakes. The prisoners are well-conditioned here, sir. I even seen some of the older ones hit the ground on occasion when I'm on the radio, like they got flashbacks of a war going on. Bombs and such."

"Well it ain't no good," the Warden chided. "It ain't no good at all. I gotta rifle but I ain't gotta man who knows how they used. And I gotta priznah who beats up childrens and robs them generous elderly persons and mishandles women and now he's on the run to go and do more of the same. Now I ask ya, son, what good are we doing out here?"

"We could pick him up, don't you think?"

"We could, but then we break the rules too. The rules we got inside the fence is important for all concerned. What kind of message is bein weak if it gets around? As far as I can see, he out there thumbing his nose at us. And we already know what he has to say about society."

"I can't just shoot him sir, like he's a wild boar or something."

"I know ya can't, Marcus, and I understand, I do. Is my fault, kay. I trusted this priznah with his good record here and look how he puts me in this awkward position with ya."

The Warden placed the barrel against the steel support that was his previous claim. He then horse-collared the guard by the neck. "Let me show ya somethin'," he said. "Go on, have a look-see."

The guard raised the rifle and eyed the scope.

"Whaddaya see?"

"Well I see the guy standing there looking up at the sky like he could use a swig of water."

"*Priznah.*"

The guard averted his eyes from the target. "The prisoner, sir."

"Whaddaya see, *inside*?"

The guard peeked up at the Warden. *"Inside?"*

The Warden touched the barrel and smiled. "Whaddaya see when ya look inside that makes ya hesitate with that trigger on this winny here. This fine piece of machinery."

"I'm not too sure what you mean by the inside, sir."

"Yer conscience, what's it sayin to ya?"

"Not to shoot."

The Warden patted the guard's back. "Of course it is. And it should, kay. Yous a good man Marcus, is why I hired ya. A real good-hearted man."

"Thank you sir."

"You go to church?"

"I take it sometimes here at the prison when things get too busy. I know I'll be attending during my double shift come Christmas, that's a given."

"Good good. *Thou shalt not kill*, is what yer thinkin'. I didn't even have to ask ya but I did. Otherwise is just a priznah standing there in yer way to doin yer job. A priznah like that one right there. The kind of priznah who does such bad things to women, childrens and them helpless elderlies. A priznah who takes advantage of the good things we got goin on and makes it his business to mess it up for the rest of us. That make more sense to ya now, Marcus, about the inside?"

"Yes, some."

"Good good. So don't kill the priznah then, just make a wound. A little flesh shot as a reminder to what the rules is. Yous a champion in the long range. If yous so good, make a wound. There ain't no rule about that from you know who."

"A wound sir?"

"Like they teach the police. You better than them. Is why I hired ya."

The guard retracted from the scope and looked at the Warden with obedient eyes. "I guess I could go for a leg shot," he said.

"A leg shot is good, Marcus. He'll be with the nurse and we don't have to pay for the state transport and you don't need to lose that raise of yours. Good good, the leg is perfect. Now . . . let's see what they all says aboutcha. Is it true that Marcus is the best with the long range in Cochise cownie? Well, now, I tell ya, is what I came up here for."

I THE LAST OF SPRING

1 A NEW PLACE

HIS RIGHT FOOT was a bloodied mess. He couldn't see the blood seeping out from the heel, how it soaked through the sole of his sneaker and trickled down into the dirt. For Gavin was flat on his back and he'd been that way for some time trying to figure out what had happened. The desert sun slipped across the sky in full of his breath. His lonely world, it seems, his only thing. A world with nothing but rock and sand and open spaces to run through. Someplace hidden where the unknown tears right through rubber and flesh when you least expect it.

Age sixteen was supposed to be his year. A year with his driver's license in hand and destinations to ramble about in a Jeep with wheels made for all road terrain. The year wasn't supposed to include six months of living in isolation. Or, at six months and two weeks, nursing a bum foot and figuring out how long it might take to make it back to his trailer. A trailer with no foundation in the ground and located on a mound of dirt forty miles north of Sierra Vista. A new place one million and forty miles away from Gavin's former self.

He closed his eyes and counted to five to relieve the tension in his mind. With two hands under his thigh he tugged to a seated position and opened back up. There a bit of strength returned in him. The returning was like a sign for the last of spring. The end of one thing and the beginning of something other. He placed his hands at his sides and thought about how he might stand up on his good leg, searching for answers along the borderline of native scree.

He was too far out, too far gone to make it back to his trailer before the sun would give way to the dark.

Not but a few hours before, Gavin had followed the path out from the northwest trail of his campground until it rounded him back. He'd stopped at the turn and thought about what could be out there; out beyond the smothering creosote, the unknown territory he'd failed to investigate too many times before.

What was out there was a sea of thin brush that didn't open up for a few miles. And he'd made his way over that brush until it scattered and died in a volcanic display of porous rock and red dirt.

Eventually, he had come upon another path. And so the runner inside of him ran faster than he did from the start until something had made him tumble to the ground.

With a worry about snakeskin blending into dirt he spotted a shiny object out of the corner of his eye, pushing out from the ground at least two body lengths away. He crawled over to it and dug it out of the ground. The object was in fact a large arrow tip with the designs of a bird on one side and a fish on the other. The sides of it felt smooth in his hands.

He chucked the arrow tip into an island of brush and slid his left knee up to his chest to get a better foot on standing. After a minute, he made it up on his good leg.

With the leg operating as it should he tried to find balance with arms spread like wings but he soon fell victim to gravity, saving his face with the strength in his hands and arms.

Gavin adjusted to where he was able to stabilize his left foot again. Extending his right leg he rubbed it from the knee down. There he tested the pain of his injury, moving his foot back ever so gently to feel the heel. Pressing forward the blood in his sneaker felt like stepping down on a wet sponge. And with more weight added to the press he experienced a cold unaccustomed.

In the cold and dusk he thought about the long distances he had run. Mile after mile from his metal shed to Sierra Vista and back, each mile passing a little easier than the last.

His mind ran from the marathon-highway to his family, particularly about how his family tree had been removed by the roots. And how he had to pack his things in the middle of the night for someplace he'd never heard of before because that's what his mother had said they were going to do.

Up until the night his life changed, his memories had always been good. If he could bring himself to picture any of the good he might pull in the grassy backyard where he played one-man football with the laundry as his net. Or the way his mother tended to him whenever she found him scraped and bruised. In his former life she was never very far away. And when he reached for her, she reached for him too.

He could feel her words coming. Words that winded the broken paths he had run to meet him head-on at his anger and hurt. How selfish she had become in the year that was supposed to be about him. Thinking about his mother and her changes and all of her demands made him want to fall back to the ground. Just lie there in the dirt and let the dark of the Sonoran Desert move in and consume him.

He was sure her words hurt more than his foot.

Jesus is Lord, she'd say, *and his work is the only offering. Don't hold your hands up to the Lord, Gavin, without a heart set on anything but forgiving.*

GAVIN MANAGED to make it up to the Rock Gardens campground an hour and a half later with a Palo Verde branch as his support.

He sighted his mother in the fire pit glow, sitting atop the steps of his trailer with her back pressed against the door. His feelings for her changed ways hovered above the flames, readying for a burn. He backtracked some, both in his mind and with his feet.

She stood up and brushed her arms, clearing her throat. "The son I have," she said, "I no longer know." She then picked up a cushion from under her and positioned it on a fallback wooden chair next to the fire. "You've got to be hungry," she added, retrieving a book from under the chair. "That's the one thing *I do* know, kid." She dusted the dust cover. "There's something special here I made for your punctual nature: grilled iguana on a stick."

Gavin moved to the light post approximately ten yards from his trailer. As soon as he came under, the bulb flickered and died. He heard the electric buzz meld with the drone of the generators, a much flatter sound from the center grounds. He eased over to his trailer's front steps, sat down on the middle step and put the white shirt that hung at his waist around his neck. He smelled beans. In the mix was the sagebrush that surrounded his modest living space. He saw his mother buried in a book she had cradled between her legs. She thumbed the pages.

After a few uneasy moments, she turned to the fire. "Allow the dead to bury their own dead," she announced as if she were preaching to a packed congregation. "But as for you, go and proclaim everywhere the Kingdom of God."

Gavin rolled his eyes, wiping the grime of his day from the back of his head. "Nancy . . ." he said. "How do you bury somebody if you, yourself, are in the ground, dead?"

The crackling of the fire picked up. She returned to the book, flipping through more of its dog-eared pages. "I will follow you," she said. "But first permit me to say goodbye to those at home."

Gavin broke the branch in half and tossed the pieces into the fire. Standing on the tiny porch he leaned against the door. "You never said goodbye," he said. "You just left."

"What I said was every day but Sunday, kid. That's not a goodbye."

"Barely a Sunday," he said under his breath.

She used her finger for a book-mark and looked over at him. "I didn't leave you," she said. "Let's put that one to bed this instant. Nobody left no one."

He felt his right knee. "What if I had got bit by a rattler out there, would you have even been able to find me?"

"That's not gonna happen."

"It could," Gavin said. "Some old geezer told me that if one doesn't come after you that you're bound to step on one of their heads. He said their bodies get dumped all over the place without the ends. There's plenty of rattler heads out there that ain't even buried."

"*Aren't* buried," his mother quickly corrected, shifting in her seat. "The King's English when you address me, and it's not a request."

Gavin bent down and untied his laces, keeping one eye on his mother. She got up to tend to the food and he bowed his head as low as possible.

"You make it sound like we're surrounded by snakes out here. Like you can't do anything without first getting their permission. So you know, kid, creatures that crawl on the ground try to avoid you when you got the Holy Spirit. And you got the Holy Spirit."

Gavin sat back down on the step. He slipped off his right sneaker to inspect the damage to the sole. He ran a hand over the hole and wiped the bloody bits of sand on the side of his jeans. "I could've gotten bit," he uttered. "So, that's all. There's no place to go if you get bit."

"So don't go there."

"Where?"

"Out in the desert."

"We're in the desert."

"What I mean is . . . out where no one can find you if you get lost and something happens."

"I wasn't lost."

"You know what I mean."

Gavin thought in fragments about what irked him the most.

"You go too far anyway, kid. You could stay close to here or find something else to do."

"What else is there to do?"

"You could run the access road to up here, and then down to the bridge and back so you're where people can see you. You don't have to go out far like you do, always having to make an adventure of things." She moved a spoon through a pot of beans and measured out her seasoning. She then stabbed at a hunk of meat with a fork. "And I don't want to hear about your plans again to go hitch-hiking from place to place. That's not a joke to me. Not until you're eighteen do you have the right to even think like that. I'm even thinking twenty-one on that one."

Gavin lifted himself up with the help of the porch rail and used every muscle in his left leg to make a path around the fire. When he came around, he took to the empty chair. He picked up the book and flipped through it as he comforted, wondering why his mother wasn't watching him. "Did Jesus ever heal a one-legged man?" he quipped.

Her eyes came alive as she stared downward. "When was the last time we bought you shoes?" she said.

"Why?"

"Because I'm your mother, that's *why*. You have other shoes, where are your brown ones?"

Gavin looked up at the endless amount of stars in the night sky. He started a count in his head but soon gave up on the fruitless endeavor. Every star, though, had a bundle of other stars to point to. "Jesus went everywhere in bare naked feet," he said, his eyes still on the stars. "Maybe I wanna be like him, just don't call me a *Christian*."

The spoon fell out of her hand and so she repositioned the hand to her hip as the waist of her acid jean jumpers came in an inch. "How do you know what he did or where he did it?" she said. "The Bible I got for you looks like it's never been opened."

"It's by-"

"By the way, I don't want to hear you ask me *why* again. I don't have the time or patience for uninformed politicians, even one who happens to be my son."

"I read the book," Gavin said.

"Oh really, what did you read? Let's see . . . I'm in Ephesians, can you give me a summary?"

"A summary of what, the boy and his horse?" Gavin wrapped his shirt around his injury like he knew what he was doing and what he was talking about. "There's the apple and that lady, the man with the boat and the camel and the-"

She swooped in on him and hovered. "Please go on with your lecture," she said. "This is getting interesting."

"I didn't read everything," Gavin said. "I didn't find what I was looking for so I quit. It got way boring."

"Please explain to me your seeking of entertainment in the Good Book."

"The word *Christian*, I was looking for it and-"

"And you thought what, Gavin? Please don't stop now, you're on a roll. This is better than the Gospel Hour and 700 Club combined. I can't believe I'm finally getting a religious education. And to think, it was always right here for me. All I had to do was ask my young son because he knows about everything."

Gavin looked straight ahead, the other trailers only shards of metal under a crescent moon. "I thought I would see it," he said. "But I didn't see it anywhere, so, that's all."

"So you thought you'd just stop looking, was that your thought process, to quit when you're satisfied with your way of thinking?"

"No. I just didn't see it, so . . ."

She nicked at the ground and exhaled a few expressive breaths around his ears. "You won't find what you're looking for because you're looking in the wrong place."

He stood up to test the pressure of his right foot in the soft dirt. "Is that what you said to Dad?" he said, collapsing back into the chair. "That he was in the wrong place?"

"You know that's not fair."

"Neither is this. Being here since my birthday, on my own."

"Your life isn't fair, is that it?"

"Kinda, yeah."

"Is there anything else you want to say to me before we eat?"

Gavin thought for a second. "Yeah, do you always have to be preaching?"

"Preaching?"

"Yeah, like, do we always have to be talking about the Bible now, like we're in a Sunday School or something?"

She smirked. "Would you prefer that I take you to the service at the Fort, use the gas to drive up here early on Sunday and miss the meals I've got to prepare for the week?"

"That's not what I mean."

"Well, we could sit there. The two of us. We could sit and listen to the preacher they got go on about everything under the sun but the Word and shout prayers that take forever and a day and dance around because the Lord isn't smart enough to figure out what each person needs. We could go and do that, kid. I could close up shop and forget about those new recruits who don't really know what they're hungry for. I could do that."

"You don't need to get upset."

"I'm not upset."

"Well, that's not what I want."

"So what do you want from me?"

"I want things to be back to normal. It sucks that this thing is the same size as my room back home."

"Back home?"

"Yeah, back home."

"This is your home. St. David is your new home, kid."

"That's what sucks."

"What *sucks*, as you put it so well in your own English, and in the words of your TV programs, is that you're looking at things that are behind you."

"I like those things better," Gavin said. "Forward sucks."

"Forward sucks?"

"Yeah, forward."

"Okay then, Isaiah 43."

"Is that a verse or the name and number of a football player, Nancy?"

"Don't get smart with me."

Gavin grinned. When she stepped to the side, piercing her blue eyes into his affable browns, his grin ended.

"Isaiah is something you should investigate if you want the right answers. Your mother is referring here, not preaching. In fact, I will no longer speak to you about this. I'll leave it up to you to read what you want to read and think what you want to think from here on out. I can see that you're old enough. If you've got a question, I've got an answer for you and the answer comes direct from the Good Book. You've got a copy and if you want to talk some more about it, kid, we can open it up, together, and next Sunday when I come back. And so you know, the word *Christian* is in the Bible three times. The one word you will find, that is, if you choose to really look and can forget about yourself for once is the word *follow*. Your mother is a *follower* of Jesus. If anyone ever asks, she's a hardworking F.O.J., got it?"

"F.O.J.?"

"Follower of Jesus, that's right. You can see that he says it clearly to anyone who will listen with their heart: follow me."

Gavin thought about the Bible she had presented to him for his birthday. That bitter cold first day of January. Not a Jeep like his father had hinted about in the months prior. But a Bible, one with his two initials on the inside cover.

"And one more thing, kid. Your father may not be here right now, but I know for a fact he wouldn't care for your ideas, regardless of the situation. By the time he comes back, I hope you've done some more reading. That is, I hope you do so for your own sake."

She turned away and plated a portion of the meat on some white Corningware. She then tossed a flat piece of wood into the fire and went inside the trailer. After a minute, she reached her hands through the door, brushing them together in the warm air.

"Now . . ." she said, "before we eat, wash your hands. And for the love of a silver dollar, put on a clean shirt."

"What about my foot?" Gavin ached.

Lights around their neighborhood reduced.

"Keep your voice down," she hushed, eyeing his foot. "Alright, what about it? It's bundled up in your shirt, so what, are your toes cold or something?"

"I've got a hole in it, a nail got me. You can't tell that I'm suffering?"

She licked the print of one of her thumbs and ducked back inside the trailer. Just left him there with his own broken self. Before he knew it, she was pointing her head out the kitchen window. "We've all got to suffer in some way or the other," she said. "You wanted to be like Jesus. That's what you said to me. Your words, kid."

He looked around the north area of the grounds that was his little plot of land. There were only a few lights remaining from the nearby trailers. He counted four before giving up. "Jheezus . . ." he uttered to no one other than himself.

Before Jesus it was a man with a cassette tape that could heal the smokers of Southern Arizona. His mother had a box full of those tapes, but he'd never once witnessed her struggling. There wasn't even one cigarette that he could point to.

2 PRIVATE

WHEN GAVIN AWOKE it was 3:58 in the morning by the digital clock on his bedroom floor.

He fanned out his arms and legs on the single mattress and stared at the paint peels dangling from the ceiling. He heard a door shut. Another door then did open. Weathered hinges just begging for a splash of WD-40. When he rose and stepped toward the bedroom window, his right leg gave way to the floor and the rest of his body followed. He crawled over to the window frame resentful his condition and laid to rest under the light of the F-150 he knew was readying to vacate.

The Ford cranked and wallowed and then sputtered some before it finally bellied over. Gavin's eyes blinked rapidly before slowing to match the meditative hum of the truck's underbelly. Shutting his eyes he turned a cheek to check the time in his mind. He added two minutes to what he'd seen before and opened back up. A little game he played to occupy his thoughts. He found nothing but the same as before and so when the clock did welcome the new hour, the Ford roared.

Later in the morning, with the sun on the rise, the clock buzzed the gunk between his ears.

Gavin shook off the tired to find himself sloped against the window wall of his bedroom, his right arm preventing his head from plowing through the carpet. He used the sill of the window to stand up as he focused in on his pale-blue foot. What it looked like at the arch was anybody's guess and he wasn't in any mood to bother with a bend. He cautioned well the injury and gazed out the wide frame with anguish written all over his face, his thoughts hampering any and all motivation about the day.

He entered the washroom east of his lot ten minutes later and selected the middle of the three available stalls, removing his sneakers. He pulled back the curtain and rolled up one leg of his Levi's.

There were two large buckets of water at his disposal. He spat in one. In the other he drowned his stale toes and scooped water in his palms, showering his face. Then he felt as best he could where the gash was at the heel and thought about his next run. He cancelled his plan to tackle the highway after school due to his body pleading with him for just one day of rest. He emptied the bucket and himself. And for a peaceful time he considered nothing but the water leaking out into a faint maroon.

The only boy on grounds exited the stall, a full-size mirror in the corner capturing his every move. He gimped over to get a closer look at his face, wondering if he looked any older than he was. Not one hair that he could spot until he touched the hairline. Would anyone even notice him in this place? He attended to the hair growing wild over his ears and waited for something to interrupt his thoughts.

A knock at the door saved him from himself.

In the mirror reflection he saw a man with a fuzzy beard in a Members Only jacket. The beard smiled at him.

"Do you have any duct tape, Mr. Sandis?" Gavin asked.

"You can never have too much if you ask me."

"Can I get some before school?" Gavin said as he turned to face the real thing.

"Depends. This an emergency?"

"Not really."

"Well, then, I got some fresh rolls in the back of Sunny, but she got stuck down the hill last night after blocking the entry from some trespasser. Some red-haired fella who kept telling me he was looking around for a place to stay, so was his story in the middle of my flashlight. Had to roll her off to the side to make way for the rest of us tax dodgers. If you want, you can hustle down there and raccoon through the crates yourself. But be careful."

"That's okay," Gavin said. "I'll get it later."

"You sure?"

Gavin faced the mirror.

"I'll get her moving today, and when you get back from school, you make sure to stop on by and there'll be a roll waiting for you. You want a full roll in plastic, you got yourself one."

"Alright."

"Anything else?"

"Nada."

"That means *nothing*, so you know."

"Yeah, I know."

"I missed your mother yesterday. Got tied up with the deliveries among ten other things. She doing well with her catering business?"

"Yeah."

"You doing okay?"

"Yeah."

The conversation paused.

"You know any other words than just, *yeah*?"

"Yeah."

"What are they?"

Gavin spun around. "What?" he said with a confused look on his face.

"Do you need anything for that foot, is what I said."

"My foot is fine."

"How come you're favoring it then?"

"I'm not."

"You get a spine?"

"I'm fine."

"You sure?"

Gavin didn't speak.

"Are you thinking about covering up a sore with some duct tape? If that's the case, I got plenty of Band Aids and gauze. You need some alcohol rub diluted in water. The rub with water is the best way."

"It's the muscle that aches, that's all."

"All that running will do that. You run too much. You're not a jackrabbit, you know. And you need to gain some weight, not sweat it all off. A boy your age needs bread and loaves of it. What did your mother bring for you this week?"

"She brought bread."

"Well Good."

"Mr. Sandis?"

"He is me."

"I'm going to be late and I need to brush my teeth." Gavin looked at his index finger, his own version of a toothbrush.

"Oh right, not one ounce of a problem, I was just leaving. I'll get out of your hair. Too bad about the trail."

"What about it?"

"It isn't wide enough to drive Sunny down the back. Otherwise, I could drive you to school."

"Your truck is stuck, remember?"

"Well . . . it was a thought, is all. Well, I got plenty to do and you're off to school. So have yourself a good day and report back to me later, Private, and collect your supplies."

Gavin watched the beard disappear behind the door. He took a few thoughtful steps and hand-combed his hair without the help of the mirror. Then he placed his hands on a shelf where there was a pan of water and a tube of toothpaste. He moved a finger in the pan, removed it and layered it with fluoride. As he fingered his teeth, his mind, like the lower half of his right leg, numbed.

EARLY MONDAY EVENING, Gavin found Sandis outside of the old man's trailer – seated in an old man chair at the foot of an old man fire pit. An orange sun twisted lavender, setting the western horizon for only those aged enough to care.

Gavin approached the pit with the sun on his back, his heel feeling better the more he walked on it. He noticed that Sandis was covered in a mess of shavings. When he moved in closer he could see little flakes curled in the folds of the old man's beard. "Is that for an arrow?" he asked.

Sandis kept his eyes on his handiwork. "I'm not sure what it is just yet," he replied. "An arrow is a good idea. I'd have to carve a bow, so that would be quite the challenge." He made some digs. "Come to think of it now, I remember seeing a bow made from an elephant tusk, so anything's possible."

"Okay."

Sandis looked at Gavin. "Where is it you run off to all day anyways, school ends at what . . . o-fourteen hundred?"

Gavin shrugged. "I go to the river mostly. It kinda goes on forever, I guess."

"So you got yourself a destination."

"I guess so."

"The river, huh . . . well that's where I'd be too if I was your age and in wee bit better shape. Maybe one of these days I'll go with you on one of your little journeys."

Sandis grabbed a lengthy plank of wood from behind his feet and jabbed at the fire with it. He then tapped at the side of an ancient wrought iron bench that was on his left, motioning with his eyes for Gavin to take a seat. "You know that sound you can hear if you listen real close before the dawn," he said. "That's the river."

"I don't get up-"

"That reminds me, Private, you're mother squawked at me on the high-band earlier, said you need to tell your teachers that your grade history report from your former school will be in your hand by next week. She'll bring it with her on Sunday. I gather she forgot to tell you that on her visit here yesterday."

"*Teacher* . . ." Gavin informed. "There's just one teacher at the Corte School."

Sandis cleaned his Swiss Army Knife by his pant leg. "Well," he uttered, "the thing you need, you'll have."

Gavin stretched his right leg out across the bench. "It's not a big deal," he said. "I don't think it matters much anyway. Miss Prey has me speak out her sentences. She said she likes the sound of my voice. She told me it's like the spring."

"The spring is ending soon, so you better hold onto it while it lasts."

"What's that supposed to mean?"

Sandis grinned. "Your voice, it will turn to winter sooner than you think. Just wait until you have to shave."

"I shave."

"Every day?"

Gavin pinched his lips, answering the question with a brow.

Sandis accessed the corkscrew. "That's when you know old man winter is coming for you. When you got to shave each and every dang day and it becomes a pain in the you-know-what to do."

Gavin picked up some pieces of wood from around his feet and tossed them into the fire. "You don't need to check on me tomorrow," he said. "Miss Prey told us school was gonna be closed for the day. I guess there was some dust or something. One of my friends, he and I are going over to the Square, we're gonna go see a movie, maybe even two."

Sandis brushed at his beard. "I needed those," he said as he moved his eyes to the fire and then out to an empty spot between his trailer and the next hunk of metal to the west. "As you can see, we're not exactly living out in the wild blue yonder."

"Sorry."

"Gavin, I know this place isn't exactly an amusement park, but it's no retirement community either. There's things to do here, fun things."

"All the people here are old. They all have gray hair or no hair. What's there to do up here when you're my age, sleep all day?"

"Thanks . . ." Sandis said, raising only his eyes.

"For what?"

"For describing me to a T."

"I wasn't talking about you."

Sandis chuckled. "Right, okay. You ever been to the jeep graveyard before?"

"Where's that at?"

"You know where Tison Yard is, it's maybe . . . four klicks to the west of there."

"The metal place?"

"Roger that," Sandis said. "Some of those old jeeps run too, so long as you give them a good kick in the head." Sandis stood up and wiped the shavings from his lap. "What I'm saying is don't let the river bore you," he added. "Man can only get so much nature before he turns into tree. You can't exactly hug a cactus, know what I mean?"

Gavin placed his elbows on his knees, cupping his chin. "Sometimes it's fun to go shoot guns," he said devoid of any conversational tone.

"Where do you do that?"

"My dad took me out once to shoot at the dunes. When he comes up here, we're gonna shoot bottles, that's how come I got all of them saved up under my stairs."

Sandis picked something out of the bed of his truck. "You have been a real help around here with the maintenance," he said. "I will most certainly give you that." He tossed back the something. "Well . . . we won't be doing any shooting around here, so let's come up with something else." He returned to his chair and leaned back, crossing a leg and folding his arms. "I'm thinking now that I could pick us up a bow and arrow set next time I'm at the corner shops. There's a Graydees right there. That'd be a good test of your skill, don't you think? How's that sound for a cherry pick, you interested?"

Gavin collected a small rock and launched it over the lengthy trailer that was stationed in front of his own. "What kind of guns do you go shoot, Mr. Sandis?"

"I don't."

"You were in the Army."

"Indeed I was. I do have some recollection of that, now that you've reminded me."

"What kind of guns did they give you?"

"The kind that ain't built for weekenders."

"Shotguns?"

Sandis didn't say anything.

"Machine guns?"

"Yeah, sure, machine guns if you want. Got one of those handed to me on my first day. The sergeant looked at me and said: welcome Private, here's your dang machine gun, now go to work."

"Really?"

"No, not really."

"How about grenades, did you ever throw one?"

"Oh, sure, all the time. I was a pitcher for my unit's baseball team. We played all over Korea against the enemy on our days off. Baseball with hand grenades. Never had so much fun."

"I'm being serious."

"So am I. I wouldn't joke about my grenade playing days."

"Did you ever throw one, for real?"

Sandis leaned in on the pit. "Well almost," he said. "Let's just say I got some thrown in my direction, if that counts. Most coming to me special delivered courtesy of the US Army. But that's alright, I got out of the way. I was lucky. Some guys . . . well, they weren't as lucky as me." He let go of his carving to the flame with no regret. "You eat yet, Gavin?"

Gavin shook his head.

Sandis got up and grabbed a pair of binoculars that were draped over the back his chair. He pointed the sights at two trailers crammed into one lot over by the main gate and made some adjustments. The old man then moved the sights over his sandals and did some further adjusting. "How about I go nuke us up some Salisbury steak?" he said. "I got two in the hopper for you and a Hungry Man with double mash calling my name."

AN HOUR LATER, Gavin entered his trailer and immediately crashed on the couch. He rested there for a time in the light of the snow from the television. When a rainbow of colors blurred horizontal, he adjusted the rabbit ears and rotated the channel button. Only two channels were working. He settled on the one with the best picture and returned to his favorite piece of furniture, letting his right leg drift to a pillow on the floor. He tuned out the boredom of his runner-less day and began to snore.

A few ticks after midnight and he dragged himself from the couch to the bedroom. He had to turn sideways to enter the room at the tail of the trailer so as to avoid a cardboard box in the way and when he corrected he tripped over a stack of maps and magazines. The materials as well as his body splayed on the floor. As he gathered back the materials his eyes targeted The Highways and Byways of Southern

Arizona. With every map he flipped through the pen markings of his father reminded him of his lot in life. He studied the circular land claims and arrows leading to the nearest gas stations and measured the distances as best he could by finger and thumb.

Gavin turned his record player on. A seven inch record on the dial then did skip. The scorching needle burned a hole through the speakers, penetrating his ears. He moved the needle to the outside and adjusted the volume. Post the bass and drums, the first verse of a numbered song played to his audience of one.

> *I waited patiently for the Lord*
> *He inclined and heard my cry*
> *He lift me up out of the pit*
> *Up from the miry clay*

He clenched his fists and squeezed his eyes to save from crying. The first line of the second verse came on as his fingers reappeared. *He set my feet upon a rock and made my footsteps firm.* The line helped to keep his tears in check. "I will keep running no matter what happens," Gavin uttered. "No matter what."

He clicked off the record before the end and clicked off the light and made his way over a land mine of cotton to rest his sixty-eight inch long body on the mattress with no box spring under it. In the metallic moon a poster tacked to the separator wall sparked renewal in his eyes. A man in a red and white uniform ran downhill and with a football in his direction. *Maybe the* Saint *in St. David has purpose,* Gavin thought. *Maybe if St. Louis could see me run as fast and as far as I can they'd want me to play football for them. That could be me up there with the football. The* Saint *in St. David could mean something. It could be special.*

3 HIGHWAY MILES

TUESDAY MORNING broke under the cover of dark clouds.

Gavin drew in the stark weather through his bedroom window and put on a wrinkled pair of jeans and a clean white shirt. He doubled up on socks for his right foot and kept the left foot bare. Slipping on his sneakers he attached a piece of duct tape under the sole of his tear to ward off spines and rocks and any fabled snakeheads that might try to enter.

With a plate of leftovers half-digested he opened his front door to a glass bottle of rubbing alcohol and a plastic container of Coppertone. He placed the bottle inside the door and then lathered the lotion over his face, neck and arms, squeezing out a good portion for his elbows. He tossed the container onto his couch and closed the door, using the key from the lace around his neck to lock up. With the key tucked to wear he ran from his trailer like the injury to his heel had never occurred. In his back pocket, a collection of five and one dollar bills folded to make for about twenty.

Before he could think to breathe, he found himself on the other side of the bridge and connected to the south highway. The first signs of civilized life on the 80 motored into his view. Cars slowed on approach to St. David with headlights dancing to the thundering of a storm. Taillights raced over his back with body parts flailing in the wind. To the south was a promise being made for a cloudless day, and travelling in that direction looked to be about as good a decision as any.

Several miles on the highway came and went, until, at about the halfway point to Sierra Vista, Gavin stopped after realizing he'd drifted into the lane. He eased back mid-shoulder, traffic south, and stretched his arms above his head. He yawned ever-long as a lone hawk banked in the high winds.

The colors of the landscape converged inside of his head as he bent forward to breathe better the dusty air. For a moment he considered a return to St. David. And for another he scoffed at his dream to run with a football as a dust devil spun out of control. He picked up his feet and picked up the pace. And as the little devil restricted, Gavin picked up his head.

The fort supply depot was closing in from the distance.

Gavin thought about how far his legs could go on full burn. And he thought the same for the dollars in his pocket. There were the fifty-cent books the depot was famous for along with the dollar record piles that had everything but the country and western junk of the radio. He remembered the Walkman with red headphones. The last time he checked, it was on special. *Special,* he thought. Maybe more, maybe less.

He slowed his pace to tune into a group of birds in the middle of the highway. Then it was only him and a mother with the full of her yearning. Gavin tried his best to give warning to the absolution of oncoming traffic, but the birds offered him no reward. Every last one of them kept their creature eyes to the line, ignoring the manner in which his human hands were moving. There was no traffic coming. For the birds could feel sounds over a hundred miles away. The only sound he could hear was the music beating in the back of his head. Music that had been with him since the beginning of his journey. Music with lyrics that burned on him like the sun of an endless desert. *He set my feet upon a rock and made my footsteps firm.*

Those lyrics, along with a letter he kept hidden under his mattress, refused to leave him alone. The letter read:

Mary,
I miss you like you'll never know.
I hope you like this song as much as

I do (40). It reminds me of the poem
Footprints that you gave to me on the
day I graduated Basic, the one I carry
with me to this day. I know now that
God carries me when I can't carry
myself. It is especially hard with the
things that I am asked to do for my
country, but my footsteps move
toward you. I believe the thought
of you stands with me through
all of my loneliness and because
it is so true in my heart now, I know
that I sincerely love you. Please wait
patiently for me my love, as the song
says. Until we meet again, my heart
will be alone. Will you?
I hope that you will.

He'd found the letter one day not long ago at the depot. It had fallen out of the sleeve of the seven inch record. The record with two songs, one of which was titled by a number – 40. It was a number that could mean anything. The distance between cities. The age when a person starts living. It was possible the numbered song had many different meanings. And to Gavin, the letter and the numbered song, and the place he's come to know as St. David, all of it had a special meaning that he could not quite articulate.

A HALF HOUR PASSED and Gavin wasn't one step closer to his destination than before. He had exited off the shoulder, to an opening that led him astray into the unprotected desert. On a large rock he set his feet to better his view.

With all the dust it seemed likely that military planes were in exercise on the airfield. But no planes were in sight and so he turned back to spy the highway of cars and rigs and passenger trucks. There he found the colors of his adventurous mood.

He sloped down the rock and made his way back to the highway. He waited until traffic cleared and walked out to the middle of the flattest stretch he knew. *Doesn't matter how far,* Gavin thought. *Doesn't matter there's nobody but you. Keep moving. Forward could be good.*

His thoughts made him close his eyes and smile in one big breath to tempt the fate of his situation. He believed that if he was to survive the next ten seconds then every tick up to the last could somehow be transcribed. When the count proved good he shuffled back over to the shoulder refreshed in the eyes. He decided for the first time to use his thumb instead of his legs to do the work.

With a thumb he greeted an eighteen wheeler at forty seconds post his mark, thinking nothing of his escape. A compact car then flew past reckless of the legal limit. Shortly thereafter, a sedan tapped the brakes on approach. Then it gassed off. A mix of cars and trucks continued to come and go in both directions as time squandered in the heat.

When he noticed something slither out the corner of his eye and twist into a hole the diameter of a paint can, Gavin searched the desert. Dropping his thumb he dug in a pocket, searching for something in there too.

After a minute, he put his thumb back out, diverting his eyes from the peeking sun. A wind grabbed hold. Before he could break free and catch the motor hum, a sudsy can of soda came flying at his chest.

SEVERAL HOURS LATER, a funnel cloud hovered over Rock Gardens.

Sandis was busy latching down the last of the trailer restraints when his lunchbox-sized flashlight flickered and died. He set the flashlight down, produced a military style timepiece from his pocket and rubbed a thumb over the glass. He waited there with one knee in the dirt until the time displayed exactly 30 over 1700 hours. He started a count from behind his beard as lightening flashed north-river. On the fourth count, the lights that encircled the grounds all shut off.

Sandis kept his count going and when he got to double digits, the reserve lights came on in a slow fusing burn.

With the reserves operating as they should he handled his flashlight and scrambled over to his truck and sifted through the bed for spare batteries. After giving up the hunt for the right size, he turned over the engine, backed out of his lot and positioned the headlights over by the area where he'd been working. There he noticed Gavin's trailer to be about as dark as the aching cloud formation above so he put the truck in park and lights on low and exited the cab with the engine still running.

He tapped on Gavin's front door with the brim of his flashlight. When there was no sound from inside he drew it up to the kitchen window and clicked the rubber button multiple times in vain. Then he dropped it, gave it a swift kick and hustled back over to his truck.

Rain drops appeared on the truck's windshield the moment he got behind the wheel. The pattering sound was like a box of tacks spilling over the glossed shipyard wood of a 19th century attic. The rain became a radiant dance within the confines of the cab and so the former soldier soldiered for a time to take it all in like he was lost in the mud and memories of battle.

He gripped a hand around his neck and mowed upwards as the rain thinned. He then rolled the window down halfway and reached out to test the moisture. The cloud then dumped a box of picture nails. Sandis woke from his reverie to roll up the window and plot his next move. He zipped open the hood on the back of his windbreaker and positioned it just right by the light of the driver's mirror. Twisting the rearview he sat there as if he were a captain at sea monitoring the crest of twenty-foot waves. After the down pour he drove out through the north gate and bogged down the hill, keeping his foot heavy on the brakes the entire way.

When he made it to the bottom of the hill he eased out to the pavement and idled in the muddy tracks of his Goodyears.

Sandis stationed in the damp and the dark and dialed in any reports he could find over the AM radio. When a report about a flood went to commercial, he amped up his headlights, lowered his wipers a notch and pulled out a pipe from the pocket of his windbreaker.

Stepping on the gas he reached inside the glove box with the pipe in hand and rummaged through a stack of papers. The lighter he was searching for fell to the floor. He stretched as far as he could in an effort to retrieve it, but it was to no avail. Frustrated, he put the pipe in his mouth and two hands to the wheel and thought how he might get the thing without getting wet.

Sandis set the pipe at his side and blinked at the barely visible bridge. When the black road came to light a figure appeared in line with his hood ornament. He stomped on the brake pedal with both feet as he jerked the wheel left in a fraction of a second. The truck came to an abrupt stop on the bridge guardrail and his head did the same over the steering wheel. Luckily, his forearms helped soften a good portion of the blow. Pulling back, he touched his bloody nose.

The figure he had managed to avoid was staring at him right outside the passenger window. Sandis buckled his seat belt and adjusted the rearview. "What in the doggone heck were you doing?" he said, his loud voice mostly housed in. "You were in the middle of the dang bridge, Gavin. Jesus, Mary and Joseph."

Gavin retreated a few steps, folded his arms and faced the mist. He took a few sad breaths and trudged back to the truck. Overly cautious with the door handle he leaned and said, "Why'd you just do your belt?"

Sandis ignored the question. "What in the doggone heck were you doing on the bridge, Gavin? Answer me."

Gavin lowered his head.

Sandis wheezed of adrenaline.

"Here I am . . . promised your mother I'd take good care of you. Sat there and told her I'd look after you like you were one of my very own, and this is what happens."

Gavin flopped down on the passenger seat. He dragged the shoulder belt across his chest and flung it back. "You're not my dad," he said, his eyes traveling out beyond the splinter in the windshield and down the foggy bridge road.

Sandis looked at his nose in the rearview. "Guess what, Private, I never did have any of my own brood. But I'm here and your father isn't, now is he?" He looked at Gavin. "So where is he, got any idea?"

Gavin clung to the belt. "Out at his job," he said.

"His job? What kind of work keeps a man so buried that he can't even be with his own family?"

Gavin hesitated. "Land," he replied.

"What do you mean, *land*?"

"It's what he buys. Sometimes he doesn't come back until it sells if it's a big deal. And he's out buying something bigger than all of St. David. That's how come he's not here right now, I mean, it's what my mom told me anyway."

"Why are you here, Gavin?"

"Because my mom brought us here."

"What I mean is, why did you leave Sierra Vista in the first place?"

"We just left."

"You just left?"

"Yeah. She said that he was gonna be gone for longer than the usual and that we were moving to save on things."

"How long is, *the usual*?"

"A few weeks."

"You know how long you've been here?"

"I don't know, a few months, maybe." He knew. And he knew the total sum of days.

"Try six."

"Okay, six."

"On your own."

Gavin put a hand on the door.

"Doesn't seem very usual to me," Sandis said.

A grinding came over the front end of the truck. The fan belt whistled and then expired.

Sandis pinched his nose with one hand and pressed in some bits of glass in his side mirror with the other. "I'm gonna need some headache powder," he said. He looked over his shoulder as if there might be some traffic backed up behind him. "Well how about it Private, you think you got the skills to back Sunny off this dang rail before me and her go for a swim and take you with us?"

"I don't have a license."

37

Sandis smoothed his temples. "You see any dang badges around here?" he said.

Gavin looked out the side window.

"Cops . . ." Sandis said. "You ever seen any weekenders with badges around here?"

"Umm . . . no," Gavin uttered. "I've never seen a cop up around here before."

"Scootch on over," Sandis said, unlatching the belt that should have been with him from the engine start. "I need to go have a look at what all the damage is."

Gavin exited the truck.

Sandis slid down the bench seat and out through the passenger door and used Gavin's shoulder from an arm's length away to help stand up straight. "Your mother told me you were chomping at the bit to drive," he said. "Told me you even got a Polaroid of a Corvette. I hear you stood next to it and the owner threw a hissy fit."

"Yeah, so . . ."

"So that's what I call ambitious," Sandis said. "First time I learned to drive I was twenty-four years young and in the thick of it. The thing I had to learn on only had a couple gears. Had to use it to set off land mines and transport stiffs across the God forsaken 38th parallel."

Before he entered the truck to get behind the wheel, Gavin looked at the dark road that led back to the highway; to the pavement with lines he'd used so well to forget about his anger and hurt. He thought about taking the highway to somewhere other than the supply depot for once. Somewhere in Mexico. Anywhere, really, that was far enough away from the life he knew in the dirt.

4 CHOKE

THE CORTE SCHOOL was a little more than four miles north of Rock Gardens. He ran as fast as he could, racing across the school's dusty lot and up a ramp to the double-wide nestled a stone's throw away from the river bank. A black dog curled against the classroom door let him know he might have to stand alone in the corner. Gavin managed to open the door without bothering the dog and went inside. The pristinely dressed Miss Prey turned to him mid-sentence. "Runner," she said, shuffling her papers, "please letter for us the board."

Gavin plodded over to the blackboard and picked up a piece of chalk and wrote the entire alphabet in lowercase cursive.

A boy at the back of the room who looked to be about ten years old raised his hands. "Why is the *c* like the salty sea?" he said, moving his arms up and down like a wave.

"Like what?" Gavin said, disinterested and glancing over at Miss Prey. She smiled with her lips closed and cleared her throat. "He means to say, Runner, why do they sound the same but are different?"

Gavin looked at the boy. Shrugging he said, "I don't really know."

"Are you a penguin?" the boy asked.

There was some laughter about the room. Miss Prey hushed backed the chatter. "You mean *Pilgrim*," she said, arching her neck in an attempt to look down on the boy. The boy sunk in his seat. "Teza, you go lie down in the corner for speaking out of turn. Coloring in the book will come much later for you now because of that hole in your head."

The classroom quieted as Gavin located his seat.

"And let there be two ears and a mouth," Miss Prey stated. "These are the things your spirit-father has given to you. He missed to say to be used in such a way as is the proportion. Two ears, one mouth."

She studied her students. After a few more moments of utter quiet, she pushed away from the desk and rolled her wheelchair over to the door. "Older ones," she said. "Follow me." About half the room stood up. Gavin opened the door and helped wheel her down the ramp and over to a small patch of grass that was roughly ten yards from a shallow pool of the river. A mix of boys and girls stood next to Gavin and their teacher under the shade of some cottonwoods.

Miss Prey wheeled herself over to the water. The group rightly followed. Apart from Gavin, they all had formed a line. She positioned her chair back around and faced the group. "What is it you see on the other side of the river?" she asked.

"Treezzz . . ." an anxious girl with ankle boots said. "Tall treezzz, Mizzzy Prey!"

Miss Prey cupped her hands over her lap. "And you can only see with your big eyes, little lady. But what if you were the size of an ant? It has two eyes like you. What do you see now with your tiny creature eyes?"

The same girl tested the temperature of the water. "Mizzzy Prey," she said. "It feels like pee. Can we move the rocks again?"

Most of the group giggled. Miss Prey singled out Gavin amongst all the noise. "What is it you see on the other side, Runner?"

Gavin made quick work of his surroundings. He then gazed above his head, at the cottonwoods extending a good portion of their age on him. He felt the relief of the open space as he sucked in a breath. "The water . . ." he answered, pointing toward the middle of the river. "If you were that small and looking in that direction, then you could only see the water in front of you. It would be hard to see the other side of the river."

Miss Prey nodded at Gavin with an approving smile. She pulled out a drumstick from the side of her wheelchair and tapped on the metal hub. "Future generations . . ." she said. "What have we been studying?"

"Plymouth Rock," a different girl said, one with a pair of coke bottle glasses.

Miss Prey tapped on her wheel a few more times and loudly cleared her throat. "Is it better to read the story in the book or to be thinking of the story for those who really lived it?"

Aside from the river, there was silence.

"Both," Gavin chimed in. "I mean, that's kinda the way you've been teaching us. Since I've been here, that is."

Miss Prey observed the faces enamored by Gavin. "And with the showers there are beautiful flowers," she said. "Now why is it important, older ones, to read the story in the book and to think of the story for those who really lived it? Some teeth I haven't seen in a while, and not the Runner, please."

A young man with clumps of facial hair clapped.

"Neddy," Miss Prey said, "please, share your thoughts with us."

The young man drew a circle with a piece of chalk on a small board he held in his hand. Gavin considered it a decent sketch of the sun.

"The eyes . . ." Miss Prey said. "The eyes are looking, aren't they, Neddy?" The young man knocked on his board and she tossed him a piece of wrapped candy. She spun her wheelchair around to grace the water with her presence.

"Neddy is saying the eyes are important because we can only see things one person at a time. Nothing is exactly the same for all people. Even when we are here together we each see things a little differently."

The young man made a noise and she spun back around.

"The people of Plymouth Rock saw things differently, didn't they? Were they not on the other side of the water before they arrived? Do you really believe they all saw things exactly the same along their journey? The answer is *no*, and it is the same as the spirit leaving the body. *No* - you are not just your body. You are a spirit using the body. Now that we know this, and we already knew this, can any living spirit teach to me who wrote the book we are studying?"

"The Pilgrims!" the girl with ankle boots said.

The young man called Neddy shook his head and made a sad face.

"Not far," Miss Prey said. "But think now, harder this time, who wrote the book we are studying?"

Neddy was about to write something on his board, but he made a confused look and put his chalk back in his pocket.

"*Nobody*," Gavin offered, somewhat unsure of his answer. "Nobody who was there anyway." He thought Miss Prey might ignore him for speaking up but she opened her eyes much brighter than before.

"What do you mean to say when you say *nobody*, Runner? Please say."

"What I mean to say is . . . is that you can't write a story while you are in it because it is not a story. When you are in it, it is your life, so someone other than the people who experienced Plymouth Rock must've written the story long after. I saw the printing page, it said 1960. If they had the chance to read what the writers of the book believed, what they thought their life to be, I bet they wouldn't be too happy. I bet they wouldn't agree with it more than some general facts. Like the names of the boats and other things like that."

"And with the sun comes more of the sun," Miss Prey proclaimed with a grand smile. She wheeled into the middle of the group. "Older ones, do you understand what the runner is saying about this?" Most of the group nodded. Nods in all directions.

Then one of them pointed at the river and said, "The rocks we made have some fish!"

All of the group but for Gavin ran into the shallows of the water. Miss Prey wheeled herself over to the very edge and took a good look for herself. She raised her arms and motioned for Neddy and Gavin to lift her out of her chair. The two lifted her out and carried her a couple of lengths over to where the rock formation was. Sure enough, a collection of juvenile fish.

They were all up to their knees in the water when Miss Prey said with much joy, "Did you hear what the runner has said? He said: *Nobody. No-body*. This is important. This is what our thoughts can do when we allow them to speak to us."

WHEN SCHOOL ENDED for the day, Gavin went over to the river

bank to be by himself. He stood there and stared out at the docile waters with his mind running the highway.

There were noises coming from behind his head, sounds familiar to his ears; engines cranking and voices in different layers and decibels. He let what was behind him dissipate, choosing instead to concentrate on the things he could see and touch.

Stuffing his hands in his pockets he walked a few steps over to the very edge of the bank and spat in the water. He slid off his right sneaker using the rubber toe of his left, placing his double layered foot on the ground. He then removed the layers and slid his bare foot on top of a river rock and spat once more, watching little ripples form and rocks under the surface clear. He gave the cool surface his weight and thus it returned a warmth to his veins and spidery tendons. He forgave the pressure and set free a face that was equal parts pain and surrender.

A mid-sized truck painted a fire engine red pulled into the parking lot. The truck had low end white striping with long side mirrors. Gavin glanced at it just prior to easing out from the shallows with his left sneaker submerged and his right foot moving from one smooth rock to another. After a minute, he stopped to tickle the waterline.

A man with a black motorcycle jacket glorified of patches exited the truck. He headed up the ramp and opened the classroom door.

Miss Prey wheeled herself through the doorway and the man helped her down the ramp and across the parking lot. When her wheelchair came to a stop they exchanged a few words in a moment that made them both smile. She raised her arms as if to submit to her spirit to the sky and the man lifted her up and out of the chair with virtually no effort, setting her down on the back of a small horse. The man untied the horse from the daggered post it was roped around and led it up the exit road and over to an opening in the brush; the black dog nosing in on the horse's tail all the while.

Gavin occupied his thoughts by skipping rocks.

He'd collected a good deal in his pockets over the lunch break of Chigustei bread and small game and was down to his last rock that was just flat enough to make it over to the other side of the river. He side-armed the rock and watched as it skipped one time before plunging dead-center. He grew bored without anything left to do and so his mind turned to his father. *He would have told me where he was going,* Gavin thought. *He's not doing one of his land deals. He's run away. He's done what I feel like doing.* His thoughts fueled his anger. *So will you do the same? Are you that brave?*

To let go of his father he imagined detaching the canoe from its line at the back of the double-wide and taking it north until the river dried to dirt and the dirt mashed under pavement. The highway lines he could follow to somewhere better.

His mind returned to the first day not long ago at his new school by the river. How the older kids had tried to convince him that the river went all the way to the ocean. He knew different. He knew the river ended near Casa Grande because it's what his father had told him when he was younger. He also knew the river was born out of the nothingness of Sonora Mexico. And for some strange reason, the river flowed north.

Trudging back through the shallows and over to the grass, Gavin sat down and listened for any sounds he hadn't heard before. An hour went by without him moving much more than his head and neck. There was a good deal of shade over him and for the first time since he could remember he didn't feel a little chill when the sun cradled the west.

He got up and walked over to the trailer where he'd spent a good portion of his day. There he crouched to make his way between two rotted boards under the ramp. After a few minutes, he emerged from the crawlspace head-first and with a canvas bag in hand. He then returned to the spot where he had been for the past hour and slipped both socks over his right foot. The one called Runner then pulled out a hefty firearm from the bag and took aim out over the water.

IT WAS PITCH DARK by the time Gavin made it back to his trailer.

He could see that the lights were all on inside and he thought for a second that his mother had changed her ways and come back to him. Before reaching for the door, he considered the possibility of her making a meal to celebrate a return to their previous life in Sierra

Vista. *Would the* Saint *in St. David mean nothing now if we went back to normal?* He pondered his future as he tried the knob but it wouldn't turn. Footsteps came to the door.

The door swung open and Sandis stood before him. Gavin immediately flung the canvas bag behind a shrub at the back of the trailer.

"What are you doing here?" Gavin said. Sandis troubled with an answer.

Gavin made his way to the kitchen in a hurry. "You can't come inside without me being here. Is my mom here?"

"The bulbs . . ." Sandis finally said, closing the door. He then bowed his head and palmed the door as if to keep something uninvited from entering. After a long moment, he pushed back. "I got to fixing all the bulbs in the lots and I knocked for a day and a year and then used my set of keys and let myself in. And then I got busied up with work. You know you had sixty watts going in the back? Sixty watts is way too heavy."

"You let yourself in to change the light bulbs?"

Sandis nodded.

"And you have a set of keys to my house, and all the other people's houses, I mean, trailers?"

The old man continued with his nod.

"Do you go in when they're not there?"

Sandis stilted in his dungarees. "Not usually," he said. "Well no, it's not at all common for me to enter a residence other than lot one-eight, so no."

"How come you came in mine then?"

Sandis brought a fist to his lips and coughed. "Like I said, the bulbs. The bulbs were out. Well, they were close to going anyways and I was busied and so that's just what I did. I apologize, Gavin, for letting myself in. You're the man of the house and I should have waited or come back later. You're right."

Gavin looked at the ceiling and all around. "I want you to leave," he said. "I'm really not too happy with all of this."

"I was hoping we might talk. You think we could talk?"

"Talk . . ? Talk about what?"

Sandis sat down on the arm of the couch, sliding his hands up and down his pant knees. "We had a guy in our unit," he said, extinguishing his breath. "Frankly, Gavin, there were two who had . . . we'll call it, emotional issues. Fact is, they couldn't deal much with the situation taking place around them and they just about lost it. Well I take that back, they did lose it. I mean their laces came untied."

"So what's that got to do with me?"

"Well for starters, I got on the fort channel this afternoon to speak with your mother about what occurred last night on the bridge. What occurred didn't sit too well with me, I'm afraid."

"Nothing happened."

"That wasn't *nothing*," Sandis said as he folded his arms. "I got concerned about your welfare and couldn't sleep. Your welfare stuck with me and I'm not talking about the basic kind of needs. I kept thinking that you needed to talk to someone. You know, someone other than me."

Gavin inspected the contents of the refrigerator. He poked his head in the freezer for a second or two. "You don't have to worry about me Mr. Sandis," he said. "My life is totally *bueno*."

Sandis went back to creating friction on his pants. "Your mother had mentioned to me that your grandfather was in the Army. She said he came all the way from Oklahoma and joined the conservationists out here and then spent most of his time fighting the krauts in the second war."

"He was in the Army, yeah, that's about all I know."

"Did you ever talk to him about it?"

"What, the Army?"

"Right, did he and you ever have a conversation about it? I'm thinking from the way your mother spoke, maybe your father was in the service too. A legacy is what I'm trying to get at here."

"My dad was in the National Guard, but I don't think it counts. I think I saw him in his uniform maybe one time but I'm not really sure. My grandfather was in the Army, yeah, and he was from Oklahoma, but I really don't know much about him other than that because he died before I was born."

"I'm sorry to hear that."

"Sorry about what? I never knew him."

"Right . . ."

"Could you leave me alone, Mr. Sandis? I'd like it if you just left, no offense. If you want to leave some bulbs for me, I can put them in myself."

Sandis planted his feet. "Not one ounce of a problem," he said. "Not one single ounce."

Gavin pretended to arrange miscellaneous items in the kitchen. He did his best to keep his eyes pointed at the floor.

"Gavin?"

"Yeah."

"You know I fought in the war, right, we've talked some about that?"

"Yeah, you were in the one fought at Hawaii."

"Well not exactly. I was in Korea. You ever heard of Korea before?"

Gavin didn't answer.

"Korea's the war. It's the real war."

"The real war. Got it."

"You ever seen that show on TV, about the doctors in the war?"

"You mean, MASH?"

"Right. MASH."

"I've seen it, yeah."

"It's funny, right?"

"Kinda, I guess."

"Well, that ain't it. War ain't funny and it ain't no joke. War is war."

Gavin unwrapped some food on the counter. "So where's Korea at if you want to talk about it so much?"

"About thirty years behind me," Sandis said. "But what I'm trying to get at here, in my own jumbled up sort of way, is that war ain't funny and it ain't anything but unfair."

"War is war."

"War is . . . well, exactly right."

"Why are you telling me this now?" Gavin said, sawing his food.

"Because your mother wants you to join the Army when you finish

47

school. She didn't say it in so many words, but that's what I heard from her. She asked me my thoughts on the subject and I gave her my two bits. I think I gave her what she needed to hear."

"What did she need to hear, Mr. Sandis?"

"Would you be given the tools to succeed out in the world as a grown man for one. Would the Army help give you a path and such. She talked benefits. Women always want to know the benefits. Something you'll learn about later on. She took out a pen and paper and wrote down plusses and minuses."

Gavin kept busy at doing nothing in particular with the plates and cups on the kitchen counter. "No one can make me do what I don't want to do. Maybe I want to do something else. Maybe I want to play football in the pros, or maybe I want to go to Mexico. No one can tell me what to do. I can do whatever I choose to."

"This is a free country. When you turn eighteen, you got that right."

"Damn right I do," Gavin said as he stepped out from the kitchen and over to the television. "You can't take that freedom away from me."

Sandis scratched his beard, chuckling.

"What's so funny?" Gavin said.

"Sorry . . . I think I just had me one of those moments. The freedom you got, it's just funny to me when I think about that. Give me a moment here."

Gavin pinched his lips.

"Take a seat on the sofa for me, son, will ya please?"

"Are you leaving?"

Gavin sat on the couch with a game show and a soda the size of a bowling pin. Sandis, however, stepped between him and his chance at twenty-five grand.

Bowing only so much Sandis gazed at Gavin with a somber look in his eyes. It was then Gavin noticed the black band that Sandis had wrapped around his left bicep. Not a band to hold material for a fix-it job or a pipe when your pockets become overwhelmed. But a band to signal the end of a life and a new time to mourn.

5 TAKE IT EASY

WALT ESKIN sat and sipped his Mormon Tea as the world outside his wickiup swayed.

He fixed his browns on the myriad of bricks that made up his chimney, following their lines until a drop of rainwater landed in the valley trenched across his forehead. He reached under his table set for one to feel at a stack of animal hides. When he found a hide of his liking, he dragged it outside to the dark hours before the dawn.

He stood amongst the form and fauna, looking like he was listening for something and offering a palm up to the cobalt sky. He then tested the hide over his head for a minute before trusting it to the roof.

With his eyes satisfied to the stability he collected a jar by the entry and back-handed the hide that hung in his way to get at the tea kettle.

Like a religious ceremony he poured the watery night into a piece of metal that had, at last generation, been formed by an Apache blacksmith. He returned the metal to flame and returned to his empty cup, his big hands looking like they might crush it.

Time passed.

The kettle huffed.

A world of paved roads outside the weaving walls.

When the wind moaned, the kettle did spoke.

In the billowy steam he whistled like a sweet little bird. He stopped his whistle soon after the start, glancing at the back of the room. Refilling his cup he hummed a few bars sold of a smile, turning to song. *Take it easy . . . take it easy . . . don't let the sound of your own wheels drive you crazy, lighten up while you still can, don't even try to understand, just find a place to make your stand and take it easy.*

He plucked notes on the air-guitar.

Well I'm standing on a corner in nowhere *Arizona-*

A noise at the back corner of the room interrupted his tune.

Walt moved to a cot in the back corner and dropped to a knee, feeling at the beads tapered around a white blanket. There he studied the blanket weaves as if they might provide insight into the one curled underneath. For a minute or two he closed his eyes and raised a palm and listened for something outside, or something from deep inside of him.

He moved back over to the fire and placed a hand over the wire to feel the burn. He removed his hand much slower than he should have and unbuttoned his flannel. Barefoot in jeans he flexed his arms up and down in rapid succession and made some loud breathing noises. And then for a minute, he just stood there in the firelight stiff as a board.

The weather altered.

Walt ignored the winded whirls with a fist held over the flames. He counted out to ten and switched hands. Then he started his count all over again.

After the burning he wrapped his hands up in the flannel and gently rocked in his chair. He tucked his arms under the table and nodded over the piney air until his breathing cleared. Merging his fists together by the smallest fingers the veins in his arms became dirt roads through an old desert cleared.

He turned his wrists over to a multitude of scars, pressing his knuckles together as he dug his thumbs deep into his sternum. A pain in his eyes did reveal. He guarded his breath and contemplated his next words, denying the pain he felt from reaching his neurons.

Walt let go the pressure and looked across the table at a string of hides on the wall. With an ease about him he danced with a skeleton dancing in a carcass and battled with Apache warriors and their axes in a rifle battle. He sat there for some time with the fire listening, imaging it all. "My only weakness," he said. "Is the tops of my skin."

6 RUNAWAY

"You breathing in there?" a muffled voice said over clapping hands.

Gavin wiped his tired eyes and stretched his body out as far as he could across two lawn chairs to the point where his rear was about in the dirt. A white blanket covered the upper half of his body and he gathered it in and up to his ears. He yawned without making a sound and shaded himself from the beard.

"I'll be right back, Private. So don't you move a muscle."

He ignored the instruction and gazed out at the mid-morning sky, his eyes following the jagged lines of clouds curling to the south. He yawned once more with passion.

His shaking out from the heaviness of sleep caused him to lose position between chairs and so he dropped to the dirt and just sat there with his hands clawed and his eyes bloodshot.

When he figured out that he wasn't going to be lifted out of the situation any time soon he pushed up from the ground and grabbed the chair at his back, elbowing up on the cushioned vinyl. Somewhat comfortable, he looked at his naked toes. A spray of water at the back of his neck then made him flinch. "What's your problem?" Gavin said with one eye closed.

"You're among the living, good."

"Where am I?"

"You're where you-"

"What?" he said in an argumentative tone.

"You are where you are sup-"

"Where's my shoes?"

Sandis put a hand on Gavin's shoulder after dropping his bucket of water. "How about we get a grip on your handle first and then we'll go from there, okay?"

Gavin looked like he might respond. He didn't.

"You like coffee? How you like yours, one big pillar of sugar I bet?"

Gavin sprung out of the chair. He regretted the action as soon as he felt bits of gravel and spines at his feet. Quickly he stepped on the edge of the blanket for relief, yanking the other end up to his chest. "Where's my mother?" he said, checking around for stray bulbs of cacti.

Sandis gestured out in front of his body with his hands in a push-up position. "Okay, now you are-"

"Where. Are. My. Shoes. Where are they? Why've you taken them away from me?"

"Just settle, Gavin. Nobody has taken your shoes." Sandis pointed at the water tower about twenty yards away. Gavin only grimaced. "See," he added. "They're right over there."

"Where's my mother? Where is she? What time's it? What's the day, today? And what's the time?"

"Today is Thursday, and you're at home. You're where you're supposed to be, okay? You remember talking to me last night, right?"

He only heard his mangled thoughts. "I don't live here," Gavin said.

Sandis did a quick scan of the grounds. He came back to Gavin. "Well . . ." he said. "This is where you live. You're where you live, alright." He raised a hand above Gavin's head. "By the looks of it, I believe you hit your noggin on something, so just sit back down and let me get some-"

"This isn't where I live, asshole."

"Listen to me now, just sit back and-"

"This place is a dump," Gavin said. "I don't live here. You're lying to me, geezer."

Sandis opened his mouth like he was going to say something but then he bit his lip. "Right," he uttered.

Gavin eyeballed the old man. He felt like he wanted to hit him. Hit something. Anything. "Bring me my shoes, asshole." The request rolled off his tongue as if he were being polite.

Sandis turned a cheek from Gavin and gathered himself. He then jilted his head around to work out a strain. "I'm gonna let that one slide," he said. "You're hurt. And you're hurting." He spread the lawn chairs out and took a seat on the one where he could observe the grounds the best. "Go on now, Private," he said, pointing at the empty chair. "Take a load off."

"No."

"You need to sit."

"No, I don't."

"I know what you're going through right now. There's a couple of stages. Right now you're in the stage of shock. And slowly, but surely, you're drifting into the chasms of disbelief."

"You're full of shit, you know that? Where is she, what did you do to her?"

"Gavin listen . . ."

No response.

"Gavin."

His thoughts scrambled.

"Gavin."

"What?"

"You're having trouble understanding what happened to your mother, I get it. But do me the favor and sit your butt down because I don't have the legs to go on a scavenger hunt again in the desert with a dang flashlight made and manufactured by drunk Chinamen. Can you promise me you'll sit down and listen to me and not run away when I talk to you this time?"

"Did you hit me?"

"Of course not."

"Did you hit my mother?"

"What?"

"You heard me."

Sandis almost laughed. He then thought for a second. "I'm going to stand up and face you now," he said. "And if you ask me again if I hit you or if I hit your mother, I might just make that a reality, the one that's in the first person kind."

Sandis stood up and moved within a foot of Gavin. He placed his hands on Gavin's shoulders without any interference.

Gavin lowered his head and felt around on the lining of the blanket. "Where is she?" he asked, in a voice as soft as the fabric.

"It's like I said to you last night, son, she's not coming back. And right now, at this very moment, it might be the only time in your life that you'll have the opportunity to let it go. Now is the exact time to let it go. Scream if you want. Just let it go. She's not coming back, do you understand me? She was brought to the infirmary inside the Fort midday yesterday, unresponsive. They confirmed with me this morning that it was a stroke. She had a stroke and she choked to death on her own vomit, that's the report I've been given. There's not a thing you could have done about it, Gavin. Do you know that? Not one dang thing."

Gavin huffed and cranked his legs, his anger denying him from any singular focus.

"You know what a stroke is?" Sandis said as he secured Gavin better by the arms, taking a chance at being shoved.

Gavin brushed away and sat in the lawn chair. He folded the blanket into halves in a distant stare. When he was done he snapped his fingers and pointed at his sneakers.

"You're not getting those things unless you speak to me and tell me you understand what it is I'm saying to you."

"I understand."

"What did I say then?"

"It was a stroke."

"Right. A stroke."

"And she choked on her own vomit."

"Right."

"And there's nothing I could have done about it."

"Right. Well, okay then, how-"

"And you're an asshole for keeping my shoes over there from me with a bunch of spines in the way."

Sandis looked over at Gavin's sneakers, folding his arms. "That make you feel better?" he said. "Your kind words?"

"Bring me my shoes and I won't swear at you anymore."

Sandis went over to the ladder of the water tower and retrieved the pair, releasing the stuffed socks to the cleansed air. He spread it all at the runner's feet. "Now . . . " he said, "if you put these dang things on and bolt off like you did last night, I'm gonna go retrieve my high-powered and sit in this chair up on the Jacuzzi we got here and pick you off and take you out of your misery. And then I'm gonna go inside and make myself a ham and cheese sandwich and enjoy the thing and get on with my day and my routines. Now, that's what I plan to do. So what about you, what are you planning on doing?"

"You don't have a high-powered," Gavin said with spite. "And when you were in the Army you were a stupid cook or something. I bet you couldn't touch me because I'm too fast anyway for an old man with a bunch of hairs in his ears and nose."

Sandis chuckled, backing up as he did. "That sounds like a challenge to me," he said, adjusting his overalls. "Like what you're saying to me is fighting words, and that I better come prepared."

"Maybe, yeah. I got your challenge right here."

Sandis gripped his bands. "Well lace up those dirty shoes then poor boy, and we'll see how far your mouth takes you on a dimes worth a petrol."

Gavin grabbed a sneaker. "I'm not poor," he said. "You think I live in a stupid trailer, that's a joke. You're a dipshit and you're the one who's poor. You're the one who's stupid. You choose to live out here, not me. No one knows who you are and your stories are all bullshit."

Sandis rocked in his shoes, his brown rubbers half combat. "God you're focused," he said.

"What's wrong with being focused?"

"Nothing, if you ever made it about someone or something other than yourself. You could take that dang spotlight you shine on yourself and shine it somewheres else and give us all a big break. Your compulsion is a bit hard to take sometimes, you know that?"

Gavin wiped the bottoms of his feet and stepped into his sneakers. He tested them out lace free before picking up his socks. "I'm leaving," he said. "As soon as I can get some food and get rid of this stupid headache, I'm outta this dump for good."

WHEN ALL OF THE RACKET outside his trailer died down, Gavin peeked his browns out from behind the kitchen window blinds and waited for something else to happen. A small plane sputtered overhead and then nothing happened for several minutes. At twelve-twenty in the afternoon, Rock Gardens turned into a ghost town of metallic siding and sunned-laundry.

Gavin had found a legal pad stashed amongst some of his father's things and so he'd penciled a letter of several pages and addressed it to Sandis. With his own eyes and hand he wanted to explain as best he could his personal story.

He attached the letter with a generous piece of duct tape to the outside of the front door. Closing the door without locking it he set off in the direction to where the old man had discovered him earlier.

When he arrived at the spot, just yards from the start of the northwest trail, he searched around for the white blanket. He then noticed one of the chairs propped up on the deck of the water tower. He gazed at the chair for far too long before making the decision to keep moving and to forget about anything and everything for the day, the night, and the days yet to appear.

Hiking down from the south he spotted Sandis hauling trash containers in the same direction. In a flash he crumpled to the slanted Earth, removing his white shirt in order to keep his body as much a part of the landscape as possible. He huddled there over his knees and took mental notes as the sun warmed his shoulders.

A delivery truck rumbled over the bridge. The truck made its way to the base of the hill and parked beside Sandis's Ford F-100. Gavin watched Sandis transfer supplies from truck to truck and then take a break on the gate of the Ford with a book in one hand and a pipe in the other. When Sandis finished with his pipe, he climbed back inside his factory girl and gassed up the hill.

Gavin lurched to the base like he was on a recon mission. When he made it to the flat dirt he checked his position and cover. A small gray lizard scampered at his sneaks. He moved his eyes from the high grounds to monitor the creature but soon lost it to a hole the size of a quarter.

Gavin ran at half speed from the dirt to the pavement of the bridge road. As soon as he stepped on the highway connector he bolted east. After a hundred yards or so, as quick as he'd begun, he slammed on the brakes.

He felt for the first time that running might no longer patch his anger and hurt. The thought of his mother, his father, and his trailer in the dirt, impossible for him to let go. Every question in his head forever unanswered.

He approached the bridge in a funk as his thoughts continued on to the shores of somewhere Mexico. He wondered what life would be like for an American there. He so desperately wanted a few more birthdays added to his sixteen years. And for the first time in his life he no longer wanted to care.

The wind picked up from zero. It played with his bangs. Those fine black strands with hints of auburn. He thought to pick up his feet before deferring all motivation to sorrow.

When he came to where the wood beams of the bridge connected to the pavement, he saw a man in a leather jacket attaching something to the foundation. Gavin hopped up on the beam that was at his left and took a few steps and then hopped back off.

"Don't do that," the man said, keeping his eyes to his work.

"Do what?"

"What you just did. Don't do that."

He felt the twisted metal of the crushed guardrail that was his doing and leaned over. "What did I just do?"

The man tossed a tool into the bed of his truck. "It is weak already," he said, his shoulder-length hair bleeding into black leather. Gavin thought the jacket was much too warm for the weather. "If you see it as I see it," the man continued, "you will see it weak and splitting. You will see it with little support for what it truly needs."

Gavin kept tight lipped as he backpedaled across the bridge. When he made it to the east end, the man yelled something in his direction. Gavin ignored the man and opened a hip, continuing on in his particular gait of emotions governing his feet.

The man got into his truck and cranked the engine. He shot west toward Rock Gardens and made a U-turn after about a quarter mile stretch, racing back toward the bridge at a high rate of speed. The truck crossed over in a split second, skidding parallel with Gavin.

The man stuck his elbow outside the window and shifted up the wheel shaft. He sat there with his left boot on the brake and his right tap-dancing on the gas, the wheels blowing smoke from underneath. The needle on the RPM went over three thousand and then it leveled back to two. Gavin focused in on an elbow patch. "Where are you going?" the man asked.

Gavin took in the nature, and the smoke. "South," he said.

"Like a bird?"

"Maybe."

"How far south?"

Gavin turned a cheek. "As far as Mexico."

The man clicked on the radio and changed the station dial. "It is not safe to hitch rides," he said.

"Who says I'm hitching."

"You're walking?"

"Maybe."

"You got water?"

"Yeah, the river."

"The river, that's not a plan."

"Are you my guardian?"

The man paused. "I will say I am not him."

"Then who cares?"

The heavy old motor revved, the engine a work of refined tuning by the temperament sound.

"I am Walt, second son of Chief Ez."

Gavin inspected the running boards and white-wall tires, backing to the narrow shoulder some as he did.

"I am going to the rounded corners," the man said. "If you want, you can ride shotgun."

"Where's that at?"

"South."

"Close to Sierra Vista?"

"Close."

Gavin turned to spy the highway about a mile and a half east.

"No cars."

Gavin pinched his lips.

"After hump-day you got the out-of-work drunks and truckers behind on the load."

"So . . ."

"So be careful. You never know who you'll run in to."

"What about you?"

"What about me?"

"Who are you?"

"I am Walt, second son of Chief Ez."

"You said that already. I meant, what do you want to give me a ride for?"

"I see an empty seat to my right. What should I do, wait for it to be filled?"

"That's not an answer."

"A question then. What is a car with no driver?"

"A car."

"It is metal and parts not moving. What is a seat with no sitter?"

"An empty seat."

"*Empty* is a good word. With no driver, we are left with material things, aren't we?"

"That makes no sense."

The man gassed the engine. The bridge road a drag strip until it linked to Highway 80. "You can think about my words on your long walk to Mexico. Food for your thoughts."

Gavin thought about hamburgers as the engine pulled him near. "What about the back?" he said.

"What about it?"

"Are you thinking that it needs to be filled?"

"Do you not see the tools?"

Gavin raised on his toes. The man greeted the opportunity to spy the runner's tape.

"Yeah, I see them," Gavin answered.

The man smiled as he messed with the sun visor. He then gripped the steering wheel and tested out the wheels. "The tools," he said, looking at the road ahead, "are in the right place. I will say they are right where they belong. *Empty* is a good word. What about you, what in your cup needs filling?"

7 LAST GAS

WHEN GAVIN AND WALT pulled into a Texaco station just south of Whetstone the clock on the pump read one-sixteen in the afternoon.

"Last gas," Walt said.

Gavin felt his pale in the passenger window. "Are you a father?" he asked.

Walt put the truck in park and tested the motor a few times before shutting it off. A greasy teen rushed out of the garage with a rag in hand. Walt waved the teen off. "You can always start over," he said, turning to Gavin. "Your vow of silence, you get many tries."

Gavin pressed a thumb against the window and focused in on the red that surrounded the nail. "So are you?"

Walt changed the radio country to more of the same. "It is true," he said.

Gavin gazed out beyond his reflection, into the light of the mellow afternoon sun. He had an unusual thought and fought to keep it to himself. "Is it fair for a child to die, Walt, you know, before their parents do?"

Walt clicked off the country twang. "Is this your burden, you lost a brother . . . a sister?"

Gavin wouldn't turn. "It just doesn't seem fair for a young child to die, that's all."

They watched a motorcycle chug into a parking space next to the garage on one leg.

"Some things in life can seem to be unfair at first impression," Walt said. "Some things . . . show no reason."

"So it's unfair."

"It is not what I say."

"I think it's unfair."

The greasy teen held up a sign about an oil change. Walt shook his head in response. "It is not far then," he said.

"What's not far?"

"Sierra Vista."

"Oh . . ."

"And your thoughts. They are not far from the truth."

Gavin sat up straight to get a good look at himself in the corner mirror. In his head he aged one year.

Walt cased the gas station. "How young is young?" he asked.

"Like ten," Gavin said.

"I see."

Walt tucked the ignition key inside his jacket pocket and then moved his hands atop the wheel, drawing in a considerable amount of breath behind his grip. "Let me say to you then: there was an old woman, her name was Essa. Essa had survived the great rifle attack. When I was a young one, Essa would gather all the little feet to share stories. Her big story was that her mother had brought comfort to her and the other young ones when their camp was being burned. Essa's message, the one from her mother, and the one I say to you now, was that they were to experience the promise of a great love. Her mother's words were not to hide the young ones from the fear of death, but to reveal the truth."

Gavin adjusted his body so that he was no longer barricading himself against the door. He messed with the radio dial. "Why do some people get to live so long and others don't?" he said. "I met a man once out on the highway pushing a grocery cart who told me everything he owned was in his cart. He told me he was a hundred years old."

Walt grinned. He removed his hands from the wheel and made a shape with his thumbs in his sternum and his index fingers like an arrow tip. He then drummed at the horn. "What I say you say is: what is love? Is that about right then?"

Gavin shifted back toward the door. "I don't know," he uttered.

"Love is as it is written. There is no greater love but for a willing death before a friend. Do you trust this?"

Gavin drew in a thoughtful breath. "I'm not sure my mother ever loved me," he said. "I know my dad wouldn't have left us if he did. If he didn't love my mother any more that's fine, but he didn't have to go on and leave me too, not say goodbye."

Walt hummed in a humorous manner, tapping his fingers.

"It isn't funny," Gavin said, looking at Walt.

"A child knows of his mother's love," Walt said. "Do you not know this? Are you really that blind? Your excuse is an eagle scratched out your eye, is that it?"

Gavin kicked the glove box. "I'm not a child," he said.

"Says you."

"Says me?"

"And not him."

"Who?"

"The one who is laughing with me. The biggest comedian of them all."

Gavin paused. "Who would that be, Walt?"

"The one who gives us raindrops to drown our thirst and oceans we cannot drink and rivers that bleed into dirt only to bleed from the dirt somewhere we cannot see. The Living Spirit."

"Living Spirit?"

"Yatasay. You call him God. You hold your hands up to the sky like he is a bird and looking down on you and not inside. It is not as it is written and so you go on and do your own things. This is why you get pooped on so much."

Gavin pressed every digit of his weak hand against the side window. He could see the lines of her face there in the glass as he made a circle. He remembered a picture he'd seen in a scrapbook somewhere. A picture labeled of two lovebirds who shared every last detail.

Walt folded his arms, resting his chin to his chest and sharpening his tone. "The water on your eyes," he said. "Does it not burn?"

"I don't know, I guess, maybe a little."

"Wipe your eyes."

Gavin wiped away his memories from the window, continuing with a wipe to his eyes. Walt faced the scene left of his window. Unrecognizable cars on cinder blocks. Scrapped engines under tarp. A baked yellow desert with mutt brush and flecks of green.

"The water on your hand . . . does it not taste of salt?"

"I don't know," Gavin said, rubbing his nose.

"Spit that into the ground."

Gavin opened the passenger door. He tried to follow Walt's instruction, but his mouth was too dry.

"Now . . . " Walt said, "get out of the truck and dig a handful of dirt and offer it up to the wind. I say this to you because the wind is the only thing you can say is real because when it catches the dirt it touches you. When you are done, go and punch that machine by the house of cars and bring to me a cola that has the cherry." Walt dug around inside his jacket for change. He placed a few pieces of silver on the dash. "Go on now, Runner," he added. "I am filled up with thirst speaking big things to you."

THEY ABANDONED the truck at the back of the gas station and headed down a narrow trail toward the open west desert. They walked in silence for a good twenty minutes before Gavin slowed to look behind him. The red and black Texaco sign was about the size of a shoe box. The cola machine lassoed him by the neck.

"Look at me," Walt said.

Gavin faced Walt.

"To the side of me. Pick a side."

Gavin scanned the scenery. *It's the stupid desert,* he thought. *There are no sides.* "The pretty desert," he said. "Thanks so much for showing me, Walt."

"Look now at those things on your feet."

Gavin looked at his road-worn sneakers. "My feet, okay," he mumbled.

"They're on the road that once challenged my back and hands. I will say it was the challenge that almost defeated me. To make the roads that moved the wood. The roads that moved the wood that built up the place where you live and everywhere else you run."

Gavin cared little for the speech. "That's what you wanted to show me, this old road? Why didn't you just tell me that at the beginning? I thought we were going somewhere different, like you said back there. Somewhere I'd never been."

Walt pointed southwest. "Have you run up there?" he said. "I know the answer, so don't say. Say if you want to say, but the answer is *no*. No, you have not."

Gavin leaned left. "What, the mountains?"

"They are more like hills."

Gavin leaned a bit more. Then he steadied back, shaking his head.

"See if you can make it all the way up and back to where it is we stand. To make first place. There are rocks on the top that don't look like anything you'll see on the steps you take. Find something that stands out and make your return. See if you can make first place."

Gavin glanced at his right sneaker, rolling it over. The duct tape looked to be about as durable as scotch tape. "This road goes all the way up there?" he said.

"It splits. And when it does, choose right."

"So when I get back, we can leave?"

"You could leave right now, you have your legs."

Gavin rubbed his stomach.

"Are you really that good, that they call you - *Runner*?"

Gavin made a serious face, drawing back the hair over his ears.

"If you're not a runner, we can find out. We can find you another name."

"I already have a name," Gavin said.

Walt sat on the ground.

Gavin put his hands on his hips and took a few eager breaths. "First place, huh?"

"First place," Walt said. "No *huh*."

AN HOUR LATER, Gavin throttled down to half his speed on the last leg of his run. When he got beside Walt he went to the ground like a dog with the sweat of the sun covering him complete. He remained at eye level with Walt until the wind in his chest returned from vacation. The choice to go right nagged at him as he thought about his winning time and mentally accepted his award. The choice to go right seemed a lot rockier than the choice he would have made on his own.

Walt opened his eyes after an entirety and finger-raked the dirt. "So . . ." he said. "You got first place, good job."

"How do you know I . . . I haven't even . . . even given you the rock, maybe . . . maybe I didn't even get it."

Walt meditated on the cloud swirls. "Did you?"

Gavin coughed. "I think so . . . yeah . . . I think." He reached into his front pocket for a shiny black rock and tossed it in front of Walt. Walt picked up the rock and looked at it like it was the next thing to meditate on. He then threw the rock to stand out someplace else.

"It is like I say, Runner. First place."

"What times it?" Gavin said.

"Later than it was before."

"What time did I make?"

"Probably a good time, if I had a watch on."

"You weren't timing me?"

"No."

"How did I get first place then?" His mind sprinted the route. And his hands jabbed. "You have to beat a time, Walt. That's how the thing works!"

"You were first to run, and first to place, so you got first place. It is not different from how I say."

Gavin's forehead and cheeks flushed bright red. His neck strained. "You could have told me you didn't have a timer," he argued. "You could have told me that because I would not have run that fast. I busted my ass for nothing. Thanks a lot."

Walt got up off the ground, brushing the dirt from the jacket he'd used for a cushion. "You think I tell numbers from the sun?" he asked.

"I don't know what you do."

"I do many things. I do not tell numbers from the sun. The sun goes up and it goes down. And it rises in front of me."

"The sun rises from the east, Walt, everyone knows that."

"The sun rises in front of me."

"Whatever . . ."

"You got first place."

"I know what that means now. Absolutely nada."

"I will say also that you get the prize handed to you by the people with no legs at the V.A. They say you're a winner when you say you run first place."

Gavin slicked back his bangs with a wicked grin. "Can I ask you something?" he said.

Walt nodded.

"Promise not to get mad."

Walt nodded again, locking a wrist with one hand behind his back. The jacket tucked under his muscular arm.

"Do you drink?"

Walt nodded once more.

"People at my school, I mean at my old school, they said Indians like to drink."

"It is true. Indians are big drinkers."

"That's what people said."

"The people were right."

"You're not mad?"

"I do not get mad at the truth of words. Any anger I have is burned from my memory before it scars."

Gavin's brows came together over his nose. "What exactly does that mean, people with no legs at the, the . . . what did you say?"

"The V.A."

"What do you mean by that?"

Walt put on his jacket. "You have legs, true?"

Gavin looked at his sneakers. The white about gone to brown. "You know I do," he said.

"And you run a time, you don't know what time, but you run a time, true?"

"Yeah."

"What I say is that you walk in the veteran's hospital in Sierra Vista and you see people who cannot walk in front of you, and you tell them you run up a hill. You say you did this just the other day, and they look at you and your legs, as you do now. Do they ask you what time you made?"

Gavin picked up his head. "No," he said. "I don't think so."

"What is it they say?"

"I don't know, Walt, this is stupid."

"What is it you *think* they say?"

Gavin shrugged. Although drained of energy, he considered a dash for the pavement. He thought that Mexico might be too far for his legs. He thought the same for the highway. Walt cleared his throat.

"They say thank you for coming. They say thank you for your visit. And one will say to you that you bring up pictures in their mind of their son. They say nothing about time. Time goes away and they feel better. They forget they have no legs or no legs that work for the time they talk to you and they feel better because you are there and the son they have who does not visit disappears. You give to them some time without the pain. This is what I have been thinking about since you have been running to make first place."

The runner kicked at the dirt.

"Did you know I was capable of thinking such things?" Walt said. He kicked the dirt more. "No," Gavin answered. "How would I?"

"Deep thoughts then."

"Deep thoughts?"

"Yatasay. They are good."

Gavin folded his arms. He didn't want to take another step. He pictured his lungs the size of sandwich bags.

"What is it you are thinking now, Runner?"

Nada, Gavin thought.

"Bet I can tell you."

"You can't know what I'm thinking, Walt. But if you want to know, nothing at all." His mind sprang to the Walkman at the fort supply depot. He pictured the poster he had bought there. The one tacked to his bedroom wall. The one with the man in the red and white uniform, carrying the football.

"You are always thinking something. Bet I can tell you."

"Okay, what am I thinking?"

"It was stolen."

"What was stolen?"

"My watch."

"I didn't ask you if it was."

"I know."

"So why are you telling me that it was?"

"Because you wanted to know."

"Know what?"

"You wanted to know when the injun in front of you would use his money for once to buy a watch instead of whiskey."

WALT CRANKED the motor and pressed the gas until the two came together. "It is sensitive," he said. "Sensitive like me."

"What kind of trees are they up there, Walt?"

"Green ones."

"You don't know what kind?"

"We planted them long ago. We planted them when I was about your age, when we made the roads and moved the wood. I do not know the name."

"Was that the conservations?"

"It was."

Gavin clicked his seat belt. "There's a sign at the camp about them. My grandfather was in them too. How come they planted those kind of trees in the desert?"

"To make it more green and less brown."

"That's the reason?"

"People needed jobs is the reason. There was no work when I was young. It was of no difference what color your skin was, there was no work. So the government made work."

They drove out to the highway and headed for Sierra Vista. Walt dialed the radio. He hummed along to a song that came on after a brief commentary. "This is a good one," he said.

"You can drop me off before we get to the signs," Gavin said.

"I will take you where it is you are going. Where will you stay at night if you're going all the way to Mexico?"

"At my old house in Sierra Vista. If there's no one there, I know a way in."

Walt thought. "And if the old house is a new house for somebody else, where will you stay?"

"Outside."

"Outside?"

"Yeah."

"What if it rains?"

Gavin shrugged in his filled seat.

"The desert is cold at night, no matter the time of year. You know how to make a roof from the trees?"

"No."

"Much like a friend, I will say, a good one takes two years."

Gavin gazed at the speeding brush. "I have my two feet," he replied. "Besides, it doesn't look like it will rain for another year."

"You ever sleep in the desert at night before?"

"I've been sleeping in the desert, for the last six months, by myself."

Walt kept in line of the road. "Good point," he said.

When they reached the mile marker before the Brass road exit, Gavin undid his belt and leaned forward. "You can drop me up here," he said.

Walt took his foot off the gas and then reapplied after a few seconds, bringing the speed back up to forty. An obnoxious horn screamed at him from the rear. He gestured with the back of his hand at a vehicle about to tag his bumper. The vehicle gestured back and rambled over to the left lane. Walt stuck his elbow out the window and smiled at the passerby like the sun was in the very center of his veneers. After an ugly word or two in his ear, he winked at Gavin.

"It is not his age, the sign he makes with his hand, and it is not his IQ, it is the size of the penis of his wife's lover."

Unabashed, Gavin let go of laughter. "You say some funny stuff, Walt, you know that?"

"Humor is all you have sometimes. Do you not know this?"

"Yeah, I guess."

"The angry man has nothing."

"The angry man?"

Walt checked his rearview as Gavin turned to a catchy sign for Dee's Restaurant on his side of the highway. "When that car passes," Gavin said, "you can pull to the side and I'll get out."

"The question you had asked me before, Runner, about the young one."

"What about it?"

"I will say it was good."

"Thanks . . ."

"What I say is that someone your age would not think to ask such a question. I know my son would not think so deep."

"How old is he, your son?"

"How old are you?"

He thought about sixteen and how it sucked worse than all of his previous years. "Seventeen."

"Same age minus two years then."

"Fifteen?"

"You can do math. I've heard good things about the Corte School."

"You know I go there?"

"Not for sure. But I will say that you do. You like to run and you're white."

"I guess some people know that."

Walt increased his speed to fifty miles per hour. "I will bet on two things," he said. "One is that you are hungry, and the other is that you have never had the tacos made by the vendors at the back of rounded corners."

Gavin eased in his seat. "You bet right," he said.

"I will stop then and we will eat. You can run all you want after that. Maybe you go more than Mexico. What is more I don't know. But maybe you do."

Gavin's stomach grumbled. "That sounds good to me," he said.

"I will say one more thing and I will shut up. You will watch me eat and I will not speak. I will enjoy the warm of the sun and the tacos and rolled beef, and all the extra sauces. And if you let me, I will enjoy the company. I will say one more thing before we eat and I will shut up. You will not hear from me a peep and if you poke at me with a stick I will not say one word. Just one more thing to say for now, Runner, and that is all."

Gavin hugged his knees and looked at Walt. "What is it you want to say to me?" he said, his mind open and curious.

"I will say those tacos are the best in the west and that those beaners really know how to cook up a storm. Some of them I call friends. Those who wink at me when they call me a blanket-ass to my face."

8 FOXHOLE

ON FRIDAY, Gavin stepped out from his trailer and into the blaze of the late morning sun. He had made the choice to move one day closer to the summer rather than to remain on the couch that served him so well for a part-time bed.

He contemplated the choices that he'd made over the last forty hours, one of which was the choice to run down into the flat valley with a gun in his hand. And another choice, equally as brash, to head for the Mexican border without knowing one single person or having an ID that would allow him legal entry. His choices were flush with emotion, yet he couldn't quite grasp how easily his emotions led his feet. Gavin only felt the bitterness inside of him as he squeezed the rail of his porch for answers about his situation. What happened in the desert after hearing the news of his mother? He desperately wanted to remember. Where was his father? He let go of his questions and let go of the rail, considering a run for the highway instead of the school for Apache kids by the river.

He rotated around in the cared for dirt three hundred and sixty degrees. The temperature felt half that with the way the heat emanated up from the ground and radiated off the siding to absorb all the moisture in his skin. The intense glare made him dizzy. He saw spots bounce and then disappear before his crusted eyes. In an attempt to lighten his mood he told himself the summer might melt his body.

When he adjusted well enough, he noticed a small stack of canned goods under the steps. He collected the cans in a sack made from his grimy shirt and struggled back to the door. With a foot inside the trailer he tossed the cans onto the couch with an easy touch in his motion. Then he shut the door and removed his shirt and swung the key that was strung by a lace around his neck so that it hung at the middle of his back. He put the neck of his shirt over his head and, fitting his ears, stood there for a moment with a hopeful face testing the temperature of the sun once more.

Gavin walked in the direction of the main gate, to the northeast.

Two residents were huddled next to a trash barrel adjacent the gate and when they saw Gavin coming they flicked the last of their cigarettes and separated. He tried, but he could only figure one of their names. He stopped a few yards short of the gate to secure the lace of his tape-free sneaker. The lace was too far gone to even try for a center knot so he pulled the line down a notch and simply knotted the ends.

When he looked around from the low ground he could see there was a good deal of trash that hadn't yet found its way to the containers. Cola cans and cracked beer bottles and specks of debris from who-knows-what kind of things. To top off the mess, there was a small rodent lying dead as a stick near the edge brush. The thing had black, bulging, sunbaked eyes. Gavin collected as much trash as he could and dumped it into a container. Then he marked off a few paces, aligned his hand with an imaginary goal post and gave the rodent a swift kick. He shouted "Goal!" as it sailed over the back of the hill in two pieces.

Out of nowhere a loud bang cracked through the dry air and so he made his way around one of the gate posts and down the hill to further investigate the noise. After a half-minute, a familiar Ford F-100 with its newly distorted front end made its way around the last turn. Gavin let the truck pull up to his side.

"Just my Browning," Sandis said with a slight grin. "I like to set it out the other window and take out those old Saguaros. You know, the protected ones."

Gavin stood speechless.

"That there was a joke, Private. Sunny gets upset with me when I don't treat her to the rich man's petrol. So she backfires on me now and then. I tell ya, Sunny, she's a jealous girl. But heck, aren't they all?"

"What's petrol?"

Sandis mumbled something to his thousand pound girlfriend. "Just a fancier name for gasoline," he said.

"Got it."

Sandis styled his beard in the corner mirror. "I got your letter," he said. "I tell ya what, that was one helluva story. One helluva story." He eyed the boy. "You ever think about turning it into a picture show?"

Gavin raised an eyebrow.

"I was out at the 76 earlier and I got to thinking about it all pretty deep - the drive does that to my mind sometimes. I guess I never did know your mother but for a little while. Was she really like you wrote about, when your family lived in Sierra Vista?"

"I wrote what I did, Mr. Sandis, because it's what I know. It's how I see things. And it's the only story I know."

"You wrote some odd stuff."

"My life's been odd."

The transmission growled. Sandis arched over the steering wheel, caressing the dash. "Easy . . ." he tendered.

Gavin continued on for the bottom of the hill. Sandis shifted into neutral and the truck rolled backwards.

"Wait up a minute," Sandis said, bending his head and elbow out the window.

"What for?" Gavin said.

"I'm intrigued. You got me intrigued."

Gavin put his hands in his front pockets and slant-planted his feet. Sandis shifted into park and shut the engine down.

"She had swore off God, is that so?"

Gavin shrugged.

"I'm asking you, Gavin, because I read the thing front to back. Are you regretting your story now, sharing it with somebody else?"

"No."

"Okay then. So . . . no God?"

"Yeah," Gavin mumbled. He decided not to bury all of his feelings. His hands came free. "She told me that since I was at a school for

Episcopals, and that they had mandatory church during school hours, that that was enough God for the both of us."

"Right."

Gavin obliged with his eyes.

"What about your father, you didn't say much about him at all?"

"That's because it was me and my mom since I can remember. My dad was with us on most weekends and he always made it for my birthday and my mom's birthday, and their anniversary. He promised that he'd never miss those, and he never did miss any until my last birthday."

Sandis exited the truck and grabbed hold of a smooth rock from the bed, tucking it behind the left rear tire. "You got any idea where he is?" he said as he looked at Gavin from his vulnerable position. "Today, as we both live and breathe?"

"No, but I know he's gonna come and get me just as soon as he can." With that, Gavin lied to his unofficial guardian, and to himself. He had already lost faith that his father would ever return.

Sandis rose, swiping his palms. "I suppose you're used to going at things solo," he said. "Can't say I agree with it, somebody your age. But it's just the way things turned out. Wouldn't you agree?"

Gavin didn't speak. His eyes moved around like there was some action going on behind the old man. There wasn't any.

"Was your father the one who put you in that school, for the religious teachings?"

Before Gavin could respond an old jeep with different colors of spray paint motor-boated by. Sandis did a one-handed salute with a wave combination at the driver. The old man got nothing in return. He smiled at Gavin and waited on a reply.

"My mom was the one who wanted me to go to the Episcopal school because my grandfather did something there. I guess my grandfather told her I was gonna go there and that was it."

Sandis ran a hand along the rail of his truck. He bent down and picked at a paint chip near the wheel hub. "So let me see if I got this straight - your mother, she just made pottery all day?"

"Pretty much, yeah. I used to watch her."

"And her working at Fort Huachuca like she went and did, with her food cart, right after you moved up here was . . . how did you put that again?"

"Like two different people."

"Right, two different people."

"The first night we got here, she cut her hair so it was shorter than mine even. It was like looking at someone I'd never met before."

"You said that she baptized herself in the river the next morning, is that right?"

"Yes."

"Huh . . ."

"Why?"

"Well you can't do that. You can't baptize your own self."

"She did."

Sandis made sure the tire pressure and tread was up to speck with one of his stubby thumbs. "And before the two of you came up here, she had no religious beliefs whatsoever."

"No, I mean, yeah. Yes."

"She didn't believe in God?"

Gavin nodded.

"She didn't believe in God? Or she didn't believe in anything, including God?"

"Just God."

Sandis stood up satisfied of the tire condition. "Right," he uttered into the distance. Gavin folded his arms. Sandis did the same, stepping to Gavin.

"Your mother, she ever tell you I'm from Blanchard, Oklahoma?"

"She said Oklahoma."

"Nothing about Blanchard? The float parades?"

"Just Oklahoma."

Sandis scratched the back of his head. "Us Oklahomans, no matter what, we stick together." He returned to his fold. "I respect what you had to tell me, Gavin, I really do. It's not up to me to tell you what to do or how to go about doing it. If you think your father didn't come back because of how much your mother changed by coming up here, her finding Jesus and so forth, well, that's entirely your business. If you want my opinion, though, I'd say it's likely she changed so drastically because of something he did. I think there's a lot more to it than meets the eye. He might have pushed her away, made her change."

Sandis reached into the bed and rearranged items. He unlatched the gate and flipped over a large crate. "I cannot find my dang signal pistol for the life of me," he said. "It just got up on two legs and waltzed away. Maybe I'm losing it, I don't know. They say the desert does strange things to your mind."

"Signal pistol?"

"Right. My M-8."

"What's that?"

"It's a signal pistol."

"Okay . . . what does it signal?"

"Well, for one it's supposed to signal the Fourth of July for the kids who float the river. I've been doing it for a few years now right over the bridge and I can flat tell you those Indian kids go nuts. They think it's just about the best dang thing around and I sure as heck don't want to disappoint them this year. You know how hard it is to find an M-8? First things first, they don't make them anymore. And second, the rounds they got need to be imported. I get one round on order at the Fort and I got to make the drive down there to get it. It ain't like going to K-Mart, Private, they ain't got lay-away."

"What does it look like?"

"You ever seen a .38?"

"No."

"A .38's got a short barrel, real short. Well the M-8 is like its mean older brother. A real rebel. And the round looks like a dang rocket."

Gavin pulled the shirt off his head and put it on. He tucked his hands into his back pockets and glanced behind him. Then he dug his right toe in the ground like he was a pitcher on the mound deciding his next pitch. "Mr. Sandis," he said. "Can I ask you about something?"

"Shoot."

"Is an *athist* the same as a person who doesn't believe in God? Is that what they go by?"

Sandis stopped what he was doing. He tilted his head for a moment and then went back to the materials in the truck bed. He picked and put away for a solid minute without saying a word. "*Atheist*," he finally said as he peered through a metal nut between his thumb and index finger. "*Atheist*, Private. Three syb's, not two."

"Okay . . ."

Sandis tossed the nut into a cluster of nuts and bolts and opened a canvas bag, feeling around the inside. "There ain't no atheists in foxholes, though," he said. "So you got to remember that to consider if they ever did exist in the first place."

Sandis zipped up the bag, lit his pipe and sat down on the gate. He indicated for Gavin to take a seat next to him but Gavin didn't bite. "Thing is . . . " he continued, "is if I put you in a foxhole, and your name is Gavin, and you come from such and such place, you're gonna be the same person as you were before you got put in that pit, only now you're gonna feel a lot closer to God. You believe in God and that doesn't change, you just feel more now because you're in touch with your mortality. Sorta like stepping outside of yourself and realizing that you ain't really the bee's knees. The birds don't sing when you get up in the morning, if you get what I mean.

And so then, at the very moment when you understand that you could die, you grow stronger in your belief that there is a God. The part of you that makes those hairs on the back of your neck stand up kicks in to let you know you could take a bullet to the head before you ever had the chance to say your goodbyes to your mother, the very person who birthed you in them pains as you cried when you came into the world. You cried then, and now, in that foxhole of yours, you also cry. But you cry out to God in a different sort of way because you ain't got time for tears what with all the adrenalin moving around in your blood. It might be confusing, Private, what I'm saying to you here, but keep with me, there's a point I'm making, promise.

Now, I take this atheist fella of yours, and I go and do the same thing. I throw him down in that foxhole and as soon as mortars start shellin' he gets busy adding up two two's to four that it ain't the TV that's making all the noise. He starts to think about his mortality for the first time since his ego had got a hold of some big opinions in his ego-driven world. And because he's under attack now he begins to look outside of himself for something bigger than himself to bring him back to solid ground. He looks to God to lift him out of the pit he's in since he can't do squat but pray he'll make it out alive. And so he does just that, he says a prayer for the first time in his life, a real righteous one, something of meaning that can be heard by the man upstairs. Mortars makes good on bets for mortality, is the thing . . . something we used to say."

Gavin absorbed the talk as best he could. "Alright . . ."

Sandis dug in his shirt pocket. "Sorry to have to give you such a lecture on the topic, but you got me thinking about something I hadn't thought about much in a long while. You have a real knack for asking good questions, you know that? You, Gavin, are one original thinker."

"Thanks . . . Mr. Sandis?"

"He is me."

"What exactly is a foxhole used for again, what's it designed for?"

Sandis leaned back on the gate with one hand and opened his eyes up to the changed sky. He took a dry puff from his pipe and let out a relieving breath. "Well . . ." he said. "I suppose you could say - in layman's terms - a foxhole is a place God puts some people in order to communicate."

9 SOMETHING OTHER

WALT SIPPED his tea and set the cup down on the bread cloth that was his coaster. "You like to run?" he said.

Gavin fidgeted around in his chair.

"How far have you run, in a single day?"

Gavin looked around as if something other than what was directly in front of him might require his attention. Walt gentled the cup around his scars, checking the contents.

"Usually when someone comes to visit me, they don't try *not* to speak," Walt said.

"Who comes to visit you out here?"

"My son. And you. You are my second visitor this week."

"Does he go to the Corte School . . . is he Joseph?"

"That little beaver doesn't belong to me," Walt said, taking a drink. He cradled the cup over his lap. "It is good then," he added unto himself.

"What's his name?"

Walt poked his tongue around his mouth as if he didn't want to answer. "Cheis," he uttered.

"Chase?"

"Say it like you're on the bottle. Like it's closing time and you want another. Cheizzz . . ."

"Where does he live?"

Walt breathed. "With his mother."

They heard a whistling like that of a vocally gifted bird. A razor-sharp squawk followed in doses. Walt got up from his chair and walked over to the front of his wickiup. He slid by the hide and went outside.

Gavin leaned and confiscated the cup of tea, taking a whiff and a baby sip before setting it back down. He made a sickening look and pushed the cup back out of the range of his fingertips. His thoughts remained as solitary as the room he was in. And the place he lived. After a few minutes, Walt returned in a cheerful spirit. "It is good to have friends in the sky," Walt said, pulling out his chair.

"What friends?"

"Birds. It is good to have them as friends."

"Birds are your friends?"

"Sometimes."

"Do you have any human friends, Walt?"

Walt noted the position of the cloth and cup. He made sure to arrange them back as they were. "Anyone who can give you the warning of snakes, I will say, is a good friend. One with the company you should keep."

"There's a snake outside?"

Walt took a satisfying drink. "There was."

"What kind of snake?"

"The kind that slithers around on the ground."

"What I meant was, is it a rattler or something? Does it have circles or spots?"

"I know what you meant," Walt said. "It has fangs, how's that?"

Gavin teemed of disappointment. "I thought you knew everything about the desert."

"What makes you think that?"

He swept the room with his eyes. "Oh I don't know . . ." Gavin said. "Maybe it's because you live someplace where there's no people and your house looks like a shack. Like it could be broken to bits in a strong wind."

Walt stirred and stirred and stirred. "This I built with my hands," he said. "If you could focus, you would see that it uses the wind. It uses the wind and it uses everything else that it needs to do what it should. That is a lesson you should learn from it. Take from your environment and use what it gives you to fulfill your needs."

Walt moved to the back of the room. He reached into a dresser that ended at his waist and pulled a box out from the top drawer. He returned to the table and set it down in front of Gavin. "It is for you," he said. "Call it a gift if you want to."

Gavin opened the box. Inside was a mug with a picture of an eighteen wheeler imprinted on the cream ceramic with a caption that read: "Take it where you find it and if it ain't that good keep on rollin' till you do". Gavin looked the whole thing over. "Thanks," he said.

"It is for the tea."

"I don't think I'm having any, it kinda smells like burnt rubber when it's hot."

Walt laughed. "Tell me," he said, "how far have you run?"

"In a single day?"

"One single day."

"How far is it to Sierra Vista and back?"

"About forty miles one way, at least."

"So that, yeah. The last time I did that run my clock was about to go to the AM, but I got back before it did and that was in the same day."

"And you run every day?"

"Yeah, what else would I do?"

"I don't know, what else would you do?"

"There's nothing to do except run. The people at the camp, I'm not sure they even come out of their trailers. They all live like turtles or something."

"Good thing you love to run then. If you ask me, you're in the right place for that."

Gavin took a second in the conversation. "I don't love to run," he said.

"Why don't you? You do it every day of the week and you run to places normal people have to drive to, including me. I will say that is a love you cannot see, otherwise the legs would say no thank you."

"The legs would say no thank you?"

"Yatasay. When I walked the farthest, I will say I walked to

Mexico, and my legs never forgave me. I don't like to walk far these days and the last time I went for a run somebody was shooting at me."

"You got shot at?"

"I did."

"Did you get shot?"

"I did not."

"Why were you getting shot at, Walt? Who shot at you?"

"I will say someone who was not my friend. But that is another time and another place and some things are not meant for the ears and you are too young."

"I'm not too young. I'm seventeen. I can drive."

"You can run."

"Wait, how far is it to Mexico?"

"Far."

"And you walked the whole way and back?"

Walt got up to replenish his cup. "Ask my legs," he said with his back to Gavin.

"How come you went to Mexico, Walt? Is that what they make Indians do when they're young, like a mission or something?"

Walt poured from the kettle. "I am not an Indian," he said.

"You're not?"

Walt stopped mid-pour. "I am an *Apache* Indian. Apache first, Runner. Always Apache. Like the alphabet, A is first."

"Okay. Why did you go if it's so far though?"

"For a change."

Gavin took to the gift given him, turning it on its head. "What does your son want to do when he is older, Walt?"

"That is a good question," Walt said, having topped off his tea. He returned to his seat.

"Thanks. What did he tell you?"

"I meant, *that is a good question*. I'd like to know for myself. As it stands, he is far from his future."

"Well . . . what do you want him to do?"

Walt slid back in his chair and reached for something on the spread-grass floor. His hand came back up empty. "So the thing you do the most, you don't love to do it, is that about right then?"

"I guess you could say it makes me not think about things that I don't want to think about. The more I run the more those things go away and I don't really think much about my legs or how far I'm going. I don't think much about anything."

"You could think about something that you like, something you find is, *good*."

"I'm not sure anything is good."

"Nothing good in your environment?"

"Not really."

"Would you say, when you run, you feel angry, that nothing is good?"

"Yeah, I would say that."

"I see. You sound like someone I know, one of my other visitors. He has the same hair as you. He does not have the same pasty skin. He does not have a vein like you in the arms and he looks like he could blow away in the wind. It is a mystery why he is named after the strongest of trees, the oak. But for that, you have to ask his mother. He is not as strong as this dwelling, the way he is built. He has one thing going for him, I will say, but too bad for him he is not in the right environment to make the one thing he wants in his life to be true. When I drive to visit with him we drive around. Sometimes we get ice cream and sometimes we just look at the designs of the buildings and play the radio. In all that time, he has not seen anything in his environment where he can make his one dream come true."

Gavin leaned in with his heart. "What's his dream?"

"It's too bad that I am the only one who can see it. Far too bad."

"What, Walt? Tell me."

Walt took a moment. "It's too bad, Runner, there isn't a place where he lives for a comedian to go and stand up in front of strangers and work at his comedy."

Gavin scaled back in his chair. He wasn't expecting anything close to what he'd just heard. "Your son wants to be a comedian, like on television or something?"

"Yatasay. He has not told me this to my face in so many words. But one day he comes to visit me and he sits in the same chair as you and he was holding his head down talking real slow and I wondered what was wrong and then he closed his eyes, barely making a peep and he seems like the water from deep in the ground was to come through his eyes at any moment. And then he said he had something important to tell me. Said he was hurting real bad inside and it was an ugly thing to him that he had to tell anyone, but he had to tell someone or else he was going to die. 'I am being torn apart and I can't hold it any longer,' was his statement to the court, which was me at the time."

"What did he say? What was it? What made him feel that way?"

Walt made a serious face. As serious as Gavin had seen in the short time he'd known the strong Apache.

"Cheis looked me right in the eye where you sit and said to me: 'Old father, I need to pee something awful. My pants are on fire because of your tea.'"

THEY HEADED outside when it was near sun-down. Hung from a skinny tree ten yards from the hide was a snake with its head and tail excised. "Are you going to eat it?" Gavin asked.

"So you think I am a medicine man like the one you see on TV with the bald head? He lives in a shack. He talks in circles and he eats what moves on the ground in front of him. You should see this man, you say to your friends. He's a hoot."

Gavin clued in to Walt's own brand of humor. Truly, he thought he might be talking to his only real friend. The few friends he did have in Sierra Vista seemed like a world away from this isolated place. How could he tell anyone he lives in a trailer? He couldn't breathe a word because of the shame he felt about the subject. The way his father had left without telling him where or for how long was an even tougher subject for him to manage.

"I don't think you're like that," Gavin said. "But isn't that what you're gonna do with it though, like skinning it and eating the meat?"

Walt deliberated the body. "If I eat that thing what do I get?" he said.

"Full."

"True. What else?"

"Snake meat inside of your belly that makes you full."

"*Belly* is a good word."

"*Belly?*"

"If I eat that thing, and it moves around on its belly, it is part of me. I do not want to move around on my belly. So if you ask my opinion, I would rather the desert open up and swallow me whole."

"It looks like you're preparing to eat it, that's all. Like you hunted it and it's your food."

Walt felt the end. "It is here because of my friends. I am giving it to them to feed off of. They are the creatures. I am human and have different needs. And I have a shopper's discount card at rounded corners where I get my own food." Walt picked up a long stick at the base of the tree and used it to poke at the snake. "It is also two birds with one stone," he added. "A meal and a warning."

"A warning, for what?"

"I say to you, Runner, what is it you are thinking?"

"Right now I'm not thinking of anything."

"You are always thinking something."

Gavin backed a couple of steps away from the tree. He tilted his head at the snake and pointed. "Okay, I'm thinking about what kind of snake that is? That's what I am thinking."

Walt placed the tip of the stick onto Gavin's right shoulder. "Now . . ." he said. "What are you thinking?"

"I'm thinking . . . why do you have that on me?"

"I know."

Gavin looked at the snake and then back at Walt. Walt imitated the action. They stared at each other for several seconds. Who had the deeper browns? Then Walt cleared his throat. "Pay attention to what I say now. Could say *rain* or *bird* or *rainy bird*. Whatever I say . . . you think what?"

Gavin mumbled.

"You think what?"

"I don't know."

"I say *rain*. You think?"

"*Rain . . .*"

"I say *bird*. You think?"

"*Dumb bird.*"

"I say comedian who likes to run, you-"

"Yeah, I get it Walt."

"And if you think different from what I say I hit you with this stick. So, pay attention and forget about the chirping birds and the wind moving that banished thing and the Apache with a stick on your shoulder and concentrate on the word."

Gavin's browns darted the dirt. "Wait . . ."

Walt brought down the stick.

"How can you tell what I'm thinking?"

"That is a good question."

"You mean, you don't really know?"

"I mean, it is simply a good question. I am impressed."

"Thanks. So how can you tell what I am thinking, for real?"

"It is easy," Walt said, raising the stick. "I just ask."

WHEN THE SUN NO LONGER FELT LIKE SHARING they went back inside the wickiup and reunited in their seats at the table. Walt had brought with him a piece of wood for the chimney. He'd snapped it in two with his hands and kindled it for the fire.

"It is almost time for me to rest," Walt said. "But before you go and do what you don't love, I want to teach to you one more thing. This is important, so I need for you to keep focused and not let your mind wander all over the desert like I saw it do outside."

Gavin sat in solace three yards from the fire.

"The fire, Runner, when you look at it, what do you see?"

"Umm . . . the fire."

"When you close your eyes, close your eyes, can you still see the fire the same?"

"Kinda, yeah."

"You need to close your eyes not halfway."

Gavin closed his eyes. "Okay, I can see the same thing," he said. "About the same thing, anyway."

"Why is it that way? Open your eyes now. Why can you see the fire almost the same, yet your eyes were closed?"

Gavin took a breath and thought. "Because I just saw it and it was right there, like a picture. And then I saw it in my mind the same and so it was kinda easy."

"This picture . . . ever think that where you live looks like a picture?"

Gavin laughed. "Oh, I get it now," he said. "Where I live, I should appreciate it. All the beauty that surrounds me. Me and my beautiful trailer. What a bunch of crap, Walt."

"Close your eyes. Like the fire, pull a picture of what it is you think you want made from your environment and hold that picture in your mind, in front of you."

Gavin kept his eyes open. "This is lame," he said.

"You are without want?"

"I'm without want."

"Close your eyes."

"I want *not* to do this," Gavin said with one eye closed. "That's really what I want. Why do you think I want something?"

"You are a human, true?"

"No, Walt, I'm a bird. Yeah, I'm human."

"Humans want. So close your eyes if you *want* to be invited back. I ask that you respect me. If you do not have any respect for me, you can leave at any time."

"I respect you."

"Do you?"

Gavin closed his eyes. "I still don't think this means anything," he uttered with a smirk.

"Hold the picture in front of you, Runner."

"Like the fire, right?"

"The fire."

"Alright, give me a second . . . okay, I have it, I think."

"Don't think. Pull."

"I kinda have something, I guess."

"Pull."

"I don't-"

"Pull!"

Gavin squeezed his eyelids shut. He held his hand over his eyes and took a few deep breaths, clenching his teeth. "Okay, okay," he said. "I think I got it like, like a good picture."

"Hold it."

"I can't . . ."

"Hold it . . . hold . . . and . . ."

"Jheezus . . ."

"Let it go."

Gavin wiped his forehead. His breathing filled the room.

"Did you let it go?" Walt asked.

"Yeah, I let it go."

Walt brought a fist to the table, like a gavel. "We both can see the fire in here, true?"

Gavin nodded. "Yeah."

"If you never had accepted my invitation, but I let you know there was a fire inside of here, would you believe me?"

"I wouldn't think that you're lying, why would you?"

"The picture you pulled," Walt said. "Can I prove to you that it is - *not true*?"

"No, not really, you can't."

"And why is it so?"

"Because I see it, that's why."

"So it is true then, you agree?"

"Yeah, but it's not the same. The fire is right there, I can see it, the fire is real, I can go touch it."

"Do you want to go touch it?"

"Of course not."

"It would burn."

Gavin nodded ever so slight. And unsure.

"Like your eyes," Walt reminded.

"Not like my eyes."

"A choice then."

"What choice?"

"To burn your eyes or your hand."

"That's not a choice."

"You have a choice in everything, Runner. Not choosing is a choice."

Gavin handed his hips.

"Turn your chair," Walt said, pointing. Gavin turned to the back of the room. "What do you see in front of you? Please say as I am blind. The injun who pounds whiskey in the twenty-four hours you say is his free time."

Gavin inhaled his desert life. "I see a dresser, it has silver shiny handles and I see some pottery, and, there's a broom. You have a stack of clothes, and a bed with a pillow. There's some really large books with gold looking ends. Fancy books."

"Close your eyes."

Gavin kept his eyes open.

"Are they closed?"

"Yeah." He closed them with a warm thought of a blanket in the far back of his head.

"Can you see the fire that was in front of you?"

He thought about his mother and didn't answer.

"Is the fire the same as before? Anything different, different colors or flames shooting through the roof?"

"No, it's pretty much the same way I saw it before, Walt. Nothing changed." *The story of my life for the last six months. Going nowhere.*

"Face the fire now that if you put out your hand and walked straight ahead would burn your hand and make you yell out like an angry man so there would be no doubt left in you."

Gavin turned back to the real. He opened his eyes.

"The fire in front of you," Walt said. "You can leave here and you can see it. You can run back to your home on wheels and sit in bed at night and see it when it is not there. I think you can agree to that and when you leave you will prove it to yourself. You don't need me to teach to you anything more about it."

Gavin's mind picked up things that hadn't stood out before. The details of the room. Intricate designs on the bricks and artistic weavings decorating the walls. He felt comforted for some reason.

"The picture you pulled out of your mind, how could I say to you if the picture is truth? You can see it without touching, only you. And the more you pull, the more it becomes true. So, Runner, one day, because you believe, your picture appears in front of you and you can touch it with your hand. It is part of the environment and has been made for you. The big thing I say is: is if the fire is true in front of you first and in your mind second, is it not also true that it can be the other way around, to see it in your mind first and then touch it?"

Walt placed a hand on Gavin's shoulder, walking with him to the front. They stopped at the hide.

"Walt," Gavin said. "How old are you?"

"Take away the fingers of one hand from seventy."

"Sixty five?"

Walt displayed his hand. "You have four fingers and a thumb, Runner."

Gavin looked at his own hand. "You don't look that old," he said.

"My recommendation is to start drinking tea at a young age and to stay away from the cola. Do your best to stay away from the cola. The cola, I will say, is no good for you."

Gavin frowned. "How come you let your son tell you you're old to your face? Isn't that being disrespectful?"

Walt smiled. "You mean to say he called me '*Old father.*' That is not old unless the father has one foot in the grave and has wrinkles and can't walk straight. Picture a man with a cane. Then he is that way, old like the dirt he walks over. Does he not own the dirt he tramples? *Old father* - it means grandfather to someone from your people."

"You're Chases' grandfather?"

Walt nodded. "Cheizzz . . ."

"You said he's with his mother, right?"

"It is what I say."

"Did his father leave him?"

Walt struck the hide and scoped his immediate environment. Only he could see the snake attracting the birds and little creatures winding to feed. Only he could see a darkness coming. "His father is not like him," he said. "His father is not like him, and, I will say, I am not him."

II A SUMMER OF RECORD

10 THE SPECIAL

THE OFFICE boasted a grand view of the desert from the second floor of the prison. Nothing but dirt and pockets of sand to the left of the bay window. When the prisoner entered the room, the Warden rose from his leather executive and strode to the front where he took a seat by the door. "Sit sit," he said, pointing at some metal chairs with a paper cup in his hand.

The prisoner sat down on one of the two fold-out chairs that was offered and crossed his legs. After a few tense moments, and with only the ceiling fan making a sound, the Warden looked at him. "I hear you was in the Navy, did I hear correct?"

"Yes Cap'n."

"Yer record says different, it makes no mention."

"It wouldn't, Cap'n. See most of them things I was doing to serve my country was deemed classified and I swore an oath that I can't talk a lick about nothin' but them first days of gettin' my butt chewed to kingdom come. You could run my numbers at the motor vehicles even and all it'd say was that boy was one wild son of a gun. A real rebel, but one that got hisself a cause. That much I swear to."

The Warden creaked a wry smile, kicking up one of his Shincoe custom boots onto the last available chair set between the two of them. He sipped his coffee, keeping the cup close to his chest and slightly under his chin.

"Truman's Navy *is* what saved my hind," he said, nudging the cup forward like he might spill it over. "Is how I got saved, ya hear?"

"Yes Cap'n."

"Yes what?"

"Yes I understand."

"Do ya now?"

"Yessir."

The Warden tickled his bola tie. "Good good," he said. "I was beginning to think you wasn't payin me yer undivided attention."

"I-"

"Yer what now, priznah?"

The prisoner inched out his barrel chest. "I don't know . . ." he uttered.

The fan clicked. And it clicked some more.

"Yous a born again?"

The prisoner inched back. Resting his pale arms over his robust gut he said, "I was only born once, Cap'n. In 1932."

The Warden comforted his other boot on the middle chair. "Good answer," he said, keeping the cup a breath away from his lips. "Good good."

The prisoner attached his eyes to the Warden's boots. Next to the Shincoe branded S logo under each of the heels was a forty penny nail. He maneuvered slowly to come back level with the Warden.

"Only a Navy man would know how to press his shirt so good," he said. "If you don't mind me sayin as much, Cap'n."

"That much I don't mind," the Warden said as he glanced over at a black and white picture on his strong oak desk. Set inside of a white frame, it portrayed a group of young men with flattop haircuts all decked-out in Hawaiian shirts. One of them, much smaller than the rest of the group, toted a gun in one hand and a drink with an umbrella in the other. The Warden let his cheek linger.

"Ya got any idea how many Army grunts it takes to shine a pair of them sam uncle boots?"

"No sir, that much I don't figure for, Cap'n. Which is it?"

The Warden squared. "Go on shooter . . . give us a guess."

"Yessir, five . . ."

The Warden shook his head painfully slow.

"Yessir, two grunts then. With two pairs of them greaser hands."

"Is a trick question, Ensign, kay."

The prisoner looked into the aqua blues of his commander. "I give up," he said, shifting.

"With yer hands in the air I'd wager."

The prisoner lifted his hands over his head. The chain between his wrists wasn't more than an inch from his forehead. He raised a yellow brow and flashed his yellow teeth. The Warden grinned at the gesture.

"The trick is that the Army don't pay grunts to shine boots so a shiner ain't gotta worry."

"Yessir," the prisoner said, bringing his hands down to rest at his gut. "That is a trick, and a good one too if you don't mind me sayin so, Cap'n."

The Warden crumpled his cup and tossed it into an empty trash can and used his hands at the back of his head for a pillow. He looked out the designer window taking on the new desert morning. "We got a different thing goin here," he said, scratching his temple. "Shit if I felt the need, I could take priznah's at that Army base up around the bend."

The prisoner lowered his head and wiped at the side of his face. He slacked out from the chain and slicked his thin bangs over his long bald spot. Under the long blades he scanned the room like a man absent a conscience - without much movement from the muscles in his neck and superior the animal head decor. He fixed his grays on a picture portrait of a lady.

"She's a real beaut, Cap'n," he said. "I jumped ship once, almost had me a missus."

The Warden reached back and picked a white cowboy hat from a generous selection of hats on the wall. He examined the stitch, pressing it in and around with one of his thumbs. He licked his thumb as fast as a cat might lick at its paw and repeated the pressing. After holding it above his head and inspecting the brim, he re-hooked the hat. "Yer record says ya got boys," he said.

"I got me two, yessir. Not with the same little 'rita, but I got me two." The prisoner laughed and the crow's feet around the Warden's eyes tightened. "Two that come ready with them papers."

"Uh huh . . ."

"One of 'ems a real trooper too. He prolly gonna be out here one day working for you, he's got that kind of motivation to succeed and all. The other . . . well, he's got the notion to follow in his old man's footsteps and become a pirate; joining the Navy just as soon as his momma will let him free from her teet."

"How about we speak a little business," the Warden said. "You mind?"

The prisoner raised his cheeks and faced the door. Then he tilted to the little man interrupting his morning chores.

The Warden brought his boots to the floor and leaned in. "Ya like how yer times been goin up to now, shooter, up to this here conversation between the two of us Navy boys, one of which claims to be some kind of secret agent?"

"It's been goin better than at county, yessir, that I can say. You know Sheriff Rey don't even turn on the water sometimes. The Sheriff, he'll even cut it off on a scorcher of a day and make you rinse in the troth just when you done-en soaped up."

"County is rough," the Warden said as he handled his knees. "That much I heard." He tapped his belt buckle. "But the Sheriff ain't got automatic weapons at his disposal, now does he?"

"Nah, Cap'n, that-e don't."

"Well he don't."

"Yessir."

"Ya ever seen that sanitation worker buildin' his own specialized units or with some of the real estate I got under my boots?"

"No sir. He don't got none of what you got, any mule that comes down here can see that just as plain as day."

"That's what I know," the Warden said as he turned the back of the middle chair around, resting his forearms over the neck. "What else I know," he continued, "is you like the job you been doin with the paper contracts we got. You keep writin' about the good things in here and you keep hushed up on some of them riots that pop up on occasion, them kind of things happen all over the place, kay."

"You the boss, yessir."

"This place is all about trust, kay. Ya keep that in mind when ya got yer fingers on my typewriter. Remember now - is my typewriter. And just like everything else ya see around here, is got my name on it."

The prisoner nodded and the Warden eased off the middle chair. "Bunch been spendin' time with ya on them spellin' errors?"

"Some, yessir. He don't need to as much these days, but he does, some."

"Good good. Good things equal to good things for you as well when it comes to the things they provide at the state. So maybe ya put something in yer articles about gettin' an education in here."

"Yessir."

"The way I see it, yer time in here can be Sun City or it can be spent with the pipefitters in the yard. Now . . . which is it you prefer?"

The prisoner uncrossed himself. "I've got this notion," he said with an expression cooling the room. "I'm in Rocky Point pennin' my own big story for the silver screen, like Jimmy Dean."

"Ya got nine and a half more years to pen whatever the hell it is ya want to, shooter, so long as ya get right the program. Now looky here - not one of these guards is wise to you scratchin' a deputized man of the law, a junior deputy as a fact. Yer luckier than a jumper countin' sheep under a shade tree that that boy had a whole mess of pride to survive some of that copper he got to the spine, ya hear."

The prisoner didn't move a muscle. He forgot to breathe.

"Combine that with the fact that them tree huggers at the state don't like to serve ribs or executions no more and I gotta believe that there's one lucky-dumb sonofabitch settin in front of me. What I hear from you, shooter, is thatcha wanna retire in peace, thatcha gone and done some thinkin' that you ain't had done before 'cause of yer time under my care. Sounds to me like you gotta mind set flat to the horizon, and that's just fine and dandy, if ya ask me, witchya ain't, but if ya did, I'd say is what a Navy man should be doin despite the mistakes he's come accustomed to. It ain't too good a retirement though, what with that number stamped to yer chest, now is it? Ya hearin' my words, Jimmy Dean? They gettin' through or should I just be calling you number four-zero-four-two from here on out?"

The prisoner submarined in his chair. He raised the handcuffs and plucked at the badge stitched to his dark-blue prison issue shirt. Bringing his chin close to his chest, he eyed the number. A number with no name attached. "I ain't no mute, Cap'n," he uttered. "Them words of yours . . . they through."

The Warden moved his rosy round face more over the neck of the chair and let out a breath. "Good good," he eased. He then made a pistol with his right index finger and thumb and pointed at the prisoner. "I'm glad to see we're making some progress out here in the boons, shooter."

The prisoner waited for his release with the tap tap tap of a toe.

The Warden switched from prison boss to job creator. "I'm wantin' me an insider, someone I can trust to run the Specials unit so the state can see that what I been building out here, is, in fact, the future. The future is about priznah's taking on more of a responsibility to rehabilitate themselves and less of a responsibility to go and fuck up the simple shit they supposed to get straight. Is gonna be about priznah's who behave and less guards to keep on the payroll, ya hear?"

"Yessir."

"Ya know how much it takes to turn a guard into someone wearing the same silly uni as you?"

"That I don't know, Cap'n. Which is it?"

"Not much."

The prisoner worked to control his breathing.

"Ya poke someone long enough, and they gonna bleed, kay. They gonna change, and you can then make 'em do as ya please. They then part of the mold. Remember that, and don't forget: these boots I got on is special made by them foreigners overseas."

"Will do Cap'n. You right, them boots of yours is nice and they got a shine no grunts is gonna observe. Yessir, it's just like you say. That's what I know too."

The Warden booted back his chair to the wall, unhooked a hat of his pleasure, and walked over to the bay window. He crossed his arms. Two hundred feet or so from his right hand view and another forty feet up stood the tower guard at his post. After a long thought, he took to his regular chair. He elbowed the oak and pointed with his hat.

"How'd ya like to be wearin' them Rio boots you was in when ya rode in here, Jimmy Dean?"

The prisoner straightened up.

"Rios is what I wear, Cap'n. I don't much like them rubbers they issue here 'cause of how they squeak in the hallways. Them rubbers ain't my style."

"They squeak like an alarm, don't they?"

"They make a noise, yessir. Like an alarm."

The Warden picked up a red pen and studied it with his hands like it was the most important thing in the room. "And that boiler ya been in," he said. "How about we go on and set you up in the cable box room over at the Holidays Inn. That sound like a winner to ya?"

"Yessir, it do. That done sounds like a real winner to me."

"Good good. You go on and get with Bunch then, he's adept at what we gonna do with the Specials. You keep an ear to the cement and if things go like they should, I'll start refferin' on you by yer name and not that number. That'a deal?"

WHEN THE WARDEN finished writing in the prisoner's record he picked up the telephone and picked at the lint on his shirt. Within seconds, two guards stationed in the hallway entered the office and escorted the prisoner down the stairwell to the first floor.

The hands of the clock outside the main entrance pointed to eleven thirty.

As the Warden reached under his desk to remove one of his boots, the tower guard fired off three rounds in rapid succession into a stack of hay bales at the center of the yard. The first of three meal servings for the day had officially made it out of the kitchen.

The Warden gathered the file folders strewn across his desk and exited his office, heading for the stairwell. At the first floor door he tightened his tie in the metallic reflection of the aluminum plated door. The ravenous image there he did adore. He arched his neck up with his hand still to the tie and peeked through the little window in the door. Before he could press the buzzer on the door, a guard opened it like a bellman might at a high priced hotel, with one hand on the door and the other directing the Warden right through.

"'Day, Captain, deliveries arrived, right on schedule."

The Warden brushed by the guard. "Where's Bunch?" he said as he moved through the narrow hall that split one way to the main entrance and the other way through a double door and out to unit A; the unit for prisoners with more minor offenses of record.

"The lieutenant is up at the lounge," the guard replied with a tone of hospitality in his voice.

The Warden kept to his forced gait. "Tell him to get with me pronto, wouldya?"

Letting go of the door the guard walked briskly to catch up with the Warden. He reached and touched the Warden's right shoulder.

"We got some folks up front sir that say they drove in all the way from Tulsa, for visitor's day. It's something of a log jam up there right now. The lieutenant has got his hands full of complaints. Word is they got an RV in the lot taking up a whole mess of space."

The Warden rotated around on the heel of his left boot. He tipped back his hat and smiled up at the guard. The guard was somewhat tall and thin with dark eyes that darted nervously around the hallway.

"You new?"

"Sir?"

"You. New."

"No Sir. I been here since the first of the year. If you call that bein new."

The Warden held out his briefcase. The guard obliged and grabbed hold of it.

"Two hands son."

The guard clasped both hands around the handle. A twitch of strain made the veins in his neck rise to the surface of his smooth skin. "Where we headed to sir?" he asked.

"What day we got down this month for visitor's day?"

The guard released a hand and scratched his chin. He then quickly returned the hand to brass. "Visits is the 28th," he said.

The Warden motioned a finger up to the ceiling. The guard's eyes got wide as he heightened the case.

"What day is it today?" the Warden asked.

"Tuesday. Today's Tuesday. Tuesday, the 23rd. June 23rd, sir."

"That's what I know."

"Sir?"

The Warden stared at the guard's hands. "Higher son," he said.

The guard lifted the case as high as he could.

"That make ya uncomfortable?"

The guard smiled from the side of his face. "Not really," he uttered. "This is easy. I might look thin but I got a 225 pound bench."

The Warden unlatched the locks on the handle end of the case. He opened the case and removed a Dumont hand-held radio with a red face plate that was secured by a band. The guard remained steady. The Warden re-latched the brass and then turned the knob on the radio, pressing the button. "Marcus," he said. "Marcus come on . . ."

The Warden put the radio against his chest and whistled a peppy tune. There was much static over the air. Then a break.

"Captain," a voice on the other end of the radio said.

"Marcus, put two in the feed and three when I come back on and say, kay."

"Done, Captain. What's the-"

The Warden clicked the communication dead. "What time ya punch off yer shift?" he said, itching at his arm with the antenna.

A bead of sweat trickled down the side of the guard's face.

"I'm off the rotation when the B's finish up with lunch today."

"Stay put," the Warden said. "I'm gonna go have a seat and talk with my laborers on the reddy. I'll get back with ya real soon."

TWO RIFLE SHOTS had closed the barred double doors that secure the main entry.

Only a handful of prisoners had made it into the cafeteria, but those who did were quickly corralled and housed in the yard before they had the chance to get any food on their plates. The Warden had waited in the hallway for over half an hour with the bugs that resemble cockroaches with no wings. He'd talked on the radio while the guard held up the case like there was an invisible table under it he wasn't allowed to come in contact with.

With a face wet with sweat and worry the guard attempted to get a glimpse of the Warden. The case fell by the fraction. Before it could lower any more, a flurry of shots rang outside the hallway. Shaken, he collapsed to his knees.

The Warden approached the guard to touch a shoulder other than his own. He pressed the flesh between the shoulder and neck, squeezing for a solid three count. He then removed the guard's hand from the case and continued down the hallway, his boots the only audible sound in the passageway.

The clock outside the main entry displayed a quarter past noon.

The Warden stood in the break room - an extension of the visitor's lounge separated by a wall near the front of the facility. Only one guard was in on break: a beefy looking man who wore brown leather gloves that had holes at the fingertips. Aside from the gloves, the guard had a patch on his shirt that made it known he was different from all the others on the prison payroll.

"So these tourists . . ." the Warden said. "How many was they?"

"I'd say a baker's dozen give or take. Half of them was women with babies."

"They take a calendar?"

"Calendars, I believe they each took one."

"Uh huh . . . and the Rice Krispies I heard cracklin' in the milk?"

Lieutenant Randall Bunch turned around in his chair with a big smile plastered on his face. He closed the hot rod magazine he'd been leafing through, fanned it under his chin and set the gloss down on a burnt orange card table. His face grew serious as he folded his arms. "Yeah . . . the snap, crackle and pops, they made those babies cry something awful. Man oh man, it was some kind of scene."

The Warden didn't speak.

"It cleared the room right quick is what it did. Before you know it they crawled back into that tank of theirs. Probably had to hitch on back to whatever hick town they was from because of the highway gas prices and tax they got to pay on stocking supplies up in here."

The Warden stepped to where the house calendar was tacked to the separator wall. He reviewed it. Each day before June 23rd was marked with an X. "Was they runnin' a Comanche?" he said.

"I don't really know."

"You get a sign made?"

"For the lot?"

The Warden turned slightly.

"No, not yet."

"Where'd ya fire yer gun?"

"Where else. In the yard."

"Ya swap it?"

"It's already been taken care of."

The Warden spun like a dancer. "Has it now?"

Bunch felt the table with the fingers of one gloved hand.

The Warden pulled out a pair of reading glasses from his shirt pocket and put them on. He removed his hat and held it behind his back with one hand. "All of them just tourists," he uttered as he used a pen secured by a string on the wall to write in something on the 28th of June, Sunday. Bunch stood up and leaned his girth to look over the Warden's shoulder.

"Extra tents . . ? We don't usually fill up but two."

"Well I get the feeling it's gonna be a blaze around here come noon. When July comes a callin', I believe we all gonna fry up in here."

"Since when do you care so much about the comfort of others?"

The Warden removed his glasses and gestured with them at the uniform drifting away from his personal space. "I think ya got me confused, *Randall*, with some of them politicians in the papers. The Wardens at them other prisons. Them caretakers. This here's my real estate, ya hear? And if I wanna have my own shade, well, I believe that's what I'm gonna do."

Bunch went back to the plastic molded chair that was his regular throne and reached for his magazine. The Warden tucked his glasses back and set his hat down on the table. Bunch took to the magazine merely as a distraction.

"I think I'm gonna have a swill of lemonade under there too. That I believe would make for a comfortable day. I might even sell some to them single mothers. Them ones who is pretty enough."

11 THE LONG RUN

GAVIN RAN OFF Highway 80 a klick before the Olde Rail exit, twenty miles north of the Naco, Mexico border and pulled up his white shirt, covering his face. Removing his shirt he rung it out with both hands like it was an old dish rag. In the seclusion and triple digit heat, he mopped the sweat from his chest and shoulders for a hundred-plus breaths.

The mineshaft that was his destination was another half-hour from his vantage point and so he used a narrow dirt road to guide his tired legs slightly above a walking speed. As the sun gave way to the western bleed, Gavin came upon a sign for Cold Drillers Mine.

His neck was burning like a torch when he entered the mouth of the mine but it soon cooled with a rush of cold air that whisked past him. The cold slowed his forward progress a bit as it mixed with the outside heat to thicken in a standing swirl.

Gavin put his shirt back on and traversed deeper down to where specks of the light were leading him. He came upon a stairwell constructed of planks of wood that shortened the more he descended and so after three minutes he found himself on the flat ground again, looking back from whence he came.

Drops of water trickled his ears.

He crouched to feel for rocks on the ground, gathering some in his hands and tossing them into the dark. More water sounds. By the splashing alone he rendered a gauge of the water depth and rose with arms outstretched, heightening his senses with each and every footstep.

The water chilled him as the tape under his right sneaker worked against his will to fend off rocks and everything else he wanted out. He reached as far as he could and touched his fingertips against what felt like a lead pipe. The form he found thin. Thin, but incredibly strong.

As he pulled, a stream of water rushed out over his knees. Gavin crouched in his virility to let the water run wild and free over his mouth and hands. For the first time in a long time he felt right at home.

HE EMERGED from the mine an hour later and made his way back to the highway with a sense of renewal in his stride. The only traffic that he could see buzzed in the direction of Bisbee. He picked up his feet and drove his arms. A guiding breeze did dip and encourage him.

When he made it back to Rock Gardens it was officially a brand new day. Ten past twelve to be exact when he entered his room and checked the alarm clock.

He stripped down to his underwear as he moved to the couch and turned the television on without a care as to who or what was being broadcast. Continuing on to the kitchen he opened the freezer door of the sixties-era refrigerator and pulled out a package of steaks, keeping his head in the man-made blizzard for a time.

Gavin shut the freezer and turned the knob on one of the two electric burners and separated the steaks, panning two strips in a pan that looked as if it had been through a grease war. It took a few minutes for the swirl-burner to cause a sizzle. He stood there lost in thought all the while.

He focused in on his mother, about how different she was before the last time he saw her, and how different she was from that point to when he was a child. The way her short hair had made her unrecognizable. He missed her ever so much. But more so, he missed the old version of her. He missed the person with long hair, the one person in his life who was easy to talk to. What was he to do about money when the cash stashed under the trailer ran out? Cash in shoe boxes. Cash and other valuables that belonged to his father. A month before she passed, Nancy Stowemeyer Reeves had told her only child that these things needed to be protected. Gavin had listened to his mother with great intent, but he failed to include himself in that speech.

His thoughts turned to the long run of the mine. He mentally recorded it as a record. How many miles he wasn't exactly sure, but far enough. No walking and counting the dashes or thinking about hitching a ride. Only running above mid-speed and hoping for something new in his life to discover. And not one single thought about running away from the life he lived in his desert trailer.

Gavin moved the drapes to take in his environment. Closing his eyes he imagined the dirt to be a field of trimmed grass, the outer lights as bright as the sun. He laced a pair of cleats to his feet as his trailer melted away in the heat - heat that dared not burn. There he took hold of his picture in the way Walt had instructed him. There he pulled his dream from nothing to stand out in the middle of a concrete stadium. In his hand, like the man on his bedroom wall, he carried a football. After the most concentrated two minutes of his life, he let go of the picture and opened back up. And with a breath of belief, he tucked back the ball.

12 FANTASY STORY

"We was tasked with rescuin' prisoners of war, see, in foreign places the ground grunts couldn't get at based on the way the waterways was. We'd get in and out right quick and save as many lives as we could, that was the mission. Saving the lives of American soldiers was priority numero uno."

"What did they call you, the name of your secret naval group?"

"That's classified."

"This was during Nam?"

"This was '76-'77, 'round near."

"Sure it was."

"I got the story down pat, lieutenant. A beginning, middle and end, right there in your hands. How I done and went about rescuin' a brother in arms on a dangerous mission. I was the leader, see, and as the leader is always out in front leadin' away at the charge, I got into a fix faster than gettin' into them panties at the drive-in thee-ater, and I had to fight my way on out. You know, I had to fight my way on out without my squad coverin' my back. I almost done near lost my head. It's all right there for ya, a snap-shot of what I'm puttin' together for the movie business people."

"And that's what you brought to me, today - Tuesday of all days - the very day I got to distribute the work up at the Sierra Vista Eagle and Miner Times - your story about a one-man search and rescue mission?"

"It's a great story people are gonna want to read about."

"I'm real sorry, man, I am. But that ain't our business. We got contracts we got to fill on the labor and the labor is to type what the papers want us to type. In a manner of speaking, typewriter leverageability here is only about ten percent. We got human interest stories, and that's all agreeable, but we don't do stories on prisoners. We do them about the prison itself or we do them about other things, things like the weather."

"People don't want to read about the stupid weather."

"I beg to differ with you on that one, man. I think you'd be surprised at how many people do, in fact, love to read about the weather. Bring me something about the monsoons or about flood levels and I'll be sure to submit it."

"I'm bored."

"Yeah, so, this is prison."

"I'm flat done with the follow-ups, lieutenant. I ain't no ambulance chaser."

"Reporter . . ."

"Well I ain't one of them neither."

"No one's asking you to be anything, man. Just return to your seat over there and punch the little letters on the typewriter within the guidelines of what's required and that's it. Five hundred words within the guidelines and we can move on to the next article. You get lost, you check the cork board for approved topics."

"You could give me a different job."

"You already got the best job we offer."

"What about you?"

"What about me."

"You got a good job, sitting there at your desk reading your magazines all morning like you do. No offense, Lieutenant Bunch, I know you in charge here, and I got a helpin' of respect for a man as successful as you, believe me. You second in command to the Cap'n, and I know how that works 'cause I had a second in command myself. I just want a different job now, that's all I'm sayin."

"No."

"No? Why the hell not?"

"Because I know who you are that's why *no*. I put you in the cafeteria or the woodshop or in the back with the horses and sooner than later you disappear, or worse, you disappear and return with a gun."

"That ain't like me."

"So you've been rehabilitated now, is that it?"

"I am the first of the Specials. Now I even got two under me and right soon I'll have a third. I think I've done fixed my bad ways myself, yessir. But if you ask me, *rehabilitated* ain't the right word. *Rehabilitated* ain't apply to me. It's a misdiagnose."

"I'm still saying *no*. The Specials is a controlled environment and so is this little news room we got set up. Listen, man, you can walk out the door and flip the lid on the head. You can go over to the coffee pot and turn it on and fill it but you can't mess with the heat. And most important of all, you can sit and type out the pieces we are contracted with the papers to write for their articles and no one will even know the friggin difference."

"Cap'n said no one knows my histree, lieutenant."

"No one does."

"It sounds like you know more than the average. Any other guards know about me? Anyone else know what you know?"

"How about a magazine then, man, would that help fill up your void?"

"You think a magazine would take my mission story? Which one are you talking about, Soldier of Fortune? I done like that one the best."

"A magazine for your leisure is what I'm talking about here, man. I got some back issues of Drag just taking up space over in the paper drawer. They got the leggy car wash models on just about every single page."

"Sorry, lieutenant, but I ain't up for any leisure readin' today."

"How about some pictures then?"

"Of what, the weather?"

"Of the girl next door flashing you her tits."

"T and A, huh . . . thems any quality?"

"It's pretty friggin good."

"Pretty good . . ."

"Yeah, man."

"Hmm . . ."

"Whaddaya say then, man?"

"I'm thinking here . . ."

"Don't think too long because this offer ain't bound to last."

"Shit . . ."

"Shit what, man?"

"They all teases."

"It's the good stuff man, trust me. It's the good stuff that's got the cover on the cover when it comes in the mail."

"The cover on the cover . . . that there a used copy?"

"No man, I got the Wall Street friggin journal in my lap like some jerkoff money dealer. Yeah, it's like I said, the good stuff."

"They got any real stories in there?"

"C'mon man, will you quit busting my balls about your mission story already so we can get on with things today? I've already had a bitch of a morning having to deal with some of the staff I've got to babysit, and I sure as hell don't need to add another name to my benefits list. Just take the magazine already. Whaddaya say, can we get on with things this morning and get our topics together?"

"You ever find yourself in Greenhall, Arizona, lieutenant?"

"I can't say I've had the pleasure of stopping there for more than gas."

"Well there ain't no girl next door there. We got girls, yessir, and, well, they the kind that live all over the place."

"So no on this little sweetheart then. You sure? She's got a friend."

"I ain't the man who pays for the peep show. When I party, that's exactly what I do, party."

"This girl here looks like she likes to party."

"Yeah, I can see that."

"C'mon, man, you're breaking her heart. She don't take rejection too well. And you'd know that if you read her spread. Just take it and don't make me push her on you like I'm some kind of friggin prison pimp."

"I already got me a little 'rita, lieutenant. I even got the sister writing me now. I ain't that hard up."

"Hard up, *yet*. Just wait until your second year kicks in."

"I'm a patient man."

"They don't visit."

"That's 'cause I don't cross my lines. I'm careful with my business, that's just how I run things. Prison ain't a good place to have people on the outside losing their shine on you. You got friends on the inside and none out, well, you got more bars than you can handle."

"So take it, and, if you want, August when it gets delivered and after it's had its first official read through."

"C'mon, man, you're killing me. Just take the thing."

"Alright."

"Well alright then. Say, how many words did your mission story come to anyway – I'm curious?"

"I ain't mess with the count 'cause it ain't like the write-ups and shit like that. The shit just done pours out of my mind, I swear. But the count of them pages there come to . . . shit, I believe they come to 'round nine, maybe a dime."

"Long for the paper, huh?"

"Not the Sundays. Sundays they got long ones."

"I forgot about the Sundays. You read your mission story out loud to yourself?"

"No."

"You should."

"Why's that, lieutenant? I already know it, that's how come I wrote the fucking thing!"

"Watch your tongue, man. Make sure you check that number on your chest next time you feel like swearing at me."

"Well I wrote it, sir, and I ain't understanding so good why I should read it out loud when I know it. It's for other people to read so they can know my name when they turn it into a movie. I even got a list of actors who can play me in the lead. I ain't too familiar with their histrees yet and I need to get familiar 'cause it's gonna take a man's man to reinact me. And James Dean died long ago on the highway. So I'm gonna want some extra time this week on research. I believe I deserve some extra time. Well, now, how come you laughing at me?"

"I'm not laughing, man, sorry."

"I ain't been laughing none about it."

"I know, man, I know. You got yourself a parole hearing coming up though, don't you?"

"Yeah, 'round four years from now."

"Well, then, there ya go. You know you got twenty free minutes to say whatever it is you want to say at your hearing and not get interrupted. You even got yourself an audience of educated people. So read the story out loud some, man. So you can get it down and tell it when the time comes. Maybe then you'll drum up some interest about it."

13 A PUZZLE

WALT WADED IN THE MIDDLE of the river with his hands fanned at his sides like the oars of a rowboat. He faced the mass of leaves filtered near the school bank and baptized himself. Averting a wisp of wind he heaved a rock into the shallows. Before he could attempt another throw, a voice came out of nowhere. He brought a hand to his ear so the voice might repeat.

"The water makes you more thirsty," the voice said. "You can drink and drink and it doesn't ever fill you up!"

"Say again?" Walt said, searching. He waved a hand at nothing and at no one and prepared for another dip. "Come in," he added in a voice that carried west with the changing wind. "The heat today, Runner, is not your friend."

Gavin appeared from the rear of the Corte School grounds and glided to the river bank. He sat down, removed his sneakers and sprung back up. He then slogged in the water over a bed of familiar river rocks. When he came within reach of Walt he scooped a hand and tasted the river. "The water doesn't fill you up," he said, animated. "You want to keep drinking more and more of it. It's kinda hard to stop once you get started."

"So you went and found it then."

"Yeah. How come it tastes so good?"

"I don't really know. Maybe because nature knows more than man. But who cares, it is really good, isn't it?"

Gavin didn't say a word. He scooped up more of the river for his skin.

"Would you say it was worth the trip?" Walt asked.

Gavin smiled.

Walt dipped for a rock and brought it to his bare chest.

"What's with all the rocks?" Gavin asked.

Walt elevated the rock to his chin. He bounced on his toes. "I am getting rid of stuff," he said. "Cleaning out the closet you might say."

"What stuff?"

"Stuff that's your own. We all got stuff."

"Is it heavy?"

"Is what heavy?"

"That rock. It looks heavy."

Walt dumped the rock in a way that said it didn't quite measure up to his standards. He ducked under the water and motored his feet at the surface, right in front of Gavin's giddy face. After about ten seconds, he broke the surface with a rock the size of a loaf of bread. He spat water out with his breath.

"This one, Runner, is . . . it is . . . this one is the weight of the world and then some."

"I don't think you should hold that one over your head, Walt. It looks way too heavy."

Walt rested the rock on his right shoulder. "That is a good one," he said. "Something I will keep to memory. *Don't hold over your head.* It is a good lesson for me." He carried the rock over to the school bank, dropping it in the shallows. Gavin watched and followed.

"So what's next?" Gavin asked.

"You tell me."

"I thought about it on the run back. It just came to me. I figured it out, I think. I think it's like a puzzle."

"What is?"

"What we're doing. It's like putting together the pieces of a puzzle so you can discover something without being told to your face. Like when teachers start preaching to you in school so you don't pay attention all that much. They teach best when they allow you to teach them."

Walt looked around the shallows. "That is deep," he said.

"I know. So what's next?"

"What I will say is you watch too much TV."

"Where am I gonna go next?"

"Hmmm . . . *what is next*, let me think what it is I will say . . . what I will say . . . hmmm . . ."

"I'm thinking it has to do with the water and the rocks. Like when I was on that small mountain, it was a rock that was different from anything in the desert and I found it. Who would be able to notice a rock that's different in the desert? And the water at the mine is the same water from the river, but you can't drink it here, so you have to go underground to discover that. People don't know it's there so they think that the river won't give them any water to drink. People don't know it can provide for them. Like at the camp, they have to have a water delivery."

Walt studied the scars on his forearms. Beads of water on top of his memories. "You think of this all by yourself?" he said, keeping his eyes on his skin.

"Yeah."

"I will say you watch too much TV and it is no good."

"You don't have to tell me everything, Walt. Just tell me what's next. You know, I could've made it to Mexico."

Walt looked at Gavin. "Is that so?"

"I think so, yeah. This river starts in Mexico, Walt, did you know that?"

Walt gazed up at the splendor of Cottonwood overhead. And Gavin followed once again. Walt faced the runner. "Punch me," he said.

Gavin leveled back. "What?"

"Punch me in the gut. It is a challenge for me."

"I'm not punching you, Walt."

"You should."

Gavin stepped to his left, backing as he did. He then sat down, confused.

"I will say once more, Runner. Punch me."

"No."

"Trample the Earth."

"I don't want to."

Walt paused as did the breeze. "Where's your father when you need him the most?" he said.

"What did you say?" Gavin snapped.

Walt went back to the Cottonwood. "It needs no same words. The words, they are like the air now, or the wood in the water, or your thoughts. They float."

Gavin got to his feet. "Don't talk about my dad or my family."

"You want to punch me?"

"Just don't say anything about my family, Walt. Why do you want me to punch you so much? Why would you even say that to me?"

"I will say you are looking for something that is not there."

"My father's still here," Gavin said.

"You miss my words. You have two ears but cannot hear. You act as dumb as the runner bird. I am concerned the two of you are one in the same."

Gavin took a half step toward Walt. He readied himself for his first ever punch on another human being. He then thought a punch would be rendered useless on a man as big as Walt. He wondered what to do with the rush of adrenaline.

"The runner bird?" Gavin finally said, not really caring about his words. "What's that supposed to mean, Walt? I thought you liked birds. 'Birds are my friends,' you said, Birds do this and they fly around. Blah blah blah, - the stupid birds."

"Make no mistake, Runner, I am not friends with the runner bird. He's so dumb he sticks his head in the hole of a gun and flaps his wings. I have no time for dumb friends."

Gavin put his hands on his hips. "I guess we're not friends then," he said.

"Maybe I will punch you in the gut so you get my message."

"I'm not afraid of you."

"You're not afraid of anything, are you?"

Gavin huffed. He looked at his feet and then over at the classroom trailer. A few moments floated by.

"Looking for something?" Walt said.

What does he mean by that?

"The spark gun. You won't find it there."

"How do you know about that?"

"I know things."

"Was it Joseph?"

Walt frowned.

"Where's it at?"

"In my possession."

"I need it back, Walt."

"What for? It has no big bullets. What is the good of the gun to you with no big bullets?"

"I just need it."

Walt folded his arms. "It is the soldier's gun. The soldier in the Members Only jacket. The one and only member I will say."

"You know him?"

Walt smirked. "The soldier will find it back in his possession soon."

"You can't tell him."

"We're not friends."

"I can't believe you took it."

"I do not take what I do not own. I own what I own. And I live right where I live."

"How did you get it then?"

Walt looked at his own feet. "It was at my boots. And my boots were near the anger of your head. And if you knew anything about eminent domain then you-"

A rifle shot rang out. Leaves fluttered in the multitude of green that was the eastern bank. Gavin watched a small animal scatter in the brush near an Ironwood tree.

"The natives are getting restless," Walt quipped as he moved toward the classroom. "We should be somewhere else."

"I'm staying right here."

"Your choice."

Gavin hustled to get in front of Walt. "You're not going to get shot at Walt, this is America."

Walt viewed the eastern bank and then did the same to Gavin, from pale feet to small shoulders. "This is border-bunker Arizona, Runner, and you've never been shot at to know any different."

"You're really worried about some hunters way on the other side of the river?"

Walt collected a small rock. He glanced up at Gavin and shifted in his position, gathering his thoughts in detail as he soothed and spat a drip to better his grip. He pitched the rock and watched it take two hops atop the surface and land dead to where the animal had been a minute earlier.

"What I worry about is you," he said. "You don't even know how to think the right thoughts, and your concentration is way off. You know not what I say to you. A gun is a simple device. You, Runner, I will say, are the complicated one."

14 THE HERO FATHER

THE BOY picked up the receiver. A voice on the other end of the line said, "Dew drop."

"Dad . . ?"

"Your mother around?"

"No, uh . . . she's still at work. How come there's no commotion in the back?"

"I got my own penthouse now, that's how come. When you visit next time you ask for the Specials unit. You can even say you're here to see the Cap'n. Them guards will come runnin' after me."

The boy got quiet.

The prisoner leaned in his chair over a cherry wood desk and collected a grainy cup of coffee. He drew in a quarter of the brew and placed the cup back down, licking his lips. Palming his head he gazed out the window at the long strip of grass he'd mowed as part of his duties. The air conditioner clicked; it worked to cool the nine hundred square foot room down to eighty-one degrees. Outside, the heat had yet to peak. At close to four-thirty in the afternoon it was still climbing well over the hundred degree mark. He opened the desk drawer to a Penthouse magazine and thumbed through it from the back. When he came to the hot letter section he brushed at his crotch a few times.

"You been workin'?"

"About as much as they'll allow, yes, sir."

"How much you got socked away so far?"

"So far . . . I got about one-fifty saved up, maybe a little more if I get some parts sold this weekend."

"That ain't enough, it ain't nearly enough. What about your older brother?"

The boy coughed. "Half-brother," he uttered.

No reply from the prison line. The boy could feel his father's weighted stare from eighty miles away.

"Cordis said he doesn't want to get involved, sir. He thinks people are gonna get hurt. He said that it'd be a shoot-out."

The prisoner flipped some pages. "What about you?" he said. "You got any reservations about the mission?"

The boy cleared his throat. "I don't want to sir, but it's not like we have any other choice. Every time they say they're gonna let you out, you get put back in. It's not fair. Nobody but us two knows how bad you got framed, Dad. Even the FBI won't help you like you said they're supposed to help their own undercover people. How come they can do that?"

The prisoner fixed his gaze on an advertisement for premium liquor. With his eyes he shot the whiskey.

"You need to get yourself prepared and man up and not worry so damn much. You got your eye on a ride yet?"

"I spotted a van close to school. It's in a carport for most the day then every so often some lady comes out and drives it around for a few miles and that's about it. It's mostly there. Another month and a half and I can get my permit. Mom said she'd even take me up to Sierra Vista on the very same day."

The prisoner aimed a finger-gun in the direction of a guard on watch outside of his window, standing against one of the other units. "You get with the plumber I told you about?" he asked.

"No sir, not yet."

"The two of you need to get together on that van. You could get a call from me and we could be ready to go in forty-eight hours. We could even be set to go in twenty-four."

"We don't have to wait on the visits?"

"Not here, not while I'm in the Specials unit. I been put in charge of everyone but the little piss-ant Warden. I could even have you come and stay at my penthouse here and we could go for a hunt like I had done promised to you before, if there was somethin' to hunt around here we could, shit . . . well, that's somethin' we could go and do. But there ain't nothin' here but the dirt and some skinny-ass birds that crap all over the yard."

"Really?"

"I even got that Specialized waitin' for you when you come and pick me up, just like the one from the mailer catalog. The hunts'll be ripe up north. We're gonna go after all that tail, so you remind that to your older brother."

The boy mumbled and let out a deep breath. "You know he wants to be a cop now," he said. "You know that, right?"

The prisoner rummaged a pair of tweezers from the center drawer and twisted a mark.

"Dad . . ?"

"What's on your mind?"

"Umm . . . I hallowed out the cooler, so when the guards search it they won't find much but some sandwiches. I figured I'd even stick in some bad tuna."

"How come you think they'd search it?"

"Because they always search, sir."

"Well, you ain't livin where I been livin. You make your old man for a mule now, is that it?"

"No, no sir, I don't. I know they respect you. They don't search me as much as all the others, but they still search. I haven't brung a cooler in before so I thought that they'd have to open it up."

The prisoner gripped the receiver with angst. The scorpion tattoo over his right hand and wrist came to life. "Yeah," he uttered, "they would."

"Why are you getting upset with me? I've done everything you've told me to. I promise to get the plumber on the phone, I left him a message already."

The prisoner pushed the dirty magazine away with a dirty hand and picked at some chips in the desk. "You know who I am, don't you?" he said.

"Yes, sir, I do."

"And you know why I am where I am, don't you?"

"Yes sir. You got framed for something on purpose so you could clean up all the bad people on the inside. They had to make it look legitimate. But how come they don't let you come out now?"

The prisoner paused. "That's about right."

"Why won't the FBI come clean about it now, Dad, it's been-"

"There's too many bad people in the world, that's how come. What'd I done remind to you about the heroes of the world before?"

The boy drew in a deep breath. "That they are few and far between sir," he said.

"And your old man, who's he?"

A knowing pause from the boy. "A hero, sir."

The scorpion relaxed as the prisoner let go his tension.

"That's the truth and the truth don't ever lie, son. A hero has got to sacrifice and that's precise to my arrangement with my country, *sacrifice*. No matter what they says about me. I'm the kind of man who goes to war to fight, you got me? They make statues of me while I'm still breathin' in the free air. And they sure as shit is gonna make a movie about me. You're gonna see me on the silver screen like I done saw Jimmy Dean when I was your age, believe that. I'm the kind of man who takes care of things that ain't easy. These guards, they all work for me. When you come on the visits day that I tell you to next, you remember that so you don't sweat a drop. You keep that cooler covered up like you had planned because these guards ain't as smart as me. Some of them get outta line now and then. I can't be everywhere. You make sure to cover that mister up and when I give you the signal you get it in my hand and I'll take it from there. You my second in command, you understand me?"

"Yes sir, I do . . . but Dad?"

The prisoner returned to the magazine, spreading the centerfold out in full before his eyes. The featured pet for the month of July. "I'm list-nin," he said.

"You need any bullets for that Specialized?"

The prisoner slowly moved the receiver to his other ear, ditching the naked lady. He stared at the floor. "Come again?" he said.

"Bullets . . . you need any-"

"I ain't no mute, boy. I'd done heard ya the first time. You the Warden now, is that it? You lookin' up at me and gettin' wise?"

The boy held his breath.

"What I done preach to you about my damn guns before?"

"That you only hold .45's, sir. Only .45's with ivory grips."

"Yeah, and why's that?"

"Well, sir, 'cause it's like you always say: a cowboy is the law when the law ain't in sight."

"That's about right. You ever seen me wearin' any of them buster browns you got tied to your feet?"

"No sir."

"What you seen on my feet then if I ain't got any of them busters tied on?"

"Boots. Only Rios. That's what you said. You said to make sure to bury you a foot in the ground so the tips of your Rios might be admired by anyone who might pass."

"Only Rios is right," the prisoner said. "You got two good ears on you, boy. If you find me with boots made by them foreigners overseas you just figure the man who stood before me, well, it ain't turn out so good for him." The prisoner slid the receiver down to his chest and arched his neck to get a good look out the window.

"Dad . . ? Dad . . ? Is the time up now?"

The prisoner brought the receiver back to his ear. "Alrighty dew drop," he said, "Listen-in. I'll get with you when I'm about ready. You make sure you workin' and prepared. You get a game of stick goin with your older brother and you make squared to get the drain man on the horn. I know I can't be there to give you your first drivin' lesson, but I'm gonna need you to practice with your mother in her Galaxie if the drain man don't feel like picking up the phone. I only got one approved number right now from inside my penthouse here. You ready . . . yeah, I know you are. Don't be scared now, son, your old man will be the only one holdin' on to a gun when the time comes. Oh . . . and If I hadn't made the mention before, I like what you had done to the cooler, that there was some slick thinkin'. Your old man had given some thought to that before, but I like the fact that you and me is on the same page about that."

As soon as the prisoner finished speaking he did a one-armed pushup with the receiver brought to the desk. His window was his and his alone across the strip of grass and from two guards finishing up a smoke. And a third performing stunts with a stack of food trays.

Having stored the mag he clicked the line dead and moved over to the panel of the front door and stood there with his chest stuck out like he was about to get every inch of his seventy-four measured for a suit.

If only the boy could see through the prison window of lies. To see his father acting obedient and waiting on the only thing he really loves, his special eats. No one could see, though, the true nature of the mercenary, or the FBI man or whatever-role he chooses to play. A man living in a prison penthouse simply because of the magazine handed to him. How easily he owns what suits him. A sociopath and his fantasies. His hunger for fame. And the un-told number of lies that fail to register within him a heartbeat.

15 THE GAUNTLET

WHEN GAVIN MADE IT to Contention High School it was ten-forty in the morning.

The sun bore the black under his feet as his ears tuned to the slaps of drum sticks over snares from somewhere in the immediate distance. Wiping the sweat from his eyes he scanned the scene to see if he could locate the origin of the beats.

He kicked off his sneakers, resting his bare left foot and double-sock right on a cool patch of grass next to a sidewalk that had words and handprints formed within the foundation. He stood there trying to make sense of it all. He then took a seat, rolled up the legs of his Levis and rubbed his shins to sway the strain of about twenty-two miles from his calf muscles.

The school quieted.

Sprinklers in the middle of the football field hummed and wetted the grass. And then, one by one, the devices expired in the heat. He reapplied the duct tape under his right sneaker before slipping it back on. Then he peeled off a strip he had stuck to his right denim thigh and covered the laces with it. He laced up the other, forgoing any available tape, and accessed the sidewalk all the way over to a welcome sign.

There were a dozen or so vehicles in the parking lot.

He could see how the vehicles, in various states of upkeep, waited in the white morning sun for their drivers to return. *It must be nice to get in your own Jeep and drive wherever you want,* Gavin thought. *It must be nice to get a Jeep for your birthday instead of a Bible with your initials and some Dairy Queen.*

Gavin parted his bangs and bitterness as he let go a Jeep with all terrain tires and a Skoal Tobacco sticker on the bumper. He continued along the sidewalk. Next to the Jeep was a black and silver Chevy truck with a rifle rack and some sort of monument relegating the hunt from the rearview. Aside from a few street cycles, he envied most of the machinery in his asphalt view.

He headed for a water fountain he spotted across an ocean of concrete. There he drank for over three minutes before coming up for air. The water, he found, was nowhere near as refreshing as the water underground. Nevertheless, he was glad the fountain was there and working. He took in a final mouthful and spat it out and breathed back the warm.

Rejuvenated, he walked to where the concrete led him to the double doors of a square building. He pulled the handle on his strong side, went inside and stood in the foyer. In range were trophies and awards and placards of things displayed in a large glass case along the back hallway. He was taken in by the sight and with the way the lights overhead seemed to capture the glory and history of it all. The display case was taller than him, about six feet from the ground up.

Gavin nosed in on the one and only thing that had woke him up from his couch earlier in the morning.

The glass fogged and so he wiped his breath away and cupped both hands to buffer the glass against his forehead. He searched the case all over. About a minute went by without much calling out to him. Nothing standing out in his mind. He then heard a couple of loud bangs followed by amplified music. And rubbers in the hallway.

"You're the Indian runner," a voice from down the hallway proclaimed.

Gavin kept to his buffer.

"The Indian Chief said you were going to be here, and, well, here you are. How long have you been waiting? Sorry, it's just that we've been in the wrestling room looking at film and I lost track of time."

Gavin didn't move.

"Son."

"Yeah."

"You can check out those trophies later all you want. I even got the key. You don't have to crack the thing."

"I didn't crack it."

"Son."

"Yeah."

"Back up from the trophy case, will ya please? We had that special made. It took us over a year, and half a dozen or so brownie sales, to have it paid for."

Gavin eased back from the glass, turning to the voice. The voice was in fact a sturdy looking man with a decent sized potbelly. The man wore a white shirt and light blue slacks with green and white tennis shoes. "I'm not an Indian," Gavin said direct to the slacks.

"You're from the Indian school, the court, correct?"

"*Core-tay*. The *Core-tay* School."

"Excuse me. *Core-tay*. My apologies."

Gavin tucked his hands into his jean pockets, leaving his thumbs to stand out.

"I can see it now, you're white. A little sunburned, but white. They don't get sunburned like you and me."

"Who?"

"Sorry . . ." the man said with his wrists dug into his hips and hands flared back out. "I just lost my train of thought. It was the hair. The hair got me I suppose and I didn't even think about it. Sorry, my mistake."

Gavin went back to his previous position at the case. "Like I said, I'm not an Indian."

"Not a mix?"

"No."

"You're white, and you go to an all Indian school?"

"I am. And, yeah, I do."

"No other white folks, just you?"

Gavin tapped the glass in protest.

"I guess the Indian Chief didn't tell me that. I'd just assumed that you were. And we know how that goes, don't we?"

"No, how does it go?"

"I make an ass out of you and me when I do that, that's how that goes. And that's not me."

Gavin didn't speak.

The man repositioned his hands to grip his hips and flexed his chest. His pot belly disappeared. "You're near the San Pedro, correct?"

"The river, yeah, down by there, in St. David."

"We don't go down there much."

"Okay. He's not the Chief, so you know."

"Well . . . as I was saying . . . what's your name?"

Gavin hesitated. "Runner," he said.

"Runner?"

"Yeah."

"That some kind of tribal name they gave to you?"

"Maybe."

"Well, okay then, as I was saying, we're finishing up with some film and I'm waiting on a reel and in just a few shakes we'll get started."

"Can't you just give me the key so I can look for myself?" Gavin asked as he faced the man again. "I'm not gonna touch anything, promise."

"You want to look inside the case, while you wait?"

It is why I ran here and not to the depot on a Saturday, Gavin thought. Then he said, "Wait for what?"

The man glanced back over his shoulder for a moment and waved at someone vying for his attention. He eyed the floor upon return. "I can see the first order of business we got today is to locate you some cleats," he said. "Those kicks just look sorry." Gavin rolled over his right sneaker. The man squatted and swatted at the shiny concrete with his right hand like he was brushing eraser bits off a school desk.

"That duct tape you got around your shoe?"

"Yeah," Gavin said, rolling back.

"These your fulltime shoes?"

"I run in them. I do Cross Country at my school. They're real good for that." Gavin wasn't privy to the fact that only Class A schools in Tucson competed in the sport that required special running shoes. He simply felt embarrassed about his tattered wear and wanted to change the subject.

The man settled into a catcher-like pose. "Well after we get your cleats done," he said, "we need to rustle up a helmet for your head and a uniform and get out on the field before it starts to flood later this afternoon." He conferred with his calculator watch. "Looks like we got about two hours."

Gavin wiped his restless hands.

"You wear a size ten, ten and a half, maybe?" The man stretched his back as he rose.

"I came here to look at the case," Gavin said. "I'm not sure what you're talking about exactly, sir, sorry."

"The big man that came to see me, the Indian Chief, he told me something entirely different."

"What did he say?"

"He said you were coming up here to play football, that's the arrangement we made. He came to see me and we had a meeting and he convinced me of something."

"He said I was coming up here to play football?"

"It sounds to me like you don't want to play?"

"What, football?"

The man aired out his crew neck. "It's *Runner*," he said. "What you want me to call you, correct?"

Gavin put his hands behind his back and closed in on the display case. There were pictures of football teams that lined the entire middle shelf. Black and white panoramic photographs of young men from different decades. Only one photo was in color.

"Well . . . " the man said, folding his arms, "whatever the Indian Chief is to you, he was downright convincing in what he had to say to me. He told me you might not be prepared to play, and that you can be defensive, but whatever you said, he said to make sure to tell you one thing." The man grinned as he brought a hand from his fold up to his chin, his eyes fitting Gavin for a uniform.

Gavin forgot about what it was he had come to find in the hallway. "What did he say?"

"The Indian Chief said to tell you, and I'm quoting the man here:

'You look like a girl with that long hair and you're definitely a girl if you run away from the challenge.'"

GAVIN LOITERED about the fifty yard line draped in a blank white jersey striped of green and yellow around the shoulders. With all the padding on his body and the temperature ready to boil he felt sick to his stomach. He slowed his breaths and did his best to shun the image of puke chunks floating around in a cereal bowl.

When he let go his stomach he saw them make their approach.

The man had changed into an all-green ensemble, head cap to ankle. Confident to his stride were four boys in dark-green jerseys identified by big yellow numbers. Gavin added the digits. Forty-four, twenty-four, twelve, nine. He divided to find the average. He couldn't figure the average to the number stuck in his head and so he started over in reverse. Nine, twelve, twenty-four, forty-four. He doubted his place in the world and his place on the white line and thought about what might exit his mouth over the next minute of his life.

The man and his chosen numbers formed a semicircle around Gavin. "How's the fit?" the man asked with genuine care.

"The cleats hurt," Gavin said, thinking he'd swallowed a highway bug.

The man adjusted his cap. "I went through all of our extra equipment and, unfortunately, the best I could find was a size nine."

"Do you have some scissors?" Gavin asked.

"Scissors . . . for what?"

"To cut out the tops around the toes."

The yellow numbers all screeched like a bunch of wild monkeys. The man hushed them up. "We can't cut those cleats up, son," he said. "I'm afraid it's the best we can do with what we got. You'll work them in just fine, trust me."

"I'll give him my cleats, coach," number twelve said. "No problemo."

"You're six foot three, Hagerty, and what, a size thirteen?"

"Dude's a clown, coach," number twelve replied. "Let him have some clown shoes to wear."

The man hugged number twelve with an arm, whispering something into his plastic ear hole. Number twelve then made a beeline for the sideline and the other numbers rightly followed. The man folded his arms. "Don't mind them," he said. "They're just sore they got to be out here before two-a-days start."

"What position is he?" Gavin said.

"Quarterback."

"What position am I gonna do?"

The man stole a look of his team stretching out on the sideline. "Have you ever seen eight-man football played before, Runner?" he said.

"I haven't seen any football played in person before."

The man looked at the fit of Gavin's pads. "Your father . . . excuse me, the Indian Chief, he said you liked St. Louis."

Gavin shrugged, barely.

"So you're at least familiar with the game then, good. That's eleven on eleven, professional. The St. Louis Cardinals play the same game as everybody else, for the most part. Down the ranks of high school and juniors, eleven is the norm. Around here, though, we play eight on eight. We play eight because it's a faster game and not because of the enrollment. Enrollment has something to do with it, but we like the speed of the game."

"Speed, okay." He imagined scoring with the ball untouched.

"So what I'm going to do here is teach you some of the finer points of the eight-man game. That's part and parcel to the agreement I made with the Indian Chief."

"What position?"

The man rendered his legs like an umpire behind home plate. "Do you know how to snap the football?" he said as he used his right hand to simulate the motion. "How the quarterback gets the ball right from the get-go?"

"I know what a snap is, I'm not stupid."

"Perfect," the man said with a clap. "Show me then that you know how to get low and push through with your hips after the snap, keep your hands up now." The man demonstrated one time.

Gavin put a hand on the ground and successfully repeated the action he'd been shown. He then stood tall in his no-number jersey. The man gave him an approving smile.

"So, by definition, the snap is the start of the play, the initial possession of the football. The quarterback does not need to possess the ball from that point on which is why - as the Indian Chief pointed out so clearly to me - the ball can be fumbled as it passes hands between him and the center. So, if the ball is rolling around on the ground, it's a live wire and the defense can possess it if they get to it first and take a step. In our game, we allow advancement on the change of possession. Where the defense gets the ball is where they can possess it and score if they like so long as they don't go to the ground with your hand on them. Are you following me on all this?"

Gavin held his gaze on the collection of yellow numbers. After a moment of idle thought he acknowledged the man with a nod. Then he drifted back. There were about as many players on the sideline as labeled on the quarterback's chest. He felt less bothered by the dry heat.

"Son," the man said with the snap of a finger.

They look big, Gavin thought.

"Son."

But who around here is faster than you?

"Runner."

"Yeah," Gavin uttered, facing the man.

"Listen to me now, this is important."

Gavin made available one ear.

"We got a drill we call Oklahoma. How it goes is two players lie on their backs ten yards apart. When I sound the whistle, the fastest player to the ball tries to grab it and go. You win the drill if you can possess the ball first and not get tackled, or, you win if you can tackle the other guy when he gets the ball. It's real simple, you want to get to the ball before the other guy to give yourself the best chance."

"The drill is called Oklahoma?"

With a tip of the cap the man signaled for his quarterback to toss him a football. In a matter of seconds, one arrived right in his bread basket. The man nestled the ball between himself and Gavin, in the fifty yard line grass.

"You're gonna lie on your back on the forty-five there and the other guy is going to be on the other forty-five behind me, ten yards apart."

"Why's it called Oklahoma?"

"It's just what it's called. Now pay attention. If you've never tackled anyone before, I believe, the drill is what we need to do first. I explained to the Indian Chief that if you couldn't win one battle in the gauntlet, we'll scrap the whole thing altogether. I can't have you on my field if you're just gonna get run over and can't protect yourself. I can't have you as a liability, you understand me?"

"I understand. What's a gauntlet?"

"The gauntlet is where one guy goes against all the others in the drill I just mentioned, at least eight, one right after the other. If you're not in shape, you're not gonna last very long. You need to win at least one battle in the gauntlet to play in the run-through we got for you. The Indian Chief and I both agreed on that prior to you being here."

Gavin removed his helmet. "If I'm the snapper," he said, "I don't think I'll even get touched all that much. I want to run with the ball. Which one of those guys over there runs with the ball?"

The man rose from the turf with the football tucked under his arm. "Thing is son," he said, "you can run with the ball all you want if you can possess it after snapping it. You're gonna want to snap it as far as possible to give yourself the best chance of coming out of your stance and going back after it. Exactly how fast of a runner are you?"

Gavin thought about what he'd just heard. And he thought some more. "I'm snapping to myself?" he said, thinking his question sounded ridiculous.

The man scratched at his cap.

"That's correct. If you can make it through the gauntlet like we just talked about, yes, that's the plan. If you win just one in the gauntlet, we'll run-through some plays against you, the one player of the court school."

Upon learning the news that he would have to snap the ball to himself if he could make it through a gauntlet of players, Gavin felt like for sure he was going to throw up.

With nothing more than his pride he took a knee to test the sting in his toes. He slipped off his right cleat with a wince and searched every jersey in his midst for the number he wanted to wear. The number he found nowhere. As he switched knees to make the other foot bare, he thought about all the anger he'd defeated out on the highway, alone.

16 SUBMISSION

THE WOMAN on the other end of the line stated her case clearly. She wasn't going to add a connection out just because of something called the "Specials." She'd never heard that term before. And she only had one approved number for the prisoner speaking to her. One approved number and only one time a week, on Friday.

"Ring me up the regular operator, honey."

"I'm sorry I can't do that," the woman said.

"Where you from? I wanna know when I speak to you next where you from so I can know where to send my flowers out with your name on them. And since I ain't know your name and you like hidin' that from me, it's gonna be Honey bee on the card. A Honey bee, sweet like that sweet voice of yours."

A buzzing infiltrated the line.

"Well . . . that's not gonna happen."

"Honey bee, Honey bee, where's my pretty little Honey bee? You remember that song?"

"I don't think that's a song."

"Sure it is. Honey bee, Honey bee, where you been hidin' your sweet, sweet honey from me?"

The woman typed something.

"You writin' me a love note over there, Honey bee?"

The woman burst with laughter. "Yeah, that'll be the day," she quipped.

"So now you got requests, okay, I can do requests. *That'll be the day when you say goodbye, that'll be the day when you make me cry, that'll be the day* when we get high."

"I'm not asking for any requests, but I can tell you that's not how that song goes."

"How does it go?"

"I really shouldn't be talking to you."

"Why not?"

"I just shouldn't be."

"No one's list-nin. I know for real that there ain't no recordins goin on because of your boss man the Warden and how cheap he is. You tell me what you want and I'll be that man. You tell me, Honey bee."

"I don't want to hang up on you."

"Well you is a good girl, that I can tell. Ain't nobody gonna tell me otherwise."

"Thanks."

"You like mister James Byron Dean?"

"Who?"

"James Dean, you know who, Honey bee."

The woman expelled her breath. "Oh I don't know."

"Well, you like how he looks? All that life, the world in his hair."

"The world in his hair?"

"Yeah, you know, that pretty boy face, that college boy look."

"I think I saw a picture once, but I forget it."

"You ever seen that old picture, *Giant*?"

"No, that one's not familiar to me."

"Well that's me. He got my face on the silver screen. He got my hat and my stare and my boots and my hair."

Not a word from the one without the felonious record.

"They all says I look like him. From about my teen-age. I even get some stares at me now. You like how he looks, you like me. You like famous people, right?"

"I really have to go. I'm sorry."

"I know you don't, Honey bee. Good girls is shy girls. At least that's what I'd heard."

"I'm going to get this call coming in, hold on."

The woman switched the line and a minute passed. The prisoner excitedly chattered his teeth and breathed heavily. She came back on.

"Alright, sorry about that."

"Don't apologize to me. Never apologize, can you promise me?"

"Look . . . you are a charmer, but I can't keep talking to you. I've got a job to do."

"Well it makes me sad, you leavin' me. If you was with me now in my penthouse, the comfy one they got for me here, you'd see me cryin on you."

"Don't say that because I know it's not true."

"It's how I feel inside. I feel things inside."

"Maybe your stomach is upset like last time."

The prisoner sighed something fraudulent.

"Look," the woman said, "just so I know . . . and maybe, just maybe, when I get off my shift later, I'll go to the new library they built up at fort center where they got just about every kind of magazine even though I don't think I've ever even seen it before. What's the name of it again?"

"Soldier of Fortune, Honey bee. They gonna be the first one to print my mission story before it goes to the silver screen."

"Well I won't make you any promises. But if I come across it, I'll write the address down. That is, if I can even find a copy."

"Well now I know for sure what I been feelin' inside is true."

"I still think you need to get your stomach checked. So take care of yourself, and don't ask me again. If I get it, I'll dial you. And only dial me on your call day. I'm hanging up, okay?" Her voice sprinkled sugar. "By now."

The woman hung up the phone before the prisoner could get another word in. He held the receiver to his beguiling ear to see if she might return. She didn't. He ended the one-way connection with the index finger of his scorpion hand and leered out the window at the empty sun of the late afternoon.

"Yeah . . . *bye now* back at you, Missy True."

17 BAGGAGE

THEY floated north river at the speed of a walking bird. "Say again, Runner, what do you see?"

"It's too hard," Gavin replied in angst.

"Hard how?"

"The noises. I just can't concentrate at all. Everything is louder for some reason. And the sound the water makes is even starting to bug me now."

Walt removed the stunted paddle from the river, resting it over his lap. He recessed in the last branch of shade as the canoe diverted debris. "Now," he said, "what do you see when you are in the middle of the football field and the light is shining upon you as it is now?"

Gavin continued to scout blind over his environment. He sat up straight and made a serious face for only the water glaze to see. In a split-second his concentrated energy expunged before his body. "Jheezus . . ." he cried, dropping his head in defeat.

"Take it off then."

Jheezus.

Gavin removed the black bandana covering his eyes. When adjusted to the clear light he gathered in his surroundings only to discover many of the same things he had seen nearly an hour before, at the start of the canoe trip. The mass of river sticks on the banks hadn't decreased by one dead stick. And the ridges leading up to the eastern grassland looked only steeper. He squared out the bandana at the corners and rolled it over until the fabric thickened around itself.

Then he fastened it around his head like a biker might, or an Indian on television with a spear.

"There is something I smell that is not supposed to be here and it has been with us since the beginning. Only now, with no flowers or trees, it is heavy. What is it in your hair, Runner? What is the shampoo you use?"

"I don't use shampoo."

"What is the soap, the spring of the Irish people?"

"I don't use soap."

"What do you use?"

Gavin thought about his old cowboy washroom. "Water," he said.

"You need more than water to keep from the dirt."

"It's Coppertone."

"Copper?"

Gavin looked over his shoulder. *"Tone,"* he said. "It's sun lotion, Walt."

Walt put the paddle in the river, port side. Gavin lifted his legs and maneuvered around on his plank to look at the one he wanted to learn from.

"Am I allowed to ask a question now?" Gavin said.

"No."

"I don't want to think any more about what I see when I close my eyes. The only time I ever come close to seeing what I want to see is later, always later, when I'm tired and all I want to do is sleep."

"I will say it is your mind playing tricks on you. Your mind is filled with trash. And it must be emptied. Same as a can of garbage, no difference."

"My mind isn't full of garbage."

"Turn off your TV. Nothing there about your dream."

Gavin flustered. "Could you speak English for once Walt, please?"

Walt smiled. *"English,"* he said.

Gavin grabbed the sides of the canoe, rocking it. The Apache only paid attention to a long scar on his bicep. Then, the Apache closed his eyes.

"Ask me now, Runner, what it is I see and I will not say the water or your anger as it prances in front of me."

Gavin waved his hands out in front of his face. Walt paddled in perfection.

"How come you tricked me?"

"Tricked you?" Walt said, opening an eye.

"Yeah. You told me there was something different that stood out in the hallway of the school. 'Find what stands out,' is what you said."

Walt saddled back the paddle. "And you found nothing?"

"What I found was that I was really there to play football. No wait, I found out I was there to play against their entire team, by myself."

"So you accepted the challenge in the ring of fire?"

"The gauntlet."

"Did you pass?"

Gavin pictured the hit that ripped a sleeve. "No," he said.

"Not one in the ring of fire?"

"Why do you call it - *the ring of fire*, Walt? That's not how it goes."

"How does it go?"

"You lay on your back and wait to get creamed. That's how it goes."

"I see."

"You told the coach I liked St. Louis, why?"

"Because you do."

"No I don't."

"Were those not your words to me in my dwelling? When you drank all of your tea, and half of mine?"

"I told you I liked the *Saint* in St. Louis, like St. David, that's all. That it was kinda cool. That it might have a special meaning because of where I happen to live."

"Not a big deal then."

"I looked stupid and got laughed at."

"Who laughed at you, the hillbilly?"

"You mean the coach?"

Walt nodded. "It is what I mean."

"He was pretty nice to me."

"Hillbillies are generally nice I will say."

"It was some of the players who were the assholes. Not some - all."

"They are mean."

"Assholes."

Walt paddled by a floating flower. He judged the decay. "The offspring of hillbillies, I will say, are generally not nice."

"Where do you get *hillbillies* from, Walt? There's no hills over there."

"It is a state of mind. I take it you did not notice all the four wheelers and gun racks?"

"I don't know."

"Any cars there with names like fee-yacht?"

"I don't know."

"*Hillbillies*."

"Stop calling them that!"

"You're right. *Rednecks* then, sorry."

"No, not rednecks, not anything."

Walt put the paddle out starboard, guiding the canoe east. "You're defending them because you live in a trailer. How sad."

Gavin grabbed the sides, resisting the turn. "You live in a shack, Walt, you know that right? You talk in circles, you're probably drunk right now, and you throw rocks for fun. People think you're crazy."

"Who does?"

"I don't know, just some people."

"Name one."

"How about the coach, he called you the Indian Chief? He made it sound like he had something against Indians."

"Hillbillies and Indians are friends."

"Friends . . ? You are drunk. Is that whiskey you're blending in your tea these days, Walt?"

"They are both rednecks. I will say that is what makes them so. Common things, Runner."

Gavin scoffed. "You can keep joking around all you want," he said, "but I'm the one who was in the wrong place and had to be there by myself and take it. Forget you if you thought I was gonna run away. I don't run away from anything."

"Not your dream."

"What, Walt, getting my butt kicked in the stupid gauntlet? Or, what, running back to this shithole with some of those assholes honking at me and calling me things and ditching them in the desert because they're all a bunch of stupid assholes who can't run as fast as me?"

"Playing football. No longer the dream, not worth it."

"Sure, whatever."

Walt dug deep in his paddle, setting course back to the Corte School.

"It is a step and you have another. The nice man in the green, who I will not call a redneck or a hillbilly or a sheep-chaser because you are offended. Did the nice man give you a bag for the equipment?"

Gavin paused for three long seconds. "I had it, yeah."

"What do you mean, *had it*?"

"When those assholes started following me on the highway, I had to ditch the bag when I took off in the desert."

"You could not carry it?"

Gavin looked away.

"You know where it is?"

"Maybe."

"You need to go get it."

"I don't know why because I'm not gonna need it."

"It is not like the whiskey you say is in my tea."

Gavin looked straight. "What's that supposed to mean?" he said.

Walt slowed his paddle. "It wasn't cheap."

"You bought the equipment for me?"

"And the bag, yatasay."

"Why?"

"You prefer to play football with no equipment?"

"I prefer not to play football at all."

"I see."

"Are you saying, Walt, that there's another gauntlet somewhere else I get to go to and make a fool of myself in?"

"I am not."

"Good."

"What I say is that you have what they call a 'scrimmage' at another school on Saturday. And if you have no equipment, you can't play."

"A what?"

"If you decide to go, ask the Sulger coach my word if you want repeating."

"Where's the school?"

"You remember where the mine is, the place of your puzzle discovery?"

"Yeah, how could I forget it?"

"Run the same direction, but take the turn where the tires of the road bend."

Gavin remembered seeing a gas station about an hour before the Olde Rail exit. One pump and a wide assortment of tires for sale.

"I can't play one-man football, Walt. That's impossible. Football doesn't work that way."

"It is not what the eight-man rules state."

"Just because the ball is live doesn't mean you can run a play. If you snap it, they can just pile on top of you or pick it up and score. The best you can do is just snap it and pray you don't get killed."

"Not your dream."

"No."

"Never was."

Gavin didn't speak.

"The *Saint* in St. Louis means nothing to you anymore."

"I'm sorry I even told you about that. I should have never even said that."

Walt raised the paddle above his head for a stretch. "I found the listing in the papers. And I am ashamed to say that I borrowed the paper from the lawn of some suburbanites near the Square. There are the Saints in the place by the warm waters. Saints of New Orleans is what they call themselves. St. Louis has meaning then. St. Louis and St. David have meaning together."

"No they don't."

"They do."

"Not to me."

"Why is it you say this now?"

"Because it's just stupid I ever thought of something so stupid."

Walt paddled a few lengths over gloss. "No deep thought is ever stupid," he said.

"Why does it even matter, Walt? It's not like anybody in the pros will ever notice me. I can't snap the ball to myself and I can't throw it to myself and I can't play against a whole team by myself. You need to be on a team to play football."

The canoe drove itself.

"Anything you *can* do?"

Gavin put a hand in the water. *Even the stupid river is hot,* he thought. Then he said, "I think I'm getting a headache from just sitting here in the sun."

"We are moving," Walt said, ever prophetic. "In the right direction, at the right pace."

Gavin felt the heat of his jeans. The bits of copper made for presses and buttons. He hated everything about the summer.

"That reminds me, Runner, the fireworks celebration of pale America has come and gone with nothing but sticks of pinon to set fire to."

Gavin pulled the bandana off, undid the roll and wiped it over his face and neck. He smelled his sweat with little relief. "Just call it what everybody calls it, Walt. You don't have to make a joke about it like you do about everything else. Not everything is a big joke. And you don't have to act so different all the time, you know."

"*Different* is a good word."

"I'm sure it is."

"If I give you the spark gun, will you return it to the soldier?"

"I can't just give it to him, he'll think I took it."

"You did take it."

"Yeah, but I can't do that."

"Can you make it so he finds it? When people get older they can accept the appearance of things that had once disappeared. Place it somewhere right in front of him and watch for when he trips over it how he scratches his head for an hour."

"It doesn't have a bullet, Walt. Remember - the gun with no big bullet speech you gave me?"

"I do."

"How about the seat with no driver?"

"That was a good one."

"Now you're going against your own words a little bit, don't you think?"

"I do not."

"Jheezus, Walt, you can't argue now against your own words!"

Walt felt the waterline. "The spark gun has a bullet," he said.

"How does it have a bullet?"

"You put the bullet in the opening and lock it."

"I meant-"

"I know what you meant," Walt said, shaking out his hand.

"How did you get a bullet in the first place?"

"You mean after you fired the last one?"

"So you saw me fire it, so what?" What happened in the desert after hearing the news of his mother? His memory was as dark as that particular spring night.

"I have my ways, Runner. And I know some people. Unfortunately, though, the bullet came too late."

"You set up a scrum, or whatever, with me against some school that's like in Mexico. You must have your ways."

"It is for the good of you to be challenged. And it is football. As for the rules, they state: a team from any school under two hundred enrollment in Cochise County is eligible to compete in Class C." Walt welcomed the radiant blue skyline. "Know that there is no definition anywhere of what constitutes a team. There is also no definition of the start of a play. One player can play. Many things I have learned about the eight-man game just by contemplating the nature of the fumble."

"One player can't play, Walt."

Walt embraced a defenseless oak.

"Are you gonna let me borrow your truck then?" Gavin asked.

"What purpose will that serve?"

"If you let me use your truck, I'll go pick up your precious bag and I'll drive to wherever it is I'm supposed to go get buried in the dirt. I'll go there if you let me drive your truck, no problem."

"That has no purpose."

"What *does* have purpose, Walt? Anything?"

Walt released the tree from his sights. "You not outrunning a truck," he said, smiling.

"What?"

"You run, Runner, you have time to think about what it is you are doing. You can keep running or your legs can say no thank you. I will say that every step is a choice. I put you in a truck and that has no purpose. I put you in a truck and you truck-it to Mexico and sleep in the bed. When you want to run from your future, your dream, you take the bus. There's a Greyhound waiting for you at the border, in Greenhall."

18 GREENHALL, AZ

THE BOY picked up the receiver and listened for a time without speaking a word. He finally breathed. "Yes sir," he said, deflated. He raised his eyes to the ceiling of his lengthy trailer and rested the receiver on his shoulder, strumming at the coil as if he were attempting the stand-up bass. The voice on the other end of his tiny world blurred sentences together. The anger in the words. He brought the receiver back to his ear.

"Yes, I did . . . just yesterday, yes . . . yes, sir, I did."

There was a heavy rap at the far front door.

"Hold on, sir. I think somebody's up front for parts." The boy tried to move but was forced to listen for another minute about price increases to his inventory.

He hustled over from his living room through a connector of two by fours, heavy tarp, and quarter-inch plywood to access the other trailer nearest the street - a trailer of modest proportions that was being used as a storage locker for a variety of motorcycle parts. There were boxes of spark plugs stacked about the carpet in pyramid forms as well as leather seats and reflectors. He made his way through the mess and opened the door, ever so slightly. "Yes ma'am," he said.

A weary old lady and a man many years her junior stood side by side on the front porch. The lady had a long gray face and black strands of ratty hair. She wore pants that looked to be the same as her shirt, only in an upside down fashion. The man at her side was unnoticeable in every imaginable way.

"Rents today," the lady said, extending her hands as if taking communion.

"My mom's not home yet, ma'am."

"Don't ma'am me, child. We ain't runnin' no charity here or day care and we got rules. The rules is no dogs that look like ki-otes or feral cats. And no damn childrens."

"I'm in my teens, ma'am."

"I know that ain't likely the truth," the lady said out of the side of her mouth as she lit a cigarette.

The boy tried to rescind the door but junior wedged his foot in the way. "You work at the Dairy Queen dontcha?" junior snickered. "I know for a fact they don't hire adults due to the wages they got in place. That's a fact that I know."

"Is it late?"

"Is what late?" the lady said.

"Our rent."

"Not till we get to the end of the day with no cash in hand it ain't."

"When's the end of the day, ma'am?"

"Six-thirty is when the office closes-is-is up for the night," junior interjected.

The lady aired her smoke. "After six," she wheezed, "and I might not take it till Monday." She flicked her ash, smirking at junior. "Plus an Abe Lincoln or two, taxes child."

"Should be five-thirty at the very latest today, ma'am."

The lady enjoyed a long drag and then flicked the ash like it was an action prerequisite her speech. "And we don't stay open one minute later neither," she said, pointing with her stick through a cloud of smoke.

"Have we been late before or something?" the boy asked, fanning a hand in front of his kind face.

The lady looked at junior. Junior removed his Velcro-clad foot from the door as she smacked him in the arm. "It ever come late from them before?" she barked.

"No, uh . . . that's a fact, nu-uh mums."

"What about him ma'am?"

"What about him?"

"He's your son, right?"

Junior folded his arms, nodding. "That's a fact," he said. "It is a fact that he made there, mums."

The boy put his body in the door to shield his parts. "Pardon me for saying so ma'am, but he lives with you, and he's a child."

"He's a damn grown-up with a real payin job just over the border and he's got a girlfriend and his girl has got a damn job too."

The boy dropped his head, tapping one of his brown shoes. Then he popped back up. "Is he not your child?"

The lady looked confused. Time stood still in the Friday sunset launch. A dog howled and howled before it got choked.

The lady parted her old lady hair with her old lady smoke-hand. "Don't speak to me with that educated tone you got. I ain't like it when people speak to me like they educated and I ain't. I own this place, child. I own it and make my payments to the Mexican bank in person. I give them dollars, child, not pesas. They don't have to come looking around for me. They respect me due to the dollars I got."

The boy didn't speak. The lady stomped on her cigarette and backed away from the door in the comfort of her specialized orthotics. She looked to her right and then to her left, then straight ahead. "Six-thirty," she said, pointing with a fresh cigarette. "And not one minute later, curly."

WHEN THE BOY came back to the receiver the line was dead. He clicked the handle of the base and double and triple-checked the connection by saying "Dad" multiple times into the honeycombed hole. He then reached to the center of the Formica table that was his mission central for an envelope that had the familiar black stamp. SSVC in block type. "Specials" and "4042" scribed by hand.

He removed the five pages contained in the envelope. One of the pages was a handwritten note with instructions. The instructions stated that he was to wait for the second letter which was set to arrive sometime next week. The second letter was to complete the pages of the mission story. *Get all the pages together like theys numbered and I'll get with you. You need to make copys, at least in the dubble dijits since we aint got no copyers in here at our dispolsa. You need to mail out to all the locals and state papers so they can know about me before you come for a visit. I'm working on puttin adresses together for you. It's about time you man up. I'm dam proud of you. Dam proud. A-dios.*

19 GLASSES MAN

GAVIN SOLDIERED on his own five yard line.

The football gravitated to the ground thirty yards in front of his bulky shadow and he watched it sputter for a second or two in a spot of over-seeded grass. Eight players in his field of view save for one made their way in a full sprint to where he was, their fists gutting the high noon heat and their dark- blue numbers adding up to a thousand or more in the mind of his ever changing world. Gavin swiveled his head and tuned into their fury. He sucked in a deep breath and held it close to his heart.

The ball went untouched.

The lanky kicker, number eleven, hovered over the dead pig with his hands in the air like he was a parolee caught with a gun in one hand and a handbag in the other. Contorting in his gray uniform he glanced at the official beside the rubber kick-tee, a good fifteen yards behind his crooked back.

No whistle heard.

Gavin glided forward two yards. Pistoning his hands and feet he cocked his head. Before he could blink, a forearm zoomed at his chest. He managed to avoid the full force of the blow with a juke to the left, however, when he came back right; he saw that his right ankle had been trapped in the snare of number thirty-three. Gavin kicked with his free leg and attempted to reposition.

Nothing changed.

When he raised his head, in a manner more instinctive than

anything else, another forearm clipped his right shoulder pad. Gavin jolted left in an effort to anchor his sneaker better in a patch of dirt and when he came back square the last thing he could see was a crossbar in the middle of his facemask. And then, for a time that could have included all of his years, everything inside of his world blossomed into roses and plaid.

Every mouth in the crowd had gaped in response to the complete vulnerability of the hit on the boy in the long-white, no-number jersey. The solo player laid to rest with a bouquet of yellow flags at his funeral.

Things were still plaid and strange when he lined up to face the Sulger offense on his own thirty-two yard line. He thought it was for the first time, defending the yardage behind his taped-up sneakers, but it wasn't. It was his second stint on defense and the score after thirty seconds in the scrimmage was seven to nothing. The nothing recorded for the one-man football team from some Indian school by the river.

Gavin yelled something guttural and grabbed at his knees and tried in vain to convince his lungs to go along with his plans to fight the eight players lined up against him at the snap of the ball. He thought he might dismiss the cadence altogether and just wrap his hands around the neck of the quarterback; a player with the same build and number as the asshole kicker.

The back-official in the black cap grabbed Gavin by the shoulder pads and helped him to a three-point position. "Keep your head up," the official whispered as he knelt beside Gavin and held up a hand to hold off one of the other two officials. "If you can make it to the half," he added, "at least you'll get the chance to kick." What Gavin heard was: *Can't make a snap.*

The whistle blew and the quarterback delegated in brief under center. Sulger snapped the football. The center dug into Gavin's shoulder pads in an instant, driving him back a solid three yards. Gavin had done a decent job of planting his feet when absorbing the hit, but he'd crumpled under the weight of two hundred plus pounds and a pair of calves that resembled jackhammers. Flat on his back again, he twitched his eyes at the chained Doberman snarling over him.

Gavin heard the whistle squeal inside his skull. He rolled to his hands and knees and spat in his facemask. Then he leaned back and surrendered his limbs up to the dotted clouds. With the saliva about to come back on his lips he unsnapped his helmet so as to lessen the pressure. Inside his bars he cursed the heat as well as the player who found it necessary to add a little dance to his score.

Sulger had scored on an out pass - a play that resembled two athletic boys engaging in a simple game of catch in the backyard. Or at the beach.

When Gavin slid his helmet back over his ears, the husky tight end, a player with a neck roll the size of a small inner tube, clipped him with a driving knee to the lower left region of his cranium.

When he woke twenty minutes later, Gavin found himself alone and on his back with his legs straddled over a long metal bench. He felt the rivets stab at his back and so he sat up and scratched himself as best as he could in the area he felt the most irritated. He side-saddled the bench and got to his feet, feeling the back of his head as he worked to right himself. In a nasal breath he dizzied to the turf. There he crawled on his own like a boxer down for the count.

He soon managed himself back to the bench and sat on the ground with an arm around the metal and a knee to his chest. In a daze, he scanned the dreary scenery.

A group of men were huddled together in the middle of the playing field. Gavin could see them conferring with one another like they were in a heated negotiation over the sale of a new car. One of them kicked at the grass in his direction. When he turned his attention from the group, he noticed a wiry looking man out of the corner of his eye coming toward him.

The man came in close and squatted on the tips of a pair of red and white Tiger athletic shoes. He wore large glasses. As he plucked the grass, his glasses slipped down the bridge of his nose and so he rightly pushed them back, clearing his throat. Gavin thought the glasses resembled the window frames of his trailer.

"You're from St. David?" the glasses-man said.

Gavin said nothing.

"Can you hear me?"

Yeah dipshit, I can hear you.

The glasses-man snapped his fingers.

"Yeah. I can hear you," Gavin uttered.

"You okay?"

I don't know dipshit, are you okay? "Yeah, I'm okay."

"Okay, what's the day?"

"Okay."

"Tell me the day."

"Okay."

"You think you can stand up for me?"

Gavin's gaze went out beyond the frames asking him all the questions.

"Try and stand up for me, if you can."

"Today's my birthday," Gavin said, barely moving a finger. "The day, today, is my birthday."

"Really . . . your birthday. Well Happy Birthday."

Dipshit. "It's not."

"What's not?"

"My birthday."

The glasses-man reached into the chest pocket of his alligator shirt and retrieved a small pen. He flipped open a notepad the size of a wallet and scribbled something to bleed out the black ink. He pushed his glasses back up the bridge of his nose with his pen hand and dated the note for Saturday, August 8th. He wrote under the date:

Sulger Vs. Indian Corte (St. David)
Indian Corte, one player, first game of its kind on record (no check needed)
Player name:

"Can I get your full name and middle initial?" the glasses-man said. "No middle initial is fine, too, if you don't want."

"No."

"No, what?"

"No middle name."

"Okay, what is your name?"

"Good question."

"It's a standard one."

Gavin smirked. "Standard for what?"

"Reporting."

"Reporting what?"

"The local sports news beat."

"TV news?"

"Print news."

Gavin sniffed, wiping his nose with the back of his hand. As soon as he dropped the hand he noticed a streak of blood over the knuckles. "So print that I don't have a name," he said. "I gave it up."

"You took some pretty big hits out there, do you remember any one hit in particular?"

Gavin brought his other knee to his chest and gazed up at the distant sky. "I wonder if it will ever rain again," he said. "The rain would be nice. I miss the rain."

The glasses-man clicked his pen, tucking it into his shirt pocket. He used his frames in a way like they might magnify the ground. Then he pointed skyward with the pair. "That up there is the brewing," he said as he wiped away the sweat from his forehead. "The brewing, though, it won't do much but growl for another few weeks. It's how I got it playing out in my head anyways. We got a bet going at the paper for the exact day. I got Monday, September 7th. Fifty big on the 7th for the brewing to break."

"What's . . . *brewing* mean?"

"Monsoons. The monsoons are brewing right now as we speak. Soon they'll break open. And by *soon*, I'm saying it's gonna be the 7th of next month."

Gavin massaged the back of his neck. The left node on the bottom of his skull felt about twice as large as normal. He winced with complete contempt for his opponent.

"So, your name, you gave it up, sure, fine. I've heard weird before, I have absolutely no problems with weird. What's your mother's name then, let's start there?"

"Let's not."

"What am I supposed to call you then, for my readers?"

Gavin tried not to think too hard. "*Runner*," he answered.

"*Runner*, as in, you run?"

"It's what I do."

"You run, okay, well, that's a start."

"I'm a professional at it."

"Like I said, I'm fine with weird, but c'mon, you gotta give me something to go with here. You know those people over there don't know your name either. There's not a soul here with you and you're wearing a jersey halfway down to your knees, with the sleeves in pieces, mind you. And to top it all off, you don't even have a number."

"It's weird, I know."

"Where'd you get the uniform, the Corte School?"

At least the glasses got it right. "You know about it?"

"In a round-about sort of way, yes. It is for the . . . the . . . how can I put it . . . well never mind. I can tell I'm just vomiting in my mind right now. It's not very professional of me to say the wrong words when I don't know for sure what I'm talking about."

"The LD's," Gavin informed. "For the disabled. You can say it, nobody cares."

"Let's go with that. That's what I was trying to say."

"You know it's not because of the water, why some of them have problems. You know that, right?"

"I didn't say anything about the water."

"It's not the water, they don't drink from the river. And most of them don't have any problems at all."

The glasses-man sat in the grass, biting his pen. He tucked the pen back in his shirt pocket. "Mother Mary, it's getting humid," he said.

"Why are you wanting to write something about me in the first place?"

The glasses-man removed his frames and brushed his forehead with the back of his hand. He laid the notepad down in the grass and then scrubbed the pair with the end of his shirt for half a minute. He retrieved the notepad, sliding his frames back on. "So . . . " he said as he flipped to an empty page, "do they call you *Runner* at the Corte School?" He clicked his pen.

Gavin didn't speak.

"You name yourself that?"

Gavin turned a cheek and thought about not touching the ball.

"I can't put down *Runner*. It's too vague. Runner what? Runner who? *Runner* doesn't work. I know you're not an Indian. I knew that even before your helmet got popped off by that big nasty. So here's where I'm thinking about going with your back-story: you were born in Germany, okay, and your parents left the Army base there to live at Fort Huachuca when you were two. You grew up in Sierra Vista and you've got a thing for running. Your given name is John."

"No it's not."

"*John*, as in . . . the Baptist. It is, now keep with me. Your parents were missionaries at the Army base in Germany, that's why you were born there. When they finished with their work overseas they moved on to a new base. Your goal in life is to follow in their footsteps because that's what you know. You're a missionary in training who got lost at the Indian school and the juice of the story is to find out why you're playing one-man football instead. The first time ever on record, by the way. You got lost and strayed from your purpose. Interesting story if you ask me."

"You can't write that," Gavin said in a mild protest.

"Freedom of the press. You've got to love that about this great country of ours."

"It's not true. You can't put what's not true about me in the paper!"

The glasses-man hid his expression well inside of his notes. "So let me ask you, *John*, straight up – what's it like being a German? And B, what's it like being on a one-man football team, does it ever get lonely out there?"

Gavin squirmed around on the ground. "Why are you doing this, making up stuff about me? I don't even know you."

The glasses-man shrugged. His notepad slipped out of his hand. He let it rest. "Give me something I can use then," he said. "I have to write something because never in my time beating the small town heroes with fluff pieces did I ever once consider that the game of football could be played with only one man, check that, one boy. One against eight. Never did that thought occur to me. I mean, why would it? But you know, *John*, you don't have to snap the ball to anyone but yourself to play the game, do you? The thing is live, that's what you taught me today. You taught me that perceptions can be changed."

Gavin straightened up. "I didn't touch the ball," he said.

"That one is crystal clear, *John*."

"My name is not, *John*."

"That one isn't so crystal."

"I didn't possess the ball, so it's not like I even played. You've got to possess the ball to play."

"I'd say you played."

"What kind of story are you wanting to write? Me getting flattened or me getting crushed when they should have blowed the whistle?"

"Neither."

"So what kind then?"

"We do all kinds at the Eagle, *John*. The ones we don't do are the ones we should be doing, if you get my drift. This might be one of those stories. One player against eight. First ever game played that way."

"It isn't a game if you don't play on Friday or get the ball. Today is Saturday, it's a scrimmage. It doesn't even count."

The glasses-man smiled.

"So why does it even matter? Why would anyone want to read about me not touching the football?"

"It matters because I'm not over there talking to the quarterback right now about their home opener in a few weeks. I'm over here talking to you, that's why it matters."

Gavin pushed away from the bench and rested in a prayer-like position on both knees. He felt the slick grass that had played so well against his need for the right size cleats. "Do you do headstone letters at your paper?" he asked, his frustration about things easing a bit.

"I think what you're referring to is the obits. We do obits, sure."

"How much is an orbit?"

"Obit, as in, *obituary*."

"Yeah, how much is one of those?"

161

"We charge twenty-five cents a line, same as classified. Most come to about a buck-fifty on average. An additional forty cents to bold the line or a nickel for a single word, I believe."

"Where's the paper at?" Gavin asked.

"We're right in the heart of Sierra Vista, off of Marker."

"Can I bring it to you, tomorrow, the money, for an obit letter?"

"We don't open again until Monday."

"Okay, Monday, what time?" He could run the distance before the sunrise and be back in time for lunch.

"You want to place an obituary in the paper?"

"Yeah."

"Who for, yourself?"

"My mother."

"Your mother?"

"Yeah, I want to write a letter for my mother. Can I buy one with five lines with a bold, maybe?"

"Hang on," the glasses-man said, gesturing with his hands. "Are you just making this up because of the stuff I said?"

Gavin rubbed his palms up and down his thigh pads. "I don't invent things like you," he said.

"Now I feel bad."

"You should feel bad for inventing things."

"When did this happen?"

"A few months ago," Gavin said as he peeled away the pads at his hips to help his skin cells regenerate.

The glasses-man stood up to check the field over his thin view. The scrimmage that had taken place for two minutes of the first quarter was long forgotten. Rows of bleachers, like metal sold for scrap. When he turned around, his subject was standing tall and admiring his expensive running shoes.

"If you want," Gavin said, "I'll give you my mother's name. Her name is Nancy Stowemeyer."

20 PAYROLL

THE WARDEN REMOVED his rancher's hat and stared at the branded S stitched in the lining. He waited there with something running back and forth through his voracious mind. Like the answers to all the questions he'd been asking himself were to reveal in the beaver and under the hallway light. He handed the hat over to a feeble-looking guard and entered the Captain's Office inside the wire of his forty acre prison.

Lieutenant Bunch followed and shut the door.

After a minute, Bunch opened the door and kicked a laundry bag over to the soles of the hallway guard. He then ducked back inside.

"Lock the door," the Warden said.

"It's a lot cooler in the hallway," Bunch said. "The friggin humidity . . . what's it like, friggin eighty out today?"

"Ears lieutenant."

Bunch secured the door and rounded his cap.

"We need fans or somethin'. Somethin' like the tents with water sprinklers on 'em. Somethin'."

The Warden bent an arm on the strong oak desk and scratched at his temple like he was counting the cards of a blackjack dealer a yard in front of his nose. "You sound like my second," he said. "With her it was always *somethin'* too."

Bunch wiped the sweat from his neck and fanned himself with his cap. He flubbed his lips. "You're a real saint, you know that."

The Warden massaged his silver head. "Hava seat, Randall."

Bunch remained. The Warden reclined and slid off his right boot.

"Go on, sit your big butt down in the chair."

Bunch obeyed his commander.

"What did it have to say exactly?" the Warden asked, his capillaries stringing.

Bunch cleared the microwaved burrito in his throat. "Yeah . . . so the obituary was just her name and the husband, JD. Then it said somethin' real polite about how the two of them was lovebirds and where they had met along the way. And then under it was a real tender moment, like reading a poem."

"A poem?"

"Yeah . . . it said somethin' about waiting patiently for the Lord to show and how the Lord heard her cries and how he answered her. Something of that particular nature anyway."

The Warden stiffened in his executive. "You get a copy?" he said.

"It was on the plates."

"When's it gonna run?"

"The Eagle runs on Wednesdays."

The Warden paused. "Just her name and his and some religious babble, huh? Well, it ain't got me too worried."

"So it's done."

"Not exactly. It seems the ol' guard ain't showin' up for duty these days and he don't like answerin' his phone."

"He's still on the payroll."

"I know."

"Blackmail a part of Red's agenda now? What, he ain't earn enough doing your dirty work outside the yard?"

The Warden scratched at his ear. He crossed his good leg. "Ya got to have demands in that kind of business, Randall," he said. "And in a ways, you got to have some smarts, too. Nah . . . I think he's just bein lazy."

"Lazy people make demands sometimes."

"I know."

"What are you gonna do about it then?"

"Well I'm thinking."

Bunch smiled a little. "You look rattled," he said. "I can't say that I've ever seen you rattled before."

"I ain't rattled, Randall."

"So what is it?"

The Warden took a moment and then slammed a fist on the desk. Papers and pens scattered. "The ol' guard ain't have my permission to kill the broad, Randall, that's what. You happy now, cousin', gettin' yer questions answered just as soon as them interrogatin' words of yours leave yer big mouth?"

"Relax . . ."

The Warden pushed back from the desk. "I am relaxed," he seethed.

Bunch settled his cap back on his head. "It's the friggin humidity," he moaned. "You mix in the desert heat and it makes people go batty."

"I can't have two dead," the Warden said, turning to the window. "Two from the same family ain't no good. It ain't no good at-tall."

"Look at it this way: that's two people that can't do jack-shit with the evidence that cowboy collected on you."

The Warden pointed at Bunch. "On us," he reminded.

Bunch didn't say a word.

"I wanted the evidence, Randall. I wanted it here in my hand, kay. The Dear John Letter we sent to her was perfect. But the ol' guard ain't get the evidence to me like he was supposed to. Now he's using it against me by not showin' up for duty. I don't know what he's got in his hands and that ain't settin too well with me."

Bunch wiggled his form around in the chair. The Warden swiveled to the full panorama of the prison desert. The room went silent for a minute.

"Red's lazy," Bunch said. "I agree. He's dumb but he ain't stupid. If he starts making demands we can just say he's involved too. So we bluff some and bring his ass back here into work on a bonus. You more than anyone should know what a wad of cash can do. All it takes is one single patrol on B during workout and he's got an accident coming when we slip up changing the locks. Problem solved."

"It ain't that simple," the Warden said as he swung back flushed like he'd been out in the sun too long without the shade of his hat. "I can't have another accident inside of here. At least not until that damn cross-dresser at the capital gets served his walkin' papers." He put a finger back in Bunch's swollen face. Bunch observed the dead on the wall.

"You know I'd like to shoot that damn cross-dresser myself right between the teeth but I ain't had to get my hands dirty since I was in the Navy. Nah . . . I'm thinkin' somethin' else here entirely. I'm thinkin' I get me someone I can rely on to take care of this piece of business, somebody real special. I can't afford to have things goin further south than they is, ya hear? That much I can't tollar, kay."

21 NAKED

THE FOOTBALL FIELD for Clawson High School looked like a landing strip for crop dusters. The school itself was someplace else entirely. The same could be said for the goal posts. Somewhere out beyond the green of fertile seed to the north were classrooms for a student body of about one hundred and fifty.

Gavin approached the field of dirt in a cautious gait, his duffle bag slung over a shoulder and his fate over an hour late in survey of the barriers. Within range of his silver plaster was a school bus the age of his fridge parked next to its vinyl interior. A trailer or two from there was a tractor next to a billboard that had manual slots for keeping score.

Letting go the bag he slid off his sneakers and removed his shirt and jeans and stood in the middle of his fading dream with nothing but two socks around his right foot and his underwear in plain view.

He ran a finger under the band of his whites, separating himself from the burn and his choice to take on another team.

What options are there? Gavin considered.

They're not gonna kick you the ball, so what are you left with? Anything?

Not giving a shit about the ball is an option.

Anything you can *do, like Walt says?*

You could let the ball go wherever the hell it goes and forget about the whole stupid thing and just use your legs to get to the kicker and wipe the stupid smile off his face. Your speed equals a greater velocity as it factors your weight the faster you run; you learned that in eighth grade physics. You also know the faster you pump your arms, the faster your foot speed. You don't have a team, but you've got physics. And you've got better speed than anyone. You could use your speed and the force generated and your helmet like a missile.

Is that what you really want to do?

What does it really matter if you aren't allowed to run with the ball and they can't see you leave everybody in the dust, and score? Nobody is watching. Nobody cares. You know that right? The Saint *in St. David is just your imagination playing tricks on you. Why did you ever think that was even important in the first place? Why did you think St. Louis would even give a shit about that? How could they care when they don't even know your name? Why would anybody care if they can't see you and don't even know who you are? Nobody is out there on the road with you. Nobody can see how far and how fast you run. Your father leaving you is what's real. He's gone and he's never coming back.*

What are you gonna do about it then if these assholes decide to show up? Are you gonna blast the kicker under his chin or worry about him not kicking you the ball?

"Ghost!" a voice called out in his direction.

Gavin had to circle twice to find the body attached to the voice. A wire with the frames that reminded him so much of his trailer appeared near an opening in the green. Those big frames attached to a body in desperate need of more meat on the bones.

Gavin directed his legs and equipment to where he thought his sideline may or may not reside. He put a hand on a hip and looked up at the blank sky and guessed at the time of day based on the degree of rays that penetrated the cracks of his fingers. He thought the sun was at one o'clock. Maybe forty over. *Walt told you twelve thirty, remember?*

He counted the time between his stab at the present and the time he last saw his clock digitized. Three hours, give or take. He thought about how he had used a thumb and index finger on one of his father's maps to plot the distance from St. David to Clawson as he'd debated the run on the bridge earlier in the morning. How the wind had tried to steal the map out of his hands and take it to the water in an effort to settle the debate. He thought about how the thumb and finger trick was no way to judge the distance and time to go somewhere when you can't even measure your own speed. How that was simply dumb. With no credit to his stamina or fortitude he stepped into his pads.

The glasses-man walked along the sideline chalk. "You get hung out to dry on laundry day or what?" he joked.

"What?"

"Ah, never mind, what were you doing?"

"I wasn't doing anything."

"I could see that. But why were you just standing there half-naked? Don't you care that somebody might see you?"

Gavin did a quick scan. "There's nobody here," he said.

The glasses-man bent down and laced up his Tigers like he was afraid they might be cut from his feet. "Clawson was here," he said. "And I'm almost certain they're on their way back now. When you didn't show, they sent someone out to route twenty-seven."

"I know," Gavin said, tightening his belt.

"How do you know that?"

"It was an asshole in one of those Bronco things."

"Yeah, that's right. I don't know about the asshole part, but yeah, a Bronco."

"The guy pulled up and asked me if I knew where the field to the school was like he wanted directions or something, but then he took off after saying he'd give me a ride. And then I sprinted after him and he stopped and then took off again. He kept on doing that and I saw him turn and almost get stuck and I kept on sprinting and I got a rock and threw it at his piece of shit Bronco. Then I fell."

"You fell?"

"Yeah, in a pit."

"Are you alright?"

"I don't know. I guess that's why I wanted my jeans off. Because it's so hot out and my legs were hot. I was burning up."

"Are you ready?"

"For what?"

"The game, your second official contest."

Gavin adjusted his thigh pads. "It's a scrimmage," he said. "It doesn't count."

The glasses-man retrieved his notepad from his back pocket and flipped it open and dated the little page for Saturday, August 15th. He touched the tip of his pen to his tongue and scribbled something. "It's your second game," he stated, fingering his glasses up the bridge of his nose. "It's how I got it in my head anyways, and to tell you the truth, my readers won't even know the difference."

"Why did you just call me Ghost?"

"Because it's your nickname now, short for - *The Ghost*. Of St. David. It's got drama written all over it."

"No it doesn't."

"Well, I'm not going with *Runner*. And you won't tell me your real name, so it's what I got."

"How about you don't go with anything."

"Your last name isn't *Stowemeyer*, is it?"

Gavin turned a cheek.

The glasses-man speculated Gavin's feet, pointing with his pen. "You got two socks on one and none on the other. How come?"

Gavin went quiet to his padded knees and sifted around the bag for his helmet and shoulder pads.

"You know you don't have any control over your nickname, you know that, right? Nicknames are given to you by other people."

"I don't like it," Gavin said.

The glasses-man balanced on his toes and breathed in the scenery. "All we need now are some wind gusts," he said, mostly to his own ears.

"What do we need the stupid wind for?"

"For the clouds to come in and brew up some more moisture."

"Oh right," Gavin said, "your monsoons."

"Can't you feel the dry heat down there?"

"I can feel the dry heat everywhere."

"Well there's more moisture in the air now and when the wind picks up it stirs again. And like a pot on boil, it works to blow the lid off."

Gavin fell from his knees to the side and sat in the dirt, peeling strips of duct tape from his second skin. "I hate the stupid wind," he said, fitting his right sneaker and layering it with tape. "I hate it more than anything."

"Can I give you a lift back home after the game?"

"It's a scrimmage."

The glasses-man removed his frames and forearmed his forehead.

"I don't think so," Gavin said.

"Why not?"

Gavin thought for a second. "It's not part of the plan I got."

"What plan?"

Gavin didn't speak.

"Is your plan to keep running long distances to play in games that aren't really games in your mind, with no team? Is that your plan?"

"Maybe."

"Why can't I just take you? I need to get more background for my story. I need to paint the picture and I need more materials to work with here."

Gavin rose and dusted himself off. "I think you can paint a good enough picture in your head," he said. "Just close your eyes and put yourself there. Close your eyes and pull the picture in and hold it until you know it's real."

"You sound prophetic. You make that one up by yourself?"

Gavin tilted his head with a thought about Walt.

"Well I tried that already on my drive up here. I almost went up to St. David, you know, this morning, to look for you."

Gavin lifted the bag to locate his blank white jersey with torn sleeves. The jersey was balled up to about the size of a softball. He grabbed it and let it expand in the heat. "Don't follow me again," he said.

"It's a free country."

"I know. But just don't." He thought about freedom and a certain old man who looks after him.

"Put yourself in my shoes," the glasses-man said.

"I can't do that," Gavin said.

"Just try, alright. I need to see you run those miles and I need to see how it looks out on the highway. I need to know how long it takes and what you do when you get back home and where you live. I want to see that and compare you to the other people around. Do they notice you? Do you notice them? Do you run off-road like when you ditched me after the Sulger game? Just think of me as a camera in the background."

Gavin reached to his feet and retrieved his shoulder pads and latched the straps to the plastic protectors over his bare skin. He struggled as he pushed his head and hands through the jersey. "Can you help me?" he asked.

The glasses-man moved behind Gavin, who he thought of only as The Ghost, and pulled on the jersey. He lingered there, his face stoic behind drab fashion. Gavin spun around. "Thanks," he said.

The glasses-man stilled to the twenty percent moisture.

"What?" Gavin said.

No reply from the lover of Budweiser beer, one woman and overpriced words.

"What is it?"

The glasses-man smiled like something hidden from his point of view had just been revealed to him. His look was one of enlightenment.

Gavin grew anxious. "Tell me?"

"Well I just told you to put yourself in my shoes and then I thought about it the other way around. What it's like to be in your shoes, you know, how you might feel about things."

"Oh . . ."

"I'm sorry I said that, it was selfish of me. I don't know what it's like to be you. I'm wearing about the best running shoes money can buy, and I drive everywhere. And I'm genuinely sorry about your mother. That must be a really tough thing at your age. I can't even begin to imagine."

Gavin observed plumes of dust to the north. "One week from Monday," he said.

"One week from Monday?"

"Yeah, I'm back in school. We can meet then."

The glasses-man took a knee and smoothed the tape on Gavin's right sneaker. "Sounds real good," he said. "So where exactly is the Corte School? How do I get there?"

"Just go to the statue at the Square," Gavin said. "Walk from the trail there to where the trees start, and go from there until the river. On that day, I'll meet you. We can meet at three. And don't leave if I'm late, okay?"

"Sounds to me like an exclusive. You can bet I'll be there."

"I don't make bets," Gavin warned.

The glasses-man smiled wide.

"At three, okay? And make sure you don't leave if I'm not there."

"Okay, Ghost. If you're not there, I'll be waiting patiently. Patiently like those nice lines you gave me, for the obituary."

"You swear you won't leave?"

The glasses-man jockeyed in his stance. He viewed the white line in the dirt and then the boy with the hopeful stare. His glasses were dusted over the norm and so after a wipe from his shirt he held them up to the sun like the optics might render things more clear. In that moment a story within him was born. Something much bigger than his work. He peered at The Ghost for the first time with 20/200 vision. "I swear I'll be there," he replied. "I promise you I won't leave."

22 CITIZEN BAND

SANDIS EASED SUNNY down the access road of Rock Gardens with his free hand moving through the channels of his high-band. He veered her west, to the open desert, at the very moment she recoiled. He played the gas and let go the dial and smiled like a child as he readied his forearms for a path he claimed as his own.

He whooped and hollered and swallowed the axle strain. A hundred yards later and the bumps melted to a buttery spread. He managed his excitement and managed the band and checked the bed for any crates absent their place.

Highway 90 appeared like an oasis thirty minutes later.

Sandis nosed out to the pave and waited for the traffic to clear. When it was safe, he crossed over the northbound drift and gunned it south. A familiar voice called to him over the channel. "Desert Fox," the voice said. "Desert Fox, hit me one time."

Sandis brought the portable mic to his lap. "If there's a fox in the desert," he responded, not looking at the road ahead, "he is me."

"There you are, old buddy."

"How you getting along?" Sandis asked.

There was a long pause, and a wind shear.

"You mean with the wife or just in general as a guy feeding off the legal system?"

"With everything, of course. And that intel I'm needing on one JD Reeves. Aged forty-five years give or take. No military record other than weekend volunteer."

"Things is pretty decent, can't complain."

"Good to hear."

"What's all the noise?"

No immediate response from the highway. "Hold tight," Sandis finally said as he moved his right hand to the steering wheel and used his left to roll up the window. "There," he added. "Sorry, I'm driving."

"Roger that."

"So anything?"

"Well, yeah. I got a hit on a JD Reeves out of Sierra Vista."

"That's good."

"Well I wish it were. Because that's all I got really. There's one department store card pinned on him. But no activity, though, for over a year. Get this: he's got a gas card that was active for every single week up until last December. The man was a guzzler."

Sandis thought there out on the open road. "That's when I'm told he checked out of this desert life we all got going here."

"I referenced motor vehicles."

"And?"

"Well they got about zero registered under that name. There's an outdated CDL card though. You didn't mention he was a driver?"

Sandis thought some more. The first bits of traffic raced by his forty-eight on the meter.

"I'm pretty sure he hitched around on the circuit in his line of work. He was a land scout, I'm told. So I'm thinking all that open land and no roads. Relying on truckers and motels to make his way to and fro. I'm thinking now he might have played that card as a parlay."

"They call that kind of thing gypsy riding around these parts."

"In most parts I imagine," Sandis said.

The voice over the channel muffled. Sandis used the time to clear the allergy out of his nose. He broomed his throat.

"I do believe that's about what it was. But this man had his fair share of responsibilities, what with a wife and a son and all. I just do not think he'd just get up one day and ride on out of here with all that hard work under him. From what I can tell, he was better than that."

"He could have hitched his way out of town pretty easy with that kind of lifestyle. But again, that gas card of his has not been run since mid-December. It's been frozen since and right now it's sitting tight in collections."

"Good luck with that one," Sandis joked.

"Yeah, good luck."

Sandis consulted his beard. "Well it ain't too normal of a behavior for skipping out on things when they seem pretty good if you ask me."

"That it ain't, old buddy."

Sandis brought the speed up to legal. "Well keep on it for me, and maybe something will pop up."

"Where you headed to?"

"Going down to Fort Huachuca. I got a few favors left with a friend of mine there and I'm bound to use one or two."

"Roger that. Hey?"

"I'm here . . ."

"Why not contact the police? File a missing persons? Put them to work on this for free."

Sandis hesitated, tapping the brakes. "Hold the phone," he said. "I'll be back in a jiff." He dialed channel 19. The information channel was all concerning of the local traffic. Sandis waited a minute for any word about the weather. He got nothing but a stock tip before dialing back the open channel. "What does it look like outside your window?" he asked.

"Same as yesterday, two Chevy's on blocks and weeds instead of grass."

"How's the weather up there?"

"Same as yesterday, hotter than it need be."

"Any clouds?"

"Well I don't know for sure. Why you ask?"

"It's way too clear right now. I can see Sierra Vista better than I can see five feet in front of me."

"So?"

"So if it's cloudy up in Benson and clear as a bell down south that's a recipe for monsoons. I didn't secure any of the trailers before I took off. I even forgot about mine."

"Is it thick?"

"Is what thick?" Sandis said.

"The air."

Sandis rolled down the window and stuck out a hand. "I'd say so," he said.

"Thick and clear, cloudy and dry. You need cloudy and thick. And even then you need the dry heat to swoop in and try and overcome them both. Muscle them out of the way."

"So it's cloudy up there, but dry?"

"Dry as my bank account, Fox. And, well, yeah, now that I look at it, a bit overcast."

"I'm gonna sign off now," Sandis said.

"So . . . no cops."

"No cops."

"Any reason in particular? Other than them being about as smart as a roadrunner?"

Sandis waited with a grin. "I don't like paperwork."

"Well that's a lie."

Sandis sniffed as he searched for a tissue. He found one in his pocket.

"JD's wife never did make contact with them. She moved out of Sierra Vista faster than some people cash their paycheck. So there's got to be a reason. Although, I never got a single confirm one way or the other."

The voice over the channel chuckled. "You know, maybe we should consider doing the weather for people like us? I might be able to reserve us some time if you're interested."

"Maybe."

"Think about it some, old buddy. We both got years and years of experience."

Sandis packed away the tissue. "Right," he said. "And the faces for radio."

"Hey . . . careful now."

Sandis gripped the wheel. "Well I like that idea. The dimwits on TV don't know what the heck they're talking about half the time anyways. Always dancing around with an umbrella like Fred Astaire when the sun oversleeps. I'd take an Apache friend of mine with a stick sooner than I'd take one of their million dollar satellites. That's for darn sure."

23 NO MAN'S LAND

GAVIN HELD BACK ten yards from the river bank, kicking rocks. "I'm not sure what you mean," he said. "Why do you want to know anyway?" He took a seat on a plot of grass and massaged his right shin.

The glasses-man fronted him with a ballpoint pen and a checklist of questions. "Let me ask you then: why football?"

"Do you know who number twenty is for Clawson?"

"Number twenty . . . that one doesn't ring a bell . . . so football means . . ."

"I hate his guts," Gavin said. "Whoever he is, he's a big asshole. Can you say that I say that?"

The glasses-man bent down to be eye level with Gavin, giving his long legs a stretch. "You like living out here?" he asked in a warm voice.

Gavin settled his anger over getting jabbed in the groin under a pile of Clawson players. "It's ok, I guess," he said.

"What do you like about it?"

"Well . . . it's quiet. I can think, I guess."

"Anything you like to do other than football?"

"Run."

"Running huh? Anything else?"

"Me and my friends go and shoot guns sometimes. We go out with my dad. My dad's an expert with guns."

The glasses-man penned something. "So where exactly is the Corte School from here?" he asked.

"It's a few minutes down from here," Gavin said, pointing south. "But the water is high right now and it's too fast to cross over."

The glasses-man rose to the west. "Across the river," he said under his breath. He came out from under. "Is that where you live also, on the other side?"

"On the other side, yeah."

"Interesting . . ." the glasses-man remarked, scratching his chin. He glanced at Gavin. "Just you and your father, huh? You have any siblings?"

"My dad, yeah . . . it's just the two of us." Gavin got to his feet and walked over to the water.

"Can we go see him, your father? I'd sure like the opportunity to meet him sometime. And by *sometime*, I mean today."

"Today, no, we can't do that, sorry, he's busy."

"How about next week? We could get some shots of you with the football."

Gavin skipped a rock with skill. "I don't have a football," he said.

"Simple enough," the glasses-man said, bringing his pen back to paper. "We'll supply the pigskin. Our photographer at the Eagle makes it a point to have every known sport residing inside of his trunk. How can we get to you?"

"You go past the bridge like you're going straight into the desert. And before you do, you take the dirt road that goes up the hill, where the dirt is kinda orange, that's how you know."

"That camper area?"

"Yeah, the road goes up to it there, but then there's a trail that goes down the back. My house is kinda far from there, but you can see it after a while if you go down into the lower part of it and keep walking. The house is a real house with a chimney and it doesn't have any wheels. It's not a trailer. I don't live in a trailer."

"Sounds isolated."

"Yeah. We like it that way."

"What about sprints, you don't need a team for that, why not compete?"

Gavin bent down to get a feel for the water temperature. He caught his profile in the gleam as he turned to the frames asking him all the personal questions. With a wet hand he came back up and parted his bangs, many things inside of him reflecting.

"How long have you been doing newspaper stuff?" he asked with one eye. *Is he blind behind those things?*

"It'll be ten years this December, no, wait, November."

"So when you were my age you wanted to do that?"

"You could say so . . . sure, you could say that. I had won a photo contest my senior year, black and white, Honey bee on a plastic flower. It got a mention in a lot of the papers. It even went national for a time, so it kind of took off from there. They used to call me *Ansel*."

"Is that what you go by?"

"It's what they used to call me."

"What do they call you now?"

The glasses-man scratched his temple. Grinning he said, "So you want to know my real name, is that it?"

"Unless you want me to call you what you just told me, *Hansel*."

"Ansel. *And-Sell*."

"Got it. *And-Sell*. And Gretel."

"It's Dean, okay. My name is Dean Toombey. See, it's not so hard to share things."

"Okay, *And-Sell*, I mean, *Dean*."

"You didn't see my name and picture at the top of the article I wrote about you taking on Sulger, next to the obituary?"

"I didn't see the article," Gavin said. "Or the letter. Or your name. Or your picture. Or anything."

"I've got a copy in my bug you can have. If you're interested in checking it out, that is."

"That's okay. I already know what it says about me. It says he never touched the ball. But he sure can take a beating, that kid."

Everything stilled but for the river.

"Just so you're aware, we've never published an obit on the sports page before. That was a first at our little rag. We did that at the very last possible minute."

Gavin turned to the water, placing his hands in the pockets of his tattered Levi's – weathered jeans that appeared more black than blue.

"You don't really care about that do you?" the glasses-man said.

Gavin closed his eyes and let the white noise rush his ears. He felt the warmth of the late afternoon sun prick his forearms. "I care," he said, opening.

"I have to say, I find that funny. Not funny haha, but, you know, funny ironic."

Gavin spied the west bank. "Why's it the ironic kind of funny?" he asked. He really wanted to know.

"I say that because I get messages at the office and letters and I even get presents sent to me on my birthday. Some parents find out my birthday and send me presents so I'll write articles about their kid."

Gavin shook out his legs as if they'd fallen asleep on him. "Do you?" he said, facing the glasses-man.

"I don't take bribes, no. So all their effort ends up being a big waste of their time. That is, of course, unless their little hero winds up doing something special, but that never happens. That's how come I find it just a tad ironic that you could care less about being in the paper. You probably could care less about being on the front page of the paper I'd imagine."

"What's *ironic* mean exactly?"

"It's hard to explain. Well . . . let's say for example that you like to run."

"I don't like to run."

"You don't?"

"Is that ironic?"

"Well, no, that's just strange. Strange is what that is."

"Why's it strange?"

"Well for one, you run to the schools you compete against. And B, you run more than anyone I ever heard of before or have seen in person. You'd have no problem . . . no problem making a track team. And you could probably be on a track scholarship somewhere in your near future if you were at any other school. You're saying that you don't like to run, yet you do it so much and you go so far. That to

181

me is very strange because I can't imagine doing something to such an extreme when you don't love it, let alone even liking it for that matter. When I was in high school, I used to skip the days when they timed us for the mile. Mention running the mile to me and I still get a little queasy."

"Was it one of the schools around here?"

"This was in New Mexico."

A batch of birds skimmed the trees. One landed on a large branch about to sever. The glasses-man typed out scenes.

And like a pistol shot in a crowded room Gavin said, "Where's your camera, Dean?"

The glasses-man fumbled around with his notepad, and his lips. "Umm . . . let me ask you," he muttered, jotting down his own name. "What is it you hope to gain from playing by yourself?" He breathed in the trees and suffocated his emotion. He focused in on his profession. "It's not like you can run a real play if they ever kick you the ball and let you line up on offense to snap?"

"I don't know," Gavin replied. "Like I said to you before, it's just what I thought I wanted to do."

"When did you get the idea to play football as a one-man team, and how in the heck did you ever think that was going to work?"

"How many more questions are you gonna ask me?" Gavin asked, annoyed.

"I think people have a lot of questions. It's real unusual what you're doing, so naturally, people are curious."

"I don't know why people would want to read about me not touching the football."

"The more I learn about you, the more interesting the story. At first I thought you were from St. David - and we've never done a piece on anyone from St. David before, mind you. But now I find out you're living out in No man's land. And when I think about that one, that's almost as good as being a one-man football team. It has all the makings for an original story."

"What do you mean - *No man's land?*"

"You live somewhere west of the river, but before you get to the northern connecter that they're building up to Benson, right?"

"Yeah."

"I'll bet my four aces the Corte School is all trailers, like the camper area is, am I right?"

Gavin forgot about the day. And he forgot the gut-check he wanted to hand number twenty. "Yeah . . . so?"

"So you can't build anything on that land, that's why I call it *No man's land*, because it's unincorporated. There was a big fight over that place years ago. Officially, I think they call it a protected territory."

In response to hearing the news about where his trailer really resided, Gavin felt shaky. His wild dream of running with the football and being discovered by the professional team with the Saint in their name, being special, flashed before his eyes. He saw himself on the poster in his bedroom. And he saw the poster burn from a hole in the middle.

"It's not St. David if you live on the other side of the river?" Gavin asked, in a trance.

"Where we are right now, this is really where St. David ends. If we were to cross the river from here we'd be in a place that has no official name." The glasses-man nudged his frames. "Huh . . . the other side has no name. When I think about that now, I find that incredibly funny."

Gavin gulped. "Funny ironic?"

"Absolutely."

"Why?"

"Well because you're telling me you have no name. And you won't tell me your real name, so the place you're in is a lot like you. The place you're in has no name too."

24 SQUATTER

GAVIN LOCATED WALT'S truck near the scrub littered area north of the Apache's wickiup. He made his way to where the dirt widened to double the size of the path he was on and approached the truck to peek in the passenger window, pressing in the handle with his right thumb.

"Jheezus," he moaned, flapping his hand.

The scolding metal of the handle had burned in him a valuable lesson to think first before acting and so he backed away with much regret, kicking the hunk of shit with crap whitewalls and no-good bumpers.

Sucking the tip of his thumb he captured Walt's top half in a clearing of dirt a decent sprint away. He yelled out but got no reply. He yelled a few more times. Then he cupped his hands around his mouth like a bullhorn and shouted "Yahtzee" in the upper range of his voice.

Walt remained as he was and had been for the last hour - his leathered back like a brick wall to anyone who might try and pass from the south. Gavin turned over his feet and ran up a degree in elevation to where Walt was, arriving in under three minutes.

The one with multiple nicknames raced by the one with none for a scare. The one with multiple nicknames came to a halt in his own brand of humor.

"What are you doing?" Gavin said.

"Get behind me."

"What?"

"Get behind me. Move your feet like you like to do and get behind me."

Gavin drifted south with his hands out, leading. "Yeah, sure, okay, whatever you say, no problem."

"Stay behind me," Walt said as Gavin brushed by.

Gavin settled a few yards behind Walt and folded his arms in the direction of Benson, mimicking the stance of the big Apache in denim and leather. "Do you ever get hot in those clothes?" he teased.

"Shhh . . ."

Gavin grinned. "What are we doing?" he whispered.

Walt looked over his shoulder. His jet black cheek. His one eye all-knowing.

"Did you use this road to get to the nice man's school or did you use the road of St. David?"

"I used this road, it's faster up to Benson."

Walt brought his head back square. "Thought so," he said.

"Why?"

"It is not one of my roads."

"You have roads?"

"I have land," Walt replied to the wind. "On my land I have roads."

Gavin stepped to the side of Walt. "You mean, your protected territory?" he said.

Walt scouted southeast at the vast array of creosote. The chimney of his impressively constructed wickiup. And the hill with the trailers of all his guests. "That's right," he said.

"I know it's not St. David, Walt. Why didn't you tell me it's not St. David?"

"You never asked."

"Yeah, but I told you about my stupid thing and now I've done all this stuff and it means absolutely nothing."

"Nothing means nothing," Walt said.

Nada means nothing, Gavin thought. *But whatever.* He furrowed his brows. "Why are you in your bare feet, Walt?"

Walt looked at his feet.

"You walked all the way to your home and back after leaving your truck, didn't you?"

Walt's eyes followed his prints until they died. Not a breath from his lips.

"Are you trying to hurt your feet or something, like a firewalker? Is that one of your challenges, should I go barefoot too?"

"My feet will never hurt, Runner," Walt said. "And my eyes will never burn."

"Is something wrong?"

Walt paused. Then he said, "If they connect a road around to the bridge from Benson, it will no longer be my home. My home is my land. If they pave a new road here they will pave me."

Gavin faced Walt. "How long have you lived here?" he asked.

"All of my minutes and years."

"You were born here?"

"Yatasay."

"You told me you made roads, and that you moved the wood, that you were in the conservations."

Walt conferred, mostly with his eyes.

"So why's that a big deal then, to make a new road from the bridge to Benson? Isn't that a good thing?"

Walt breathed the changed air.

"What I didn't say, Runner, is that I went to college and then on to law school when the Army would not allow me to apply."

Gavin hunched, stunned.

"It is true. I am not just the man who lives in a shack as you say. A man who talks in circles and eats what eats of the ground. A man who can out-drink the drinkers on the road. I have a degree of your law. Practiced twenty-five years. Spent three years clerking for the only ten percent native on the circuit bench."

Gavin scratched his head. "Is that how you got those teams to play against me?" he said.

Walt smiled. "No."

"What did you say to them?"

"I just stated the rules."

"The rules?"

Walt shifted his gaze. "Yatasay, the rules," he uttered. "And we talked dreams. I believe some had heard me. Others took more convincing."

"They don't kick me the ball, Walt, not that you'd even know that. They just kick it around me. Then they kick the crap out of me."

"I am sorry I did not think of that. I can't think of everything."

"It's what they do."

Walt looked through. "I believe you."

Gavin crossed his arms.

"You tell me all these things I can do, how to follow my dream of playing football in the pros, for St. Louis. To make the environment work for me when I close my eyes. A stupid dream that doesn't even exist now because I'm in No man's land and the *Saint* in St. David is for somebody else - somebody who lives on the other side of the river in a regular house and not a crap-ass trailer. Somebody who doesn't give a shit about football. I'm sorry you're upset about your precious land, Walt, I really am, but I've been doing something that is truly going nowhere. I am sorry about the road. At least you got to do things when you were my age. At least you weren't alone."

"You are not alone," Walt said.

Gavin didn't speak.

Walt placed a thoughtful hand on Gavin's shoulder. "It is not so much the road," he said, "or the builders or their plans. It is my mind."

"Your mind?"

"I am thinking thoughts that won't burn."

"*Thinking* . . . about what?"

Walt gripped. "I am not an angry man," he said.

Gavin tensed. He listened.

"My feet do hurt. Make no mistake, they are the same as yours. They are the same skin."

"I guess I don't understand what you're saying to me."

Walt took in a breath and slowly exhaled his hurt. "I can make the roads and I can move the wood. I can become a lawyer when the Army won't have me and I can protect this small land for future generations but I cannot protect my son."

"Protect your son?"

"All these things I can do. One thing I cannot do. Of these things, I would trade."

"What does your son, I mean, grandson, need to be protected from, Walt?"

Walt swooped with a native bird. "Second son then," he said. "Of a little girl with the face of the morning sun. Nita, born to me of the best day."

"Okay . . ."

"It is something I cannot prove. And I know how to prove things."

"What about his father?"

Walt didn't speak.

Gavin strengthened in his stance. "Where's his father when he needs him, Walt?"

Walt bit his lip. Then he said, "His father is the metal welder of Tison Yard."

"Why do you need to protect him and his father won't?"

"His father is not like him," Walt answered, letting go his grip. "His father is not like him, and I am not him."

"Okay, so if his father is not like him, so what? My dad's not like me. My dad doesn't run like me and he never once mentioned football or liking anything I like other than maybe BB guns. My dad's a cowboy. He likes horses and things cowboys like. He likes things that I don't."

Walt backed up a few bare feet and looked down range at his truck. He came back to Gavin. "Have you driven yet?" he asked.

Gavin eyed the truck.

"I know the answer, but say if you want to say."

"Why?"

"The final football challenge, I think you should drive."

"Where is it?"

"Not far from the place that would not have my application to the Army."

"Sierra Vista?"

Walt nodded. "I do not think it is right for you to run there. It does not feel right to me."

"Why?"

"It is just what I think."

Gavin handed his hips. "I'm not - *not running*, Walt."

"We could go get your license. There's time."

"Maybe I got my license already, did you ever think about that? Maybe I can do things that you don't even know about."

"And maybe you're a year younger than you say you are."

Gavin swallowed his spit. Walt returned the hand to Gavin's white shirt split at the neck seam.

"I know you can do many things without me, Runner. Many things."

"Yeah, but I'm not going to drive now. That time has passed. If those assholes don't kick me the ball, I know they could never run as far as I can. I know that."

"I know."

Gavin felt the drive inside that made his legs turn.

"What stands out is you."

"What?"

"In the hallway of the nice man's school. All that shiny stuff. Only you stand out."

Gavin was about to say something but he withdrew.

"You're what's different, Runner."

Gavin felt like he wanted to say something, anything, but the thought of him finding himself in the hallway of the school was too big for his young mind to fully comprehend. Walt seemed to enjoy watching his words soak in.

"Drive me then," Walt said.

"Where?" Gavin asked, half-cocked.

"Up this sorry excuse for a road, to Benson."

"Why? What are we going to do in Benson?"

"Nothing."

Gavin held his sharp tongue.

Walt looked around. "I want to put tracks on the road," he said.

"Why do you want to do that?"

"Think about this, Runner: who was it who took your legs when you wanted to run away from your dream?"

III MONSOONS UP TO THE FALL

25 SOTG

Whatever his real name might be, he is, and will always be, The
Ghost *to me. The name came to me in a dream and I like it.*

*I can see him clear as day, well maybe not this day, but clear
in my mind anyway. Him in his whites standing before me. One foot
tall, right here on my dashboard. The Ghost transposed through my
windshield in scenes that play out like a movie. His long, numberless
jersey, hanging down to his knees as he hopes for the ball. And him
on his knees right before his bell got rung. The Ghost looking right at
me. Maybe even through me somehow. His pain from that cheap-shot
to the back of his head like the rain handled by my wipers. Was he
smiling right before that hit? Smiling in the way people smile when
they know they are truly free? Like they know something the rest of
us don't? Some sort of internal secret, maybe? I got that feeling the
moment I saw that big nasty for Sulger go after The Ghost like he
hadn't been fed in a week.*

*In a way, I'm glad I don't know his real name. All I've got to do
is write the story the way I see it and let it play out in the minds of
my readers. Am I lost thinking they can imagine him in the same way
that I do? It's The Ghost on the field by his lonesome where I'm going
to start. His aloneness gets me. The imagery and solitude of a game
that's supposed to be a team sport, not one player versus eight. The
other players lining up against him are nowhere near as strong as
him. No wonder they won't kick him the ball.*

He looks weak, sure, but I'm talking mentally. The kind of strength coaches always go on about. The kind of strength most teams can't find in the fourth quarter. Hell, he's got the kind of strength most men can't find in any quarter of their lives. Will anyone else see what I see? I know for a fact that he can't see what I do. I also know that I'm supposed to see the stop-signs and not press down on the gas. Too late, there I go again, blowing right through that annoying red octagon at fourth and Marker.

Haven't you done that about a thousand times before, Dean? You realize you can't afford to get another ticket, and you sure as hell don't want to be reminded about your salary before you start writing today. That's not a positive thought like those affirmation tapes say you're supposed to tell yourself. Don't start today off depressed, you hear me? If you can't afford much, you can't afford that. Just remember the story you got in mind is a good one. The story you are going to write is going to win you a Pulitzer. Well maybe not a Pulitzer. But the story is going to bring you attention and a foot in the door at one of the big papers in the syndicate. The story is going to change things around here for the better.

Think now, real hard, before you spend your entire day hammering out this piece on the trusty Selectric. Is it the story you see happening in your head or the words he said? Like the way The Ghost wanted to talk about your photography like he was interested in you and not himself. That's how people once talked to you, hombre, and you were more than happy to share your goals with them. What happened to that guy? What made you think you weren't good enough? You won a big prize, remember? Aside from the accolades, you even got the best Canon camera on the market sent to you because of how good you were. The same kind of camera they used at the professional level. And what did you do with it when you were in college and needed money? Do you remember or did you put a block on that memory like all the other negative junk in your life? You needed money and you pawned it. I'm telling you it's okay, but the reality is is that you pawned it. It was your choice, Dean. Your choice. You're forty now and you've got to accept that the same way you've got to accept other things.

This is no longer about your parents. They couldn't help never saying they loved you. Have you ever stopped to consider that maybe they *were never loved in the way a parent should love a child? It's called narcissism, hombre, and it's not your fault. Get over it. You need to forgive and forget. And you need to move on. So what if they made you take a bus to accept your photo award and when you brought it home you placed it on the table and your mother threw it in the garbage. There are others out there who had it worse. This isn't 1958 anymore. This is 1981 and there are therapists for your problems. This is the present day, hombre, and you're a reporter and you've got a job to do and your parents are dead. There is no turning back. Either you earn more money and pay for therapy and a box of eye wipes or you drop two tears in a bucket and say fuck-it and keep with the tapes. You have a choice. If you can't get an answer from the man above, that's okay, thank him anyway for your story and meditate all day on your freewill if that's what it takes to be grateful. You got a gift, Toombey, you hear me? A gift.*

Just breathe and don't worry so much about your speed. At this early in the morning no one's rushing around like you. No one's got deadlines like you and coffee in the car and cigarettes under lock and key in a metal box in the front luggage compartment where the engine is supposed to be. Germans, they like to do things a bit different, don't they?

Remember, it's the little things that make for getting up in the morning, just like the tape says. So what are they?

Glazed donuts. Check.
Springsteen. Check.
Black coffee. Double check.
Wendy. Check.
Wendy in her winter sweater. Triple check.
The sunsets you'll never admit to loving. Check.
Writing. Check.
Writing true crime and one day getting it out of the drawer and sending it off to one of the bigs and having them wine and dine you because of how good you are. Big - fat - check.

One more light and then the Eagle. Stop lights have a way of making me hit the brakes. My home away from home, the Eagle. In a way, I'm grateful for the job I have. Give me a donut and a decent cup of Joe from the percolator and I'm good to go. All I ask is that the girls in the office keep their gossip to a minimum and let me focus. It's enough that I have to spell check myself with ink on my hands and ink on my face when no one will tell me. I was naive once to think that they were talking sweet talk about me. It was the ink and the lines on my face, and it was a running joke. But it's all okay now. I've got real lines on my face and those lines mean I don't have to take shit from anyone.

The Ghost is brave and smart, but he's completely oblivious to what he's doing. Guarded *might be the best word to describe him to readers. That, though, I should keep for myself. Who doesn't tell you who they are? Parents tell you who they think their little heroes are – they've got no issues with that. Parents are quick to point out all the adjectives when you're thinking about something else entirely like getting laid or playing whiffle ball. Crazy. How did he come up with the idea to play football by himself? How did he figure out he could do that? And who has the balls to do what he does? Is he part Indian? I know he's not. But why is he at an Indian school over in No man's land in the first place? And how in the hell can he run so far to play in contests that are merely scrimmages? How can his legs take all that pounding on the pavement before he even plays? Mother Mary, what is his reward?*

I know I love my bug. That's something, I suppose. She's a trusty German girl. She takes care of me and I always park her in this same spot here in the back corner of the lot to keep her from getting door-dinged.

I'm probably half-drunk right now. Is there a fog outside my window or is it trapped in here with me? I like the trust of familiar things. I know if someone wanted to find me, they wouldn't have to look too hard. Every day it seems, I'm in the same place at 6:25 in the morning. Well, it's 6:20, so that makes perfect sense.

There's my office on the second floor and the man that cleans and stocks the place. Almost a decade here and I still don't know his name.

Go figure. To know his name is to shake his hand, writer recluse. I'm craving a cigarette already. Mother Mary, help me develop a taste for this decaf coffee.

Today is going to be the big day, Monday, September 7th. I can feel it. If the monsoons break I'm officially fifty bucks richer and the hair of the dog that bit me last night is going to get pulled. The sky this early is a decent indicator with the way the pale yellow and gray clouds are pressing down on the streets like it's London, England here or something. You don't have to be a weatherman to know what those colors bring. Today is the day things officially change, weather related and otherwise.

Then there's the humidity. Probably approaching forty percent already. The man is waving now. Well there it is, my signal to exit a space within my control.

The air is thick and my glasses are fogged up for the umpteenth time. What's the use of the end of your shirt if it isn't being used to clean your eyewear? Should be a trivia question, I swear. If I look at things from behind my glasses does it fog up my thoughts? Is it the reason I'm dreaming about this story? Do others see things differently than I do and is that the reason why The Ghost and I are alone in all of this? I know I'm not really alone, but what about him? What does he have other than the hope that someone will let him snap the football and run back and get it?

It's time to make the walk and let go of the endless search for things, Dean. Time to plant your ass in your seat and write. Even stories about bake sales reek of fiction. It's just the business you're in. If it bleeds it leads and this one bleeds even when there's a Band-Aid. Write what you want to write, hombre. Be like The Ghost and allow yourself the freedom to follow your own thing without anyone telling you different.

The steps to the Eagle are closer than they need to be. I should just stop here and feel the mist since I haven't exactly had time for a shower lately. My writing window is foggy too. A metaphor for things, maybe. I only get a few seconds of this view, usually, if I'm lucky, from the outside looking in. Then I'm on lockdown. I got two full days, though, and I got the front page and I got the sketch artist from the police coming over. A drawing is more dramatic because you can have it come out just like you see it. It's a good idea, hombre. Remember, though, to pick his brain on the Dryden case, particularly on how they can sketch a composite of a killer when there are absolutely no eyewitnesses and only half a shoeprint in a flowerbed. How can they make sketches from almost nothing?

Today is my day because I'm focused and still a little buzzed and I feel like I could take a few hits to the head like my subject and just keep going. This is why the monsoons are bound to break open today. I called it and stuck to the date and all things have been unfolding ever since.

Through the fog of the second story window is my writer's hole. It's where I can be found outside of my bug. Stuck between books about philosophy and untimely deaths and ego-graphies of people who matter and other people who don't really add up to shit. Fucking no-names who've achieved frame by robbing the good. There's more true crime in there than I have the time for.

Up there, though, is where I'm going to plant myself like a weed and write the best story I can write. If I write a winner she might not leave. If I write something worth reading my life might change in the way that I want it to change. Mother Mary, please let it change me. One thing I know is that for the first time in my career I have a story and I need to write it so others can see what I see. I need to write it so others can dream the way I've been dreaming. Up there, on the second floor that might as well be my apartment, with the beautiful view I have of the coin laundry, I'm going to write the best story I can write. It will be a story better suited for the movie screen. A screen that's not my windshield. Something others can watch and appreciate. Up there I'm going to write the Story of The Ghost and I'm only going to take a break when the monsoons begin to flood the desert. And when I'm done with my Pulitzer I'm going to count my winnings and bury my head in Bud over at Mickey's. End of story.

26 GHOST TOWN

THERE WAS A FUNERAL PROCESSION of rigs on the south 80, ten miles outside St. David.

Gavin lagged a couple of yards from the convoy shoulder and added their numbers as they rushed by. When the last of them faded into the mid-morning dust, he looped an arm through his duffle strap and made another step toward his far-off dream.

Before he could make it up to speed, a horn screamed at the tender bone in the back of his head. He let the bag strap caress down his arm as he turned to the noise. Detaching from the duffle he took a few steps north in the stir of two boys sat in the cab of a beat-up van. One of the boys pointed at him with a rolled up newspaper.

As Gavin approached the van, a blonde crew cut in a black shirt minus the sleeves exited the passenger side. "You're him, bro," crew cut said. "You're *The Ghost*. That's you, dude!"

Gavin shifted his eyes to the driver. The driver was less of a crew cut and more of a dark buzz down to the quarter inch. The driver seemed bothered, only acknowledging his crew cut companion with an eyebrow and a defiant shrug. Crew cut smacked the print at his corduroy hip.

"You're on the front of the paper, dude!"

Gavin shut his ears, eyeing a tooth astray from the one flapping his gums. He looped his duffle back over his shoulder and scuffed off south while pretending to be interested in the bag's zipper.

The van revved and rolled. Crew cut hustled his stocky profile to catch up with Gavin. "Wait up," crew cut said, already out of breath. "I just wanna get your autograph, dude, that's all."

"What for?" Gavin asked, veering.

"What for . . ? For being famous, dude."

"I'm not famous."

"You're in the paper, dude. They got a story about you that takes up the whole front page, and the other pages, like a book or something."

Gavin kept to a breathless pace. He listened for more big rig sounds. The van pulled over to the shoulder and the driver shut the engine off. The driver then took a swig of something and patted at the horn.

"At least let us give you a ride down to Post," crew cut said. "It'd be a really cool thing, to let us do that."

"I'm good."

"You've never gotten a ride before, right, to the other games?"

"They're scrimmages."

"You don't want to come with us?"

Gavin wondered about the nickname. He knew where it had originated. He decided it wasn't for him.

Crew cut begged with his hands. "You can save your legs for the thing you just said if you come with us."

"I'm good, really," Gavin said, out of the side of his mouth.

The driver honked the horn in full and held it down until crew cut paid him some mind. Crew cut grabbed at Gavin's duffle bag. "Wait up, dude, c'mon, please."

Gavin tugged back his belongings. He picked up the pace. "Thanks for the offer," he said, drifting away.

Crew cut did a few double-takes before entering the van mid-side, via the slide door. The van lurched out to the pavement, emitting a cranking noise as it came back to life. After about ten seconds, the van rallied enough horses to get alongside the boy blessed of duct tape.

"This here's Phin," crew cut said, with one tanned arm outside the passenger window and his left thumb pointed at the driver. They call me Clay. My name's Clay."

"Hey."

"I guess you gotta run. It's what the story says. You run everywhere, that's so crazy, dude."

"I don't run everywhere."

"It says you do."

"Okay."

"You know there's gonna be a lot of people there."

"Where?"

"At the game."

"It's a scrimmage."

"They even said it might be as crowded as the big schools get up in Tucson. What do you think about that?"

Gavin spoke only to his legs as they did crank. The van rallied another horse.

"You got any people, on your sideline?"

Gavin thought for a few strides. "I don't notice the people," he said.

"Are you cool if we watch on your sideline, are you cool with that?"

"You can do whatever you want," Gavin answered. "It's your life, not mine."

The van whined. And crew cut did the same.

"Just stop for one second, dude. One second and let me come talk to you. It's important. Please."

Gavin heard the request and stretched his legs. He felt the denim of his right leg, soothing down the shin. Sweat came over his head and neck in a microburst as the bag hit the pavement.

"What's so important?" he said, angling.

Crew cut jumped out of the van and rushed over to Gavin, crouching to get close to his shaggy ear. "You know Phin, right, he's cool."

"I don't know him, sorry. And I don't know you."

"What I mean is, he thinks you're cool. He thinks you're cool and, this is stupid to say . . . but he says you're his hero, dude. You know, for what you're doing."

"What am I doing?"

"Playing football, like you do, with no team."

"Like I said, it's not like that."

"Phin won't say it but . . . you're his hero, dude. You know he can't play, right? He's got something wrong with his back."

Gavin stood up. "What's wrong with his back?" he asked.

"See how he's hunched over the steering wheel like that, that's 'cause it won't go straight. It's crooked. He can't play football. The doctors won't let him."

"Where are you from?" Gavin asked.

Crew cut fronted Gavin.

"Hodo, dude."

"Where's Hodo at?"

"About thirty miles east of Benson."

Gavin moved in the direction of his former home. Crew cut went with him in stride.

"We've been driving around all morning looking for you. And now here you are. You're right here. So cool."

Gavin looked over at the buzzed driver. He then felt the ridge of his lower back, fanning his arms. The van chugged south a few lengths and glided over to the shoulder. The brakes squealed and one of the lights flickered.

"So you guys want to give me a ride and be on my sideline, during the scrimmage?"

"If you'll let us, yeah, that would be the coolest thing."

Gavin pictured his one-man trailer. "Alright," he said.

Crew cut hopped around in his hand-me-down brown shoes. "Hey, what's your real name, dude?"

Gavin secured his bag. "What did the paper put?" he said.

"It just says that you're *The Ghost* 'cause of how your white jersey is so long and torn up and stuff and you don't have a number. That you appeared out of nowhere to do what others don't. The paper did a badass drawing of you, dude. Real badass."

Crew cut retrieved the story from the passenger seat and attempted to hand it to Gavin, who refused it.

Gavin clasped a hand around the silver of the slide door. Before he could turn the handle and sway the door, he let go of his grip because of the burn.

THIRTY MINUTES LATER, Gavin climbed out of the van to survey the history of a place he'd never seen before.

He thought he was in the middle of something, like a town street or maybe one of the old west prison camps he'd heard whispers about as a child. In his way were the remains of brick buildings and pile after pile of splintered wood. Near the edge of the area was a platform with a cross that served as one of the two face posts. The cross was over ten feet tall with a sign that warned visitors in a dark stain: TALL SINNERS LEAVE HERE short OF EXPECTATIONS.

The one called Phin glided free of any visible pains around the van. He leaned his slender against the passenger door and folded his arms. With his knuckles he kneaded his biceps. "It's a ghost town," he said. "Like you, *The Ghost*."

"What is this place, for real?" Gavin asked.

"*Tilmon*. Home of the injuns. Used to be anyway, until it got torched. Poor little injuns, thought they could take our land from us. Guess they found out the hard way."

Gavin turned around. "Apaches," he said with a serious face.

Phin pointed dead ahead and Gavin's eyes followed.

"Check it out . . . it's the injuns with their rocks and sticks coming to get us."

Crew cut exited the van out the slide and stood beside Gavin. For a moment, Gavin only absorbed the devils of dirt. Then he saw through it all to a dune buggy with red flags flagging down from where the platform was, the flags jittering in every which way. After motoring by the cross, the buggy geared in the direction of the van and then skidded a few yards away from Gavin's wonderment. It idled there, as loud as three motorcycles, before it fell silent in the blinding dust.

Gavin could make out two people seated inside the metal roll cage but he couldn't get a good feeling for their faces because of all the bars and floating debris. "It's cool," crew cut said, somehow ignoring the dust. "They're cool, right?" Before he could speak, Gavin felt a burn slit his neck. When he swung around to face the van, and the clearer air, he found a rope situated from his neck over to Phin's wayward grin. The rope tensioned and the sun peered. Gavin managed to wedge his hands between the rope and his skin, but his fingers got caught up as he tripped with a callous pull. He went to his knees rather smoothly and worked to free himself.

Crew cut put a hand on Gavin's back, tending to him like he was a physician measuring the breathing of a patient. "You weren't supposed to do that," he whispered.

Gavin coughed and repositioned.

"Get up," Phin instructed.

Gavin got to his feet, keeping his chin to his chest. He let go the rope and spat in his hands. Rubbing his palms together he righted his head and slicked back his hair.

When he saw that Gavin wasn't exactly worried, Phin tugged on the rope and jabbed him in the gut in what looked to be one complete motion. Gavin handled the gut-check a lot better than he should have.

"We're just scaring him, right?" crew cut said.

"Shut-it, autograph boy."

"Just don't go crazy on him, dude!"

Phin reeled in the rope and signaled for the two from the buggy to assist in his plan. The two newcomers lifted Gavin up and helped him over to the van. The two were older. One wore a western shirt with a lasso design and the other sported a mustache.

Phin opened the slide door. "Sit his ass down," he said. "Helmet on, like that *badass* drawing."

Crew cut unzipped the duffle, grabbed the helmet and lowered it onto Gavin's head. "Just be cool," he whispered, adjusting the chin strap.

Mustache pushed crew cut out of the way so as to stoop in front of Gavin. He tapped a finger on the dome of the helmet. "Aren't you going to say something to me, little man?"

Gavin closed his eyes.

"Anybody in there? Hello . . ? Say something, *hippie*."

Gavin clenched his fists.

"Tough guy, huh?"

"Since when are hippies so tough?" lasso added from a few yards away.

Gavin thought about the finger Walt had been given out on the highway and the thought pushed away his fear. He opened his eyes and released his middle fingers. Mustache reacted to the gesture with a palm-thrust to the facemask, an action equivalent to a stiff-arm in football.

"Don't eyeball me hippie!"

Gavin rolled his eyes and rocked his head.

"Just hold his ass there," Phin said in a controlled manner as he tied his end of the rope around the passenger mirror of the van. After satisfying a knot, he mastered a butterfly blade from the back pocket of his jeans and approached Gavin. He held the blade to the bars and scraped off some of the gray molded rubber, boring it to the metal.

A spark of sunlight hit Gavin's face, causing him to squint.

Phin tapped his blade. "All you gotta do is follow me, fag. Don't lag on me now."

"You hate injuns," mustache said. "Say you hate injuns."

Gavin kept his poise. "I don't hate anyone," he said.

Phin picked more with his blade. Mustache looked around at the group for approval of his last words. And for his words to come.

"You hate injuns, hippie, you just don't know it yet."

Gavin smirked.

"What's so funny?" Phin said.

"Was that in the paper?" Gavin said.

"What, you being a fag?"

"*Hippie.*"

Phin lowered the blade. He slid into the driver's seat and gatored the blade back to the handle case. Gavin dropped to his knees by his own accord.

"Get up," mustache demanded.

Gavin didn't flinch.

"Get the fuck up."

The key turned and the engine refused to spark.

"Get the fuck up, hippie, before I kick your hippie-ass myself all over this home of yours."

"No," Gavin said.

"You better start praying," mustache said.

"I already did that," Gavin quipped. It was true. He had been saying prayers here and there since the last of spring.

"Don't get smart with me. People that get smart with me end up not being so smart no more after they try being smart."

"That doesn't make any sense," Gavin said.

Mustache huffed over Gavin's helmet and then slapped him. He regretted the slap, though, as soon as the hard plastic shell and plate screws around the earhole beat back his hand. He made a face at crew cut, shaking out his anger.

Phin glanced over his shoulder after a successful engine turn. "What are you pussies doing back there?" he said.

"I got this," mustache answered, kneeling in front of Gavin.

Gavin sucked in the moist air.

"Now, hippie motherfucker . . . I'm gonna count to five and you better get up because we're gonna go for a little walk. Just a little walk around this ghost town, you and me. You're gonna learn about our land and forget you love injuns. And then you're gonna run back to your teepee by the river and forget about your game at Post. You got me, hero?"

Gavin let the air out of his being. He was officially done with explaining the difference between a game and a scrimmage.

"You understand?"

Gavin nodded from behind his bars.

"Good. One."

The bars didn't move.

"Two . . ."

"Wait . . ." Gavin said.

"What?"

"Where are you from?"

"What's it to you?"

"Hodo?"

Mustache looked around. He came back to Gavin. "Yeah."

"What's the school called there?"

"There's no school in Hodo. You gotta go to Contention, if you go to school."

"Okay."

"Umm . . ."

"You were on three, *James*."

"How the fuck you know my name? You don't know me."

"Clay," Gavin said like crew cut was an old friend of his. "Clay said your name a few minutes ago when you were knocking on my door."

Crew cut shrugged. Mustache scowled at every eye he could find. "Yeah. Okay. *Three*."

"How high are you going to again, *James*?"

"Five."

"Okay, sorry, go ahead."

"Three."

"You already said that."

"Four. Hippie-ass-smart-ass-injun-lovin'-mother . . ." It seemed mustache considered another slap to the side of Gavin's helmet with the way he raised his hand in the air. But by the look on his face it was as if the hand interceded. He smoothed his stache instead.

"It's nice of them," Gavin said.

"Who?" mustache said, tightening a fist at his side.

"Contention."

"What's nice of them?"

"Just all they do for you."

"What all do they do?"

Gavin thought about Walt. And he thought about choices in life. He replayed the choice to use his helmet like a missile on Clawson's kicker when the ball traveled thirty yards behind his back just as he'd predicted. "You know," he said, unbuckling his chin strap and tipping back his facemask. "Giving hillbillies the opportunity to go to school and stuff like that. That's just really nice of them."

27 40

A RAUCOUS CROWD was waiting for him when he arrived at the field gates of Post High School in the eastern section of Sierra Vista.

As he made his way through the mesh and over to the dirt track that outlined the football field, somebody yelled out the name they called him by in the Sierra Vista Eagle. Gavin continued on for the grass with his right eye swollen about as much as the cloud formation overhead. In his heart he clutched a demand. Never again would he go somewhere with people he wasn't sure of. Never again would he find himself alone. One against eight or any other number. His hands were open and his fingers twitching. Bound to his wrists were several strips of silver as if necessary to secure the hands to body.

Bitterness hurled in the wind. Words about him and his kind and the kind of company he keeps in a place he has no business being in. With all the spite came a tallboy beer. The beer whizzed past and he watched as it tagged a sprinkler head, bursting open and spraying foam like the sprinkler was active and filled with soap. *That's the real story of my life,* Gavin thought, dodging the spray. *Right there, the ball spinning around in front of me. Something I can't touch. Write a story about that because that's what's real. That's what I can see with my own eyes.*

Gavin leapt over the can and took off for the middle of the field. In a couple of ticks he was there. There in the middle, and with the host team nowhere in sight, he took a seat and folded his arms over his lap Indian style. He sat in relative quiet and observed the crowd as they consumed beer and soft drinks, dividing rather graciously to their concrete seats.

A few minutes later, an official walked up the steps from under the stadium. As soon as the official touched the track, he hustled over to meet with Gavin.

"The scrimmage today is canceled," the official said. "Based on a no-show."

"I'm showing right now."

"After an hour, in a regular game, it's recorded as a forfeit."

"I didn't forfeit."

"I know you didn't, but the clock over there says different. The other team is, I mean the other players, they're in the locker room right now undressing."

"So."

"So that's it."

"That's it?"

The official glanced back at the stadium, tipping his cap at the foundation. "Well, frankly," he said as he came back to Gavin, "it's up to the home team on what they want to do from here. They get to make the final call about all this."

Gavin turned to his barren sideline.

"Ghost . . ."

The name meant nothing to him. And so he didn't turn.

"Why do you have your helmet strapped on?"

The question was an obvious one given the condition of his eye. But the bars covered his bruising well enough. He decided to answer.

"Because I feel like it."

"Where's your other equipment?"

"It got lost."

"You just got the helmet?"

"Maybe."

"You got a mouthpiece?"

"Why?"

"Because I have to check."

Gavin leaned back on his hands. "They don't work for me," he said.

"They don't work for you?"

"They bother me. Besides I haven't had to wear one before."

The official took a knee. "How would you know if they bother you if you haven't worn one before?" he asked, fatherly.

Gavin clawed the grass and looked up at the dark clouds. He considered the threat of monsoons. Had they already happened or was this the final brewing?

"Let's forget about the mouthpiece for a minute," the official said. "You can't play if you don't have any equipment for your other body parts, period. I don't care how tough they say you are."

Gavin's attitude stirred as heavy as the air. "They have plenty of equipment," he said, pointing with his facemask. "Make them give me some."

The official adjusted his cap. "I'm afraid I don't get to make that call," he said.

"They can give me some for the scrimmage and then they can take it back. I don't want to keep it. This is my last one. After this, I'm done."

The official hung his head. Then he looked at Gavin. "I take it you've never crossed paths with Stad Parker before."

"I don't know who that is," Gavin said.

"Stad is the man who runs this program. And I can flat tell you he's not the type of man who lends anybody anything. I think the only reason a man like Stad has friends, is, if you ask me, because they're all afraid of what he might do to them."

Gavin got to his feet, stretching his legs out in the process. "So if I called him an asshole to his face, that wouldn't be a very good idea?"

The official rose, tapping Gavin on the helmet. Two hours earlier, the finger had been a blade.

"Unless you like wearing that thing as a permanent fixture then I'd say no. In no way shape or form does that make for a good idea."

"So what do you want me to do then?"

"How did you get here?"

Gavin thought about the real story. How his helmet had been used for a soccer ball. That it was the only piece of equipment left behind. "I hitched," he finally said.

The official did a double-take at the crowd.

"Normally I'd tell you to hitch yourself back home, but I don't think that's gonna go over too well with the yokels. How far is it to No man's land from here exactly?"

"What did you call it?"

"No man's land."

"How do you know that?"

"What, where you live?"

"Where did you get that name from?"

"From your story in the paper. The story says that's where you live. That's what they call it."

"I live in St. David."

"Okay."

"St. David is where I live."

"I'm not saying you don't."

Gavin unwrapped a sliver of tape on his left wrist. "It's forty miles," he uttered.

"Here's what we're gonna do: my car is parked in the teachers lot and I'm gonna give you a ride. If we can make it down the steps to the locker room without too much of a hassle, our change room is the first door. From there we can get you one of our shirts and then, hopefully, head on outta here with no trouble."

Gavin wrapped the sliver around his index finger. "Thanks," he said.

"Just walk with me then. It also might not be a bad idea if you pretended to walk with a limp. One thing I know about rowdy crowds is that if they see you're hurt, they'll likely not be motivated to inflict more damage."

Gavin backed a yard away from the official. "Thanks," he said, "but I'm not ready to go anywhere today."

"You're gonna want to leave this field, trust me. These people here think you're supporting Indians by what you're doing. Like you're making some political statement about the way they've been treated over the years by going to that school, sat where it is. I'm not sure that story of yours helped your cause to play football. It just stirred up some bad blood around these parts if you ask me."

Gavin was confused by the official's remarks. The story in the paper, whatever it had to say, was never his desire. How could he explain that the Corte School wasn't his choice? Or the trailer he had said was a house with a chimney? Or his father leaving. Or his mother giving her life to Jesus after a life of non-believing and then losing it in a heartbeat to a stroke. All of these circumstances had been out of his control. He'd tried his best to follow his dream of running with the football. His wild dream of being discovered by the team with the Saint in their name because of where he thought he lived. A dream that helped him cope when everything in his world fell apart.

He felt like crying. But he also felt like punching something or someone. He clenched his fists and turned to the crowd. "I came here for a scrimmage and that's exactly what I plan to do," he said without a shred of doubt in his words.

The official cradled his cap. "They are not going to give you any equipment," he said. "That I can just about promise you."

"What about the kickoff?"

The official put his hands on his hips. "What about the kickoff?"

"The home team has to kickoff first, right?"

"That's part of the deal, sure."

"So the whistle."

"What about the whistle?"

"You don't blow the whistle until everybody gets set in their place, right?"

The official dug a finger in his ear. "Where is it you're going with all of this?"

"Don't blow the whistle until I put my hand down. And when I do, call the scrimmage without running the first play."

The official widened his stance.

"Let me get this straight. You want me to get everybody set on the field, in their uniforms, while you, you're not in uniform, and . . . and then you want to have me wait for you to give me the signal that you're ready, and then after all that, have me draw out a long whistle and end the whole thing before it even begins?"

"It's what you have to do."

"What in the world makes you think that?"

"It's part of the rules. If there is no first play, the equipment shouldn't matter. I realized that on my way over here. I also realized I'm not really playing football with what I'm doing, so I don't want to try and play anymore. I don't want to fool myself anymore. I'm done fooling myself."

The official threw his cap on the ground like it was a penalty flag. He stroked his hair repeatedly for a minute. "Well . . . " he finally said, "factually speaking, like the one-man snap routine, it works. But in all honesty, I don't see it playing out that way."

Gavin returned to the ground, locking his arms over his knees. "If their coach doesn't want me to camp out on this spot overnight and dance around like an Indian praying for a monsoon to break, he has that option."

"Can I just ask you *why* then," the official said as he retrieved his cap. "Why would you want to challenge a man who's a full-grown bully, here, on his own field, with this kind of crowd? And why would you want to go through all that headache to not even have the ball kicked? Why are you even here if you didn't bring any equipment with you? Help me understand because I'm having trouble making sense of things here."

Gavin unbuckled his chin strap and removed his helmet, putting his black eye on display for the official. His cares ran to the goal post nearest the gates. To a kid perched atop the crossbar. "I'm doing it," he said, "because there's something important I came here to say. That's *why*."

THE COACH STOOD at midfield with his back to the west end zone and his muscular arms folded, about five yards from Gavin's viewpoint and that of the three officials. Equal parts burly and ripped, he broadened his stature as he fingered his teeth around the lower left gum.

He removed a can of tobacco from a well-worn back pocket and pinched a mound between his cheek and gum. Gavin watched the chew get packed into the back of the mouth by way of the tongue. "This must be a real treat for you," the coach said out of the free side of his mouth. "All these people . . . all this fuss about playing with yourself."

Gavin stared straight, well beyond the coach in a black shirt two sizes too small. The coach swiped his hands, eyeballing the head official in amusement.

"You tell me your real name *Cocheese* . . . and I'll give you the equipment you need to play with yourself."

Gavin turned his attention to the crowd. Only small spaces between persons were available.

"What he's asking for here, coach," the head official offered, "is just the lineup. All we do is lineup for the kickoff and then call it on a technicality. Real simple."

The coach eyeballed Gavin with disgust. "It seems a lot to go through just for a game of Smear the Queer, don't it fellas?"

Gavin's thoughts ran to the man on his bedroom wall. He planned to take the poster down as soon as he could. Without regret, he willed it to the trash.

"You said he's got something to say, Harley, and I don't much hear him making a peep over there. What is you want to say, Pocahontas?"

Gavin remained steadfast in his silence.

"See, fellas, this is why he's in the paper. They do the speaking for him. Primadonnas, am I right?"

The head official approached the coach with his hands out like a shield. "Just let him have his thing and we're done, okay?"

"Ahwww fuck-it, Harley," the coach moaned as he took a step toward Gavin and spat out a blackened tar. "I'll give him the damn equipment he needs just so I can watch him get his ass kicked. So what size shoulder pads do you wear, Pocahontas, a size two?"

"I refuse any equipment that isn't my own," Gavin said.

"Holy shit, he speaks! See, fellas, all you got to do is say the wrong thing to a glory hound and watch how he can't take it. Watch him give you the attention he's so desperate for."

"I will no longer speak," Gavin said.

The coach scowled. Then he pointed with his right hand as if it were a sharp tool about to slice into something.

"Tell this glory hound here, Harley, you tell him I got a freshman kicker who's tougher than he is."

The head official nosed in on Gavin's facemask. "What is it you want to say?" he said.

Gavin kept quiet in the promise he'd made.

"Listen to me now, Ghost. We don't have to get everybody lined up in order for you to say something. So what's on your mind that wasn't said in the paper already?"

"Ahwww just let the papers do the speaking for him," the coach interjected, tar falling out of his mouth.

"C'mon, Ghost, we're all here. What is it you want to say? You've got our ears, and the floor. The whole stadium even seems to be listening from over there."

Gavin made the grass his seat with the knees of his tortured jeans.

"I guess he's upset. Somebody call the paper. Glory boy is upset."

Gavin unwrapped the tape from his right wrist and then did the same for his left. He put the strips on his white T-shirt and stood back up, peeling a strip from his leg. He tore the leg-strip into a few pieces and then configured all the pieces on his shirt. When he was done he picked up his head and faced the crowd from behind the bars that sectioned them off from his point of view. He showed the number of his work: 40. And he held the number there for as long as it took the clouds to spill out their brew.

28 BACHELOR PAD

LIEUTENANT BUNCH knocked on the manicured arch door of the two story condo. The door opened and he walked in, courteous of an exotic throw rug in the way. He took inventory of the decor, ignoring the little annoyance with the cane.

"What's the square footage up in here?" he asked.

"You in my business of conquering real estate, cousin?"

"Just askin a question," Bunch said, keeping his head tilted to the vaulted ceiling.

"They nine hundred a piece, so what? This here's two levels, so you do the math."

"It looks to me like you're moving in."

"I got some things with me. It ain't like they plain walls."

Bunch leveled. "Don't let the Specials see you livin it up like this out here."

"How would they see me here?"

"You know what I mean."

"You call this livin things up, Randall?"

"I call it a bachelor pad forty years too late. That's what I call this friggin place."

The Warden tapped his cane. The polished support a matching piece to his slippers and robe.

"Well you ain't never been where I been. You ain't grow up in West Texas with all the oil. Swimming pools of oil is what they was, kay. This here's the maid's quarters, ya hear? I got me a maid then, so what?"

There was silence for a few seconds. Then music boomed out of the back room. Bunch turned his puffy eyes to the source of the beats and horns.

"I got some company. Three's a crowd."

"Then why did you buzz me? I still got checkouts and schedules to go through and I got write-ups galore and I'm fucking tired. And I don't much like making the hike from the other end of the facility over here for jack-shit. And I especially ain't appreciate it when I started my run before the damn sunrise and now it's gonna come back in a few hours. Fuck this place. Fuck the heat. It's friggin September already. It's friggin September 14th and ninety damn degrees out at midnight."

"Randall . . ."

"Don't make me make that fucking hike again if it ain't necessary."

"Randall."

"Why's it so fucking hot in here? You got the AC setup. Turn the fucker up if you're gonna have some company."

"Lieutenant."

"What?"

"Take a seat."

"Where?" Bunch said, moving his head and eyes all around the room. "You ain't got one single piece of furniture."

The door to the back room cracked open and a bundle of hair fluffed out. The hair immediately got shooed away. Then there was nothing but the two men together in the dim light of the shag rug room. One dressed like an old playboy. And the other, with a firearm strapped to his hip.

The Warden whistled.

"I did not know the guard was involved, yer honor, I just had no clue. That I swear to on my mother. Please be lenient on him sir, Randall Bunch is a good man. He ain't a wife beater like they says he is and he didn't let that priznah die due to lack of attention. The priznah, he hung hisself with that rope in his cell."

Bunch unfastened his utility belt and went to the floor, wounded. Resting his back against the wall he placed his arms over his knees.

"Now. . . " the Warden said, tapping the parquet, "can we continue?"

Bunch raised his head a fraction. "Visitor's day on Sunday is gonna be a bitch," he said. "We got somethin' like fifty on the list already. That's the most ever."

"It's gonna be a blaze."

"That's a given."

"I won't be here."

"Yeah, you will."

The Warden laughed, and with his cane he tapped at the side of his right leg. "I'll be here with ya in spirit, Randall."

"You got a golf game?"

"Yeah, you could say I gotta game goin on that day."

"Care to fill me in this time?"

The Warden took in some of the dead air.

"Let's just say one of the Specials and me is gonna play golf on Sunday. Instead of a club, the Special I got picked for the job is gonna have a gun. And well, he ain't gonna be anywhere near me and my country club with it. When he comes back on Tuesday, he gonna get the bullet he gave to that poor boy over at cownie, just like he deserve."

"You're sending that man out?"

"Now you're askin questions you know the answers to, Randall."

Bunch stiffened. "That's a mistake," he said.

"Why's that a mistake?"

Bunch chuckled, letting go his strain. He eyed the ring of sweat around the belly of his uniform. "He's dangerous," he said.

"We deal in dangerous, wouldn't you say?"

"Yeah, but he's different."

"I know."

"What I mean is that he's different from the four hundred plus we got controlled. A's and B's across the board. He believes the lies he tells. I mean, he really does."

The Warden laughed. "Maybe his philosophy is if ya believe it then is true."

"It ain't any damn philosophy."

The Warden licked his lips. "So what," he uttered, tilting his head.

Bunch eyed his boss. "His kind of thinking causes nothin' but trouble. I take that back. I don't know what his kind of thinking causes because I ain't never seen it before."

"Well, it ain't much a big deal. Money is the only thing. And a lot of money is gettin' your neck rubbed by the chorus line. Money will change any stupid thoughts he might have about goin back to that border town of his."

"Not in his world."

"How come you know this man so well?"

"Because I've read his stories and I've seen the look in his eyes when he talks about them. Somethin' about that look of his, I can't quite explain it."

"I've read his stories too, kay."

"I ain't talking about the write-ups we got contracts with the papers on, that ain't it. He's got stories about him fighting in wars that ain't never happened. His whole life is one big fantasy story."

The Warden thought about something. "He's full of it, ain't-e?"

Bunch reached for the stick on his belt. "This whole bullet routine sounds familiar," he said. "I'm curious, how *did* you get that poor sucker to put on one of our numbers and stand out there in the open like he was beggin' to get shot?"

The Warden did a pirouette of sorts with his cane planted to the floor and walked to the door at the back of the room. He cracked it, whispering a word or two before walking back over to Bunch. He held the handle of his cane to his chin, aiming the length at the lieutenant's legs. "Paint," he said with a childish look about him.

"Paint?"

"Yeah, a big ol' bucket."

"Okay, you got me stumped. Usually I can plot your next move and the move you got after that, but what the hell did paint have to do with that man wearing a prison issue shirt when he wasn't one of our prisoners to begin with? He worked for your land business. He was a hard working tax payer. And from what I even hear, he had himself a college degree."

The Warden lost his look.

"We was in a meeting, kay, and JD, the good cowboy that he was . . . he come on to me with his usual good deeds. How he wasn't too happy that the land he'd been gettin' for me was bein sold off more than once. Said he got plans and deeds and buyer conversations about my schemes. I ain't care for the word he used with me, kay: *schemes.* I told him that it ain't my fault they ain't got regulations in place. It ain't my job to police real estate. Well, JD, he got threatening with his words and I told him his threats wasn't needed no more. Somehow then, when he was makin his way down the hall, a big ol' bucket of paint came at his squeaky clean shirt. The only shirt we had for him to put on was the priznah kind. One with a number. It only make sense."

"Damn . . ." Bunch said. "And that man was smart."

"Yeah . . . he was."

"And he worked for you how many years?"

"A dozen."

"And you killed him."

"The tower guard shot him, yer honor."

Bunch grinned in a way that said he was more ashamed than amused. "Just like our movie star," he said.

"Exactly like our movie star."

"And the truck?"

"Truck, what truck?"

"The truck that poor sucker was driving before he got pinched. Your new Ford, the one you bought for moving hay."

"Oh, that."

"What was he doing with your truck? And why the hell did he get out of the thing and stand there halfway between here and the highway?"

The Warden raised an eyebrow. "I got lucky," he said.

"Lucky?"

"I had offered JD the truck to buy me some time, kay, so he could bring the evidence to the table, so we could make things right. And, well, Marcus, he had hisself a cold trigger finger when the number went around to the stables. I guess I just got lucky that JD went back to his good ways. How he stood there with his good conscience out in the open like he did. You know I could feel him staring at me real heavy, letting me know the truck wasn't gonna change things. Well, then, Marcus, he did his job."

"I know how it all ends for our movie star, but how's he supposed to take out Red?"

The Warden raised his cane, tapping the side of his head. "Ya know, Randall," he said, "in all my time in the Navy, not once did we drop anchor and play match game with the Japs. Is how we won the war, ya big dummy."

29 DIRTY WORK

BUNCH HANDED THE PRISONER an envelope containing several hundred dollar bills and a business card with the name Big TexAZ embossed in gold leaf.

The prisoner turned the card over and read the back - just the word "Ensign" in red ink. He tucked the card into his shirt pocket and thumbed the stack of bills, letting the envelope feather empty to his wide bare feet.

"The papers don't pay but a penny a line," he said, fanning the bills under his nose. "What am I supposed to do with all this?"

"Wait for the phone to ring," Bunch said. "I got the feeling you're gonna get a call real soon."

"A call from who, the lady with the honey in her voice? You tell her to call me. You tell her I got somethin' special I been savin up just for her."

Bunch let the door to the unit stay open as he slewed with his hands behind his back and something of a smile on the side of his face.

The prisoner waited for a minute in the doorway with the crickets and the lights from the other units clicking. He then took a few steps out to the walkway, banded the bills, and winked at one of the other Specials who happened to be spying on him from the unit across the strip of lawn. He sniffed at the bills under a palette of stars and then treaded back to unit number 1 with his gray eyes plastered to the gray concrete.

Closing the door behind him he paced over to the single bed in the corner. Lumpy and unfazed he sat on the middle edge, staring at the brass of his desk drawer. He leaned an inch toward the door and fanned the money out on a pillow like the green was a fresh set of playing cards. With his eyes and a gashed fingertip, he counted the bills. He collected a grand back with one hand and just sat there with the other tucked between his knees, staring at the telephone.

The phone didn't ring.

He sat and waited, his pale body crouched in the same position for over thirty minutes. The life in his eyes living between the phone, the television and the light on the coffee maker.

When the nine o'clock news came on the television, the phone rang. The prisoner turned the volume button down and stood there in the most occupied part of his place with one hand on top of the set and the other on the receiver of the rotary dial, looking out the window. After a long minute, the ringing stopped. He neatly stacked the bills on the desk and then scuffed back over to his bed, taking up the same seat as he had before.

He rocked back and forth with his gaze on the screenplay. News in his pestered view of a car torn in two. A delirious girl screaming in silence as the cameraman scrambled her shots. The news abruptly cut to a break. After a sprinkle of commercials about detergent and lotion and turning tired hair into a younger version of you, the news returned to the weather brief and the phone started in again on its irritating grate.

The prisoner ran a hand over the long hairs on his head, looking at the thicker hairs of his toes. He then turned to a man on the television twirling an umbrella. A look of resentment washed over his face. In his muted space he watched the man dance around the screen like a silly little puppet.

AT FORTY past nine in the evening, the prisoner woke to a tapping on his door. The sound was reminiscent of a bird with a beak bent on drilling a hole. He retired from his cozy curl, clicked the light switch and checked his face in the primered license plate that was his mirror.

He pinched the bridge of his nose and closed his eyes. Then he opened them and raised a miniature Jack Daniels to his mouth. He swallowed the packaged shot whole and scrounged around for another. He placed the empty bottle into an empty drawer of Pepto-Bismol and other samples of whiskey second his choice and managed his weathered skin over to the door. The tapping on the door continued as he opened it.

"Cap'n . . ." the prisoner yawned.

"Ya breathin' or what?"

"Sleepin' yessir."

"What time we got lights out, *for you*?"

"Ten," the prisoner answered, rubbing his gut. "But my stomach had been bothering me some and I done turned in early."

The Warden kept the gold of his cane level with the prisoner's grays. "Somethin' wrong with yer telephone? We ain't get it installed properly out here?"

"No sir. The phone works just fine."

"Then how come ya ain't answerin' my call? You knew it was me."

"I ain't hear it ring."

"Ya didn't hear it ring?"

"Like I said, I ain't hear it with that pilla over my head, the fluffy one I got as it is. I had got me one of them migraines after research and so I come back and put it over my head and turned out the light early so I could feel better. And then I got to feeling uneasy."

The Warden stepped more into the room. "Put some pants on," he said. "This here's a business meeting."

"Yessir."

The prisoner quickly located a pair of slacks and took a seat on the edge of his bed. The Warden's eyes wandered around the room, everywhere but on the prisoner. "I don't come out to the yard," the Warden said. "Let's get that straight right now."

"Not the yard. Yessir."

"And the business I partake in is either on the telephone or in my office. Like the Yankees, I always got the home field."

"The Yankees, yessir. You had said that before and I had written

224

it down somewheres. One of them things that gets me to thinkin'. Somethin' of the advice I can use for the future."

The Warden wavered about unamused. "Bunch got with ya," he said, "that's what I know. So I take it, it ain't enough? Is that right, Mr. Businessman?"

"What ain't enough, Cap'n?"

The Warden used the desk for a seat, outstretching his cane. He wiggled his right boot and comforted his rear, glancing at the motivation of green at his hip. "Yer good at sayin the right words," he said. "It ain't always a bad thing, but now yous just gettin' to my nerves." He exhaled upwards. As he squared he brought back his evening hat with the gold, rising to his five and a half feet. "The money . . ." he added. "You need more."

"More money for what?"

"Don't make me go back on my words, priznah. Yous livin in the lap of luxury out here. Don't make me take back my words."

The prisoner straightened. "I got some money come my way, yessir, but I done figured it was the papers or the movie people that bought out my story so they could go show it to the world. I figured the lieutenant done represented me to the right people after I let him read my mission story."

The Warden's face reddened to a shade brighter his natural tone. "Oh that's right," he said. "I forgot, yous famous."

"It's just what I thought."

"Excuse me, yous famous. I got things mixed up, and for that I apologize. My mistake. I understand now, I do. I should be waitin' to get a call from *you* from now on. When ya sign off on yer visits list we get yer autograph. Well I shouldda known better. You don't need to explain no further to me."

The prisoner didn't speak. The Warden half-spun and tapped on the television.

"Pretty soon yer gonna be coming through that screen, Jimmy Dean."

The prisoner dropped his head.

"Pretty soon they gonna make yer movie, *movie star.*"

The prisoner remained as the Warden putted with his cane. "The money," he said. "Is yer first paycheck."

"My paycheck?"

The Warden moved over to the dresser housed under the license plate mirror and rummaged through the items contained in the top drawer. A razor and some soap. Some unopened letters and letters waiting to be stamped. He went down a level. "Go on and keep it," he said, sniffing a bone dry bottle of Wild Turkey. "You can spend it within the confines of the facility. I don't care."

"I don't wanna keep it."

The Warden relinquished the bottle.

"Go on, keep it. What I hear from you loud and clear is ya don't want ten times that to go and spend at yer leisure at places that aim to yer pleasin'. We can keep the monies in house so you can keep on gettin' yer fix of coach whiskey and cheap cigarettes. And them hot Mexican dishes you bug the cooks about. But you ain't no businessman, that's what I know. Ya ain't a man who knows how to take advantage of the skills he's got. Is a shame, kay, a real shame."

The prisoner lifted his head with a pinch of confidence. "What kind of skills I got, Cap'n?" he said.

"Well it don't matter much," the Warden said, caning toward the door. "Yous like a bull rider with no bulls to ride. You outta place. This ain't yer time."

"If you don't mind me sayin so, Cap'n, this here plan of yours is working. I got my hands full keeping it all in line like you had instructed me. The men we got in the Specials now is almost all self-managed. Kersey has painted every one of the inside of these here units. Senna is making sure we got all the meals delivered, and in order. And if there's a problem, he takes it direct to the deliveries and bypasses the guards. He comes to me with the inventories and we go through them line by line and I done turn in the reports to the lieutenant. We can even assist with the construction of the new units you got that foundation for. You know you got not one but two good carpenters in here. One even got his card."

The Warden turned from the door. *"Card?"*

"Yessir, one even got his card. His Woodmans."

The Warden sat down in the desk chair with his back to the prisoner. "Yer talkin' names now and I only know numbers," he said.

The prisoner opened his mouth more than the usual setting. Nothing came out.

"Well I ain't gonna argue the point. You sound like my second. When she wasn't fussin' with me she was fishin' for compliments. The two of yous-"

Loud words outside interrupted the Warden. Chatter in layers. Then came a rap on the door.

"Everything alright?" a small guard inquired. The Warden grimaced at the guard and the guard immediately backtracked. The guard then shut the door and walked past the window with a radio glued to his ear so as to hide his face. The Warden swiveled around.

"Ya got skills others ain't got is what I'm sayin. You can handle a gun."

"Yessir. That I can do."

"What'd they do to ya first when you shot that poor boy over at cownie?"

"I got put down on the lock, I can't recall as to how long and such, but it was long."

"And then what'd they do to ya?"

"From there it was to the judge and then to state."

"Pretty fast."

"Fast. Yessir."

"And state . . . it better than cownie?"

"Yessir, state is, by a long shot."

"That's what I know. Yer moving up in the world, shooter. Let's say, now, for shits and giggles, I put this gun in yer hand and ya go on and shoot one of my guards. What happens then?"

"I shoot one of your guards?"

"Uh huh."

"That there looks like a .38 to me."

"It looks like one to me too."

"It loaded?"

"It might have a bullet or two. Let's say is got a full chamber. Shits and giggles, now, kay?"

227

"I wouldn't touch that gun, Cap'n. And I wouldn't shoot at one of your guards. I done learned my lesson."

"Let's say ya do."

"If I did, and what I'm saying is . . . I wouldn't. But if I did, I don't think there's a lock or a judge or jury or nothin'. Somethin' bad would take place. Somethin' the papers don't get reports about. Nothin' for the files."

"Nothin' for the files is right."

"Yessir."

"Now . . . let's say I give ya this gun here and ten times what's in yer paycheck and I let you cowboy on outta here in them Rios yous was so tickled about on entry and letcha go to work on them skills of yers. What would ya have to say about that?"

The prisoner cleared his throat. He wiped his nose. "Ten beans and a special?" he said.

"Ya get ta slip out and slip back in, like a furla."

"I guess there ain't nothin' too bad about that, Cap'n. What I gotta do then to earn that big money?"

"You already earned that big money."

"How'd I earn that big money?"

"You shot a guard, remember, over at cownie? Sheriff Rey's place for the undesired."

"You're gonna give me all that loot because I shot a guard?"

"You earned it."

"No one ever told me I earned money for my actions before. The judge, he said my actions was that of a man with no concern. He had a psycho-man examine me."

"He wunna mine?"

"Who, *the judge*?"

"The guard, cousin. The one taking disability from the state and crawling on his hands and knees."

"No sir. I know that-e ain't."

"Well he ain't. So ya earned that money then. Yer actions tell me somethin' much different than them so-called experts and theys opinions, kay. What they says to me is I got someone I can rely on. A man who can be counted on to do what others can't. Ya even told me you was in the Navy. That took balls to say to me. In fact, I believed yer words just as soon as they came outta yer mouth. Is a real skill if ya ask me."

"That's not what the psycho-man had to say about me. The man, he-"

"Who cares what some shrink thinks? Yous a man of action, that's what I know."

The prisoner clenched his lumpy toes. "What's the gun needed for Cap'n?"

The Warden caressed the chamber.

"This here's a tool for negotiation, kay. There's some negotiatin' I gotta do that I can't be present for. Call it a buyout. I need ya to go to work for me and come back and get yer bonus pay. Ain't nothin' ya can't handle."

"There's more?"

"If ya want, there's an extra ten I got tucked away on successful return. I'll even give ya another weekend on the outside if alls is squared."

The prisoner stood up. "You gonna leave that mister with me, Cap'n?"

The Warden looked at the gun with indifference. "Yeah, but ditch it in the river when yer done."

The prisoner licked his lips and wiped his sweat and took note of the temperature setting on the wall. The Warden placed the .38 on the desk and spun it around.

"How long it take ya to make that kinda money in that tourist town of yers, Greenaverde or somethin'?"

"*Greenhall.*"

The Warden flashed a weak smile.

"I only seen that kind of money come to me on my missions before."

"Yer missions, ya say?"

The prisoner nodded.

"Uh huh . . ."

"When am I supposed to be leavin' on this here mission, Cap'n?"

"On Sunday," the Warden said, leaving the chair. "As ya know, we got the visits coming and there's gonna be a whole lot goin on. I'll take care of things that arrange for yer transport. It'll take the guards a day to search the inside and another to search the desert. After seventy-two hours I'm required to phone it in. I believe by Tuesday morning we'll find ya somewhere over by the mountain. Then we just have a meet and greet and write in yer record. You'll be back with the B's for six weeks and then back here at yer conda, excuse me, unit. I'll even say that you was out gathering rocks for the rock garden we doin in front of the Specials entry. Like yous the landscaper around here."

The Warden opened the door and exited to the clear night and buzzed lawn of the Specials.

The prisoner picked up the .38. He checked the chamber. Cold and empty. The Warden stepped one good foot back inside the unit.

"I forgot to tell ya . . ."

"Yessir."

"Ya know how I know yous the right man for the job?"

"*Mission.*"

"The right man, uh huh . . . for the mission."

"Well, it's like you said, Cap'n. I can handle a gun."

"Nope."

"Because I pulled the trigger?"

The Warden removed his hat and held it over his heart. "Well sorta," he said. "But no."

"I don't know then, Cap'n, which is it?"

"Is how ya got the gun."

"How I got the gun?"

"Uh huh . . . how it got to yer hand when ya had one hand already cuffed to the desk in the sick room."

The prisoner swallowed some dead air.

The Warden coddled back his hat, teasing with the gold. "Now don't go spoilin' it by tellin' me, Dell. There's just some things that is better left to the imagination, kay."

30 THE BURN

SANDIS let himself into Gavin's trailer with the barrel of his Browning Auto-5. He set the shotgun on top of the television and clipped his keys to the loop on the right most side of his pants, bundling them together with a rubber band. He moved to where Gavin was sprawled out on the couch, in the low glow of a channel-test broadcast, and gently shook him. "Wake on up," he said.

"What's going on?" Gavin asked with a purple eye.

Sandis let go of the weary. "Okay, wait, just wait now . . . hush up for a second." He listened intently with the Browning on his eyes.

"What is it?" Gavin whispered.

"Quiet."

Ten seconds passed. Sandis accessed an M1917 revolver from the outside pocket of his Members Only jacket. He handed the revolver to Gavin, stock ways. "The thing's not loaded," he assured.

"What's this for?"

The old man paused. "If I go outside, make sure you got one hand over the barrel and the other on the trigger."

"Why?"

"Listen to me. One hand on the barrel, over, not under. One on the trigger."

Gavin thought to speak. Sandis held up a hand and quieted him.

"Just do as I say. I'm not sure though, if I'm going outside just yet. But if I do."

"What's outside?" Gavin asked, barely in a whisper.

"Some people we don't want to meet. And I'm doing my best right now to make sure they don't want to meet with us."

They heard shouts and bottles breaking and heavy motors in the distance like you might get at a drag race. Gavin got up from the couch. Sandis pulled him back down by the wrist.

"What's going on outside?"

Sandis eased his way back to the Browning. He felt the 16 gauge recoil in his hand as he took a knee by the window. With the barrel he made his view better by the treatment. He eyed Gavin.

"Some uglies torched something. I think they torched the landlord's place."

Unsure as to who or what Sandis was referring to, Gavin fiddled with the revolver. The revolver was more of a relic than anything else. It had the look of a museum piece, like it had been lifted right out of a glass case.

"I got as many people on lockdown as I could," Sandis said, spying through the frames.

Gavin hunched over to the window. There they both saw the beams of a flashlight on the silver of their common neighbor's exterior.

"Who'd they torch again?"

Sandis didn't reply.

A middle-aged man meandered between the trailers. Sandis put an index finger over his mouth and winked at Gavin. The trespasser stopped for a moment and then retreated.

"Okay, good," Sandis said. "They can't find their way around in the dark. That's good."

Gavin nodded like he knew what Sandis was talking about.

"Listen, I'm gonna get up behind that guy and fire off two rounds. It's gonna pop his ears something awful since his teeth ain't readied and clenched. And while he's in a panic, I'm gonna herd his sorry ass over to the gate. I'm gonna show him the way, and when his buddies see him, hopefully they'll do likewise."

Gavin's browns fully agreed with the plan. He wondered who the landlord was if it wasn't the old man in his trailer with the shotgun.

"Where's that duct tape you put all over your body?"

"In my room," Gavin answered.

"This whole thing is your dang room."

Gavin didn't speak.

"Well wherever it is. I need you to hurry up and go get it."

Gavin stayed close to the floor as he moved through six of his nine hundred square feet. He returned a minute later with a half roll of duct tape. He took to the couch and rolled the tape over to Sandis. "There's a flashlight in the cupboard," Sandis said, retrieving the tape with the barrel. "Right above the stove. I need you to get it for me. Quiet now."

Gavin stood up without realizing. "There's a flashlight in the cupboard?"

"Right. The batteries are inside the coffee can. Do me the favor and register them for me, will ya?"

Gavin continued on to the kitchen. He knocked over a colorful plastic plate that was on the counter - artwork of his family house he had painted as a child. He collected the craft and opened the cupboard. Sure enough, a flashlight on the top shelf. And two batteries in a coffee can he had not once considered opening. He returned to the frames by the door practically in a crawl.

"You hear any more than two shots, I want you to meet me at Sunny. You copy me on that, Private?"

Gavin nodded.

Sandis lowered the Browning to the floor and taped the flashlight to the barrel. "Listen to me, Gavin," he said, most serious.

Gavin cleared his scattered brain.

"Every action, every single gosh-darn action, has an equal and opposite reaction."

"Okay."

"That means, if these guys decide to get brave, we're taking Sunny for a ride in the desert. I can take her west, right through this place between homesteads if need be."

Gavin didn't speak.

Before Sandis opened the door, he turned to Gavin and said, "Keep your white shirt off like you do when you try to hide from me, but put on your jeans and running shoes."

GAVIN WAITED for over ten minutes in his sneakers and jeans before his curiosity had got the best of him. With the revolver tucked away he opened the door and looked for any action, head first with the rest of his body hesitating.

He jumped the steps and jetted through the garden of rocks that surrounded his fire pit, spreading ash and shards of cattle bone. On auto-pilot he moved to the washroom and went inside and ran a hand in a pan of water. He drank from the hand and wiped his bangs back and around the ears. He then grabbed the revolver and inspected the hammer, placing one hand over the chamber as he pointed toward the door. He actioned his left hand back and forth, imagining for a time he was a cowboy like the kind who battle Indians on Saturday morning TV.

When he tucked the revolver back in his pants, a shot rang out in the distance.

Gavin reached for the revolver but it had already dropped down the back of his pants. Securing it by his sneaks a second shot sounded louder than the first. He left the washroom in a panic and bolted back past his trailer and around his neighbor's lot.

He slid into Sunny and tried to think. *How many shots was it? One or two?* Two shots proved good enough for his anxious mind and so he sat there with a hand over the barrel and his blood coursing about as fast as it does in anticipation of running with a football.

Five minutes and an eternity he did wait. In that time, Gavin had witnessed only one other old man not named Sandis investigate the noise. He worried for the first time that Sandis might not return.

Isn't he the landlord here?

Gavin exited the cab to make his way around two other trailers that were just west of his position. He heard another shot, followed shortly thereafter by two more blasts in rapid succession. He caught a few flashes out of the corner of his eye and followed the light. After a minute, he was within twenty yards of the water tower. There, in the flicker of the outer lights and inner stars, he spotted the old man. Sandis waved him over with the barrel.

"What are you shooting at?" Gavin asked.

Sandis didn't respond. Gavin repeated the question.

"Sixty degrees or so, into the black, left to right. Like there's two gunners up here, not one."

Gavin noticed a faint glow in the desert. "Did you target a tree?" he said.

"I'm not that good."

"What's that burning?"

Sandis lowered his aim. "They torched the landlord's place. They torched it real good and that's all that's left of it. I don't think he made it out in time. God danget, I think he was asleep." Gavin shook his head, not fully comprehending what had taken place.

"Who torched the landlord's place?"

"I don't know, there was a group of them, maybe five or more." Sandis put a hand on Gavin's bare shoulder. "Listen," he said. "I need you to go get a box of Federal shells for me. I got a box inside on the coffee table."

Gavin shuffled off five yards toward his home without a chimney. Then he turned back around.

"Aren't you the landlord here, Mr. Sandis?"

Sandis spat. "Just about every dang day."

"Who's the landlord?"

"The Apache," Sandis answered.

"The Apache?"

"Right."

Gavin froze. "What Apache?" His heart skipped three beats.

"The Apache who owns this land and doesn't charge us any rent, Walt Eskin." Gavin slowly absorbed the information. *Walt-*

In an instant, the iron in Gavin's blood seared. He couldn't keep losing people in his life. Without warning, he made a move for the trail. Sandis, however, had other intentions. With what seemed like very little effort, Sandis put out his left leg and tripped Gavin. It was pure artistry in motion, possibly a patented move by the old man and former soldier.

Sandis dug a knee into Gavin's lower back, placing the Browning lengthwise across his neck. He pressed down.

"Let me go," Gavin demanded as he tried to push up. Sandis only applied more pressure.

"Get off me!" Gavin's anger and adrenaline disrupted any thought to roll. Still, he wasn't going anywhere.

"Settle . . ." Sandis said in a strong voice that was foreign to Gavin.

Gavin attempted another push.

"Just settle."

Gavin settled.

"If you work against me, I can adjust your vertebrae along the Thoracic curve. You'll be in the hangar for a week. You move inch and you won't play in another game."

Gavin moved his fingertips. With his lips practically in the dirt he said, "There aren't any more scrimmages to be in."

Sandis scouted the situation.

Gavin turned his head. "Why are you doing this to me?" he said. He received a slight burn from the barrel in response. The metal hurt, but he didn't breathe a word about it. Sandis relaxed a bit.

"Did I ever tell you what I wanted to be when I was a youngster?"

Gavin thought about the question for a moment. He found it hard to concentrate on anything other than the condition of his friend. He believed in his heart that Walt must be alive. Walt, after all, was the strongest person he knew.

Sandis smiled at his own thoughts. "I had this wild notion I was gonna be this big radio star. A wild notion if there ever was one."

Gavin tried a delicate push. He then submitted.

"Well I had every thingamajig with a speaker and a dial you could find. Let me remind you, there wasn't much we could afford back then. But I found a way to get my hands on just about everything that was available.

"I practiced and practiced my routines and drove my parents nuts. I pulled out the insides to an RCA we had our dimes into so the stations would turn but the sound didn't come through when you got to a channel I picked for myself. 1040 on the AM. 1040 is what I liked. My father, the man about disowned me when he found out.

"But I made it so you could hear all the regulars and then hear me like it was all happening real-time in my world. Then I'd cover myself under the table and reel off reports. I'd get the reports together for the day and repeat them back to any family member of mine who'd listen." Sandis relaxed some more but Gavin didn't try anything. Gavin was tuned-in with both ears.

"Then came the day I had the chance to host my very own show. A local thing about horses and the like. That kinda thing. Now here's the real kick in the pants: when the chance came, I tell ya, I gave it up. Right, I let it pass me by. Don't ask me why but I can remember it like it was yesterday. I was on my way to the radio station, and a real fussy Christian neighbor of ours who was driving me there turned on the radio. Some gospel speak. Well for whatever reason, I jumped out of the car I was riding in. Just jumped out of the thing. Somehow or the other some dang thing had come over me that made me feel I didn't want the opportunity. So I gave up my one and only dream, right there. Just flat gave it up."

Gavin let the dirt take him in.

"Next thing I know I'm in the Army. Gettin' kicked around in the ass. Our drill sergeant, he thought we were a pack of mules. Actually, mules probably got treated better. But I had this weird thing happening inside of me. Something that said: if you survive, you got purpose in your life, Gene. So I thought that if I'm going to be fighting in any dang war, then save me. Right, God, *save me*. You know, Gene. For once, show me you care. I'm here, so now's your opportunity. Well I think I thought that thought for a whole twenty-four hours. Then it was half days on from there, see."

Sandis removed his knee. Gavin rolled over and looked at the stars. "What did you do?" Gavin asked in a cool breeze.

"What did I do?"

"Yeah?"

"I went to Korea. Got me a wife named Sun-Ja and came back a certified bachelor for life."

Gavin moved a hand over his heart.

"What I'm saying to you is that we got choices. You understand that?"

Gavin nodded from his dirt floor.

"It wasn't your choice to be here, right?"

Gavin shook his eyes more than he did his head.

"But you made a choice to do something about it?"

"About it?" Gavin said.

"Right, lemonade from lemons is what I'm saying. Something good from something . . . not so good."

"I didn't do anything good."

"You put that little school on the map by trying to do something for them. That's good."

"What did I do for the school?"

"You put them on the map. Got some decent people out there excited. Playing football."

"I never played. It never worked."

Sandis dusted himself off and Gavin repositioned in the direction of the burn. "No regrets," Sandis said.

"No regrets?"

"Right. Anything you do, you try your best, you don't quit. Even if it doesn't work out like you had planned."

Gavin thought about the fate of his friend.

"These uglies, and I've come across a few in my day, they were out looking for you."

For the first time Gavin's heart mourned for his mother.

"Forget about, *don't quit*," Sandis said.

"What?"

"Well I just don't like the negative aspect of it now that I think about it some. You take away *don't* and you're left with *quit*."

Gavin considered his own choice words.

Sandis considered the tape on Gavin's sneakers. He took a break from all the heartbreak and pointed a finger.

"Whatever you choose to do with your life, Private, you stick. You hear me? You *stick*."

31 MINER

THE START OF FALL was officially five days away. Gavin had disappeared for the last day and a half. He'd forgotten about school and everything else in his world and spent time north-river in the hope of clearing his head.

He'd traveled well past Benson and camped in the thick blades of the river bank. There, where the water runs smooth, he captured a decent share of Gila chub under the snare of time and patience; and lightening quick hands. With a stick and some brush and a lesson learned at the Corte School, he built his first fire. The fire had comforted him through the wind gusts of a protected sun. In all the distraction, he reveled greatly the reward.

Long after midnight Friday he had gazed. Into the flames and into his heart for any reason he could find other than the one tearing him apart. Was Walt just a figment of his wild imagination? Did people enter his life and disappear before he could tell them how he really felt? He wanted so much to say the words. He was consumed with guilt and did not know what to do. Guilt, unlike anger, was an entirely new emotion for him.

THE FRIDAY MORNING SUN ARRIVED WITH A SMOLDERING.

Gavin stood aside the gray air, remembering what Walt had to say about the sun. He retrieved a sharp rock from his pocket and cut his thumb, letting it bleed so as to see and feel the hurt - an homage more or less to the scarring he'd become accustomed. The air kicked and the fire numbed. And without a twitch, the blood did run.

He thought about the sun rising in front of him no matter where he rests his head. No matter what, the sun brings with it a new day. He knew Walt had been a part of his life, otherwise he wouldn't know the things he did. He felt more alone than he thought he could ever bare. But more so he felt a newfound sense of strength. Like he could go anywhere and do anything and things would work out in the end. Even if his legs couldn't carry him, he could still find a way to get to where he wanted to go. Maybe he was really an Indian? Maybe he'd been living in the wrong colored world all along? *Maybe,* his head spun, *I'm not alone.*

When he made it back to the foot of his trailer it was two hours to dusk. There he found a barricade between him and his door in the form of a man who looked like he could roll rather easily down the hill. The round-man had whitewalls above the ears and a curl that dropped from the top to mid-forehead. Gavin gave the girth the once over. He angled an arm at the hip and spat.

"I had to knock all over the doggone place for you," the round-man said as he patted his head and neck with a cloth. "Like I was on a mission to find me a convert. Which one of these was yours. Not one single chimney that I could find. Made me a couple of friends in the process, h'ever."

"I don't know you," Gavin said.

"Yep, you don't. Shouldn't just the same. I know you, h'ever."

"You know me? Good for you. You can read. There's a sign at the gate that says no trespassing."

The round-man adjusted his body suit. "Can't say I buy the hype," he said, amused with his words.

"Excuse me?"

"The hype . . . it don't get me none."

Gavin tightened.

The round-man whiffed the air. "Maybe I'll set me up a trailer here, take it all in like they says I shouldda been doing all along."

Gavin kicked at the dirt and the round-man sucked in his next words.

"Yep . . . maybe spend a dime or two on a Big Wind when the time comes. Just me and the bride. I have got to say . . . the sunset you got around here reminds me of the posters I seen at the doctors up in Tucson. You know that cowboy art they got on silk screen and poster board? Yep, that fine art. Big cities ain't for me, h'ever. And the wait don't bother me none, not with this spectacular of God's green you got going on. Well, pardon the green, son, it don't much apply to us. We ain't in West Virginia now but for my mind. But I ain't gonna apologizin' any. In a way, I s'pose you could say I've been waitin' up here my whole life. It sounds strange, I know. Bisbee ain't a good place to retire if you've lived there all your adult life. I'm from there mostly. You retire, you go someplace else. Even a prairie dog don't wanna die at home, and there ain't nothin' that dog can't take, so, well, that's how you know."

Gavin spied his territory. "You want to write something about me," he said. "Go right ahead. I won't be around to read it." He came back to the round-man. "You can talk all you want, mister, try to convince me to tell you things, but I won't be around to read your story. You can write whatever you want about me. Print what you want, I don't care."

"I'm not with the papers," the round-man said. "And I don't much care for writin' down things. But sure, I like to read. I'm particular to mysteries, mostly. Got a thing for manuals and texts, too, if you can believe."

Gavin put his right foot on the first step and stretched his hamstring. He rubbed his shin.

The round-man brushed at his round nose. "I can see I'm in your way," he said. "This is your house and I'm in your way. What was you out doin if you don't mind my pryin lips?"

Gavin turned to see if he might catch a glimpse of Sunny. He only caught part of a crate two yards from where her tires had been. "How long have you been here?" he asked.

"Good Lord . . . an hour, maybe two. Two and a quarter if you wanna stretch."

"Just you?"

"Yep."

"You don't work in the papers?"

"Not since Breeden High School overtook the town of Dunlow West Virginia and got itself a sports page, and a decent classified I might add. Not in the print business since then, no."

"Who are you?"

"Names Conrad Workman. Most folks call me Coal, h'ever. It's what I prefer, *Coal*."

"People call you, *Coal*?"

"Yep, *Coach Coal*," the round-man answered. "Call me *nipper* once, son, and I'll forgive you, John 3:16. Call me *nipper* more than that, and you got yourself a workload of push-ups comin' your way." The round-man chuckled and bobbed. "That last little bit there was a joke," he added. "I know what you have got to be thinkin' - right now you're thinkin' that this handsome man in front of you has got to work on his deliv'ry. It's about timing, am I right?"

"*Coal*, like the kind of mines?"

"Like the kind of mines, precisely. Most folks don't catch on to that name as quick as you, but then again, most folks ain't like you. Most ain't got a full spread dedicated to them in the paper they ain't had to pay a hay penny for, am I right?"

"I guess," Gavin uttered.

"You guessed right."

"Why, *Coal*?"

"Well I'm a fifth generation miner, it's just that I don't mine."

"Oh . . . and you're from Bisbee?"

"Bisbee mostly, yep."

"There's coal mines in Bisbee?"

"No coal mines in Bisbee. Copper."

"I guess I knew that."

The round-man rolled up on his toes. He settled back. "You've got a nickname too," he said. "I gather your momma didn't name you *The Ghost* just for the sake, I mean that would be a travisy. No momma should mess the name, nevamine the daddy."

Gavin widened his eyes and dug into his stance.

"What is your real name, son, if you don't mind my pryin lips?"

He hesitated for a couple of thoughtful breaths. "Gavin."

"That's a darn good name. It's strong, but not too strong that you got to break your back workin' for a livin' to prove it. You got named right for what you're doing. But how come the paper don't know your name?"

"Because I didn't tell them my name."

"Well how come son?"

"Because it doesn't matter."

"Why don't it matter, your name?"

"It just doesn't."

"You told me."

"I know."

"Well how come?"

Gavin thought about the ball not wanting anything to do with his hands. "I guess because you're not with the paper," he said.

The round-man scratched his naked ear. "And the latter?" he said. "If you don't mind my pryin lips gettin' the best of me."

"Ladder?"

"Your last name . . . it's where you're from, son. And on the eighth day the good Lord played chess with hisself 'cause he got bored." The round-man brought a fist to his lips and soft-served a burp. "Excuse me," he gasped. "It ain't make my momma too proud when I lose my body control."

All of Rock Gardens listened. "Reeves."

"Gavin, Reeves. I like it."

"I don't want to talk about my name."

"You're right. You've got things to do and I'm in your way. And I got no time to waste myself. I waited here for you and if you ask me, life is too short to be waitin' around in the wrong place. So let me tell you why I'm standing here and not shaking your hand like I outta be. Shaking your hand is the first thing I shouldda done and for that, Gavin Reeves, I sincerely apologize." The round-man waddled down the steps, extending a sweaty hand. Gavin turned a cheek and wearily accepted it. "I'm here today because I brought you some equipment."

"Equipment?"

"Yep. There's a helmet and shoulder pads, and some pants and a brand new jersey with the number 40 - the number you wear. I hope you like red. There's some cleats too, the types that got screws. All of it ain't neva been wore before."

"I don't do football anymore," Gavin said. "Sorry."

"Well football is a team sport."

"Football is a team sport full of assholes who like to play with themselves."

"There's eight, uh . . . eight apples like you say, on each side of the ball. One man can't fail the gap else you need a levee, am I right? You agree with that statement?"

Gavin retreated, folding his arms.

"There's just one of you and you ain't much taller than me."

How far is Greenhall from the mine?

The round-man looked around the grounds. "It's a team sport, no getting around that, Gavin Reeves. H'ever, I have got to say, that hot-cakin' with the ball you had come up with to make a play, well, it's darn near Einstein in the middle grades. I've been a coach since I can remember, and in all that time, the thought about how one man can make the play with the snap to hisself, well that thought ain't neva come to my mind. Not once, son, neva."

"You're not the first person to tell me that," Gavin said, releasing his fold.

"It's Einstein in the middle grades."

Gavin rubbed the back of his neck. "I never snapped the ball," he said. "So I never got the chance to play."

"That don't matter none. It says you can play. It gives you the right to be there and I love that right as much as I love to see my bride in pearls."

"I never touched the ball. Not one time."

"Well, times change. People change. Sitchiations change. Change even done changes."

"So what's your point?"

"So we want, and when I say *we*, I include not just the team, but the humble pie town of Bisbee, Arizona. And by the town, I include the mayor, which happens to be yours truly, the one tryin to look as tall as his five and a half will allow. The good Lord, he done blessed me, but he ain't made me no tall strappin' Roger Stawback. That I had done accepted a long time ago. And as the whip cream is the real cherry, son, the twelve businesses we got in the chamber went and chipped-in to purchase that fine equipment for you to come play against us." The round-man went back up the steps and grabbed the equipment bag. "Our offer to you . . . is it the cordee school? Did I pronunce that correct?"

"Almost. Yeah, that's fine."

"Our offer to you, the one-man team from the Indian river school, is to play a real game. Bisbee and you. That's why I'm here, to offer you a real game, not a scrimmage. I'd say under the lights, but we ain't got any. We want to bring in the mine tracks, h'ever, for a Friday night, and that gets us excited. We got plenty of flatbeds with lights too if you'll deliver your team, which is you. Any Friday you want, and we're prepared to forego our aways."

"Aways?"

"We only play away games since we ain't got any lights. As it stands today, we're the only other Class C, Clawson included, that ain't got the lights blessin' our field. We're workin' on gettin' the lights like we work the mines, believe me. I guess it's good I'm a politician by birth. Momma, she had me kickin' around in her womb at the school board, bless her good graces."

Gavin looked south, toward the bridge road.

"Now you look lost. Did I lose you?"

"It doesn't matter who kicks off. I still won't get the ball, I know that."

The round-man dropped the bag. "You got any idea how many players I got on my team?"

"More than one."

"There's fifteen."

"So."

"So you know how many touch the ball?"

Gavin directed to the steps. "Why would I give a flying fuck about that?"

The round-man bent down and whispered a short prayer. Then he glanced at Gavin. "You really run to those schools?" he asked, respect flowing through his voice.

"Yeah . . ."

"There and back?"

No, Gavin thought. *I took the Greyhound, bowling ball.* "Yeah, and back," he said.

"How long did it take you to make it all the way down to Sulger from here?"

A part of him heard the word: Soldier. "I don't know," Gavin said.

"How long? Im-a keep askin you."

"Maybe five hours."

"Maybe five, huh. And that just rolls off your tongue like it ain't nothin'."

"I don't think about that stuff because it doesn't even matter."

"Well . . . " the round-man said, "we took the bus. Fifteen plus two of us coaches. The yellow submariner the whole way. Got there in under an hour. We even had sandwiches made."

"And I give a shit about this because?"

"I don't know if you giva shingle, son. To tell you the truth, I don't know why I giva shingle, but I do. I done do. Even more than knowing I do, I done got a feel about it, and when I got a feel about somethin' it's like Jesus hisself is walkin' alongsida me. And there ain't nothin' better than that feelin', son. Well now I can tell you got me preachin'."

"I'm real sorry," Gavin said as he walked up the steps, ignoring the brand new equipment manifested from his environment. "But I got other plans. Football is . . . *was*, something to me. Now it's nothing. Running is nothing either. We all can run." He opened the door.

"Humor me a story then, and I'll be on my way, promise. I got a long ways to go home now because, what I forgot to say is that I ran up here all the way from Bisbee. Slow runnin' like a turtle, but the feet turnin' over no less. That's right, Gavin Reeves, I came the whole way on my two blessed feet and let my assistant coach take over for the first time since we got in the eight-man game because you had done inspired me. I ain't been this inspired since, well, since ever. So humor me if you will."

Gavin went to the couch with half an ear. The round-man moved the equipment to stop the door.

"They got a story about you in the paper, and some of it prolly embellished because that's the way it goes in the business of hype. But it's your story and you got to accept that. The story makes you what you is in other people's eyes. Other eyes, not yours. So you got some responsibility whether you like it or not. I don't care how young.

What I really want to say after traveling all this way and thinkin' and feelin' free and seein the beauty that surrounds me and havin the bride follow behind me in the station wagon because that's just the kinda lady I got in my life, bless her good graces. What I got to say, Gavin Reeves, is we got copper in those mines in Bisbee, and it's plenty, but coals is a different story. Coals is a grown man's worry. Coals is West Virginia through and through. And that's my name. It's where I'm from son.

Now, one of my uncles . . . he got caught in the quarry and it got sealed, this was spring of fifty-eight. Never again did that God-fearing man take witness to the light of day. With the copper you can truck in and truck out and leave your worries at the bedside. No copper miner has got to worry that when he goes to work it could be his last day. The lights in the copper mines is the same as the lights they got in the buildings, flatbeds and even on the fields of some of our counterparts. The mines-is bright and the airs-is clean on the inside. In there you can breathe. But coals is a different story, much like you. *Different*, hear me? And the story is you got to go alone. You go from the early morning dark into the darkness and when you come back out, if you come out at all, it's darn near darker than it ever was. You'll see the sun one day, son, standin' next to Jesus, and maybe on your weddin' day. But other than that them days is dark days for the most. Accepting that worry is a grown man thing to do."

Gavin thought to say something, but he got stuck on the analogy.

"What's your age, son, if you don't mind my askin?"

"Sixteen," Gavin said, relinquishing his ability to hide facts about his life.

"You sure it ain't sixty one?"

"You can keep on talking to me if you want," Gavin said. "Just shut the door, please. I need to pack some of my things."

The round-man closed the door as if it were made of glass. "Where are you going?" he asked.

"Away from here."

"Out of town for good?"

"This place isn't even a town," Gavin complained.

"Let me guess. You're running somewhere."

"Walking. Then hitching if I feel like it."

"Anywhere in particular?"

"No. Just away from here."

"Whatcha gonna do when you get there?"

"Where?"

"Wherever it is that you're going."

"I care about that as much as I do about playing football, which is nada."

The round-man looked about the room some. "You didn't play football," he said. "Remember, neva making a snap or touching the ball?"

"You know, you're right," Gavin steamed. "Thanks for reminding me, mister . . . what was your name again?"

"*Workman*. Names Coal Workman."

"Thanks for the talk, but I need to pack some things and get a move on. It's been real nice meeting you and learning about your life."

The round-man took a knee on the floor like he was about to coach up his team. "One thing I will guar-own-tee is that you'll get to play against us. You'll get the ball kicked to you each and every time and you'll be able to make the snap on every single offensive play. We won't even charge at you until you got it in your hands. You want to play as a one-man team, I wanna see that it happens. We'll even run the goal line and take it all in. It'll be a battle of will. You deserve that, son."

"So what you're saying is that I can get the ball and you'll let me snap if I make it to Bisbee?"

The round-man extended a round hand. "A promise from Coal Workman don't need no ink and paper."

"You won't kick the ball short or wherever like those assholes at the other schools?"

"Wherever it is you line up, Gavin Reeves, you'll get the ball special deliv'ry, I guar-own-tee. If I got a player that acts like an apple, we gonna stop the game and take a belt right to his core."

"You promise?"

"Well it don't need a shake," the round-man said, dropping his hand. "Words from my lips is a promise done made."

"Fantastic, mister miner. You've made my day and you've just answered my prayers. I get to play football, oh wow, this is just fantastic. Somebody is gonna finally let me run a play. And you brought me new equipment and everything else I need. This is just the best day, thank you so much. You're the answer to my fucking prayers."

The round-man stood up, slimming by his inhale. "Well, it's an offer is all," he said. "Take it or leave it."

Gavin picked up some clothes from the floor and tossed them onto the couch. "Thanks for the offer," he said, pointing at the door. "But I got better things to do with my life. I think I'm gonna leave your offer right where it is. Right here in No man's land."

HE'D BEEN WALKING the night highway for over four hours when a big rig with a multitude of reflectors blared its horn at him as it rolled past. The driver slowed to the shoulder and aired the brakes, sounding the horn one more time for good measure.

When the rig jolted into idle, the driver lowered an arm outside the window and slapped the side of the door. With his head and hand he waved Gavin over to the passenger door. Gavin hustled out of his dead gait and jumped onto the step rail.

"Where you headed to, rider, Greenhall or Lavanne?"

"The one with the Greyhound," Gavin answered.

"Greenhall got the hound, she sure do. Lavanne'll put you on the slow train to nowhere. Good choice."

"Can you take me down to Greenhall?"

"It depends, you a man of the Word?"

Gavin woke his brain. "You mean a preacher?"

"A preacher, son of a preacher man. The second coming of the Son of Man. Yeah, you into speaking the Word and seekin' to grow your flock?"

"That's not me."

"Looks to me like you've been busy walking the Earth and selling all your worldly possessions."

"I've had enough preaching done to me before," Gavin said. "I'm just walking, but my legs are tired. I'm tired."

The driver checked the traffic and then Gavin. "Well alright," he said. "I'm tired of talking to myself, so we's both tired of somethin', looks like." He perused his log book and then tossed it into the back. "Come on with it then," he added. "It ain't too big of a haul down to Greenhall, I can adjust."

Gavin handed the driver his stuffed and tethered sleeping bag through the window and opened the door. He rubbed a good portion of dust and highway grime from his face as he sank into the sea of foam that was his seat. The interior rumbled as the rig came out of idle.

The driver fiddled with the knobs on the CB, raising the handle up to his chin. He looked over at Gavin with an index finger that tapped the clicker by its own admission. "At first I thought you might be Army," he said. "But I can tell by that head of hair that you're nowhere near to taking orders." He clicked and spoke some trucker jargon, barely looking at the road ahead.

Gavin raised an eyebrow.

"And now I can see you're too young."

"I'm not so young," Gavin said in a partial yawn.

"Yeah sure," the driver said. "That's what they all say."

Gavin folded his arms and leaned back between the seat and corner window. His eyes blinked about as much as the reflectors out on the highway.

The driver put his handle to bed and saddled his arms over the enormous wheel, flashing a lucky-lady tattoo. The speedometer climbed to thirty-five as he stared into the abyss of the highway.

"I can't tell you how many soldiers I've picked up in the two lifetimes I've spent runnin' my routes. I think I've heard, and seen, it all. One time I had me this rider, this was when I was back haulin' live-stock up ways from the yards west of El Paso, workin' contracts for Big Beef and Rancho, and Culp some on the side when they felt like hollerin' at me.

So I had me this rider and he looks about as straight as an arrow, like he gets his hair cut about every two days. If you can picture, a real Life Magazine soldier boy. He ain't got but pressed pants and wingtips and a collared shirt on. He's dressed up for the dance but he's a long ways away from school. But he rambles off the streets of soldier town anyways and raps on to me that he got some time off and he's going down to Mexico for a little R and R and so I says to him: well R is my middle and last name and we builded a rapport from there. He's gonna take the day trip into Mexico and hook up connections with some farmers he got put on to and build himself an operation to transport weed back into the states. He's gonna get into the marijuana business and make the Army base in soldier town his place of operation.

So I looked at this rider direct and then he looked over at me the same and then he goes on to relate to me how I'd make good money just being in the transport business. I laughed and told him I am in the transport business, and he says it ain't the kind of transport he got going and we go back and forth playing this game. And then this rider, he pulls out a pipe and loads that thing up like it's his birthday and his parents ain't never bought him a happy meal and he then gets stoned right there in front of me, telling me how much he loves to get high. Can you believe that? This rider has got to be the biggest hippie flower child that I ever seen and he looks like the senator's son from that Credence song, like when they use to bring it way back in the day. So I look at you, and your hair, and your clothes that look like they been to hell and back and it reminds me that you could be completely different from how you look and that wouldn't surprise me one bit. Ain't that the darndest thing, rider, when you think about that one?"

Gavin sank deeper into the corner. Not one single word had made it through the vibratory metal to his ears.

The driver looked at Gavin and then at the road, taking it to the limit. He flicked a switch to flood the desert at the very time Gavin cut off his own.

32 GRINGO

THE GREYHOUND STATION located at the epicenter of Greenhall's four mile radius was waking up at the very moment Gavin started to dream.

"El Paso, *quince minutos*," the speaker system said.

Gavin rolled to the backside of the bench that was nearest the travel lockers, cradling his sleeping bag under his head.

"Tucson, *las nueve en punto* . . . Albuquerque, *once, Nogales, once trienta . . . y Hermosillo . . . doce quince.*"

The destinations penetrated his subconscious. He felt a poke at his arm and brushed it off like it was just a part of the scenes running through his mind. He rolled back to the unprotected edge, swatting his nose and grumbling. When he cracked an eye in full of the fluorescence above, he found a tiny finger zeroing in on his nose. "*Apa,*" the voice attached to the finger said. "*Apa,* me. *Apa,* me."

Gavin straightened up in a half-second burst and tried to focus. *Where are you?*

"*Apa.*"

Think. Think.

"*Mijo,*" a young woman said as she slowed the finger lovingly by the collar. The young woman returned to her bench seat and sifted through a hard-shell suitcase at her side. She went back and forth with her welcoming eyes. Gavin kept composed under the spectrum. He picked up foreign words here and there from the passersby.

"What?" Gavin said after having watched the young woman's eyes dance with him for a good minute. She demurred to his shy smile. The colors of her blouse the colors of the finest Mexican spread. Red peppers and yellow corn. And the inside of the avocado falling from her neckline.

"What is it?" Gavin said with confidence.

She attended to her little boy. "I'm sorry," she said, parting tiny hairs. "It's just that he thinks you're his father. He hasn't been with his father since he was born. He only has pictures."

"Oh . . ."

"*Es de mala educacion senalar con el dedo, mijo.*"

"What did you just say to him?"

The young woman blossomed. "I told him it's not very polite to point," she said.

Gavin leaned back, stretching his arms over the top of the bench. "It's alright," he said. "He can point at me."

"*Sentarse miel, mijo.*"

"Do you know which one of these goes down to *Tijuana*?" Gavin asked.

"Down?"

"Yeah."

"*Tijuana* is not, down."

"Does one of the buses go there?"

She laughed. "Oh I don't think so."

"Where does the bus go that's a good place to go in Mexico?"

"We live in *Hermosillo*, it's nice."

"How much is a ticket?"

"Well . . . it was $12.50 for us to get here."

Gavin gazed above his head at the smoke wafting in the long-range filaments.

"Is it okay if he sits with you while we wait? I just don't think he's going to stop staring at you."

Gavin slid to the side of the bench that was opposite his makeshift pillow. He smiled at the little boy who was standing not but a yard from his bare feet. "What's his name?" he asked.

"The same as his father, *Michael*."

"How do you say: come sit with me, in Spanish?"

"*Como se dice.*"

Gavin motioned a finger. "*Como se dice,*" he said.

"No no," the young woman corrected. "If you want to know something in Spanish, remember to ask in my language first. Say: *Como se dice*, first, okay?"

"*Yo comprende.*"

"See, you know that, that's good!"

Gavin leaned forward with a finger. The little boy nosed in. When he looked at the young woman again, his heart sank for the first time in his life. A sinking much different than losing a friend or family member. What he felt washed away his guilt and opened his heart. "*Como se-*"

The young woman rose, strutted a few steps and, as if to curtsey, leaned in on Gavin's available ear. His lips had yielded to her struts and beauty. She whispered but he didn't hear a word. He only understood what love was for the first time after having been so empty. She fixed the length over his ear with care and then sat her little boy down on the bench. She smiled as if her heart was smiling too.

"He'll be as quiet as a little lamb now," she beamed. "See, he's happy."

"Where are you going?" Gavin asked in a voice just above a whisper.

"Tucson."

"I've never been there before."

"We're only switching buses. Sierra Vista is our destination. It's where his father lives."

"I'm from there."

"Are you?" the young woman said, her face aglow.

"Yes." He instantly accepted that St. David had never been his home. He also accepted that No man's land was never his land. He'd been a tourist, a tenant.

"Is your father in the Army also?"

"No."

She batted her eyes at the hurried faces about the large room. Gavin thought about how he might extend the conversation. He looked at the little boy.

"Was that how you met his father, did you do something there?"

The young woman blushed. "I guess you could say that I did something there," she said. "I was a dancer once and was doing a performance and he was the only one in the audience in his uniform. Of all the people in front of me, I only saw this man. I will tell you something, since you are so young and maybe it is something you might want to know for the future: women don't share much with men. They have secrets. One of their secrets is that they love a man in uniform. The right uniform makes their defenses weak. It's how his father got me, anyways, and he's not nearly as handsome as you."

Gavin looked at the people in the turnstiles and baggage handlers and at a man in a blue and white striped uniform who had to be either a cop or a security guard. All of the distractions bought him time as he wondered what to do with his first ever compliment bestowed upon him by a beautiful woman.

"See, he's happy," the young woman said. "And thank you, this means a lot. He is just so anxious all the time."

"I'm gonna go check on a ticket," Gavin said, slipping on his sneakers. "I'll be back in a minute." He hoped she wouldn't move to another bench. Or to a bus outside.

The young woman clapped and her little boy opened. She collected him in her hands and then set his brown and white shoes on the ground. She nodded at Gavin. "*No todos gringo es su padre*," she said. "*No todos, greeengoh.*"

"I know that one, I think," Gavin said. "What is, *gringo*?"

"I'm sorry," the young woman said. "I shouldn't have said that. But he doesn't know any other word for it."

"Word for what?"

She wiped the dirt from helpless cheeks. "*White American*," she said. "I just told him that not every *gringo* is his father. His father is not like him. His father is white, he looks like you."

The lights above burned through a fuse. People and time came to a halt and the speaker system unplugged as Gavin returned to the bench in a daze and sat with his eyes on the little boy. He understood what he needed to do. And he knew why heavy rocks had been thrown. But more so, he felt a truth resonate in his soul. He thought about the second son and Walt's ominous words: 'His father is not like him, and I am not him.' Those words helped renew his dreams. And his emotions, more purposeful than ever, pulled him north.

33 BORN TO RUN

THE RUNNER HAD BEEN ingrained in the north 80 scenery for the better part of the afternoon when a VW Super Beetle veered onto the middle separator from the slow lane south. The VW popped exhaust as it careened across the dirt. As soon as the four-manual jumped a gear, though, the engine quit. Gavin turned around to face the plethora of miles he'd conquered on love and friendship and watched in humor the frustration of the driver unfold. He twirled the shirt that hung from his waist and proceeded to wipe down his face and neck. Then he hid behind the white for a few engine cranks.

A familiar pair of frames exited the VW, moving in his direction.

"You got an official game against Bisbee! Four quarters and no screwing around. Absolutely no bullshit. And, to top off, on a Friday night. It's a real game, Ghost."

"I know."

"I know you know. I had a chat with their coach when I saw him camping out near the bridge when I went to find you."

Gavin wiped a sea of sweat from his arms. "What did he tell you?" he asked.

"He said that he told you you got a real game if you want one and that you took off looking like a hobo getting ready to hop on a train."

"Did he say anything else?"

"Only that he wants to put it in the paper, what they plan to do, so everyone knows. But more so, that you'll know. They're not going to play another game this season unless they play against you."

"I don't read the paper," Gavin said.

"Yeah, I told him that. That's why I've been out looking for you since this morning. The coach means it. He really does."

Gavin fitted his shirt back over the belt and rubbed his head of wild hair. His biceps defined well in the rays to show his growth. His sleeping bag, baggage for someone else.

"Where did you go? Check that, where are you coming from?"

"So you know," Gavin said.

"Know what?"

"My name. He told you my real name."

The glasses-man returned to his VW and opened the engine hatch at the rear. He then walked up to the driver door and wedged himself between the door and the frame. He set his glasses on the roof and massaged his temple, squinting at the fuzzy horizon.

"So you told the coach who you really are. Well that makes perfect sense."

Gavin let the motors of the highway speak for him.

"Unfortunately, no," the glasses-man said. "He didn't share that particular piece of information with me."

Gavin removed a strip of tape from a leg of his jeans and wrapped it around the base of his right knee. "Your story about me," he said, finishing the wrap. "Whatever it is, it is wrong."

The glasses-man put his vision back on. "It's how I see it," he said. "How is that so wrong?"

"Screw you."

"Screw me?"

In a snap, Gavin pushed the door between him and the frames. The glasses-man fell into his seat, bumping his head along the way. His glasses landed in the cavern between the front seats. Gavin backed up a yard and watched the wire dig around in vain.

"I should break those stupid things so you can't write anything else about me," Gavin said.

With his touch the glasses-man located his frames. He adjusted the rearview and inspected the plastic for any breaks. "I've got multiple pairs," he said. "If you think this is the first time I've had them knocked off my face, you're dead wrong."

"You put where I told you I lived, why?"

"Well, I didn't have a postal address but I painted a picture for my readers to give them a back-story, sure."

"It's not where I live, dipshit."

"You told me it's where you lived, what was I going to do, argue with you? I mean it fits."

Gavin clenched his fists. He had the thought to kick in the door but his right leg decided otherwise. He punched the glass instead. The glass broke back his hand and his eyes got red.

"What's this all about?" the glasses-man said.

"Why'd you do that? Why'd you put that in the paper? You shouldn't have done that!"

The glasses-man collected himself in his seat. "Just take it easy," he said. "Just breathe, okay."

"I don't want to breathe."

"Okay. Rel-"

"Screw you. Screw your paper and your job and everything else you got."

The glasses-man scratched at his two-day-old beard in the windshield reflection. He shut the door and rolled the window down and moved his arm back outside like he was dropping the ashes of a smoke. "Talk to me," he eased.

Gavin clasped the door and squeezed. He hung his head. "I don't want to," he said.

"Tell me the real story. What does the real story say?"

The desert breathed.

"What does the real story say?" the glasses-man asked again.

"It says I'm going nowhere and I'm alone and it'll always be that way."

"Why are you alone?"

"Because he's not coming back and I owe him. I owe him because he did this. He did this to me but no one sees. You don't understand because you write stories. You don't understand anything about me."

"I can try and understand if you'll let me. Tell me, what is it you owe your father? What son owes his father anything?"

Gavin went to his knees with his hands welded to the door, his tears flowing out like the river.

"My father left me, okay, and he's dead now because I lied. I lied and said I lived there, but I don't. I live in a stupid fucking trailer in the middle of No man's land with no one around and nobody even cares."

"Tell me . . . what happened to your father?"

"It's not what I mean," Gavin uttered, sniffing and still buried.

"What is it you mean then? I'm listening."

"My friend died and I owe him for this even though it's not what I thought it would be. I know the angry man has nothing. I know that now. And I don't want to be angry. I want to join the Army and I want to go places and I want what other people have. I want to be with a girl as beautiful as the girl I just met and I want her to love me but I don't know any more. I don't know anything because no one knows me. And my only real friend is dead. He died because of me and he was my friend. And I never got to tell him what I really wanted to do with my life."

The glasses-man placed a hand on Gavin's head. "I understand how you feel," he said, "but you are so much more than you think you are. It's unfortunate that you can't see it. But I promise you one thing, you will. I promise you that you'll see everything that I see and what other people see even though they can't yet tell you. Everything you want, everything you just told me, it's all right in front of you. You're there. You really are."

Gavin lifted his head, wiping his nose. He picked up a knee.

"You know what that coach said to me when I ran into him looking for you? You know what he told me about you, do you?"

"No."

"He said the world doesn't have many heroes left to cling to. He told me you were his hero for who you are and how strong you are and your determination. He actually used that word to describe you, *hero*."

"He did?"

"Yes he did."

"I don't feel much like a hero."

"I imagine most heroes don't feel like heroes are supposed to. I imagine they are filled with doubt and have fears like the rest of us. But they act and they don't change and they don't let anyone get the best of them. You took on eight players by yourself, without a team behind you, do you know that?"

"I guess."

"I'm here to tell you that you did and you probably didn't even think about it in those terms. You probably were thinking about how to do the right thing the entire time. Heroes do things like that. They do the right thing and don't complain. They walk with real faith."

"Then why am I like this, why do I feel this way, like it doesn't work?"

The glasses-man paused to think of the right thing to say. "Can I give you a ride to your real home now?" he said. "Only if you'll let me."

For half a minute Gavin savored his view of the highway and two ways to go. "Your car doesn't seem like it's working," he finally said.

"It'll start, you just watch. I do a trick with a coat hanger and we're good to go."

The glasses-man pushed on the door but Gavin resisted.

"I need to get out to get the motor going," the glasses-man said. "My arms are long, but they're not that long."

"It's Gavin . . ."

"What's Gav-"

The glasses-man leaned back in his seat, taking a bite of his frames. Something in him changed.

"My real name, is Gavin Reeves."

WHEN GAVIN pointed at the sign for the jeep graveyard the glasses-man lowered the sound of Bruce Springsteen's horn section and downshifted with caution.

Gavin accessed his window and felt the last of the air flow between his fingers and thought about the spring that had come and gone so fast and the heat of his challenging summer. "Did you win?" he asked.

"Huh?"

"Your bet. The one you told me about . . . the monsoons?"

The glasses-man chuckled. "Mother Mary, I was so very close," he said. "But no, I'm sorry to say that it wasn't meant to be. I was a bit premature in my prediction. Actually, premature by a few hours."

"That sucks."

"Hell, I was crushing it anyways. I forgot about the monsoons because I was so completely lost hammering out your story. You know, I taped up my fingers like football players do because of the tape you use all over your body."

"You mean your story."

"My story, sorry, I forgot."

They idled at the opening of a narrow road that had a small cardboard box with a rock holding it down and an arrow drawn on the face pointing east. The sign read: Antique jeeps, 2 miles - Tison Yard, 4.

Gavin opened the door with a taped-sole to the dirt. "Thanks," he said.

"Wait a sec," the glasses-man said, punching the tape deck.

Gavin hung outside the door with strength. "What?"

"I really need to ask you about something, so don't take off on me just yet, okay?"

Gavin glanced at the newspaper in the backseat.

"When you were at Post, why did you tape the number 40 to your shirt? Why that number and not something else?"

Gavin shrugged as he thought about the Spanish language and languages he'd never heard one word from. All the places around the world with people different than him. Different dreams and visions and spoken words. Then a final thought about being uniform, one without pads, and standing out for someone special.

"Why 40, what's the significance behind that?"

"It's just the number that came to me, that's all. I thought I should have a number."

"You showed it off like you were saying something, or trying to say something, at least."

Gavin pinched his lips, nodding in the direction of St. David. He wasn't about to share his love letter with an inventor of stories. A letter he'd found in the sleeve of the seven-inch record one day at the fort supply depot. How the unknown soldier had liked the numbered song enough to share it with someone he loved. How the song said everything about what the soldier was going through. And how Gavin related in his own special way with the author's isolation.

The glasses-man hugged the passenger seat. "What was it you were trying to say out there?"

"I gave you my name," Gavin said. "Is that not good enough for you?"

"I'm curious. Not my readers. Me. Dean Toombey."

Gavin looked at the box on the ground. More so at the rock holding it down.

"So, where you're going now, and your reason behind that, like the number 40, you're not going to tell me, are you?"

Gavin smiled at the glasses-man something genuine. "Dean," he said, "do you do favors for your friends?"

"Sure."

"Are we friends?"

"I don't know, are we?"

Gavin hung his head. After a breath, he came back up. "I need a favor," he said.

"Anything."

"I need you to tell the coach of Bisbee, the coal miner, I need you to let him know that I accept the game."

The glasses-man slapped his hand on the steering wheel and jumped around in his seat. "Hot damn that's good news!"

"What day is it?"

"Any Friday you want."

"No, *today*, what day is it, *today*?"

"Saturday."

"Saturday, yeah, okay. So this Friday. Let him know I'll be there before it gets dark."

"Absolutely, you got it."

"And Dean?"

"Yeah?"

"Nothing in the paper this time, okay? If you want to talk to me after the game, I'll give you the real story. After Friday night, my time in football comes to an end."

The glasses-man watched the boy head down the road with a heavy rock in hand for a place he believed only The Ghost could travel. In a moment stuck to forever he saw the boy veer off-road and dart between rangy cacti like they were linebackers trying to steal his imaginary football. The boy, then, was no longer.

He amped his music to the bridge and didn't let go of the dial until it was at the max volume. In his venue of imitation leather he danced along his dash-keyboard and did donuts in the dirt.

With the drums and keys and symbols and horns he bugged south at the apex before rounding his return, right through the devil of his own creation. Back to the bridge between No man's land and St. David. His story in the back seat, playing in the wind. His eyes set free of his frames. And his face set free of his years.

The highway's jammed with broken heroes on last chance power drive. Well everybody's out on the run tonight but there's no place left to hide. Together Wendy we can live with the sadness I'll love you with all the madness in my soul. Someday girl I don't know when we're gonna get to that place where we really want to go and we'll walk in the sun. But till then tramps like us, baby we were born to ruuuuun. Ah honey, tramps like us, baby we were born to ruuuuun. C'mon on with me tramps like us, baby we were born to ruuuuun.

34 GUT CHECK

TISON YARD appeared to have every brand of tire stacked into its structure.

Gavin stood with his hands on his hips, measuring the rubber walls of his brave new world. As he turned to face the highway blur, the western sun captured well the man of his becoming. He took a few steps back toward his home before an awful grinding noise tugged at him by the belt loop.

The tires that had occupied his eyes and mind disappeared. There was only a massive turbine engine. And a second turbine that looked as if a bomb had gone off inside of the fan blades. He stepped to the shattered one and felt around the abused surface, sticking his fingers into a swarm of holes peppering the metal.

The grinding only tugged at him more and with it he centered his stance and head in the entry. *His father is not like him,* he thought. The thought he repeated over and over in an effort to stiff-arm his fear.

He made his way through the maze of tires with caution and splinters of light for over five minutes, following the grinds and rips. With each footstep he thought about what he might say, what he might see. When he rounded a wide turn he found himself in a room the size of his trailer and so he stopped under a ray of light trapped between the planks above his head. He waited there for a time, preparing his words. When it felt right, he smacked his hands.

Nothing but sparks.

He smacked his hands once more.

More and more sparks.

Gavin yelled with every vein in his arms.

A worker running a roto-blade the size of a pizza adjusted the device to a lower speed and turned around. The worker cut the power and pulled the plugs out of his ears and tapped on the shoulder of a man in a hood who was working a blowtorch. The welder fought off the worker with an arm, refusing to leave his weld.

When the welder extinguished his flame, Gavin tried to speak but nothing flowed.

The welder turned and tilted, eyeing Gavin through his yellow mask.

Gavin felt his heart pump.

The welder brought his head back square and swayed his torch. Gavin thought and thought and thought.

"The angry man has nothing," Gavin uttered.

The welder didn't sway.

"The angry man has nothing."

The welder sparked his torch. And in the hiss, Gavin noticed, the worker had removed himself.

The welder dropped his torch aflame and removed his hood. "What's this noise about the angry man?" he said.

Gavin didn't speak.

"Answer me."

Gavin used every vessel to regulate the blood.

"The angry man is what now?"

He honed in on the welder's shadow-pale face.

"What the fuck about the angry man?"

"He's not like you," Gavin said.

"Who?"

"He's just not like you."

The welder rocketed his gloves from his hands. "Who's not like me?"

Gavin thought about Walt's strength in humor. And his ability to say meaningful words. His voice deepened. "He's just not like you."

The welder lunged, shoving Gavin.

Gavin kept to the ground. Then he picked himself up like he did the first day with a helmet on. "Your son."

As soon as "son" came out of his mouth, the welder punched him in the gut. Gavin bowed over and spat in the dirt on his hands and knees. After a minute, he made it back to his feet. With a cheek readied because of a preaching he'd endured, he protected his ribs and prepared for a higher blow.

"He's just not like you."

There was a deep feeling of peace in his heart after those words and it seemed to last for a long time. Inside he felt as if he were someone new. As if things had meaning again and the physical pain washed away all the internal strife he'd been experiencing.

He saw his parents and the three of them opening presents together, two weeks before Christmas - the last time they were all in the same room. Gavin soon lost out on the picture to plaid as a fist full of anger, protected by a welder's glove, came to meet him at the free side of his head.

WHEN GAVIN WOKE, the sun was somewhere on the other side of the world. He lay on his side with the soft sand like a pillow, the moonlight in conversation with the turbines.

He ached to his feet and felt around for injury. He then approached the turbine with all the holes and went to one knee delivered, realizing that everything was right where it should be. Even the turbine was in the place it was destined. For the first time, Gavin saw himself as different. Different in a good way. And he understood that he was forever altered. He thought about fathers and sons and Old fathers and their second sons as he limped off in the direction of his trailer home.

35 EMPTY SON

THE BOY stowed a Colt MK IV .45 caliber hand gun with a custom ivory grip in a red camper cooler and walked through the front entrance of the South Sierra Vista Correctional. He stood at the entry desk with his shoulders slouched. A woman with a collection of gold rings on her fingers smiled at him. "Name," she said.

"Yes ma'am, my name's Denny Land."

"I know *your* name."

"Yes ma'am."

"The prisoner you're here to see, handsome. We gotta account for every name the prisoners put down and you gotta say who you're here for."

The boy gave her a shy smile. He brushed the back of his hand over his nose and shook out his curly brown hair. If his hair had been wet, he'd have sprayed water on some of the people filling in behind him. "I'm here to see Dellson Gary Land Jr., ma'am, for visitor's day. Same name, *Land*."

The woman took her time going through a file cabinet. She pulled out a file and wrote something in it. "We got another down for the day it seems, a Cordis . . . James Dean."

"That's my half-brother, he's not with me."

"James Dean is his middle name?"

The boy nodded and rolled his shoulders back. His eyes shot to the outside, through a side window.

"And Land the last?"

"Yes."

"Well . . ." the woman said, glancing up from the file and placing her chin under the fist of her hand and palm, her elbow cushioned on the desk. "Where is he now, any guess?"

"I don't know exactly."

The woman grabbed a calculator with a roll of paper. She kept her attention to it. "Any goods to post to the name for the commissary?"

"No."

"Any requests?"

"No, no requests today, ma'am."

The woman shot a thumb over her shoulder. He followed her long red plastic thumbnail with a twitch of desperation. "Walk straight down and then over to your right," she said. "It's about ten more minutes until you can go inside. You'll have to wait in a room for a little because of all the people we got crammed in here today."

The boy stepped to the side of the desk and slung the cooler behind his back. He put his free hand behind his back, securing it to the handle. His shoulders came back as he strode away with much worry in his face. The woman excused herself from the next visitor. "Wait . . ." she said.

The boy spun around and went to his toes. Briefly, he checked over her head. Then he came down to meet with her at her painted face.

"Yes ma'am?"

"Your middle name . . . that for real?"

He smiled with a slight under bite.

"It's different . . . you get that from a movie of the week or somethin'?"

The boy shrugged and the woman treated the spearmint between her teeth. He spun back around for the waiting room.

"Oh . . ." she said, picking at her stockings below the knees. "Anyway, Dennison Audie Murphy Land, thought I'd let you know I like it. It's real masculine, sweets."

A MEASURED HALF HOUR went by with the boy glued to his cooler.

He sat in a room furnished with a dozen or so school desks and a corroded Playpen. The desks had already been taken up by some of the other visitors by the time he walked in and so he'd used the cooler to make a seat for himself and sat silently over in the corner.

A guard stepped out from the break room opposite the common wall. "People . . . " he announced in a nicotine voice and with his eyes on a clipboard, "we need to make a line, starting right here in front of me. Let's get a move on and do this as friend-like as possible."

The people formed a line. The boy watched them jostle. The boy then stood up and positioned himself at the very back, stretching his vertebrae so as to occupy his fear of a getaway chase.

The guard checked off items on his clipboard. He coughed once and wheezed double that. Then he cleared the majority of sandpaper in his throat. "When we get up to the first set of barred doors, people, I'm going to have to request that you step in one by one. From there we're gonna go through a quick check of your purses, bags and belongings. Anyone here wearing pants will also be checked thoroughly. Is that all understood?"

The people looked at one another. The collection of them included a man in a sleeveless motorcycle jacket and a woman with packages of Salem cigarettes under her flabby arms. There were at least thirty people in the room altogether, most in the same state of dreary anticipation. The majority of them acknowledged the guard with a collective mumble.

"Wonderful," the guard said in a sarcastic tone. "If this is your first time visiting your loved one here at our fancy hotel, just think of it like that movie Midnight Express. You're now in our country and are subject to our own methods of search. We have the right to refuse anyone for any reason and admitting you is entirely at our discretion. If you'll look at the wall here, you'll find that included in the house rules." The guard kept his attention to his list as he used an empty hand to point to a list of rules on a poster laminate. He dropped the hand and continued, "If you're not caught carrying any illegal substances on your person, it's real simple people - you won't

be cooked in the gas chamber after we finish up with the barbecue."
Some of the people moaned. One of them laughed. The guard finally
offered the room eye contact. "That was a little joke," he said. "All of
us here are Americans, Reagan is our new President and you're free to
ask me or any of the other guards here questions. The only right you
give up in here is the right to bear arms. I'm afraid that one don't fly
inside these walls." He looked at the faces in distress. "Relax, people.
You have to go up to Florence if you want the gas. But even up there,
they don't have the lights turned on."

THE WELL MANNERED BOY WITH THE WAR HERO MIDDLE
NAME made it in and out of the guard check without much of a
hassle. They'd opened up his cooler, but didn't touch anything or
speak a word to him. The words they had exchanged were of the
weather, how it was bound to cool off in a couple of days when the
fall officially hits on Wednesday, September 23rd. His thoughts had
been far removed from the heat or promise of cooler weather. He'd
been overrun with a picture of dying next to his father without a gun
of his own. A sweltering death in a prison yard or out on a highway
stretch with no memory of a girlfriend.

He looked at the only visitor under the watchful eye of the sun.
The temperature gauge had been moved from the front entrance of
the facility over to the yard where it was setup on one of the picnic
tables. The gauge pointed slightly over 103 degrees.

He scanned the layout of the yard and looked up at the white hot
sun. In an instant the sun reminded him to look away. He shielded his
eyes and sat down on the cooler, dropping his head. When he came
back up he noticed that a few of the guards had left the serving area
under the canvas tents and were gathering around a guard with a pair
of leather gloves that had holes at the fingertips. The group of guards
conversed for about a minute. Then they all looked at the boy. The
boy stood up, turned around and put one foot on top of the cooler. He
dug a hand down a pocket, comforting the other under his armpit. The
guard with gloves approached in gigantic steps.

"You one of Dell's?"

The boy addressed the guard with his thumbs sticking out of his 501 jeans. He agreed with his head.

"The other name on the visits list, he your brother?"

"Half-brother," the boy managed.

"He drive the two of you down here this afternoon?"

"*Up.*"

"Okay, *up.*"

"I drove myself, sir."

"What kinda car you drive?"

"A Galaxie," the boy said, his voice splitting.

The guard with gloves put a hand on his utility belt and glanced over his shoulder. He came back to the boy. "You positive he ain't drive the two of you down here today, your brother? Sorry, *up.*"

"Like I said sir, he's not with me. I got my permit, it's in the car. You can check it. I didn't do anything illegal."

"How old are you?"

"Fifteen and nine months."

"You know that permit ain't legal enough for you to go solo. You gotta have accompaniment at or above the age of sixteen to get your hands behind the wheel." The guard with gloves pulled the stick from his belt and waved one of the many gloveless guards over. A young man with barely a hair on his face raced over in a fresh-pressed uniform of brown and yellow. "Colter, can you go and check on a Galaxie for me? I believe that's a Ford."

"What color is it lieutenant?"

The guard with gloves put the stick back on his belt and looked at the boy. "What's the color?" he said.

"It's green, a two-tone. It has a two-tone with some fade."

The guard named Colter paced backwards. "I should be able to spot it like a leopard lieutenant."

The boy sat down on the cooler, crossed his arms and put a hand over his eyes. He began to sniff up his nose.

"The sun got you dizzy?"

The boy dropped his hand. His eyes were glassy and bloodshot like they hadn't been closed for more than an hour over the last forty-eight. "I don't wanna go to jail," he said, shaking in the chest and neck. "My half-brother was supposed to come with me and he's seventeen."

Both the guard with gloves and the boy looked around. The adult refocused.

"This ain't about the age to drive and it ain't about you. We ain't paid to keep an eye on boys."

The boy gathered his tears. "It's not?"

"I can assure you, it ain't about you."

"I don't understand," the boy said, arching up to get a better look at the picnic tables. "When's everybody coming out to eat?"

The guard with gloves rotated the cap on his head and nodded at a man wearing a blue T-shirt. Mister blue stood at a long angle from the boy, over by a small mulberry tree; he had his hands behind his back, like a valet waiting on the opportunity to park a car.

"Your father, he tell you any of his plans?"

"We didn't make any plans sir, I swear."

"He didn't talk to you about where he might be headed to and so forth, his excursions?"

"No sir, not that I know of. My dad talked a lot about Mexico, that's about all I know. He got us a house down there at the beach and we're gonna fly there as soon as he gets paroled. He bought us a plane, a Piper he had painted a two-tone green to match with the Galaxie."

The guard with gloves tried to keep from laughing. He cupped the dome of his cap and spat. "You all hail from Greenhall, right?"

"Yeah."

"You speak Mexican?"

"Sorta . . . I know some words."

"You got a Dairy Queen I seen, outsida that Greyhound, *verdad*?"

The boy didn't speak.

The guard with gloves studied the clothes on the boy from behind his lying eyes and silver aviators. He saw a pair of brown shoes about to fall apart at any moment; a pair of frayed blue jeans and a red and black flannel with the top two buttons missing - a shirt designed for colder weather. "And you came here solo," he said, fixing his sunglasses by the lens and support. "Parked that Galaxie of yours, and it's still in the lot as we speak?"

"Yes."

"It ain't parked along the sidewall of the deliveries area, sandwiched between two of them dumpsters?"

The boy turned a cheek.

"You got the keys?"

The boy excavated his pockets. Scraps of paper fell out as he handed over one lonely key.

Placing his right hand on his hip the guard with gloves clicked the radio knob on the side of his belt. He pressed the talk button, not losing sight of the boy. "Tarr . . ." he said. "Tarr, you readin' me?"

A barely audible voice said something.

"We still got no outs at the gate, Tarr, that still the case?"

There was some static. And then a crisp click. "Only ins is what we got on the log for today, lieutenant. The only out we got down is the Warden."

The static ended.

The boy slid a hand in the neck-crease of his checkered flannel and rubbed his shoulder. Sweat from the nape of his neck glistened in the sunlight. "When are they all coming out for lunch?" he asked. "My dad is in the Specials unit and all I see are the A's lining up. He said the Specials got their own wear."

The guard with gloves looked at Mister blue for a brief moment and then at the boy. "We got the Specials held up on watch right now," he said. "They're all in the confines of their individual units except for one. It seems the one that we got missing is your father. Now it would be damn near impossible for him to escape without the use of a vehicle, and since we ain't had no deliveries yet and since he was seen outsida the research room just this morning, he's got to be around somewhere. That beater you got is gonna get a comb through its teeth, and if he ain't found crawled up in the trunk and sweating his balls off by now, we'll find him in some other trunk, begging us for water."

"My dad is here," the boy argued. "We just talked on Friday."

"Alright, don't get yourself riled up."

"I'm not getting riled up, sir. He said he'd be here, so he's here. Maybe he's not feeling well. He told me his stomach had been giving him cramps and that he had run out of pepto."

"Alright, you make a fair point. How about I go and have a chat then with the nurse if it makes you feel any better, double check on that with her, see if we got any admits I don't know about. You see that pretty lady over there?"

The boy looked at one of the six picnic tables.

"She's the nurse."

The boy held his sorrow eyes on the nurse, the very same woman who had admitted him earlier.

The guard with gloves moved toward the picnic tables, removing his shades. On his way over, he made it a point to give Mister blue a nod.

The boy was left alone for a minute to ponder his father. A father who failed to mention that the breakout they had planned was off. An empty son with an empty look on his face. His head weighing him down to his dusty browns. Shoes that were made to match the dirt at his feet.

36 SQUARED

THE PRISONER entered the front door of Mickey's Hideaway in the heart of Sierra Vista wearing snakeskin boots under a style-wide cut. He checked and rechecked his turquoise watch as he felt the feather decorating the crown of his Rio Especiale.

When the time was right he dropped his natural hand and raised the tatted other and tickled a toothpick between his teeth, registering a verdict of the room without much movement from his head. He stayed mostly still, under the musky vents, tapping in time to a slow tune on a Row Ami MM4. When a heartache strummed for one on the jukebox ended, he eased his big body forward and sucked in his gut.

An acoustic ensemble chopped-in, towing a banjo.

The prisoner glanced right, at a bar with only three stools and a small television tucked over in the corner. The bar, parallel the street and with bottles under neon whirls of blue. He selected the middle stool with the satin-back and gave the young teamster-type behind the bar a two finger pistol cue. He split his fingers. "Double whiskey . . ." he commanded. "And make sure she's leggy on the rich man's blend. Alls I got is hundred dollar bills linin' my pockets."

The bartender removed the bandana from around his neck and wiped down the bar with it. He then reached up on a shelf for a glass and turned back around to face the sheen of his handiwork. He rummaged the depths and when he found a brand fit for the request, he stood up and poured the prisoner a drink. He finished the pour and slid the glass into the prisoner's hands. In return, the prisoner flicked back a napkin.

Destitute any expression, the bartender left the game of Monday Night Football to the prisoner and his glare. The prisoner avoided the television and the play by play commentary and just sat there with his eyes inside of neon tubing and his lips anticipating the taste of a free man's whiskey.

When the jukebox shuffled, a tall man got up from his seat at the long bar at the back of the room and headed for the dance floor. The tall man stood on the gloss for a verse and then crossed over in the direction to where the prisoner was seated.

As the tall man pulled out the stool to the left of the prisoner, he looked at the glare coming back at him from a mirror that had air brushed T & A. He didn't drop an inch. "You whored up at the Misty?" he said, expectant a certain countenance. He found he got nothing and so he smiled at his own red face. "I bet the Warden brought some in for you special like, special like them gravy over beans. So I know you ain't that bent, cowboy."

The prisoner took a slow sip of his whiskey. He held the glass in front of his face and breathed in the oak. "Eggs . . ." he uttered, staring straight ahead, and at nothing. "Eggs in the sun and gravy on top, slim." He placed the glass down and slapped the bar. The tall man sat down rather slowly. "You make sure the yoke is pretty," he continued, "and you damn well better make sure them whites is covered up mostly with gravy. If I ask you for beans, you put them on a side plate and make sure theys refried before they get to me. And don't piss me off with any damn American made hot sauce."

The tall man reached over the bar for a beer bottle. He twisted it open with one of his guilty hands and the side of his teeth and chewed the cap and spat it out. He downed a good portion of the barley. "Looks like I ain't the only one outside the prison earnin' a paycheck," he said. "Or maybe you're up here on a furlough? Like they do in Tucson for them politicians at the federal peace."

"Let loose my arm, dude."

"Easy cowboy . . . I ain't come over to cuff you. See, tonight we celebratin'."

The tall man let go of the prisoner's lumpy arm and toasted his beer to a couple of men at the long bar. The men were all standing around a pool table with a bottle of tequila and some low-heeled girls performing a primal dance with pool sticks.

The prisoner folded his arms over his glass and sighed. "Card told me you got somethin' of his," he said. "Card said you went and kicked him in the shins. So goes the sailor's story."

"For such a little man, he's a big talker. You on the payroll now cowboy, that I can clearly see. So what's it you need by coming to see me?"

"Around back," the prisoner replied, motioning at the bartender that his twenty dollar bill required no changing. He finally looked at the tall man - at the red furrowed eyebrows and brown spots pock-marking the forehead. "Card got an offer for you to consider," he said, kicking back his stool. "Said it was a special delivery for the ol' guard. *Barter* was the word he used with me."

The tall man brought the bottle to his lips, keeping the prisoner in sight with one eye as he did. He raised an eyebrow and chugged the last of his beer before hammering it down. "They outta my shiner anyways," he said. "What the hell, Dell, I got my boys here with me."

They walked across the dance floor side by side and over to the back door. Before he could reach the door handle, the tall man stumbled over a tear in the carpeting. The prisoner saved the tall man by the arm, though, just before the fall. "You was playin' the pins before," the tall man said with a loopy grin. "That was you. Why ain't you said somethin'?"

There was an oversized truck in their way to the parking lot.

The prisoner held up the gait of the tall man with an arm-bar and waited for the truck engine to turn over. R & S Plumbing labeled the truck on their view side. White letters over a worn out green. A bald man in overalls the same color as the business name cranked the engine and chugged the truck in reverse.

A Lincoln Continental with wire wheels was parked to the right of Datsun 710. The tires looked mud-dried. Aside from a motorcycle and an El Camino, the lot had plenty of available space. The prisoner pointed at the Lincoln. "That one's for you," he said, removing his hat and wiping his forehead. "She's a real beaut, ain't she?"

They walked over to the Lincoln and the prisoner opened the passenger door. There was an orange cone in the space to the right and he underhanded it into a dumpster behind a barrier fence. "Damn pot holes."

"What's this?" the tall man asked. The prisoner smiled and smoothed the Lincoln.

"She's straight out the dealer. Had to make my up to Tucson and back just to get the one with leather. Go on and take a seat, so I ain't gotta break my neck no more looking up at you, gingerbread."

The tall man sat down on the passenger seat, stretching his right leg out onto the pavement.

"Slide on over . . . give her a real feel. She'll let you squeeze her tits."

"You're telling me . . . Warden Darrell Card, got this, for me? The same Warden of the SSVC? A man who would sell his own mother a piece of his crooked land and then steal it back on her birthday?"

"That's what I'm saying. Cherry ain't she?" The prisoner squatted like a salesman confident of the close. "Check them seats, see how far they linger. Check that other winda there, feel the breeze."

"It looks a lot like the one he's got."

"It ain't," the prisoner snapped. "His ain't got the leather and it ain't got stripes. You know how he is - gotta match things is his behavior. He was real specific with me on his instructions for the ol' guard."

"So what's my end of the barter?" the tall man asked. He then dropped his eyes to the floor. "Forget I asked, cowboy, I know what the barter is." He breathed in the leather. "Card wants me to show up at the prison driving this distraction. He ain't gonna be paying me no more when I show up, though. I clock in, I ain't gonna clock back out. Like that little bastard always says, 'that's what I know.'"

The prisoner used the door to get the tall man to relocate his right leg. He shut the door and hunched down to get a level look at the tall man through the open window, resting his arms over the frame. "That one he got for you," he said. "He got me on the payroll, but he don't own me. Nobody owns me." He removed his hat and sat it on top of the Lincoln. The plumbing truck pulled into the available space, tight and to the passenger right of the Lincoln. The prisoner squeezed his body between both vehicles, making his way to the front of the plumbing truck. He then entered the truck from the rear as the bald man watched for any action in the mirror.

The bald man climbed in the back to let the prisoner take over the driver's seat. The prisoner reached under the seat and produced a .38 and pointed it over his arm.

"Time to sober up, gingerbread."

The tall man was caught off guard admiring the showroom wood grain. He clued in to what was happening, sobering up in one big gulp of breath. "Man, you is a real cowboy," he said. "I got that like I got sevens on the dice. Quit playing around with that thing, cowboy. We free men you and me."

"What I wanna know is . . . how come that little peg-leg sailor got me gunnin' for you?"

"You got my head spinnin' now, cowboy, and I don't even know what for!"

"Why's Card. Got me. Workin'. A contract. Out. On you?"

The tall man straightened in his seat. "He showed you his fake leg?" he said, stalling.

The prisoner relaxed a bit with the .38. "I seen it, yeah. He don't know I seen it. But I had. We was in his office just kickin' it one day talking shop." He wiggled the .38.

"Alright, cowboy, take it easy now. Card sent me on a little thing and he thinks that thing is more than what it is, that's all. He thinks I'm holding something over his operation, but I ain't."

"You absolute on that?"

"One hundred proof, cowboy. Forget that, brother, I'm one-fifty-one."

The prisoner regripped the .38. He pointed at the tall man's legs. "This is your life we're talking about here," he said. "Not mine."

The tall man vacuumed his options. "I tell you what," he said, "you is a real cowboy. I can see that with the way you got your hand cocked on that gun. I got me more of a pension then some of them rocket engineers I seen around here, know that before you get any ideas with that thing. Know that for real. I'm on the payroll and that's where I'm gonna stay. I tell you what, cowboy, you tell me your end and I'll work a percentage in. I gotta reputation to look after. People here heard about me. Important people."

The prisoner retracted the .38 and reached under the seat with his free hand, pulling out a radio controlled device wrapped up in wire tape. "How about some dynamite," he said. "That fit with your propositionin' me? You're sittin' on two sticks and all I need to do is press this here button and let 'em rip right through that plush seat of yours. It's up to you if you feel like talking. If it takes too long, I might start to forget I give a shit."

The tall man saw that the Datsun was much too close for an escape. He retracted his seat for cover behind the door frame and looked at his crotch. The prisoner put two hands to the controller.

"Are we gonna get into specifics now or what?"

Music spilled out the back door. A motorcycle then sped off into the quiet night of Sierra Vista. When the cycle could no longer be heard, the prisoner teethed. "We drove the rice burner here, genius."

"I guess you thought of everything," the tall man said, looking like a child that got robbed of his Halloween candy. "You even got a truck that looks like a tank."

The prisoner laughed. "And tape over the glass."

The tall man looked lost in thought.

"And two girls in the bar teasin' your buddies into their beds."

"Jesus, really?"

"I don't lie."

"What all do you want to know from me?"

"Hmm . . ."

"Don't push that button, brother. I'm begging you. Please."

"Hmm . . ."

"Damn brother, you can't kill me. You just can't."

The prisoner flicked a switch. "Alright," he said as he brought down the antennae. "Don't cream your jeans on me, gingerbread."

THE PRISONER handed off the Warden's gun to the bald man in the back seat and listened with the controller tucked between his legs. The tall man went on to explain that his business with the Warden was concerning a pile of evidence and a lady - evidence that could put the Warden in a cell custom-made of his own operation. When the tall man took a break from speaking, the prisoner cleared his throat.

"What'd this evi-dence have to say?"

"Card told me the matter was about some land deals of his. He told me that if I found anything with his name or his company, *Big TexAZ*, to collect it and turn it in to him. This lady's husband was on the take, Card told me. Said her husband had worked for him as a land scout for years. I guess this wrangler threatened Card with deeds and tapes he collected on his crooked land deals. One piece of land and a payload of buyers, if you get me. The wrangler had all this evidence and was threatening to turn it over to the lawyer that work for the state if he ain't get a real payday."

"So you went to work on the hubby, is that it?"

"No, see, cowboy, he was already dead. Card told me he was made part of the foundation. Said the wrangler told him right to his face all Perry Mason-like that the evidence he collected was buried. So I guess he buried him when he made mention of that."

"Where?"

"I gather the floor of them condos he's been building outside the yard."

"The *evi-dence* . . . where's *it* buried?"

"That I don't know for sure, brother. But what I do know is them condos is a front. And I know that wrangler wasn't twisting things around like Card said. Card's the real twister. You know he advertises his condos in the Midwest papers to dumb-fuck retired persons who like to make their down payments sight unseen?"

The prisoner requested the .38 with the back of his hand. "The Specials?" he said, feeling the iron.

The tall man relaxed in his tale, like he was earning points. "Shit, the only thing special about them condos, brother, is all the money he makes. One time I was in Mickey's here and some old fart comes up to the bar and asks me if I ever heard of Bunch street. I was puttin' away my shiner like I do from time to time and I had to spit it all over me. The old fart then showed me the advertisement for those Specials. I just about fell out of my seat."

"Tell me about the lady."

The tall man laughed.

"What's so damn funny, slim?"

"Sorry . . . it's just that I can't help it when I think of that man and his dirty deeds. If Mr. and Mrs. dumb-fuck don't have a heart attack when they find out that their new home in the sunshine, is, in fact, on the grounds of a prison - land that that little motherfucker owns outright, he brings in Mohave rattlers from Mexico and has them placed on their front porch. When the snakes finish his bidding, they get cut end to end like them retirees and their down payments. Card is devious, brother. But he's smart. He thinks of everything."

The prisoner fingered the tip of the .38. "So this lady . . ."

"Yeah, right . . . so Card was figurin' the wrangler had lied about burying all the evidence to save his own skin and I agreed so I got put on the wife outside of my shift and then some days I don't even show up at the prison and I still get paid. Well her home in the suburbs is empty and there ain't no holes dug that I can tell and I even get me a ground scanner at the Shop Ready. Then one day she pops up and I start to follow her full-time. I go scannin' around where she lives now, some RV hookup in Huachuca City, tell people there I got a hobby. I take up a spot at this place and sit for a few days just observin' her when I ain't get my metal-detector bleepin' on shit but old pennies. She don't do nothin' but iron her clothes and clean her pots and pans and sit in her truck and read her Bible. The shit just gets boring and there ain't no evidence that I can see." The tall man waited for a response, a sign of approval, anything. Ten seconds passed.

"I'm list-nin . . ."

"Yeah, well, then, one day, she takes off late in the day and I follow her to another campground up north. This place is way out the way, over this bridge west of St. David. If the evidence is anywhere it's up at this place. So I drive up this dirt road following from behind the far and out of nowhere some damn rent-a-cop in a F-100 stops me and asks to see my identification. I get to conversatin' some with this old man and it ain't turnin' out so friendly because he shows me a shotgun and tells me it's a Browning and to get the hell out 'cause there ain't no police there that are gonna come save me if I'm up to no good. How the hell this old man knows I ain't there on a customary visit I don't know, but it works on his end since I don't have no gun. So I turn tail and motor on outta there.

So I get pissed about the whole thing and I get my shiner on to feel better and I wait it out with the RV set for this lady to make her return. Well she don't. I got two more days on the lot paid up so I decide I'm gonna see if she comes back with anything. Well she don't come back until my last day. And payday ain't until Friday, neither, brother. She don't have nothin' new and it's gettin' so I'm about to lose my good mood. I'm about to go back to my woman's house, but before I go I decide I'm plain gonna go ask this bitch where the evidence is all kind and gentleman-like to save me the aggravation. I don't know, I'd been fueled up on my shiner and had been thinkin' too much about Card and how I'd like to strangle the man if he didn't have his way of employin' me like he does.

Next thing I know, brother, this lady comes on about preaching. Yeah this lady, she starts talking to me about Jesus so I changes the subject, told her I ain't got time to pray. 'We ain't at church,' I sez. She was nice but then she got under my skin when the conversatin' ain't go the way I had started all pleasant-like. I can't explain how, brother, but she's got this way like she's important. So I sez to her: 'Where's the papers and tapes your husband got that he gave to you? I know they ain't buried, but I'm gonna find them. You got pictures and such and I want them. I want everything you got with my boss's name on them. I know that's why you moved out of Sierra Vista.' Well, before you can please a whore with some green this bitch starts to shake. Yeah, she starts crying. Sez to me: 'What have you done with my husband?' Where is he and on and on and on. This bitch just goes on a tear so I had to get upset with her. You know how it is."

The prisoner scratched his head. He then instructed the bald man to retrieve his hat. The bald man concurred and exited the double doors at the rear. A minute passed.

"So you the blackmailer now, slim, is that the case?"

"I worked for the Warden one day too many, that's the honest truth, but I ain't blackmail the man. I just told him to keep me on the payroll so I could get more and more of the evidence collected so he wouldn't have to worry so much. You know what stuck with me, though, brother? The way that lady looked me right in the eye and said the evidence was her insurance, said a silent partner is the only other person who knows where it is."

"So you ain't find any?"

"What . . . *evidence*?"

The prisoner raised the controller.

"Uh . . . no, not yet."

"Where's this lady?"

"Well, that's the thing, cowboy. She's been dead."

"So you ain't got but a story then. How do you know where it's buried? We live in the desert. Some of us are gonna die here it looks like."

The tall man inched toward the passenger door. He smiled. "See, cowboy, the way I figure things is that you stuck around. I can tell by the way you pulled your gun that you is a real cowboy, and folks here, they believe all the real cowboys is dead. Either they in El Paso or on the TV, but they ain't here. I seen the real cowboy in you, though, when you was locked up. That's why I wanted to make sure you was treated the best. Made sure those gravy and beans you love so much came to you on hot plates. You ever get it served on them cold plastic moldings? That was me. I think on occasion you ate in the main, but just on occasion. The thing I'm saying is what that lady said to me. When I looked in her eyes, how her blood veins were poppin'. I could tell she was holdin' out on me. She used the words *last living relative*. Why'd she say that, make that a point to me?"

The prisoner glanced at the floor. "And?"

"Well, sometime later on her son appears. Turns out she's got a son and he's in the papers. They write her obituary and talk on and on about him like he's so special. Then they write a big ass story about him that takes up the front page and it gets people talking about him. Said his story is made for the movies. I just put two and two together from there. That's why she used those words. She ain't got it buried. The evidence is with him, up at that campground. He even lies about where he lives to keep covered up."

The prisoner's demeanor changed in a heartless heartbeat. He swallowed deep breaths, staring at the .38. After a minute, he refocused. "What's this boy doing in the damn papers?"

"It's all about him just being special," the tall man said, having missed his best opportunity for escape. "So the lady was lying to me, that's why she said last relative and such, in that particular way."

"Yeah, you had made the mention."

"So you know, brother, you ain't gotta put that gun on me again. Card needed me to figure the whole thing out, elsewise, the son would get it in all the papers. And I'm gonna get to him, it's just that his place is protected by that old bastard security-guard with the shotgun. The Warden needs me. He can't go play golf like he does every day and think he's got one over on me unless he's gonna start paying me what he pays Bunch."

There was silence for a minute. The prisoner put down the controller and felt the .38.

"Card ain't mention no son to me. And he ain't mention no lady. He only mention you. Now why's that?"

The tall man didn't answer.

"He's smart, thinks of everything."

"He does."

"Hands me this gun with a serial number, tells me how it's used. Wants me to use it on you. Gonna write in my record like I had some kind of beef with you on the inside."

"You ain't gonna use it on me, right, brother?"

"What was it you said to me, about bringing me them hot plates?"

"Uh, yeah, hot plates, so you ain't get it served cold."

"See that's funny to me."

The tall man looked drained of any words that might save his red skin.

The prisoner sparked the big engine.

The bald man strapped in and the prisoner put the .38 on the dash and rolled the window up halfway. He grabbed the controller. "I ain't rememberin' that fact so good. And, I'm real sorry to say this to you, gingerbread: but I ain't remember you."

37 HONOR GUARD

WHEN GAVIN REACHED the top of the trail it was just after three in the afternoon. There he spotted Sandis attached to two large trash bags like they were extensions of his battle tested arms. He followed the old man undetected to the washroom, collecting bits of trash in the hand-sack of his T-shirt along the way.

Sandis watched Gavin labor for a few minutes in the aluminum and styro decay as he leaned back against the rail with a can of Orange Crush under his chin. He finished off the can and went about his business of fixing a plate on the washroom door. "You're hired," he said, twiddling away with a screw-driver.

Gavin paused at the comment. "I find that it's honorable to pick up trash," he said.

"Honorable?"

"It's the word I'm going with today, yeah."

"I call it a job," Sandis remarked as he struggled with a Phillips head that only helped to shred the screw in the door. He took a frustrated breath. "Something to shake out the cobwebs."

Gavin kicked a sun-beat can of cola with his left foot. He kicked the dirt, mostly.

"Do you get paid for all the work you do around here, Mr. Sandis?"

"Do I get paid . . ." Sandis uttered as he pried the plate from the door frame with a flat driver. "Let me get back to you on that one, okay?"

"So you don't get paid."

"Not in government dollars, no."

"Why do it then?"

"Because it's something I've given to myself. I like to clean, in case you haven't noticed, and my favorite thing is to sweep."

"You sweep a lot."

Sandis stopped his work, satisfying Gavin's need to talk. "You know I got patterns," he said.

"Patterns?"

"Right, like how you might see some sad sack do his lawn in the suburbs. Some former ne're-do-well with a pencil now stuck up his ass. Patterns get me. We all got our patterns, I think. Then I got a technique. Wrists in tight with the shoulders squared." Sandis demonstrated a few moves. "Back and forth like a machine until I get a good sweat going." He stabbed with the driver. "I'll do that to start and then focus on my feet and the broom lets go and we just have fun together."

"You and the broom have fun?"

Sandis smiled to himself. "Me and the broom."

Gavin emptied his T-shirt into the container with the fresh liner. "I think it's good that you've found something you love and you get to do it," he said.

Sandis wiped a palm on his shirt. "I don't love what I do," he said, picking at his shirt like there might be a stain. "But all things being equal, Private, I make myself get up each day and do it."

"It seems like you love what you do. I mean you do this kinda stuff every day. I've never seen you take a day off like some of the other people around here. The other people here, they don't do much of anything."

Sandis handed Gavin a screw from the door jam. "Don't kid yourself," he said. "These people around here – they're professionals at doing nothing."

"You sweep the dirt, you know."

The old man said a word or two with his eyes.

"Dirt wasn't meant to be swept, it's dirt."

"Precisely," Sandis said. "I've got my routines and they're what matters most to me." He asked for the screw back with a hand. "You know, Gavin, not one living soul around here but you has ever helped me in my routines, not a one. I've never even received a simple 'Thank you,' you know that?" Sandis fogged the door plate with his breath and shimmied it clean with the elbow of his shirt.

"Thank you," Gavin said.

Sandis straightened up, tucking the screwdriver in his back pocket as he did. With his thumbs he banded out his suspenders. "Well, you're welcome," he said with a snap.

"And thank you for your service to this country. Fucked up as the country seems sometimes."

Sandis took a moment. He then went back to his work.

"I don't care if I ever get paid for the thing I love to do the most," Gavin offered.

Sandis grabbed his toolbox like he was readying himself for another fix-it job someplace else. He pulled a cloth out of the box and patted at his temples. "From what I hear," he said, "football players get paid fairly well if they make it all the way to the top. A guy I once knew, well, half knew anyway, when he finished up with his duties he went on to play for the team that goes by one of the colors. What color I can't recall, but I had heard he did fairly well for himself. I guess when your time comes around, you'd turn down the money. You're a real idealist, Gavin, you know that?"

Gavin stuffed his hands into his front pockets. "Football is not what I love to do," he said. "It's what I thought I loved. I know now that I don't love it."

"You could have fooled me."

Gavin felt a patch of cool air. "I think I fooled myself," he said.

Sandis discarded the toolbox at his feet and stood up, wiping the wood shavings from his hands. "What do you mean, you fooled yourself?"

"I think I convinced myself that football was what I wanted to do and I tried my best to do it, but nothing ever happened the way I pictured it."

"Right . . ."

Gavin thought he might explain that it's not really football if you never touch the ball and don't have a team, but he let it go.

"You know I saved the feature in the paper about you," Sandis said. "Got the only copy they had left at the 76. Gave it to a guy across the bridge to have framed. Thought it might look good above the common place here. It said you were special. You're different, you know that?"

"Different how?"

"I'll stick with the word *idealist* for now because that's all I can come up with. But it's not that. An idealist is a one way street, stuck on their ideals and beliefs of the world. You gotta give them credit because they stick to their guns when the going gets tough. But you, Gavin, you're more complex than that. I don't think you can just sit still and let things come to you naturally. I bet if I put you in a room full of idealists, you'd just hate the heck out of them, or worse, you'd make them hate you first so you'd have an excuse to leave. You like to be alone, I think. You're a loner idealist, a real desperado, like the song. When I think of you, I think of that song."

Gavin felt his head at the point where he'd placed a frozen steak until it had defrosted in his sleep. "What song?" he asked with every bit of matter in his brain.

"*Desperado* . . ." Sandis said. "Well, you're too young. It goes on about things like walking through this world all by yourself. If I can quote the line correct: *your prison is walking through this world all alone*. For you it should say running through this world all alone."

"Why would you say that to me?" Gavin steamed. "Call me a loner?"

"Because I think it's true. There's nothing wrong with wanting to be alone, Gavin, trust me. You just want it more than most, that's all."

"I don't want to be alone."

"Well, I'm of the opinion that you do."

"And my excuse is to make people hate me so I don't have to . . . to what?"

"Be yourself and let the chips fall where they may. I think you're afraid of being caught off guard so you keep to the edge. Heck, if anyone's gonna shove you, they're gonna go right over the cliff with you."

Gavin grabbed a trash bag by the neck and swung it against the wall of the washroom. Half the trash exploded out at his feet. He proceeded to kick the bag with his left foot and continued until there were tears welling up in his eyes and next to nothing remaining inside the bag. Sandis stood quietly with his hands to his bands, waiting for Gavin to calm down. The old man waited patiently.

When Gavin planted his left leg and reached down to feel his right at the knee, Sandis stepped forward. "That the *honorable* thing to do?" Sandis said as he swept trash with his boot.

"I don't like what you're saying to me right now," Gavin said, tending to his leg.

"There's nothing wrong with wanting to be alone, Gavin, believe me."

Gavin eased up. "I came over here to tell you I was going into the Army. I thought you would be happy for me."

"The Army?"

"Yeah, I'm leaving on Saturday."

"You're sixteen," Sandis said, huffing, "last I heard. And the last time I heard was on the day you arrived here."

"So . . ."

"So first things first, you need to be eighteen and a high school graduate."

Gavin searched the sky, hobbling left. "I've got a plan for that situation," he said.

"What kind of plan is it you got going on in that thick head of yours?"

Gavin smirked. "I'm going to the recruiter's office, the one I saw in Benson, and I'm telling them I'm joining. That's my plan."

"With what, your dang driver's license?"

Gavin avoided everything but the clear southern sky.

"Well I misspoke," Sandis said. "You don't even have one of those."

Gavin looked Sandis right in the eye. "With an ID that says I'm eighteen."

"You got a fake ID?"

Gavin grinned.

"Where from? Who gave it to you? Who do I get to go have a conversation with my Browning?"

"It doesn't matter."

"It does. Where?"

Gavin turned a cheek. "From some market in a huge parking lot I went to over the summer," he said.

"Why in the heck, Gavin, do you want to try and join the Army at your age?"

Gavin looked down, completely bypassing the word "try" in his brain. "You joined the Army when you were my age," he said, uninspired. "You did the same thing."

"That was 1943."

He leveled his look and crossed his arms. "So . . ."

"So times were much different back then."

"You were my age."

"I was seventeen and one week with a dang beard and all my friends were joining. Everyone was going into the Army because that was the thing to do when you had no other choices."

"Was it eighteen?"

"Was what eighteen?"

"The age to join."

Sandis collected himself with a few dry puffs of his pipe. A tenant stepped out from a snug trailer to beat the dust out of a rug. The tenant waved over at Sandis and Sandis obliged with his pipe. Thuds echoed around the nowhere town. He studied Gavin from duct tape to the scrape under his eye. "You had to look the part back then," he said. "And you don't look the part. If I'm the recruiter, I send your skinny butt back home with a box of tissues."

"I'm still gonna go."

"Let me ask you then, why do you want to join? That's the first question they're gonna ask you so you better have a good answer."

"I already thought about that. I'm joining because I want to go serve."

Sandis chuckled, snapping his suspenders.

"Annnnnck. Sorry. Wrong answer. Thanks for playing. Try again."

"Why's that the wrong answer? It's what the commercials say."

Sandis chuckled some more and then cleared his throat and swiped the length of his beard from cheeks to chin. His eyes got serious, his jawbone hidden somewhere behind all that beard. "Let me ask you another question," he said. "What do you think is the opposite of service?"

"Being selfish."

"Right. So tell me you're doing it for your own selfish reasons and I won't get there ahead of you with a sandwich in one hand and my Browning full of pellets in the other. Tell me that you want to earn a paycheck and see the world and not worry about your meals or the roof over your head. Tell me it's what *you* want the Army to do for *you* and not all that serve your country crap they shovel on television. *Be all you can be*, yeah, right, my hide."

Gavin settled his hands on his hips. "I never knew you hated the Army so much," he said.

"I don't hate the Army."

"How come you're bashing it?"

"I'm trying to knock some sense into your thick head is how come. The way you went about your football thing isn't the way you should be approaching this. You don't get any second chances when you're dead."

"Second chances?"

"Right. You go into this decision thinking like some kind of war hero, some modernized version of Audie Murphy, and you're gonna find yourself dead. Every man I ever knew in battle who was there to *serve* like you wound up one of two ways. Either in a box onboard a C-47 or in the mud at the base of the 303 with their pride buried deep."

Gavin paused in consideration of his new dream. The thought of what a shotgun full of pellets could do raced through his mind. "What's the 303?" he said.

"Let me put it to you this way: if the same pictures I got in my shoebox here at home were in those leaflets they got, you wouldn't want to join. You'd go join the Peace Corps instead and simply call it a day."

"I've been through a lot," Gavin said. "I know I can handle things."

"I'm not saying that you can't handle things, Gavin. Believe me, I know you can handle things. Think about it some more is what I'm saying. You've got another year to make the choice."

"Maybe I've got plans for my life right now. Maybe my plans can't wait that long."

Sandis itched his belly and breathed a few breaths in contemplation. He finally lit his pipe.

"What if I'm not being selfish? What if I can't be that way? What if I want to make a difference in a small way?"

Sandis puffed in Gavin's direction.

"What should I be like to join the Army if I can't make it all about me?"

Sandis gazed into the burn. "Crazy . . ." he finally answered.

"Crazy?"

"Right, crazy bad or crazy good. Either one works."

"What's that supposed to mean?"

"In my experience, I can say that bullets and bombs avoid two types. One type is the type that's born crazy, like the guy you're unsure about. The guy who talks to his gun and wants to die. This guy don't care about one living thing and a bullet is just a fun way for him to meet with his maker. The other type is the crazy partier. This guy cares about a lot of things and he's always joking around. He lives for the next big high and never wants to come down. Sometimes I think it's worse to be him, the partier. It's like the man upstairs is letting him live through the fire fight so he can have more time to think about the meaning of life. I think the man upstairs likes it when a guy like that reflects later on to see how he's been spared. All the dang party guys I knew back in my previous life are now either preachers or priests."

"So everyone who isn't like that, meets with a bullet or a bomb?"

"In my tour experience, right."

"You mean war?"

"Right."

"We're not at war."

"Not yet. But we've been in a war in every dang decade. And we just got started with the eighties."

"You can't stop me from joining."

"Listen to me, Gavin. Up until now I've honored your words. The things you wrote about after your mother died. Your own story, how you see your life as it happens. I understand some about where you're coming from, I really do. I understand you felt abandoned and you were already on your own for months. I get that. You may think your mother left you stranded out here, but you'd be wrong. She wanted the best for you and she didn't even have to say anything to me about it. I could just tell by being in her presence. If you head north on Saturday, I might just decide to fire a round at your butt and save your life."

"You can't shoot me."

"Maybe I won't. But I know the Sheriff of the county, and I could wake him up on the high-band."

"They can't do anything," Gavin said. "We're on a protected territory."

Sandis clawed his beard. "How in the world do you know about that?" he said.

"I know things."

"Well I guess you do."

"It's why I can join the Army without graduating."

"How about this then, sixteen going on thirty three, you come over at o-eighteen hundred tonight and we'll go over all of this. If you're serious, and I know you are, I've got a few things I want to show you that I haven't showed any civilian before."

"Like what?"

"Well for starters, you need to know how to handle an automatic. I've got an M-16 that I'll teach you how to load. That's right, the peacemaker of modern warfare, in your hands. Saved our hides time and time again from being out-gunned. And no, they didn't give it to me on my first day. I bought it years later, at an auction. It's something you're going to need to know how to handle, nut to bolt, eyes open to eyes closed. There's the written test that I know they still use and the physical test to prepare for. You're gonna need one solid month to bulk up and prepare and I promise you it will be well worth the time. You don't want to get rejected, otherwise you're stuck. And you don't want to be stuck, am I right?"

Gavin thought that being stuck was about the worst thing. Worse than taking hits to the head or gut. Or inhaling insults. "There's a lot of tests?"

"Right. The Army nowadays is voluntary. And right, they got a battery full. When we ain't got a President picking fights with things like missile tests, the Army likes to slow things down a bit. And they can get a little picky."

"I'm okay with all that, I guess."

Sandis puffed. "Well good."

"What time is o-eighteen again?"

Sandis stared at Gavin's right leg. "It's . . ."

"It's what?"

"How long have you been favoring on that leg?"

Gavin didn't speak.

"Gavin, be honest, how long?"

"Since about yesterday."

"Yesterday?"

"Yeah."

"Let me see you walk on it."

Gavin waited and then walked gingerly in a circular motion around Sandis, his right leg purposely held outside of the old man's view.

"How's it feel?"

"I don't know, it's just like there's a burning feeling or something."

"Right. Can you run on it?"

"Yeah." Not anywhere close to full speed.

"Let me see you run over to the gate and back."

What if I get rejected? What then?

"Gavin?"

He only heard the metallic pings of screen doors in the distance.

"Gavin?"

The sights and sounds of a colorful world outside of the brown desert pulling away from him.

"Private," Sandis snapped, smacking his hands.

"What?"

"Let me see you run on it. Over to the gate and back, quick as you can now."

38 LOVEBIRDS

A MAZDA COUPE THE COLOR OF THE SUN SHOT up the neck
of highway 80 north. As soon as it passed by the back of a sign for
Greenhall, Arizona, it downgraded and flickered the brake lights. The
driver maneuvered to the shoulder and coasted to a stop.

With a look of endless possibility on his face, the driver glanced
back through the rear window; his arm cradling the stitch of the
passenger seat as he strummed the ending to "Wonderful Tonight"
with a long and tender mane. The woman seated next to him had her
right hand on his leg and was looking back in the same direction. She
tried hard with a frown, though, to get him to change his mind.

She decided a chain around his neck was more to her interest and
moved to it with her eyes and hands. Caressing the gold of his cross
under the gold in the sun she whispered in his ear. The driver smiled
and, for a second, lost track of the man in the cowboy hat approaching
from the shoulder. His woman let go the chain, opened the vanity and
began kissing all the soft in her face.

The muffler hummed and the car rolled toward the border. When
the love song was done, the driver went from reverse into neutral and
yanked the parking brake. He then brought his docksiders to the dirt,
shutting the door with assurance in his hands and face. Twenty yards
later he raised a hand as if to introduce himself at a cocktail party. Or
swear an oath.

"Radiator?" he said, picking up the pace.

No reply. And so he slowed. "Is there a problem with your

radiator? Did it over-heat on you?" The young man planted his feet and waited on a response.

"I got a tire shot out."

The young man moved a docksider closer. "I thought you might need some water for that milk container," he said. "It looked to me like you might be running empty on both ends." His smile was all heart. "I don't have much water left, but we got plenty of beer. The beer is warm of course."

"I ain't too thirsty, thanks."

"You need a jack?" the young man asked.

"For what?"

"That tire."

"Not 'less I got a spare, and I ain't got a spare."

"That's an awful big truck you got back there, mister. Looks too big for a tow. Were you pushing it too fast up that hill?"

No instant reply. "She's big . . . yeah."

"Sorry I don't have a road kit on me."

Three yards between the young man and the scorpion tattoo. The section of the highway more desolate than the last.

"What do you need then?" the young man asked, raising a thumb over his shoulder. "I'd offer you a ride to that gas station up the way but we're on vacation and we got our bags and stuff loaded in the back."

Two yards in conversation without a step from the young man.

"What label beer you got?"

"We have Coors and some Mexican special kind that I can't pronounce very well, I'm afraid." The young man cocked his bright green eyes. "There's also a few Heineken."

"*Hiney-kin?*"

"Yeah, you want one for your travels?"

A stand-still.

"College boy."

"Sorry?"

"How old?"

"How old's . . . *the beer?*"

300

"How old. Is you."

"Twenty-three," the young man said, his voice running north.

"Twenny-three . . ."

The young man flexed his polo chest with his clean hands on his hips and looked around the highway to see if there were any other cars. An awkward moment if there ever was one. Like an actor, he began to imagine his confidence. If he'd been prey to their infrared nature, snakes in the highway brush would have felt his heart race. He backed up by the inch, his docksiders kicking rocks in the direction of his powdered woman.

"You're that good samman I had done heard about, ain't that right?"

"I think you mean *Good Samaritan*," the young man said as he opened his palms in a show of distaste. "I just wanted to see if you needed some help, that's all. You looked like you needed some water and might be in some distress. I'm sorry that I bothered you."

"Was you in the scouts?"

The young man fell his hands like cut timber. "I was, a long time ago, yeah."

"Makes sense. They teach that."

The young man motioned back to his car.

"I'll take that."

"Sorry . . . " the young man said, shaking out his hands in an effort to repel adrenaline, "but I'm not gonna give you a beer if you're gonna insult me after I stopped to help you. I can't believe I did that now."

"Your ride."

"My ride . . ?"

"You got two good ears. So listen then, why's it so damn puny?"

"What is this?"

A prison-pale gut and a silver belt buckle with the word: *Gringo*.

"This here's a .38, college boy."

"Hey . . . hey wait a minute, what's that for? Hey . . . hey wait a minute now. Just hold up, mister. You ca-"

39 SECOND SON

GAVIN LIMPED over to where Sunny was parked in deep of her tracks and dug out a long stick from the bed. He positioned it under his pit to get a feel for the support he needed and slid a hand down the length to check for splinters. The stick was about an inch in diameter and glossed with a medium stain. It had foreign words he couldn't contemplate. He ran a finger in the lines, stopping at a familiar name: Sun-Ja.

He made his way down the back of the hill in twice the time he was used to.

When he touched the flat of the northwest trail, his right leg began to lag. Thus he ruled over the momentum and hung his head, resting in the gold sunset that did beg his legs.

With his back to the gold he eyed the water tower and thought about the run of his longest day. Fifty miles one way. And fifty miles to return. He tasted the water of the well in his mind and considered greatly the reward.

He pressed on, raising his head and clenching his teeth and thinking nothing about the sunset in his particular part of the world.

When he made it to his destination in the flat valley, he set the stick on the ground and rightly followed on his knees. With one hand he removed his shirt and wiped his face and head. A light wind swooped in to heal his wayward strands. In the wind that changed on him he breathed in deep for over five minutes. He let go of concern and quieted his mind, free from any urge to turn over his feet. "I never got to say goodbye," Gavin said, in a voice much older than his years.

A flock of birds dodged fetal cacti before taking flight. He followed their lines.

"Goodbye . . . I want you to know you were my friend."

He returned to a stack of bricks guarding the summer for the very last day. His eyes climbed.

"I can see what I want and I can see it with my eyes open. I don't need to close them."

He exhaled. "I'm sorry his father wasn't like you. And I'm sorry his father wasn't like him. We don't get to choose that stuff. That's what I learned."

Gavin wiped his eyes.

"We still got other choices though," he said, convincing himself of something.

With a finger he made patterns in the dirt. He grabbed a handful, offering it to the wind.

"I'm not angry."

He wiped his nose with the back of his hand.

"And I don't want to be angry."

He spat and thought about the first time he had crossed paths with Walt. He parted back his hair, summoning the universe. He knew Walt had protected him from himself. He just knew it.

"Your second son will be alright now," Gavin said. "He's good."

Just two lovebirds in the sunset for a moment in time. And then someone said, "You always talk to yourself?"

Gavin put his left foot out, opening the hip. He rested his hands on his thigh and looked over his shoulder. He saw a boy near the trail. The boy folded his brittle arms and made a comical face.

"White people aren't supposed to live this far in the desert, you know that, right?"

"Do I know you?" Gavin said.

"White people get all sorts of skin problems even when they're not in the sun."

Gavin didn't say anything.

"And if they're in the heat too long, I'm still talking about white people here, they act like they got ants in their pants."

Gavin faced the sunset again.

"You know you look more red than me, you know that, right?"

"I guess you're not gonna answer me," Gavin uttered as he brought his left knee back to the ground, barely turning his head for a second look at the stranger with the sarcastic mouth.

The boy kicked out a leg as if it were a kickstand.

"He can't answer you, you know. His spirit went away. It needs no body where it goes."

Gavin located the stick and used it to get to his feet. He dusted off his knees, keeping the boy within his peripheral.

"You're the crazy runner my Old father told me about. I know who you are."

Gavin straightened up. "You're Chase?" he said.

"It's not how you say it, french fry. You say it wrong, like I *chase* a dog, or *chase* girls who like pasty things. It's fine."

"You could have said your name," Gavin said.

The boy switched his kickstand. "You didn't."

Gavin acted like he didn't need the stick for support.

"How come you didn't say your name?" the boy asked.

"I didn't know what you were talking about. And I didn't know who you were."

"It is not what I say, french fry. My Old father said you are good at missing the words. How come you didn't say your name, for the story?"

Gavin breathed around.

"You don't look much like the drawing."

"What do I look like?"

"Not that. You saw it, right?"

Gavin pinched his lips. His eyebrows came together.

"How many pounds are you?" the boy asked.

"I don't know."

"Are your pounds . . . bigger than one-forty?"

Gavin glanced at his own arms. "Umm . . . maybe."

"I'm one-forty-five."

"Okay. Thanks for telling me, I guess."

"You look less than me. You look . . . one-thirty-nine to me."

"Okay."

"The drawing is like you're one-eighty. In the drawing, you have muscles. Here you don't. Why?"

Gavin felt confined to a space in all the openness. "You like to talk about weight a lot, don't you?"

As the boy approached, Gavin measured him in his mind. *One-forty-five,* he thought. *Yeah, right.*

THEY WALKED TOGETHER in silence through the flat valley, back toward Rock Gardens. When the trail forked to the Corte School, the boy chose the turn. "Sayonara," he said, waving with the back of his hand.

"Wait," Gavin said.

The boy stopped. "My Old father said you don't talk much. He was right."

"He was right about a lot of things," Gavin said.

"It is almost dark, and I am not a bat. So what is it, french fry?"

"Where are you going, I mean, where do you live?"

"Mormon Town."

"Mormon Town?"

"St. David."

"Oh . . ."

"Why?"

"Just wondering, that's all."

"Anything else you want to know, Columbo?"

"What school do you go to?"

"The Mormon School."

"That's what it's called?"

"It is what I call it. Others call it the Waverly School. I don't know why they do, but they do."

"Okay."

The boy backpedalled. "Anything else?"

Gavin thought hard.

"You can ask me anything, you know, and I will tell you. Here are some things: Do Indians get sunburned? Do they like to dance for rain? Can they really get drunk off of hairspray? These are all acceptable to me."

Gavin looked away.

"Last chance for native advice, french fry."

He kept to his unfocused gaze.

"Sayonara then, pale face."

"Wait . . ."

"No I cannot piss rain. Hard as I've tried."

"Jheezus, that's not what I wanted to ask!"

"No I cannot teach a lizard to sit. No one can do that."

Gavin about broke his stick. "Just shut up for a second, will you? This is a serious question."

The boy shut up. He gave Gavin the once over for about the tenth time.

"I just want to know what *Yahtzee* is."

"Yahtzee?"

"Yeah."

"It's a game, french fry."

"No, not the game. What Walt used to say? He said it all the time."

The boy laughed. "*Ya-Ta-Say.*"

"Yeah that, what does it mean?"

"You really want to know?"

"Yes."

"You sure?"

Gavin lifted his stick and poked the boy in the shoulder.

"Okay, okay. Let's see . . . *Yatasay* . . . it means these:

I understand.

I get it, friend.

Yes, it is.

Why would you even think to not trust me?

That was a good question. Good people ask good questions.

I trust deep thoughts. And I trust you. Do you trust me?

If you can trust me, you can trust you. And vice versa.

It feels good to be connected.

It feels good to know you.

You are you. I am me. And we are here together. Where else would we be?

Only two people can have a conversation. Our conversation is the only conversation happening.

Yes.

There is purpose. There is a purpose in all things." The boy tried to bury his grin. "And the last meaning . . . what is last . . . oh yeah, last is - can I hitch a ride with you? I'm only asking because the Navajo stole my truck again."

Gavin chucked his stick. He looked up at the back of the hill like it was just another one of his challenges. "I guess there's something I want to say to you Cheis, something I've been thinking about. I don't know why, but I kept thinking this all the way back here. If I don't talk a lot, it means I am thinking something."

"Something deep?"

No deep thought is ever stupid.

"Well what is it, french fry?"

"If I say it you have to walk away. You can't talk anymore. And you can't try to be funny."

"I don't *try* to be funny. I just am. Humor is all you have sometimes."

Gavin thought for a few breaths. "The angry man has nothing," he said.

The boy nodded with respect. "Yatasay."

Gavin looked once more at the back of the hill. "When I say it, you can't say anything. You just need to walk away."

The boy folded his arms. "I am listening," he said. "You showed honor to my Old father and I will show it to you. No laughing. No making fun of your girly hair and pasty skin. Your painted eye." He nodded again. "You said my name right, go ahead."

Gavin looked at his leg and then at the boy. And at the darkness in front of him.

"What I want to tell you is that something is lifted. Not removed or whatever. But *lifted*. It is the word I can't get out of my head." He breathed in the perfect words, he believed. "Something that once bothered Walt so much is now different. Your father will no longer punch you in the stomach for looking like your mother. And there will be no pain where there should have been a mark."

40 RANGER

GAVIN COULD BARELY SEE the tips of his sneakers in the low glow of the outer lights.

He used his crutch to snake between trailers and when he made it to the one adjacent Sunny he leaned the stick against the siding and tested the strength of his right leg.

The pain he felt bordered on severe. In the burning he raised his head and clenched his teeth. And with the pain squashing his eyelids he contemplated a prayer from his mother's preachings. Something about inner strength. He dropped his head and released her words, feeling at the sear between flesh and marrow that ran along the shin; a hairline fracture unknown to him.

He turned to the muted scene behind the window curtain of his right profile and guessed at the steps he needed to take. Fifteen or so were required as he faced forward free of the siding. He gave his left leg the burden of his body as he attempted the walk in his mind multiple times.

He considered Walt's bare feet. How the Apache's footprints were probably still out there in the desert night. And how the rain, whenever it might appear next, could never wash away the memory. He then thought about the line of scrimmage like a line in the sand and how his best offense had been standing firm in his one and only position. He replayed all the cheap shots to the ribs and the shots he couldn't remember too well before things in his world went blank. He heard the slurs and thought about what it might have been like if he'd been born an Indian. For he knew the Story of The Ghost long before it had run on the front of the Sierra Vista Eagle.

To settle his fret over his next challenge, Gavin filled his head with song. And with a strength much stronger than going barefoot in a gauntlet, he walked straight ahead and up the steps to the front door like his injured leg had been magically reborn.

He knocked on the door.

Nothing.

He knocked again. Then two times more.

Before the unusual dark of the grounds, he waited. Casually he backed to where the soft glare of his trailer beckoned him. Sandis, Gavin thought, was inside again without permission.

Stuck on the routines of the old man, the door swung open. In the doorway was a lumpy hand to greet him. "Evenin' Ranger."

Gavin turned with idle hands. He took a second to think. "Where's Mr. Sandis?" he said.

"He's out."

Gavin stood there confused as the lumpy hand gave him a fast-action salute.

"I've been waitin' on ya here whiles our friend went out on a mission for supplies. He said you were gonna need plenny of supplies where it was you was headed and he done went out and asked me to keep 'round till he gets back."

"Where did he go?"

A moment of silence. The bowing of heads at a military funeral before the trumpet plays.

"He's out . . . like I had made the mention to you before."

"Who are you again?" Gavin said with distrust in his voice.

The lumpy hand didn't hesitate. "I'm Cap'n Land. Of the Army special forces command. The Rangers, Specials squad."

"You're in the Army Rangers?"

"The Specials is what we go by on the inside. Well, that's classified, so it's not like we can talk about this somewheres else. You ask me about that one in a public setting and I gotta say Rangers and let it rest."

Gavin's hopeful eyes lit up the entry.

"Well come on in Ranger. Like I done said before, I've been waitin' on ya here a long whiles."

The lumpy hand stepped to the side, paving the way for Gavin to make stride.

"You savor a beer, Ranger?"

Gavin floated in pain-free and painfully unaware. "I've never had a beer before, sir," he replied. "No thank you, this time." He stood tall in the entry, easing in body and mind as he made his way over to a recliner chair. He let the cushions take him in as he fell and kicked up his feet. He looked at the lumpy hand looking at him and then at the ceiling. Then he turned to a box full of pictures and antiquated magazines on the coffee table directly in front of him. A few pictures were laid out for display. He pressed the hand lever and, with the momentum achieved, snatched one of the prints. He studied the black and white with his left leg to the floor. Unknown soldiers in their uniform best. *Who is the old man without the beard?* He looked around in anticipation. *And where's the M-16?*

"You want the Army for your life as much as my mission pal tells me?"

Gavin reclined. "Yes sir, I do."

"How bad?"

"It's the only thing I want to do with my life, sir. The only thing."

"Your life, huh?"

Gavin responded with convicted eyes.

"So you're ready."

"I am."

"You absolute on that?"

"I have no doubt, sir." *Where's the M-16?*

"Tell me about your story then," the lumpy hand said, taking up the loveseat across from Gavin. "I wanna hear about this story of yours."

"Well, sir," Gavin said, clearing his throat, "I am originally from Sierra Vista and I've been living here at this place, well, since about the beginning of this year. I've got family, but, because of our circumstances, sir, I've been here by myself. It's just what happened and I'm okay with all of it. So you see, I'm pretty good at taking care of things and managing my own responsibilities. And I've done decent in school. When I was at my other school, I got straight B's. I never got below a B on anything and any test I've taken, I've passed. And the reason I want to join the Army is, well, sir . . . it is because I want to serve my country. I don't want any vacation for myself. I don't look at it that way. I know it's gonna be hard and I'm prepared both physically and mentally."

The lumpy hand didn't utter a word.

"Sir . . ?"

"Yeah."

"What do they do if you get hurt while on duty? Do they keep you or do you get sent home?"

"You get hurt, we put you out to pasture. Like the mules, you get put out to pasture. Bein a mule that can't go to work ain't no damn good."

"It's that strict there?"

The lumpy hand scratched its lumpy neck.

"What's the big story in the paper they got about you? What's it you got written?"

"The big story . . . I got written, sir?"

"Yeah, you sent in a story and they printed it, why? What was the big story you sent to them that made them want to print the thing?"

Gavin ran his hands down the arms of the chair. He felt moisture. He wiped his hands on his shirt and when he rubbed his thumbs together over his lap he picked up hints of beer. "I didn't send in a story to the paper, sir," he answered. "They just wrote one about me. It was their story from the beginning and it's probably one of the reasons I never gave them my name."

He saw the lumpy hand tighten. "They wrote a story about you and you ain't even give 'em your damn name?"

Gavin nodded, his eyebrows waking. "Yes, sir. That's right." A vacant stare came back at him. "Is something wrong, sir?"

"Why'd you do that . . . not give 'em your damn name for the story?"

"Well, sir, it's because I didn't think I was doing anything important like I am now. I never saw it that way. I never saw it the same way some other people did. If they want to write a story about what I'm doing right now, with the Army, I'll tell them my name. I've got no issue about what I'm doing with my life now. The Army, sir, it is my calling. The Army is why I'm here and I haven't even joined yet."

"Let me take a look at this story they got in the paper about you."

"I don't have it."

"You ain't have it?"

Gavin thought it was unusual to see someone so respected get angered. But Sandis had said the Army was picky. He wondered how long Sandis would be gone for. "No sir," he replied.

"Well what did it say about you then? What was the big, fat, important story if you're so dang special and get B's and so forth?"

"I don't know what it said, sir, because I never read it. I didn't want to."

"You ain't never read the damn thing?"

"No sir, I never did."

The lumpy hand vibrated. "Why in the hell not?"

Gavin noticed in detail the lumpy hand's tattoo. A tattoo you get when you jump out of a plane over the night desert and can't see the ground. A real badge of honor. The Rangers, Specials squad. He pictured himself making the jump.

"It's my life, sir. It's my life and I only know it. I only see it. Do you know what I mean? I am the only one in it and what I see is other things. How can I see myself? I can't. I can see the desert and people around me doing different things. I see them do stuff when they're not looking. Why would somebody look at me and want to write a story? When did that person stop living? Whatever the story is, doesn't matter to me. I already know what my life is. The Army is what I want for a lot of reasons. The Army is real and in front of me. It's right here and there are offices and a Fort and people who walk around in their uniforms. There are people who are doing the same thing that I want to do. I know it's not gonna be easy, but I'm ready. And like I said before, I want to serve. I have to be honest about that even if it means I don't live very long if there's a war. I'm ready. I know that with all of my heart. When I join the Army, though, sir, I'm happy about one personal thing. I'm just happy knowing I won't be alone anymore."

THE LUMPY HAND exited the trailer without doing much more than grumbling about having a smoke, leaving Gavin to himself and the clarity of his new dream.

An inner peace enveloped Gavin as he used the recliner to full capacity. He breathed in the life he knew was his own and smiled as loving as Walt. Everything felt good. Then, as if being directed, his eyes went to the floor, and to the right. He reached for a piece of paper. For a letter that was partially stained. It read:

To whom it may constitute a concern,

I am writing this in recognition of a young man I have come to know. A young man named Gavin Reeves. Never in my life have I seen such courage and determination in one single person. To see this first hand is a moving tribute to all of us who have served. Servitude of the gone but not forgotten sons of battle, God rest their souls.

You might know or might not, that I am a retired US Army Veteran. I had the privilege to serve as part of the 2nd battalion, 5th cavalry regiment in the Korean conflict, hereby the "Black Knights" and going forward in civilian life with hands of loyalty and the aforementioned servitude not found in a country of courts or blind dictators.

On the day of the Hill 303 overtaking, Waegwan SK, I was left for dead or worse, capture. There I lay on the corpses of my brothers and strangers with my arms tied up behind my back. My life was over and my first real prayer hand stamped and delivered, and then...

There was a Ranger.

A young man with a face I will never forget. This Ranger, he was smiling like the worst of human nature was merely the beginning of understanding. You could have thought the two of us were in some other place instead of this mess. And it was at that very moment in time I felt lucky. It was right then that I felt most alive and happy and free. That there really was a God who had delivered me. Whereas my brothers were sacrificed, I was carried on the back of this Ranger to safety. While on his back, I saw a lot of blood. But I also saw the patch.

It is with a heavy heart that I only have the image to hold onto. I was not able to thank this unknown soldier. And for that I've had much regret. I said I'd never have one single regret in my life. But verily, I do.

I am writing to let you know the name of the Ranger who saved me. His name is Gavin Reeves. Maybe it's not the same flesh and blood, but a reincarnation.

The Rangers are a select few. The kind that shun the spotlight. They turn down things most men gladly take. This letter is to inform you that you have a Ranger right here if you want him. I've had the honor of watching over him in light of him losing his mother.

Please be advised that if you come to take him away from me there might be a fight. It's just how I feel about him.

Yours in service,

Lieutenant Colonel Gene R. Sandis, US Army, Ret.
PO Box 42, St. David, AZ

As Gavin let go of the letter, he realized an important detail about the M-16: it was missing. Sandis was missing too. A voice from deep down inside told him to run. The voice triggered an instinct he had never before experienced in his sixteen years and nine months. Before he could think to flee from his seat, he was overcome by a flash-flood of adrenaline. In a monsoon of blood his nerves did swim.

When he touched the floor with his right foot, after having bound for the door with his left, his right leg shattered below the knee. Gavin's tibia bone that had served him so well out on the highway and on the fields of his wild dream, floated in jelly over the carpeting.

He clawed for the door.

With a heart beating mad he sensed something was about to happen outside of his control. His hands made it to the front door frame.

The door hinged open to the desert, uninvited. The warm of the sun expired to the cold calculation. And the carpet laid to the rest under the lifelines of his palms.

He recited the first line of the second verse of the numbered song in his head as it was all he could think to do. *He set my feet upon a rock and made my footsteps firm.* He calmed as he thought of the letter under his mattress and his reasons for taping the number 40 over his heart. The fall was yet a sprint away. But the spring, forever a marathon. Gavin's acceptance of a life lived as full as possible. His fingertips on the tips of dirty snakeskin.

SEPTEMBER '91

The book, I suppose, was worth writing despite all of the pain its subject caused. I know my pain hasn't gone anywhere. If anything, it has drifted in front of me for the last ten years.

I can see him today just like the first time I laid eyes on him. The Ghost on his knees, out there solo and about to get driven into the dirt.

Maybe it's a good thing he didn't see it coming like that final blow to the back of his head. Maybe it's good he doesn't know what I know about his ending. Truth be told, hombre, his fate met with him head-on and he didn't have the slightest chance of changing things. He didn't see it coming and there's absolutely nothing you or anyone could have done about it. Nothing.

Speaking of nothing . . . the hours upon hours of recordings offered nothing but lies and fabrications. What a waste of time and effort trying to find a reason. Any reason in the world why that man did what he did. A mountain of nothing. And still no explanation even today as that bastard lives and breathes in a jail cell in Florence with a state bent on giving him every opportunity to spread more of his lies and gloat. I don't get it. I guess I never will. Never was I a champion for the death penalty to be reinstated until the day I met Dellson Gary Land, Jr. and looked into his selfish, heartless eyes.

That is the last time you will think that name again, Dean. Remember the promise you made to yourself. You can think of him in general terms, but never the name again. And never from your lips.

His eyes revealed more than his words through those jagged teeth. That constant half-open mouth of his like a garage door one foot off the driveway. I guess a man who's always teething is never at a lack for words. Lies are words. And his words mean absolutely nothing. Those eyes have nothing good going on behind them. They're like caves with no light inside.

And then there are those whites stained yellow like his teeth. When he talked so much about eggs, and how he loves to eat Mexican breakfasts at all hours of the day, all I could think about were his eyes and how maybe they were like the eggs he wouldn't shut up about. Scrambled eggs in spoiled milk to bring out the yolky yellow. To this very day I can't eat eggs because of his lies and stained whites. And I used to love eggs in every which way.

Was I the only person to be in the same room with him and make it out alive? Why wasn't I the one who didn't see it coming? Why am I the one who's alive today, in the rays of this sunset and sitting on the steps of a stadium built for the only person I've ever met who wouldn't tell me who they were - a person who insisted on not telling me his name from the start?

This stadium is a headstone for The Ghost. A stadium built so Indian kids could play football and people like me could come and watch. A few rows of concrete and the green turf and the river not far from my ears. I want to pour a new row and write his name in the wet cement. I want to write the name Gavin Reeves *with my fingertips and get the paste stuck under my nails. And I want to build a statue out front and hand him the football.*

But I can't.

And I won't.

Some things, like the Stones sing, you got to let bleed, hombre.

The pictures are my passion and the writing my way of dealing with things. Would I have any of it without him?

Maybe one day the powers that be who killed the death penalty will experience what it's like to lose somebody close to them. A child, maybe. I'm thoroughly convinced they don't have a clue what it's like to suffer the loss. And they certainly don't know what it's like to sit across from a man who's taken, what, a handful of lives? He smiles and doesn't even blink when you say that. He smiles and all you see are those teeth.

When he gave me his script or screenplay or whatever the hell it was, I thought I was going to throw up. Mother Mary, how I wanted to throw up all over that thing. Instead of showing weakness, though, or any type of feeling - I sat there like a professional and mirrored him. I acted like I was interested just so I could get the bastard to tell the truth. He just told me what he wanted me to hear. Like he was entertaining me all the while. Bastard.

Still, the bastard made you think, didn't he, hombre? He made you do the research and write better than you thought you could. He made you do the real work that it takes to write a book. And he made you delve deeper into the back-story. You studied the demographics of Greenhall, Arizona like you were on a census missionary from the federal government. You knocked on doors and sat at biker bars and you almost got your head kicked in and you almost went broke, but you got it done. You now know more about that little place and its inhabitants than anybody, even more so than the people who've lived there all their lives. The study was interesting, wasn't it? Admit it, it was nothing like you thought and it got the juices flowing. Nothing about income or religion or opportunity. The doctor you interviewed - that man of goodwill - he made it out of Greenhall just fine and started an orphanage. He had it worse than that no-name killer. The good doctor had no parents after the age of five and about zero opportunity all around, but he decided on something he was going to do and he did it. He wanted to add value and that's exactly what he did.

Maybe what's-his-name decided on what he wanted to do with his life just like the good doctor? The research points to that but I never did get an answer despite my personal investment in Memorex tapes. It's likely, though, I never will. Does that mean, then, a man who you say has no conscience actually made a choice to be bad? Does that defeat the underpinnings of the book?

So you didn't get an answer, so what? You dug up things about a tiny fraction of society that isn't talked about much and you gave it a voice and made it into something that people want to read. Isn't this your dream, Dean? Isn't this the moment that you've been waiting for? Look at the check in your hand, hombre, and read what it says and forget for a second about that off-pink sunset you know isn't like anywhere else in the world. Forget that you walked, what, a solid five miles after leaving your car at the side of the road where the camper's place still is to sit here on these steps and make a decision. Forget about all of that and look at the check. A fifty grand advance for the No-Name Killer. Fifty grand, hombre. That's what, three times what you made in your best year reporting for the Eagle? Your true crime book is officially in print, hombre. You deserve it. No one here is telling you that other than yourself. Like your whole life, you pick your own self up, Dean. You keep imagining your parents speaking the right words. Like they never died without saying they loved you even one time. That is perfectly okay. And it's enough to tell yourself that. You are a good son and a good writer and a better photographer than you were before and a good man and a giver and not a taker. Your fifties are going to be the best years of your life.

So they like the structure of the book and they like your style of writing. It's Doubleday, *hombre. But they want the subject's name on the cover and you want your clever title. You want the No-Name Killer or nothing at all.*

But what is it you really want? Do you want to take the manuscript to that bastard and wave it in his face and say: here it is, buddy, your story for the world to see now, just like you wanted, but too bad for you no one will ever know your name. Too bad your story has no name attached to it. Watch him gloat then. Watch him squirm like he does when he gets angry. Your story for the big screen you piece of shit, right in the trash can.

It was a brilliant idea to write a true crime story from a perspective that the killer would never be named. And it was an even better idea to follow each chapter that bastard gave you with one of the truth so as to reveal a cunning sociopath. One chapter about saving lives on secret missions under the code name El Rancho and the next on kiting bad checks under multiple aliases at the El Rancho border market. It's entertaining to let readers decide without telling them much of anything. Every chapter is truth, really. Maybe other true crime books that follow will block out the name like the Watergate reports or use the NNK moniker you use in the book? Maybe other books will adopt the practice so victims will be celebrated for once?

But victims can't be celebrated when they're alive. If anything, I learned that with my first story, Story of The Ghost. I don't know how to write that story today in novel form because I don't know it outside of my own head. Besides, it's not like it's fiction. It's all a puzzle, really. And there's nothing I got really other than the image of The Ghost in white and the number 40 taped to his shirt. Why did he choose that number when he could have taped any number to his shirt? What was he trying to say? Did he think of his reward before he died, a real game with an entire town ready to hand him the football? Just like that no-name bastard, I'm afraid there aren't any answers to be had.

I think the only way an answer might come to light is if there's somebody extraordinary like The Ghost who comes along and does what he did. Maybe they don't run like a deer for miles on the highway and play football as a one man team, but maybe they stand out in a different way. There'd have to be symbolism. He'd have to play football. And he'd have to wear the number 40 because that would be telling. He'd have to have promise, but meet with a tragic ending. A life cut short before it really begins. With an ending no one sees coming. A real hero who knows nothing about playing the role. Somebody, like my own hero, who shuns the spotlight. But somebody, though, whose name people know. I'll wait for that. And when I do see it, that's the next book I'll write because then I'll know how to write the real story. Give it every word it deserves. Mother Mary, please bring to me another shooting star of inspiration with the number 40 stuck to his shirt.

So your story is long gone and the only way it can be dug up now is in your closet or on the last reel of microfilm at the county recorders. It was always your story, just like The Ghost reminded you. That was a different time, hombre. But look at where you are now, and how far you've come on your own journey. And think about all you've learned. Go ahead, author, cash that big-fat-check in your hand. And pick up your head, and look at that never ending sun.

ABOUT THE AUTHOR & ACKNOWLEDGEMENTS

This is the first novel for Charles L. Mahoney. He is a 1997 University of Arizona graduate (Political Science) and a proud former football player for the Wildcats.

Some great songs are mentioned in various forms within the book. I would like to acknowledge them and their creators.

"40" by U2
"Take It Easy" by The Eagles
"Wonderful Tonight" by Eric Clapton
"Born To Run" by Bruce Springsteen
"Desperado" by The Eagles
"That'll Be The Day" by Buddy Holly

UPCOMING

THE GRAY HOUND (2015)
A Thriller by Charles L. Mahoney

Things are a little too quiet for one investigative reporter at The Arizona Standard. With the population in Phoenix pushing one million and the crime rate in steep decline, the time feels right to take a stance on corruption; hard evidence in hand or not.

The year is 1976 and the celebration of the Bicentennial is in full swing. All crime is regulated on the western front. That is, until one rather dull news day when names are published linking the mob to a racetrack, and ultimately to a wealthy member of society - a man who prefers to remain untouched inside the barb wire of his isolated desert compound.